Ebola K:

A Terrorism Thriller

Book 2

Book Two
of the Ebola K Trilogy

By

Bobby Adair

http://www.bobbyadair.com
http://www.facebook.com/BobbyAdairAuthor

Cover Design & Layout

Alex Saskalidis, a.k.a. 187designz

Editing & Proofreading

Kat Kramer   John Cummings

Cathy Moeschet   Rob Melich

Margaret Ferguson   Linda Tooch

Technical Consultants

John Cummings: Military

Kat Kramer: Construction, Geography

eBook and Print Formatting

Kat Kramer — www.katkramer.com/publishing

Catering & Deadline Support

Bryan Ferguson (manservant)   Margaret Ferguson

Preface

Wow. Ebola K, Book 2 is finally done. For all of you who waited patiently, I appreciate that more than you know. It has been an emotional journey, and I've learned a great deal.

Before I get into the blah, blah part of this preface, let me first say as emphatically as I can, some of the characters make some REALLY BAD CHOICES that might seem like well-reasoned, even good choices, as they explain their choice in the story. DO NOT try these at home.

The characters that I hire to exist in my books don't tend to make good choices in general. It's kind of a prerequisite. After all, who wants to read a story about some guy who does everything right, never gets in trouble, drives a Porsche, and lives a happy suburban life. The most interesting thing that will ever happen to that guy is when his neighbors knock him off and run his body parts down the garbage disposal.

Ebola K, Book 2 took a bit longer to write than I expected. I did a LOT of research, reading books about epidemics, watching documentaries, and even talking a bit with a few medical professionals. I'm not going to say I got all the details right. I hope so.

Ebola and infectious diseases have consumed a lot of my waking hours for the past few months, and I can say it makes for stimulating conversation over the dinner table. "Hey, babe, thanks for making this wonderful meal. Wanna watch this documentary on typhoid over supper?"

Armed with that insight into the history of diseases, I tried to educate readers as well. One of the things I found interesting as my editors were going through the book was when one of them called "BS" on the plausibility of a certain situation in the book. It was interesting because the circumstance was a modern version of something that did happen during an epidemic a long time ago. I'd like to pretend that I'm insanely imaginative and I made all this crap up—that's true about most of it—but when you come across pretty much anything about how a government or culture deals with the stress of an epidemic, I've drawn almost every bit of that from historical events.

Scary stuff.

Another interesting concept I found intriguing to explore was the erroneous idea that rational people—when looking at the same information—will behave in the same way. This point is explored in depth in the relationship between Paul and Heidi, but the idea runs throughout the book at all levels. Businesses behave differently, cities take different approaches, as do countries, and cultures. Again, all proven out in history to make a dynamic mess for the book's characters to navigate. And with that I paint a picture of what the world *might* look like as it deals with possible realities to come.

I think that's the intellectual exercise that drew me into this story—the imaginative exploration of how societies manage change, especially when the change comes fast, violent, and ugly.

Thank your for picking up a copy of Ebola K, Book 2. I sincerely hope you enjoy it.

With that said, your feedback and reviews are valued and appreciated, so if you enjoy the book, please take a moment and write a short review and leave it on the website where you obtained the book. Links are provided at the end. Also don't forget to "Like" my Facebook page… we have a lot of fun and really enjoy interacting with readers.

And just as the readers in my Slow Burn series have enjoyed the suspense left at the end of each book — spoiler alert — there *is* a cliffhanger at the end of Ebola K: Book 2. So please refrain from giving bad feedback based on the fact that I leave you hanging. I would really appreciate it!

Enjoy,

Bobby

Previously, in Ebola K Book 1...

Austin Cooper, an American teenager, has traveled to Uganda as a volunteer in a school for street kids, just as Ebola breaks out in Africa. He becomes stranded in a small town—Kapchorwa—while watching his friends and others become sick and die.

Back in Denver, his father (Paul) and stepmother (Heidi) are worried and dealing with their own Ebola fears. Paul stocks up with supplies, and they ready themselves for the inevitable. Eventually, contact with Austin becomes difficult, and Heidi sets out to track Austin down, pestering Mitch Peterson, a CIA operative in Uganda, housed at the US Embassy in Kampala.

Unbeknownst to the world, Najid Almasi has arranged to infect his jihadists with what's now recognized as an airborne Ebola strain, sending them around the globe to infect others.

One of those jihadists is Salim Pitafi, an Pakistani American teenager from south Denver, who finds himself in over his head and having second thoughts about his involvement with Najid's sinister plan.

Chapter 1

Mitch Peterson didn't need to listen long to Austin Cooper's semi-coherent story. He got the gist of what happened to Kapchorwa—the city was completely torched by Najid Almasi's men. At first what seemed like the most frightening piece of news—that Ebola was airborne—turned out to be the least of his worries. Some number of jihadists had been in the village with no goggles, no masks, no protective suits—they *had* to be infected. Had Kapchorwa been immolated for the sake of secrecy? For the sake of satisfying Najid Almasi's ambitions?

Mitch brushed his knee with a gloved hand as he stood up. Chunks of dirt damp with vomit, diarrhea, and blood fell to the ground, leaving contagious stains on his knees. Mitch shuddered at the thought of Ebola virions worming through the denim, burrowing into his skin.

But did it matter?

If the virus was airborne—as Austin had said it was—was Mitch already past the point where any measure of precaution would protect him? He stepped involuntarily away from Austin Cooper's exhaled miasma of deadly microbes. He touched a comforting, double-checking finger to the mask that covered his mouth, another finger touched bare skin across his cheekbone, reminding him of a choice that might have already cost him his life: he wore no goggles.

It was at that moment he thought about the state of his skin in a way he'd never considered it before—in exactly the biological terms of its nature, a defensive membrane—a *compromised* defensive membrane. In a firefight not forty-eight hours ago, with guns popping and bullets sizzling the air, Mitch had scraped his knees and cut an elbow. Trivial injuries, not worth a thought at the time.

Ebola had a way of amplifying trivialities into calamitous, grotesque agony.

With the realization that his fears were snowballing, Mitch breathed deeply, sucking the flimsy surgical mask back against his lips. Never one to fall victim to panic, he knew fear was an emotion that conflated all the worst parts of risk and imagination into irrational certainties. Mitch Peterson hated irrationality. He hated fear.

He put his mind to work thinking through the problems he faced, the ones whose outcomes he could affect.

It still stood to reason that Mitch was likely contracting Ebola as he stood there. A simple calculation on bad odds would determine whether or not he would eventually die of the disease. The only way to increase his odds of surviving would be to seek out a modern hospital and convince the doctors there to do all they could to save him.

Of course, *that might still be nearly nothing.*

If Austin's semi-delirious story was legit, an ill-intentioned Almasi had escaped down the eastern road with an unknown number of Ebola-infected jihadists, and the world was in trouble.

No, not trouble. Mortal danger.

Airborne Ebola unleashed on the planet would devastate humanity. Sixty to ninety percent would die from the disease straight away. More would meet their end through starvation and consequences of the inevitable chaos to follow.

Mitch knew enough about the nature of men to know that the dark-hearted, predatory ones would thrive in a world of disorder left in the wake of an annihilating pestilence. Those kinds of men would bring suffering to the few good people who survived. Mitch knew—as he stood in the sun, turning to look down the slope at the ashen mounds of crumbled houses—that he was looking at a preview of what Almasi had planned for the rest of the world.

When it was over, seven billion people might be dead. The scant few left alive would find themselves standing in the ruins, asking what had gone wrong, asking what they could have done to prevent it.

For most, the answer to that question would be *nothing*.

Mitch *could* do something. He weighed the value of his own life against the value of seven billion. No choice between two options had ever been so obvious.

Najid Almasi needed to be stopped.

Chapter 2

Dr. Mills hurried after Mitch as he briskly skirted his way around the burned-out hospital. Mitch called to his men as he went.

"You're leaving?" Dr. Mills asked, surprise covering her anger. "What are we supposed to do?"

"*You're* here." Mitch waved a hand at the building, doing his best to maintain a rigid guise while he worked to control emotions that were none to happy with his fatal choice. "*This* is what you came to find. Didn't you plan to stay if you found an outbreak?"

Dr. Mills started to say something, but didn't.

Mitch rounded the corner. Two of his men stood by their vehicles. He ordered them to unload all of the doctor's supplies. He turned back to her. "Where do you want your stuff?"

"What?" Shock got the best of Dr. Mills. She pointed at the hospital. "Look." She pointed at the burned out school buildings. "Look. There's nothing left except blackened walls and falling roofs."

Mitch's voice softened to a human level. "I'm sorry. Please understand. I have to leave just as soon as I can get your equipment out of my trucks and get my men loaded back up."

Dr. Mills stepped back and looked him up and down. She glanced over at the men already unloading. Deducing, she asked, "Is there another outbreak?"

"No."

She looked down the road going west. "You're going back to Kampala?" Venomously, she added, "*You think you can run away from this?*"

Mitch chose not to rise to the fight. "I'm not going to Kampala." He nodded toward the eastern road. "I'm going that way."

"To Kenya?"

Mitch turned back to his men and gestured toward the hospital's front porch. It was clear of debris. "Put it all up there." Looking back at Dr. Mills, he said, "The roof over the porch is still in good shape. It'll keep your equipment dry when it rains."

"Why are you going to Kenya?" Dr. Mills asked. "You should stay here." She cut her eyes in the direction of the small town's center. "*Everybody* should stay. What you *should* be doing is calling the ambassador and mobilizing every US government resource to contain this."

Mitch put a hand in his pocket and took out his phone. "You believed Austin Cooper. You believed all that stuff he said about Ebola being airborne. You believed what he said about Najid Almasi."

Dr. Mills was taken aback by the change in direction.

Mitch continued, "I was watching you and Dr. Simmons when Austin was trying to tell us what happened. You looked like you believed him."

"About Ebola being airborne?" Dr. Mills asked. "I don't *have* to believe him. If there's the smallest chance he's right, the risk is too great for inaction." Dr. Mills was overwhelmed by her thoughts and she gritted her teeth. "Don't you see that?"

"I see exactly that."

Dr. Mills looked slowly around at the destruction. She looked up through the door of the hospital and at the charred bodies inside. As she turned back toward Mitch, her eyes went glassy with tears. "*I do believe it is airborne.*

How else does any of this make any sense? How else could all these people have gotten so sick so fast?"

"Your phone is a satellite phone?" Mitch asked.

"Uh—of course it is." Dr. Mills shook her head and drilled Mitch with a harsh gaze. "I don't understand what's going on here."

"Listen," Mitch said. "I need your phone number. My boss will be calling you a little while after I leave."

"The ambassador?" Dr. Mills asked.

"His name is Jerry Hamilton."

"That's not the ambassador," said Dr. Mills.

"No, it's not."

"You're not the cultural attaché, are you?"

Mitch focused his attention on his boot, cast a sideways glance down the road, and then turned back to Dr. Mills. "You're a smart woman. You can put the pieces together."

Dr. Mills didn't say anything for a moment as she thought about it. "You're CIA?"

"When Jerry calls, he'll have lots of questions. He'll be able to get the ball rolling to get you whatever resources you need here, you understand? Please, tell him everything. The things you know, your doubts, and your opinions. Don't leave out any details."

"I will," Dr. Mills nodded. "Where are you going?"

Mitch glanced briefly down the eastern road again. "I'm going after the men who did this."

"You have to stop them."

"I have to try," Mitch confirmed.

Dr. Mills sniffled. The tears that had been threatening to pour down her cheeks were gone. In their place was a seething fury. "The men who did this—"

Nothing else needed to be said. Mitch understood that she wanted them dead as badly as he.

"There's something else you need to know."

"What's that?" Mitch asked.

"You've got some time before things get out of hand," she said, "Ebola isn't contagious until the symptoms start. The elevated temperature, the vomiting, the diarrhea, the bleeding."

"I didn't know that." Cautiously, Mitch asked, "How long after infection do we have before these guys turn contagious?"

"Three days to three weeks."

"From what the kid said," Mitch asked, "could you tell when Almasi and his men arrived or when they left? He seemed pretty confused on that point."

"In the state he's in, I'm surprised we got as much as we did," said Dr. Mills. "I got the impression Najid left a day or two ago."

"That's my guess, too."

More of Mitch's men came to help unload the trucks.

"You're on a tight deadline, Mitch. Good luck."

"Good luck to both of us."

Chapter 3

A quick transaction of cash from one hand to another expedited the border crossing into Kenya for Mitch and his hired guns. More bills proved useless in shaking loose information about any Arab men who might have crossed the border on prior days. Nevertheless, only one road led east out of Kapchorwa. With no other leads, Mitch stayed the course.

Eventually, dirt turned to pavement, and the pavement led into a town, Kitale. Mitch followed his instincts and asked directions to the airport, a single runway in front of a moldering little terminal building under layers of flaked, chalky paint not much bigger than his office back in Kampala.

Mitch walked past a wall of louvered windows and through the open door. A man with small, weak shoulders wearing an airline baseball cap much too large for his head stopped shuffling papers. From behind his authoritative counter he smiled. "Good afternoon."

"Hello," Mitch responded.

"The flight to Nairobi arrives at eight a.m. and leaves at eight thirty-four." The man nodded to a clock on the wall and smiled again. Both unnecessary gestures; it was late in the day.

"*The* flight?" Mitch asked. "Just the one?"

"Yes, sir." The clerk showed his set of bright white teeth again. "I am locking up the doors in a few minutes. If you need to purchase a ticket—"

Shaking his head and cutting the man off, Mitch said, "I don't need a ticket." He looked out at the vacant tarmac. "What I need is information."

"About?" the man behind the counter replied.

Mitch laid his diplomatic passport on the counter and said, "I'm Mitch Peterson. I'm the United States cultural attaché to Uganda."

"Uganda?" the man muttered, looking down at the passport.

"I work at the embassy in Kampala. And your name?"

"Wycliffe."

Mitch extended a hand across the counter. "It's good to meet you, Wycliffe. I'm looking for a group of tourists that wandered off."

Wycliffe took Mitch's hand and shook. "Wandered off?"

Mitch smiled broadly. "There was some confusion with a tour company. It's a long story. The group would be mostly Arab men."

"How many?"

Mitch made a pained face to sell the lie. "I'm not sure. A few dozen. Maybe more."

"How many are you missing?" Wycliffe asked as though helping a child work his way through a simple problem.

"We don't know if they all went off in the same direction," Mitch continued with the lie. "You understand, right? We're still trying to assess the situation."

"What would I know about this?" Wycliffe asked.

"Have any groups of Arab men flown out of Kitale this morning or yesterday?"

The ticket agent's hands dropped to the counter. He shot a furtive glance out the window.

Seeing that Wycliffe was uncomfortable, Mitch reached into his pocket, snatched four twenties, and laid them on the counter. He scooted them across toward Wycliffe and without looking down at the money said, "I'd be very thankful for any help you could offer."

Wycliffe looked down at the money. He wanted it, but he was nervous about taking it, and that made Mitch suspicious. Bribery was usually easy.

Wycliffe looked back out through the windows. Mitch turned and looked through the glass slats to see what had Wycliffe's interest. All he saw was an expanse of green grass and the tarmac. Mitch asked, "What are you looking for?"

Wycliffe looked down again at the money on the counter.

"Were you here when the flight to Nairobi left this morning?" Mitch asked.

"Yes."

"Was there a group of Arab men on the flight?"

"No."

"And yesterday's flight?" Mitch asked. "Were you here then?"

"Of course," Wycliffe said. "No Arab men were on that flight, either."

"Did any other flights leave the airport?"

Wycliffe sucked on his lips and ground them between his teeth as he drew a loud breath through his nose.

"Was there another flight?" Mitch asked more firmly. "You'd know, wouldn't you? With one scheduled flight a day, you'd know if another flight went out."

Wycliffe seemed stuck between two choices. Mitch took a few more bills from his pocket and laid them on the counter. "Please, Wycliffe, I need to find these tourists."

Wycliffe looked past Mitch and through a window on the far wall. Mitch followed Wycliffe's gaze toward a small airplane hangar a couple of hundred yards distant.

"What about that building?" Mitch asked.

Wycliffe drew a long breath to stall. "I was told to say nothing of this. Threats were made."

Mitch looked at his watch. He looked at the clock on the wall. He wondered if grabbing Wycliffe by the back of the head and slamming his face into the counter a couple of times might change his mind. Instead, he scooped up the bills, and in a single motion stuffed them back into his pocket.

Wycliffe's eyes went wide.

Mitch reached over, grabbed a telephone on Wycliffe's side of the counter, and picked up the receiver. "Dial your supervisor's phone number," Mitch ordered.

"But—"

"Do it." Mitch let his impatience boil up. Why not? He stood a full head taller than dithering little Wycliffe who was about to get a few knots on his forehead.

Wycliffe held up a placating hand as he pressed a finger to hang up the phone. He looked down to the spot on the counter where the money had been just seconds before. "For the gratuity you offered, I can tell you all I know of these Arab men."

Mitch slammed the phone into its cradle, pulled the bills from his pocket, and smacked them on the counter. "Talk."

Chapter 4

The hangar that Wycliffe pointed out to Mitch had a floor of disintegrating asphalt and smelled of old sweat socks. Several garden hoses snaked around mounds of clothes near one end. A couple of empty tables stood at the other. The hangar held nothing else of consequence.

In the dimness Mitch found a wooden rod that he used to rummage through the piled clothing, looking for clues. On the barest chance that he wasn't yet infected, he didn't touch the garments with his hands. In the dark, in the damp folds of those clothes, he had no doubt Ebola virions were alive—at least as alive as a virus could be.

All of the clothing was Western and modern: jeans, shirts, hoodies, athletic shoes, boots, and even loafers. Underpants, t-shirts, and a few baseball caps lay in the mix. Everything was dirty, streaked with reddish mud, and tinted in the same red dust that coated Mitch's truck parked outside. Many of the items were stained with blood—not from the wearer's wounds. There were no holes in the fabric. Mitch guessed the blood had belonged to the sick people of Kapchorwa.

Mitch pulled his phone from his pocket and dialed his boss.

"Yeah?" Jerry Hamilton picked up before the first ring finished.

"I'm in Kitale," said Mitch. "I'm standing in an airport hanger that's got to be full of the Ebola virus."

"What's going on there?"

"I got info from the airport manager that four loads of Arab men flew out of here between the hours of two a.m. and seven a.m. yesterday morning. It looks like maybe they showered and changed clothes in this hangar. It's dark, damp, and warm in here, virus heaven. There's gotta be a hundred sets of clothes on the floor."

"Jesus," said Jerry. "Tell me the hangar was locked, at least."

"I walked right in," Mitch told him.

"Shit."

"I'm using a stick to poke through the clothes to see if I can find anything useful."

"Anything yet?" Jerry asked.

"No, but I have to tell you, I'm torn between burning all this right here or spending more time going through it."

Jerry asked, "Any idea on the planes' destinations?"

"None," said Mitch. "But Nairobi is the nearest international airport.

"Yeah," Jerry agreed, defeated.

"What do you want me to do?" Mitch asked. "I can probably get to Nairobi in five or six hours."

"No," said Jerry. "We've already got people in Nairobi coming up to speed. We'll have them at the airport hours before you can get there. You stay in Kitale for the time being. Lock that hangar down. Get yourself some protective gear, and go through that stuff. How many sets of clothing again?"

"About a hundred I'd guess."

"Holy Jesus."

"Yeah," Mitch agreed.

"There may be something there that'll give us a hint about what's coming next."

"I think we both know what's coming next," said Mitch. "This thing might be airborne. Almasi might know that, and he's deliberately infected a bunch of his dimwit zealots to export Ebola around the world."

"How certain are we on Almasi?" Jerry asked.

"I just have the delirious kid's word for it."

"I don't know if that's enough for me to get a cruise missile shoved up his ass, but I'll work on it from this end." Jerry sighed, and took a second to find his resolve. "We need to know as much as we can if we're going to stop this. I'll get a medical team sent your way. They'll quarantine the site once you're done."

Mitch wanted some assurance that he wasn't wasting his time. "That doctor in Kapchorwa told me it could be three days to three weeks before these guys are contagious, so as early as tomorrow I'm guessing. Have any new cases come up on the radar?"

"No," said Jerry.

"You certain?"

"I know you've been out in the field, Mitch, but you don't need a security clearance to keep apprised of the Ebola situation. Every time there's a new case in a Western country, the news flips out over it. Nothing new yet. Just the sprinkling of cases we've had—the ones linked to the West African outbreak."

Mitch breathed a sigh of relief. There was still a chance.

"Let me know as soon as possible if you find anything. And Mitch—"

"Christ!"

"What? What's that?"

"I found a passport. One of them dropped his passport here."

Chapter 5

Najid Almasi stood at the end of the pier a hundred meters from shore and watched a transport ship being unloaded as the sun went down. Layers of old hull rust bubbled under the paint. Pieces of oxidized metal the size of playing cards flaked off and fell into the water. The cargo ship smelled of diesel and the sweat of men who'd been hauling goods on it since before Najid was born.

Dwarfing the cargo vessel, his father's yacht, the *Basima*, sat anchored in the calm night waters of the Red Sea. The yacht's handpicked crew of twenty, along with a dozen armed men, left room for twenty-four passengers in the luxurious staterooms. Behind the yacht sat anchored another rusty old ship, a near-obsolete tanker that had been delivering fuel to small islands in the Indian Ocean until just four days ago. Now its only purpose was to follow the *Basima* with a supply of fuel and provide her with the ability to stay out to sea for years.

That left the question of food and water. The *Basima* used ocean water to cool the engines, and the steam from that process was distilled into drinking water—dual-purpose and efficient. Food, or at least what would pass for food—canned, dried, and dehydrated—had already been loaded onto a third ship in Najid's private little fleet. Plenty of other goodies were loaded on that boat, goodies like weapons, ammunition, and medical supplies.

Those three ships represented a backup plan. Najid's long-term goal: to emerge from the coming apocalypse as the undisputed ruler of Saudi Arabia, and perhaps the entire Islamic world, required that he stay in the country through the coming crisis. Only if things went badly—if the virus got out of hand, if the Saudi Army came in numbers he couldn't defeat—would he escape on the ships, and ride out the apocalypse in grand comfort on the world's oceans.

Najid shuffled slowly past pallets stacked high with bags of grain, each wrapped in clear plastic to keep the loads stable. He absently kicked spilled grains of rice between the pier's boards and into the water twenty feet below. He wondered how many bags had been torn on their journey. He wondered how much rice had been lost during unloading. He wondered, as he watched the grains fall between the boards, if one day in the not-too-distant future, he might regret wasting half a handful of raw rice.

What he didn't see in the dark between the lamps illuminating the pier in pools of yellow light, were the rats, running to keep up with the food being offloaded from their floating home.

Najid did see Dr. Kassis trudging toward him under the weight of his weariness. He'd sacrificed his sleep to stay by Rashid's bed in an effort that grew more futile with each passing hour. Rashid's health declined. No quantity of medicine, no degree of attention had any effect. Now, Dr. Kassis would be clomping up the length of the pier for only one reason. Rashid was dead.

Najid turned toward the water and leaned on a rail, compartmentalizing his grief as he watched lights glistening off the sea's surface, looking like stars on a black sky. He thought about his father, already weak from his struggle with cancer. How would his father handle the news?

Najid turned his thoughts away from Dr. Kassis and Rashid, and wondered about all those villagers in Kapchorwa. He wondered about that American boy. What was his name? Austin Cooper? Had he died as well? Had all of them died? Was it possible that this airborne strain of

Ebola was more lethal than any other before? Was it possible that instead of killing ninety percent of the sick, it killed them all? Neither Najid nor his men had seen any other survivors in Kapchorwa.

Realizing the weakness of those thoughts, Najid pushed them to the back of his mind. He couldn't afford to allow doubt to grow in a field where his crops were already sown.

He cast a glance toward one of the buildings in the compound. There, on the second floor in the space of three guest rooms converted to offices, were his computer men — hardware guys, software guys, network guys — they were all the same to him. Najid's cousin Hadi was responsible for all computer matters, gathering data, and analyzing information.

Forty-eight hours had passed since the last of Najid's jihadists left Kapchorwa carrying the virus in their blood. Najid himself had been busy during that time, sleeping little and arranging what he could to prepare for the changes to come. Now, he had time, and he wanted information. Unfortunately, Hadi had no news yet to give.

Chapter 6

Salim Pitafi awoke disoriented. He'd dozed off sitting in a chrome-framed, brown-cushioned chair in an attached group of four that made up something of a couch. The chair was of pretty much the same design he'd seen on the concourses of airports in Lahore, Nairobi, Dubai, Frankfurt, Milan, Miami, and now...where was he? Atlanta?

Yes.

Atlanta was still a long way from home, but at least he was on American soil, no longer a foreigner with an alien accent.

He stared at an expansive, glossy terrazzo floor, and his eyes followed a pattern of glaring reflections toward a bank of windows. Outside in the rain sat a couple of big twin-engine jets, waiting for a refill of rushing, tense travelers, anxious to get to their important, personal somewhere.

Was it morning or was it afternoon? The clouded sky gave no hint. With countless layovers and time zone crossings, whenever he woke—*wherever* he woke—he felt lost. His world was a series of vignettes and déjà vu variations of a place he'd been before; different enough to instill confusion in his thoughts.

Salim didn't know what day it was until he read it on his phone and confirmed it by looking at the ever-changing arrival and departure screens always hanging from ceilings, passively informing fliers of details for their comings and goings. He couldn't remember the last time he'd slept in a bed. His body was rebelling. His stomach tormented him with heartburn, his knees and elbows ached, and his head throbbed. Gurgles in his abdomen were promises of unpleasantness to come.

Salim yawned, stretched, and rolled his neck around to work off a painful crick he'd gotten when he'd dozed in his seat. Taking his bag off the cushion beside him, he pulled it into his lap, opening it to remove the envelope containing his travel documents. Searching through them was turning into a compulsion, an exercise in assertion—a claim to the tiniest bit of control over his life. Through the cumulative discomforts and pains of his ordeal, Salim counted the remaining flights until he'd reach his end. He told himself —no, promised himself—he'd then make a claim to his freedom.

Chapter 7

Paul Cooper's brownstone faced east, so his front patio was shaded by the two-story shadow of his townhouse in the late afternoons and early evenings. Paul liked to sit at the wrought-iron patio table after work, feeling the cool crispness in the air while listening to the birds and the squirrels as he finalized any leftover work tasks, checked email, or generally killed time talking to his friends on Facebook. Tonight, his laptop was open and animated browser ads tempted him to click. Inoculated against the allure of the flashy colors on his computer, Paul stared across the marigolds and deep purple petunias in the planter on the porch railing. He looked at the brickwork façade on the townhouse across the way. He wasn't looking for anything, just staring, letting his eyes fixate on the pattern of gray mortar between tumbled red bricks. The wall looked so fashionably old — a century old perhaps — but was new construction only ten years prior. The bricks were a subtle detail; one of the reasons Paul had purchased a townhome in Town Center.

Off to his right, a jogger, a woman who ran by nearly every evening, trying to keep up with her lean gray Weimaraner, no worry on her face. She glistened with sweat, absently focused on the next step, the next hill. She didn't have Paul's problems to worry over. Her kids were probably at home watching scripted reality shows, eating potato chips, playing on their iPads, and worrying about whether their overpriced t-shirts and jeans looked fashionably old and raggedy enough around the seams.

Where was Austin?

Why didn't he call?

What about that Mitch guy Heidi kept calling at the

embassy in Kampala? Where the hell was he? His assistant, Art McConnell, wasn't any help, either. He'd told Heidi— like, four or five days ago—that Mitch was on his way to Kapchorwa on other business and would call with word of Austin.

No word ever came.

Now both Austin and Mitch were gone, fallen into the African analogue of the Bermuda Triangle. Messages left for either of them were swallowed in the passive apathy of cyberspace. Art McConnell's responses, cagey at first, were now not even that. He didn't answer when Heidi called. Inquiries to other embassy personnel were now ignored. Dogged persistence hit a granite wall, and Heidi, for the moment, had met her match. Paul bet himself that by tomorrow Heidi would be calling higher-ups at the State Department in Washington. Then things would get interesting for Mitch Peterson and Art McConnell.

"Kenya closed its borders with Uganda."

Paul looked up to see Heidi with two salad bowls in her hands. She set one on the placemat in front of Paul and the other on her placemat before seating herself. "I just heard it on the news while I was making dinner."

Paul nodded. "I read a bunch about it on the Internet today. Ebola."

"In Uganda?" Heidi stretched her face into a sad look. With her smile gone, her age showed through. "I'm worried."

Paul nodded. He was worried, too. "The salad looks good." He poked a slice of pear with his fork. "Craisins, pecans—"

"I candied them in the oven, the way you like—" Heidi didn't finish. She started to cry.

Paul laid his fork down and leaned over to hold Heidi.

He held her until she sniffled what seemed like the last of her tears. She wiped her face on his shoulder and laughed about leaving a streak of snot. Paul let loose and sat back in his chair. Heidi was a crier. She cried about anything. He'd stopped being distressed by her tears years ago. Trying to make it sound like he believed what he was saying, Paul said, "Austin's probably fine. You know how he is."

Heidi smiled weakly. "Everything always works out for him. But—" More tears.

Paul leaned over to hold her through another round.

When he let go the second time and sat back in his chair, he said, "If you don't stop, our salads are going to wilt."

Heidi laughed and wiped her damp cheeks. She stabbed her fork into her bowl. "I grilled the chicken with that new lemon pepper seasoning I got from that deli Lexi told me about."

Paul tossed a chunk into his mouth. "Mmmmmm."

Heidi smiled.

"I'm sure he's fine," Paul told her again. "Thanks for making dinner."

Heidi shrugged. "You said you were tired of going out to eat."

"That's a habit that might break itself if this Ebola thing gets out of hand."

"Do you think it will?" Heidi asked.

Paul took a bite of salad and thought about it while he chewed. But thinking about it wasn't necessary. He already knew his answer to that question. He liked giving his answers the gravity of contemplation, false or not. He nodded.

Heidi laid her fork in her bowl.

Paul said, "I need to go back to Costco and get another load."

Heidi looked through the guest bedroom window, through its open door, and into the kitchen across the house. "How long will our calories last?"

At first, the question was a joke. After Paul's second trip to Costco and his explanation of calorie values to Heidi, she'd ask the question whenever the subject came up. He couldn't tell if she was serious or placating.

"We've got six months so far," answered Paul. "I'm going to get another six months' worth tonight. I think I'm going to go by Home Depot and see what they have for storing water. I don't know. Five-gallon buckets or whatever."

Heidi lightly touched Paul's hand. "Are we overreacting?"

"You see the news," said Paul, suspicious of Heidi's question and immediately on the defensive. She watched CNN all day, nearly every day. "Nearly twenty-five thousand cases in West Africa now. Reported cases. It's gotten out of hand."

"This isn't about prepping for Ebola, Paul. This is about Austin, and we need to talk about it. You need to talk about it. I know you—I can tell when you're depressed, and I don't think you're being rational."

Paul opened his mouth to rip through a rant but cut himself off. He looked around at nothing in particular while he thought about what he should say.

Heidi took advantage of the silence to repeat her favorite point on the subject. "We don't know whether Austin is alive, but we have to deal with how we feel about it."

Paul said nothing for a moment, but went back to work on his salad. "They quarantined the eastern half of Uganda today. That's why the border with Kenya got closed. Kapchorwa, where Austin was teaching, it's in Eastern Uganda."

"Paul, this would be hard for any parent." Heidi tried her best to force a smile. "Maybe...maybe you should see somebody."

"A shrink?" Paul scoffed.

"Your doctor?" Heidi suggested. "Maybe he could just give you something to help for the next month or two. You know, until we find out if—"

Paul started to say something until his voice cracked. He blinked over his tears a half dozen times, but still they escaped and rolled down his cheeks.

Heidi reached over and held Paul.

Chapter 8

Neither Paul nor Heidi said much through the rest of dinner. They washed the dishes. They put the salad dressing back in the fridge, and the croutons back in the pantry. Paul was trying to find a way to shoulder the emotional burden of a dead son, telling himself that he shouldn't give up hope, and at the same time telling himself to be realistic.

Without discussing it further, Paul and Heidi found themselves in his truck on the way to Home Depot and Costco. Paul was driving while Heidi busied herself with her telephone. They were waiting at a long stoplight when Heidi looked up from her phone and said, "We don't need to go to Home Depot."

Paul's raised eyebrows asked the question. Speaking suddenly seemed an onerous and risky exercise, risky for the possibility of losing his emotional control again and crying, like...like...Heidi.

She held up her phone in front of Paul's face. He reached up and pushed her hand back, feebly smiling. They both knew he needed his reading glasses to see anything up close.

"You're old." Heidi smiled. The two always found a way to joke their way through the hard times. Not always at first, but eventually.

Paul returned the smile. "What is it?"

"It's a waterBOB."

Paul squinted at the tiny screen. The traffic light turned green, and Paul drove through the intersection.

Heidi said, "You put it in the bathtub and fill it up from the faucet. Made of food-grade vinyl. I just ordered one on

Amazon. We can put it in the garden tub in the master bath."

"So it's like a big water balloon that fits in your bathtub?" Paul asked.

"Yes," Heidi answered. "Only sturdier. It even has a little hand pump that comes with it. I got the hundred-gallon size. That's a big tub."

Paul said, "We have three bathtubs in the house."

"You think we should buy more for the other tubs?"

Paul nodded. "Do they make them to fit the smaller bathtubs?"

"Yes."

"Order a couple more. Okay?"

Heidi looked down at her phone. She touched the screen several times, and Paul mostly didn't pay attention.

After a few moments, Heidi said, "I ordered two more. I paid for one-day shipping."

Paul nodded and weakly smiled even though he knew the one-day shipping was just a way to make him think she was on his side with all this prepper stuff. "I know I'm kind of freaking out about Austin, but—"

"It's okay." Heidi leaned over and put an arm over Paul's shoulders. "It's hard for me, too."

"I've been thinking about some stuff that's going to sound pretty crazy, but at the same time, it isn't."

Heidi sat back, worry all over her face. "What?"

"I may try to contract Ebola on purpose. I know it sounds insane—"

She slowly shook her head. A tear rolled down each of Heidi's cheeks. It wasn't the reaction Paul was expecting. He would have bet on yelling.

After a moment, she softly said, "I can't lose you, Paul. I know...I know you're —"

"I'm not depressed."

"You are. It's affecting you. You're not thinking clearly. You just can't see it."

Paul glanced at her. Here came the yelling.

"You do nothing all day but look at every stupid little rumor-mill website you can find on the Internet. You've practically stopped going to work. You don't sleep at night. Yes, I hear you get out of bed after you think I'm asleep. Paul, you're depressed. It's normal for a parent in your situation. Let me help you do something about it."

"I'm fine. This isn't about Austin." Paul wasn't sure himself how much he was lying.

Heidi sniffled.

Paul rubbed a hand over his face, took a deep breath, and launched into the set of rationalizations that he'd used to convince himself. "You know me. I'm forever the analytical type. This is about the epidemic."

"You're lying to yourself."

Paul ignored her and said, "That doctor and the aid worker they flew into Atlanta from Africa — the ones with Ebola — they lived."

"And?" Heidi asked.

Trying to shore up his belief in his argument as he spoke, Paul continued, "Only one in ten survive Ebola."

"That many?" Heidi asked.

"I've been looking at the little bit of data available, but it looks like with modern medical care, the chances of survival might be as high as forty percent. That means if you get Ebola and can go to the hospital, your odds of living are four times higher than otherwise."

Heidi rubbed at her temple as though massaging the tension away.

"Heidi, this thing is blowing out of control." Paul shook his head. In his inner dialogue, they had sounded so rational. Out loud, it was another matter. "Ebola is going to spread all over the world. It's going to come to Denver. Everybody, and I mean *everybody*, will be exposed. They'll catch it. They'll turn symptomatic, and ninety percent or more will die."

"Besides the fact that you're sounding nuts, Paul. Why would *more* die?"

"We don't have the medical facilities or staff to treat that many. At some point, there won't even be basic services. We won't be any better off than the people living in mud huts in Africa. We might even be worse off. We get our food from the grocery store. Our water comes out of the tap. At least those people can take care of themselves, grow their own food, and get their own water. If modern Western society breaks down, we can't do that. I analyze financial data. You develop professional educational curricula. The most food we've ever grown is a handful of tomatoes."

Paul took a moment to look out the windows at the blazing red Costco sign up on the building, and his eyes fixed there while he finished his point. "The people in America who get sick early will be the lucky ones. They'll get the best care in the world. Forty percent of them will survive. Those are pretty shitty odds, but they're a hell of a lot better than ten percent. It's that simple."

Heidi started shaking her head, drawn into the argument. "What about vaccines and treatments? They'll develop something—"

"No." Paul said with a certainty that bothered even him. "That's just it. The history of humanity is written in epidemics."

"Paul, the Black Death was—"

"No!" he yelled. "The Black Death is the only plague people ever learn about. They think that's the only plague that ever killed a bunch of people."

She felt her own anger rise. "Paul, modern medicine—"

"It's a joke. It's a fucking joke, Heidi." Paul's anger was running, and he didn't know why. "Do you know how many people died of the Hong Kong Flu?"

Heidi said nothing.

"A million, and that was in the late sixties. At the end of World War I, the Spanish Flu killed a hundred million people, depending on whose estimates you believe. But a hundred million, Heidi, that's like seven or eight percent of everybody on the planet. Hell, you've got seven hundred Facebook friends. That's like having fifty of them fall dead."

Heidi said, "Those epidemics happened a long time ago."

"How about right now, then?" Paul argued. "Thirty million died of AIDS, and another twenty million have HIV. Ebola comes from the same damn monkeys in the middle of Africa. You don't hear that much about all these other epidemics, because the truth is that governments don't want you to know. They don't want you to know they can't protect you."

"Take off your tinfoil hat," Heidi fought back. "What about SARS, or that H1N1 thing a few years back?"

Nodding, Paul said, "I think the government handled SARS well. H1N1 was a good job, but do you know how many people died worldwide?"

Heidi didn't say anything.

"Maybe as many as half a million. Maybe a little less. That's a lot of dead people for something we think we did a good job on." Paul stared out the window again at the glowing Costco sign.

The two sat in silence for a long, long time, Paul fuming and Heidi refusing to look at him. Finally Paul asked, "How do you shut down half of Uganda in the space of a week? Last week Uganda was fine. Now it's quarantined. That's almost like saying half of Uganda got AIDS last week. It doesn't make sense with what we know about how AIDS spreads. It doesn't make sense with what we know about how Ebola spreads."

"Those people over there are just scared. They're overreacting." Heidi turned and glared at Paul, clearly implying he was overreacting too.

"Heidi, Ebola is coming. When it gets here, the people with the right kind of immune system will survive. Everybody, and I do mean *everybody* else, will die. My choice—and this proves I'm not depressed—is to get infected early so I have a chance to live. I think you should, too."

"That doesn't prove anything," Heidi sobbed.

Paul let her cry while he stewed in his anger.

Finally she choked back her tears enough to speak. "You're scaring me, Paul. It's like you're a different person. I know you've given up hope. You think Austin is dead. Maybe if you just face up to that, it'll be a first step."

It was hard to admit, but Paul nodded. "And that Mitch Peterson guy you talked to, he went to Kapchorwa, so he's dead, too. That guy you nag—Mitch's secretary, Art what's-his-name—he'll be dead pretty soon. All those people at the embassy in Kampala, they're going to die. Then Ebola will come here."

Chapter 9

Olivia Cooper stepped off the elevator and walked down the empty hall. The night's dark hadn't yet surrendered to the morning. Most of the fluorescent lights in the ceiling were on automatic timers to come to life as normal working hours approached. The few that were on illuminated the long hall in a comforting dusk.

Olivia badged through a door to let herself into the long room housing her department's rows of cubicles. Fingers clicked softly on keyboards. Some of her coworkers were already at their desks, toiling to plug their allotment of holes in America's porous security.

The door closed behind her, loudly enough to make her cringe. She was, after all, sneaking into the building. At least she felt that way. Eric had directed her not to come back to work until next week. She subconsciously lowered her head, slinked into an aisle between two rows of cubicles, and hurried down to the one that contained her desk.

She stepped in and exhaled her tension away. The cubicle was her second home.

She sat her purse and her overpriced hazelnut coffee down, took her seat, and powered up her computer. Impatiently, she watched it go through its usual series of startup splash screens. It prompted her to log in and the computer kicked into a security scan. She groaned. The routine security scan was normally scheduled to run while she took her lunch, but several days of her absence had put it behind. The scanning software would take over her computer for at least the next thirty minutes, rendering it useless.

Olivia leaned back in her chair, yawned, and watched

the progress bar on the screen. Someone nearby sipped loudly at a hot cup of coffee. Somebody whispered a curse at a computer, probably for showing them exactly the information they'd requested, just not what they wanted. The progress bar on the computer, as hurried as it was to inch along when the scan first started, now seemed frozen in place. Never a good sign. The scan might run for an hour.

Knowing the computer would prompt her to log in again after it finished the scan, it was safe to leave it alone. Olivia stood up, looked out into the aisle, saw no one, and started to wander. Someone might be in who could bring her up to speed on the Najid Almasi project.

She walked over to the conference room she and her team had taken over prior to her absence. The lights were off. Through the glass wall, she saw the long conference room table was clear, and all of the rolling chairs were neatly pushed underneath. She stopped and stared at it for a moment, taking another sip of her coffee. She at least expected to see some evidence that someone had been in the conference room late the night before: papers, out-of-place cords, something left written on a white board.

The room looked like it hadn't been disturbed in days.

"Olivia?"

Jumping at the sound of her name, she turned to see Eric, thirty feet away, leaning out the door of his own dark office. "What are you doing here?" he asked.

Olivia smiled as she shook her head. "I couldn't stay home anymore. I was going stir crazy."

Eric scrutinized her for a few uncomfortably long seconds before he waved her over. "Come on in." He disappeared into his office.

Olivia walked over, stepped into the open door, and leaned on the doorjamb. "Yeah?"

Eric gestured to one of the chairs in front of his desk.

Olivia entered the office and sat down.

"You okay?" Eric asked.

Olivia smiled, but looked away. "I'm fine."

"Fine isn't the same as okay," said Eric. He leaned forward and put his elbows on his desk, smiling. "People who say they're fine are usually lying."

Olivia shook her head. "You know me. I can't sit around my apartment doing nothing."

"Did you go running?"

"I can only run so far, Eric. I have to stop some time."

"Yeah." Eric leaned back in his chair. "I suppose that's true."

"It's true whether you suppose it is or not." Olivia was mildly annoyed with the questioning.

Eric said, "At least you're as feisty as you've ever been. Have you heard anything from your brother yet?"

Olivia tried to keep her face blank and said, "No, nothing."

"Your dad hasn't heard anything?"

"No." Olivia gestured in the direction of the empty conference room that until recently had been her headquarters. "What has the team found out?"

Eric frowned as he twirled his pen and fidgeted with the clip.

"What?" Olivia asked.

"The whole thing got bounced to the CIA."

She tried to hide a sudden spurt of anger by keeping her mouth shut.

"Olivia." Eric used a soothing voice. "You know how it works here. We analyze data. We investigate. We draw conclusions. Our significant findings, the ones that need action, end up with the FBI or the CIA."

Olivia knew Eric was right. She was, however, disappointed for a variety of reasons, not the least of which was fear of losing the project. With the project gone, she wouldn't be able to guide the resources of her department in finding out what happened to Austin.

Into the silence, Eric said, "Imagine you work on the production line in the frozen chocolate-covered banana factory—"

Olivia raised a hand to hush Eric. "A: I can already tell this is going to be a stupid analogy. B: I don't need you to draw me a picture. I understand. I know it's a success to have the project taken over by the CIA. I can know that and still be disappointed."

"Kind of bittersweet, like when your kids go off to college," Eric said.

She shook her head. "Are you drawing bad analogies to see if you can cheer me up? Because you need to know that I don't *need* to be cheered up. I just need to work. And if you say anything else about me having college-aged children, I may throw this coffee at you."

Eric forced a laugh. "Okay."

"Okay," Olivia agreed. "What do you want me to work on?"

Eric yawned and stretched dramatically before taking a long hard look across the desk. "We both know that what you want to do is log into your computer and spend as much time as you can trying to figure out what's going on with your brother, right?"

Olivia involuntarily glanced away. "Umm—"

"It's okay," Eric said. "I'd do the same if I was in your shoes."

Olivia didn't respond.

"Let's do this. Why don't you spend the morning trying to find out what you can find out? Later today, I need you to get back to tracking the guys with American passports."

Olivia asked, "Didn't you just tell me that project was with the CIA now?"

"I'll get you plugged into their team," said Eric. "Barry is supporting them now. You'll be back in a data gathering and analysis role."

"That works."

Chapter 10

Olivia sat in her cubicle catching up on email, drinking her morning coffee, and reading through reports on the Ugandan outbreak. Most of what she turned up told the story of a government overreacting by trying to shut down the eastern half of the country, blocking all access in or out. The ramshackle infrastructure in the rural areas, in need of constant maintenance, foundered when busy hands weren't immediately on station to put failing components back together again. Information became a luxury, and rumors filled in where facts and exaggerations once held sway. The name Kapchorwa came up again and again, with almost no specifics about what had happened there except for the nearly universal reference to it as the epicenter of an epidemic.

Corroborating stories came out of Western Kenya about outbreaks in small towns like Kitale, Kisumu, and Kakamega. Olivia opened up Google Maps and zoomed in on the border region between Kenya and Uganda. The road from Kapchorwa led east around the base of Mt. Elgon and then southeast into Kitale. Further along that road lay Kakamega and Kisumu. Reports on the number of people affected were mostly dismissed. Nobody believed Ebola could spread so fast. However, one report speculated that a new, much more contagious strain of Ebola could be an explanation for what was happening both in Eastern Uganda and Western Kenya. Then, in a gush of inspired originality, the author named this speculative strain *Ebola K*.

Olivia nearly spit out her coffee as she laughed, thinking it was a good thing the author of that report hadn't been around when the first Ebola epidemic killed hundreds in Zaire. He might have labeled the newly discovered disease

Ebola Z, a moniker that would drive the fans of the current zombie craze absolutely nuts.

Getting back to business, Nairobi, with three million inhabitants, was in a state of panic. Depending on the source, Olivia found the low estimate for the number of confirmed cases at one hundred and eighteen. The scary number was the count of suspected cases. That number topped five hundred, when just three days prior, there hadn't been a single one.

She came across a heavily redacted report that had all of the earmarks as having originated with the CIA. The report was mostly concerned with a suspected terrorist affiliate—with a redacted name—who was said to be in the area of Kapchorwa. The terrorist was not confirmed exactly, but a witness with questionable credibility had identified him. Olivia knew the report had to be talking about Najid Almasi, but the thing that piqued her interest was why anybody in Kapchorwa would be able to identify a wealthy Saudi oil heir, who as far as anyone knew, had never been to Kapchorwa before.

The report mentioned an undetermined number of jihadist suspects being tracked out of the country. An addendum to the report ended in Kitale at a local airport. A misplaced passport had been discovered in a hangar according to the report. The name on the passport was surprisingly not redacted. Olivia cross-checked the name with those on the list she'd been tracking from Pakistan before her unexpected break from work.

They matched.

The ramifications frightened her to the core.

Chapter 11

Barry Middleton wasn't in his cubicle five minutes by the time he'd made enough muted sounds to alert Olivia to his presence. She came to stand in his doorway.

Barry pointed at an empty spot on the top of his L-shaped desk.

Olivia seated herself there, coffee mug still in hand. "Barry, I need to talk about the project."

Nodding in understanding, he said, "It's in the CIA's hands now."

"Yeah, I know." She pointed in the direction of Eric's office. "I spoke with Eric this morning. He's going to get me added to the team."

"Until it's official—"

Olivia tilted her head forward and looked down her nose. "It will be."

Barry's reluctance evaporated immediately.

"Don't tell me anything you don't feel comfortable with, okay? At least not until the official word comes down later this morning."

Barry nodded sheepishly.

"First things first." Olivia leaned close and said softly, "I came across a report this morning—"

Barry looked at his watch. Normal work hours didn't start for another hour. He looked back up at her. "What time did you get in?"

"I couldn't sleep." Olivia shrugged to let him know it was no big deal. "This report looked like it came from somebody on the ground in Kapchorwa. I think a CIA asset."

Nodding, Barry said nothing.

"Most of the details were redacted."

"That's the way we get 'em most of the time," he replied.

"Yeah." Olivia's face turned serious. "I'm wondering if there's any way to contact the asset directly."

Barry's expression turned suspicious, and he leaned away.

She reached over and put a hand on Barry's shoulder. "I don't want to get anybody in any trouble."

"The identity of a CIA operative is classified for a reason, Olivia. You know that." Barry looked around as though a secret agent might be lurking outside his cubicle, ready to do him in.

"I don't—" Olivia scooted back on the desk and took a moment to think of the right way to tell Barry what she wanted. "Eric has given me some leeway with my work time."

"For?" Barry asked.

"To find my brother."

Barry looked down at his lap. "Sorry about your brother."

"Barry, it's okay. I—" Olivia choked a little on her words, then quickly regained her composure. "I don't know if he's okay or not. But I'd feel better if I could find out. My parents would feel better if they knew. Honestly, my stepmom says my dad is going a little nuts."

Barry looked up. "I understand, but there's only so much we can do from here."

"Without breaking any laws." Olivia forced a smile to let him know that she was half joking. "The CIA operative was in Kapchorwa. The report made that clear enough. He moved on to Kitale in Kenya and has been making reports along the way. I don't need to know his name. I just—"

"Want to talk to him?" Barry guessed.

"Yeah," Olivia admitted. "I guess that is what I want. I just want to message him somehow and ask him about Austin."

"And with Eastern Uganda turning into a black hole, you think this CIA guy, or girl, is your best chance of finding out about your brother."

"Yes."

Shaking his head slowly, Barry said, "You know it's more than likely this guy still doesn't know anything about him, right?"

Olivia nodded, though she was pinning her hopes to the possibility of contacting the CIA asset and having him tell her he'd run into Austin, and that Austin was fine. It sounded childishly wishful, even when she thought it through. No way she could ever voice that hope.

Barry looked up at the ceiling and rubbed his chin. He picked up his coffee cup and sipped. He shuffled through the papers on his desk, as if he were looking for something. "Here's what I think."

"I'm listening."

"We can't do anything to drill down in the data and try to find out who this guy is." Barry waved his hands to make it clear that option was completely off the table. "We could both get into too much trouble over that, and by trouble, I mean jail time."

Olivia agreed with a nod.

"If, as you said, the reports tell us the locations from where this operative is contacting Langley," Barry shrugged, looked around again, and pulled an ambiguous expression across his face, "who's to say we don't come across his phone records accidentally while we're searching for calls from Najid Almasi? We know Almasi was in the area. That's how we linked him to Kapchorwa in the first place."

Shaking her head, Olivia said, "We can't eavesdrop on CIA calls though."

"Not saying that," said Barry. "They'd be encrypted anyway. If we could pin a certain telephone to certain locations in the timeframes that the reports refer to —"

Olivia grinned and asked, "How many satellite phones could be in use in that part of the world in those exact locations?"

Barry asked, "Who's to say you can't call the asset up, and just ask him what he knows about Kapchorwa?"

She thought through the pitfalls. "In the spirit of whatever law protects the classified identity of CIA operatives, calling one of them up may be illegal, but technically, I might be in the clear. It may be an exploitable loophole."

"I'll dig into the data and let you know what I come up with," said Barry.

"Okay," Olivia jumped off the desk, stepped into the doorway, then turned back around. "I won't beat you up anymore this morning. After Eric gives me the go-ahead, I'll come back for an update."

Chapter 12

Still well before regular work hours, Olivia left the building with a smile to the guard who'd seen her come in earlier. Her smile wasn't real—more of an apology for troubling him to watch her come and go. Olivia was worrying over her morning's research, specifically about the speculative Ebola K virus. She knew only one person who could tell her for sure whether the author was simply fear mongering or whether it could be something real.

Olivia crossed the near-empty parking lot, unlocked her car with the remote, and settled into the driver's seat. She took her cell phone out of the console where she kept it during work hours and dialed the number.

After a couple of rings, the voice on the other end said, "Wheeler."

"Dr. Wheeler," Olivia started.

"Dr. Wheeler?" he asked. "I thought we'd switched to Mathew already. Or Matt. You know, something social."

Olivia sighed. "I know you've got a pathological need to flirt, *Mathew*, but I need to ask you some questions if you've got time."

Dr. Wheeler heaved a sigh. "That's okay. I'm only flirting out of habit. I'm not in the mood for it this morning. Um...not because of you, mind you. I'll always be happy to flirt with you...it's just something with work."

"I know," said Olivia. "Why are you at work early?"

Dr. Wheeler laughed feebly. "You recall my employer is the CDC, right?"

"Sorry. Too many other things on my mind lately."

"Like your brother?" Wheeler asked.

"Yes."

"Last time we talked, you were worried about him. Please tell me he made it out of Uganda before the quarantine."

"No," Olivia said, letting too much of her anxiety color her answer.

"Are you in contact with him?"

"He's missing but—" Olivia cut herself off, not sure what she should say to finish the thought.

After a moment, Dr. Wheeler said, "I'm sorry. Is there anything I can do?"

After a sad, short laugh, she said, "You wouldn't happen to have a medical team in Kapchorwa, would you?"

"No," said Dr. Wheeler. "I do know the people who know the people who are trying to get into that area. I can get back to you on it."

"Thank you." Not at all expecting that, Olivia found herself choked up again with gratitude and a smidgen of hope. "I...uh...thank you."

"Don't mention it. I'd say you can thank me by having a drink with me, but even I'm not that much of a heel." Wheeler laughed a little to let her know he was trying to cheer her up.

"I know." Olivia took a deep breath to get back to an emotionally level spot. "I'll take you up on that drink, but I'll buy. I've got other questions to ask."

"Shoot."

"I've been reading reports all morning—"

"All morning?" Dr. Wheeler laughed. "Most people haven't had their morning coffee yet."

Olivia smiled. "I read something that mentioned a new strain of Ebola more contagious than previous strains. The report seemed pretty speculative to me. Do you know anything about that?"

"You're talking about the strain affecting Eastern Uganda and Western Kenya?"

"And Nairobi," Olivia added.

"Yes," confirmed Dr. Wheeler. "We've been waiting all night on samples to come in. We've got them flying from both Uganda and Kenya. Samples arrived in the European labs last night. Our plane hit some weather and got delayed. It should be landing in Atlanta any moment."

"Do you think it is a new strain?" Olivia asked. "What are the chances, I mean, that two different strains of Ebola could hit Africa at the same time?"

Dr. Wheeler drew a long, patient breath. "Actually, pretty good. Viruses mutate all the time."

"All the time?"

"Viruses are simple, elegant life forms, Olivia. They combine with RNA or DNA in a cell and hijack it for their own purposes. That's how viruses work. Just the nature of how they replicate opens them up to mutation. Take influenza, for instance. You wouldn't know it as a layperson, but most of the virions produced when influenza takes over a cell are mutations. Only a small fraction of them are accurate reproductions. Most are useless in terms of how effective they'll be at attacking and reproducing, but sometimes the mutants are more effective. Sometimes they affect the host in a new way, with new symptoms. Sometimes they transfer from host to host more easily, sometimes they kill the host more efficiently, and sometimes they kill too efficiently."

"Okay," Olivia said as an acknowledgement while she waited for Dr. Wheeler to get through the introductory matter.

"The point is, the more people who catch a virus, the more chances the virus has to mutate into a more effective strain. Africa is suffering from the largest Ebola outbreak ever. In a manner of speaking, it's never been a better time to be an Ebola virus."

"So the samples you're waiting for could be from a new strain," Olivia concluded. "What's your gut tell you on this one?"

"Just between you and me?" he asked.

"Just between us."

"If all the reports coming out of East Africa are true, hell, if *half* the reports coming out of East Africa are true, I'm afraid of what we'll find in our tests."

Chapter 13

From the air, Dallas expanded in a gridwork stain across a tan-colored sea of dead, late-summer grass. The pilot, in his pre-landing announcement, told the passengers that the temperature in Dallas was one hundred and four. Salim understood the reason why all the vegetation had withered to desert hues.

The airplane banked into the turn and started the final descent. From his window seat, Salim saw a labyrinth of runways astride six semicircular terminals. He recalled being fascinated the first time he'd seen an airport from above. He'd even been interested in many he'd seen after. Chicago O'Hare—he'd arrived there near midnight—had been particularly beautiful, with its millions of lights twinkling against a black earth.

Mostly, he'd seen too many airports, had too many flights, and awakened too many times to a wrong-colored sky, black when it should have been blue, blue when it should have been dawn. Salim was unstuck in time and place. His circadian clock sent his body messages that contradicted those sent by his eyes. Everything jumbled in his brain. His stomach was roiling. His ability to concentrate was shot. It was hard to focus his eyes when he tried to read his tickets.

Of one thing he was certain: he had an urgency brewing in his bowels.

He looked across the laps of two other passengers and gave a brief thought to climbing over them and running for the restroom at the back of the plane. He couldn't. The seatbelt light was on. The plane was landing. He had to stay seated or risk arrest by an overzealous sky marshal. He'd never make it to a restroom then.

The plane would be on the ground in two or three minutes; it might still be another fifteen or twenty before it was parked at the terminal. From there, Salim needed to get out of his seat and hustle up the gangway.

Please, let there be a restroom close by.

The diarrhea had been a problem over the past three flights. When it initially hit, Salim had been only an hour into a five-hour flight, and he'd spent a good deal of that flight locked in the restroom. The ordeal had been embarrassing. The other passengers stared at him. Some snickered as he made trip after trip up and down the aisle. He'd disturbed his neighboring passengers with his comings and goings, and he felt sure he'd disturbed the passengers close to the restroom with the unpleasant smells that escaped when the door was open.

Salim's belly gurgled some more, and cramps followed. He clenched his teeth and closed his eyes as he leaned back in his seat.

"We'll be down in a second," the elderly woman said from the seat beside his.

He smiled politely and nodded.

"Do you live in Dallas?" she asked.

Salim had been chatted up by how many passengers now? He didn't understand why it was getting hard to keep his thoughts straight. "Just visiting," he said.

"You live in Chicago?"

That's where the flight originated. But he didn't know anything about Chicago. To tell the lie that he lived there might put him at risk of being exposed for what he was.

The airplane bounced through some turbulent air, and the seatbelt tugged across Salim's lap. He winced. "I'm from Denver. I'm visiting my cousin in Dallas." That was the briefest version of his story. Why was this woman talking to him now? She'd been silent the entire flight.

"Denver to Dallas via Chicago?" The woman smiled. "I hope you saved a lot of money on that flight."

Without consciously choosing to, Salim rubbed a hand over his aching forehead as he tried to dredge up the best part of his lie, the one he'd picked up from a frequent flier on an early leg of his journey. "I'm on a mileage run."

The old woman burst into a fit of giggling.

When will this damn flight end? A little bit rudely, Salim told her, "I'm flying discount flights to maximize my frequent flier miles."

"Oh, dear." Oblivious to Salim's tone of voice, the woman laid her hand on his and said, "I thought maybe you were nervous about landing. I know what a mileage run is. I have a friend who hit a million miles last spring."

That impressed Salim as he imagined his discomfort in getting through the ten or twenty thousand he'd already racked up. "A million?"

Out the window, the ground rose closely enough to convey a sense of the speed they were traveling.

"Yes," she said, "both him and his wife."

The airplane jolted, and the wheels briefly screeched as rubber touched concrete. Wind roared over the wings, and the plane braked hard. The seatbelt tugged at Salim's lap again as he prayed that he could hold on just a few minutes longer.

The airplane slowed to taxi speed and started bumping across the joints in the runway's concrete slabs. People started clicking the clasps on their laps in anticipation of the seatbelt sign being turned off. Passengers retrieved bags from beneath the seats in front of them and situated themselves to exit.

Salim removed his phone from his pocket and turned it on. He watched the screen as the phone went through its boot process, hoping mostly to take his mind off the waiting, to think about something besides how badly he needed to sit down on a toilet.

Please, let me make it to the restroom in the terminal.

The main screen came to life. The phone searched for a signal. It dinged with the arrival of a text message—a message from a contact in his phone named *Mother*.

Chapter 14

It was a narrow bathroom stall in the terminal, and for that, Salim was thankful. As he sat on the commode, he leaned over with one elbow on his knee, the other on the toilet paper dispenser. Past caring about the noise he was making, he grunted as another cramp stabbed him in the belly.

He rubbed a hand across his sweating face. As bad as he was feeling when the airplane landed, he was getting worse. He had no thermometer, but he knew he had a fever. He ached like never before, and he was starting to wonder if the runs would keep him on the toilet for the rest of his life.

Salim shivered. Not from the fever, but from fear.

For the first time since he started hopping through airports and driving himself into a jet-lagged stupor, he didn't believe it was the loss of a regular schedule that had sent him reeling. He now feared he'd caught the disease that had killed those villagers in Kapchorwa.

If so, Salim realized, he could be dying.

With that thought came despair so real and so deep he bit his lip while he muffled a pained cry into his shirtsleeve. He gasped a ragged breath and sobbed again. Having seen so many people suffer, bleed, and wither, having smelled the stench of what flowed from their bodies, having felt trembling lips that tried to drink, having touched dying flesh, and hearing the wails of parents over dead children, Salim knew the true horror of death.

"You okay, buddy?" a voice called from the next stall over.

"Yes," Salim managed a reply. "Just...just...on my phone.

Bad news…from home."

"No good comes from looking at your phone in the john," came the voice of a man that sounded like he was smiling.

Salim sucked in a few long, silent breaths and rubbed the tears out of his eyes. He'd made a mistake in going to Pakistan. But that was just the finale in a long list of pathetic, ill-advised choices. There was no romance in dying for jihad—not for anybody or anything. He was too young, had too much living to do. Sobs threatened to overwhelm him again.

He made a significant effort to get himself under control while he stared at the floor and contemplated what to do next.

The toilet in the next stall flushed, and then beneath the wall Salim saw feet shuffle. He heard a zipper and a belt buckle rattle.

"You good, buddy?" the man asked.

"Yeah," said Salim.

"Safe travels." The guy in the next stall exited.

Salim remembered he had a message from Mother on his phone. He took it out of his pocket, not with a plan of what to do in response to the message, but more as a mental escape from the weight of contemplating his own gruesome death. He looked at the black screen for a long time without activating the device. Mother was the source of the next set of orders from his handlers, the handlers who'd put his life at risk in Kapchorwa. A thought came to him that he finally dared let himself think: he hated them.

He wanted to turn on the phone and respond to the message from Mother with every curse word, every insult he knew. Instead, he scooted back on the seat of the commode and dropped the phone in.

For an eye blink of a moment, it felt good. He'd taken the first step to free himself from his mistakes.

He told himself the thing he needed next was an attorney. When another series of cramps hit him, he realized the thing he needed more urgently than an attorney was a hospital. That's where he was going. Salim checked his billfold to see how much cash he had—a few hundred in American bills. Enough for a taxi to the nearest hospital, of that he was sure.

When he felt he'd emptied himself enough to hold it together for the time it might take him to get out of the airport terminal, into a taxi, and to a hospital emergency room, he cleaned himself up, stood, and nearly fell over from dizziness. As quickly as he could, Salim put himself back together, shouldered his bag, exited the bathroom stall, and washed his hands in an unoccupied sink.

Good God, the bathroom was crowded. Two rows of twenty stalls, at least as many urinals, and a long row of maybe thirty sinks. Still, men lined up to wait for empty spots at stalls and urinals.

Salim took his time at a sink and threw several handfuls of water on his face. He washed his mouth out and straightened up. His head pounded hard enough to knock him off balance. He looked down at the watery mess he'd made but didn't care. He was past caring about many things. All that mattered was getting out of the crowded restroom and getting through the terminal.

On shaky legs and over a floor tilting against him, Salim made his way through the obstacle course of men waiting in lines or rushing through the doorway. He exited the restroom and stepped into a throng of people scurrying at different speeds in both directions. They all seemed to be walking at a pace too fast for Salim to match. Still, he tried.

That was a mistake.

Each of Salim's hurried steps was more of a struggle than the last. Each breath was harder to draw. As he scanned the ceiling for hanging signs that would direct him to an exit and to a taxi stand, the floor seemed to come unstuck from the earth. He reached his arms out to catch his balance and fell as the world went black.

Chapter 15

"You're dehydrated," the doctor said.

Salim looked at the doctor while a nurse injected something into a clear plastic tube. He followed the line of the tube, which terminated under two bands of white tape at the crook in his elbow.

"You have a fever," the doctor continued, "one hundred and three. Do you have any other symptoms?"

Salim fought through the fuzziness in his mind. "My stomach—"

"Nausea?" The doctor asked.

"I haven't thrown up yet. I feel queasy."

"Diarrhea?" asked the doctor.

He nodded. "For a couple of days. It's getting worse."

"I'll prescribe a suppository."

Salim grimaced.

"It's best, considering the nausea," said the doctor. "Don't want you to regurgitate the medicine."

Salim nodded his consent.

The doctor said something to the nurse, using quick words and too much medical jargon for Salim to follow. He looked down at Salim and said, "I'll be back to check on you in a bit."

Trying to sit up, but failing in the attempt, Salim asked, "Am I going to be all right?"

The doctor stopped and looked back down at Salim. "You've probably got the flu. Where were you flying from?"

"Chicago." It wasn't a lie, but it was far from the whole truth.

Nodding, the doctor said, "Lots of cases of the flu up there right now."

"I'll be fine, then?" Hope was back in Salim's voice. "It's just the flu?"

"People don't understand how serious influenza can be," the doctor told Salim in a mildly scolding tone. "They don't think they need to stay home and rest until they recover, and they end up like you." The doctor pointed at the hospital bed, then waved a hand at the rest of the emergency room. "You're here now. You're young and healthy. I've prescribed some medications. We'd like to keep you here for a few days. You did pass out in an airport, after all. When we're sure you're okay, you can go home. You'll probably be fine."

Relieved, Salim sighed as the doctor walked out through an opening in the curtain that surrounded two sides of the bed.

A large, dark-skinned woman pushed her way through the curtain as the doctor was leaving. She looked down at a clipboard stacked thick with papers. "Hello, Salim. I'm Cynthia Hinojosa. How are you feeling?"

He wasn't sure how to answer. He felt terrible. At least he was in an emergency room and finally starting to feel a *little* better. "I'm okay."

"Good," said Cynthia. "I need to review your insurance and payment information. You weren't conscious when they brought you in, so we need to take care of it now."

Salim nodded.

"Do you have any medical insurance?"

He shook his head.

"You understand you'll be fully responsible for payment." Cynthia wrote something on a sheet of paper on her clipboard, and without looking back at him, asked, "You're not on your parents' policy?"

"No," answered Salim.

"Do you have a credit card or debit card you can use for payment?"

"In my billfold," he replied, "but I don't think—"

"You don't have to pay it all now. You'll be billed. Was the address on your driver's license correct? You live in Denver?"

"Yes."

"Do you have someone to stay with locally?"

Salim balked as he thought about whether to tell the lie about visiting his cousin. "The doctor said I'll be here for a few days."

Cynthia cast an angry glance back to where the doctor had passed between the curtains. "You may be well enough to go home this evening."

Chapter 16

Much of the emergency room visit was a blur. Salim slept a lot and woke to prodding and poking from nurses. Cynthia Hinojosa came several times to his partitioned area and pressed him for more information. The credit card in his wallet, the one he'd been given by his jihadist handlers, had been cancelled. His debit card on an account he'd had since he was sixteen, which was still in both his name and his father's, had been closed, probably by his father. Cynthia Hinojosa had no valid card number to write on her forms, and that caused her immense consternation.

Through the weight of her persistence and continual disappointment in his responses, Salim resorted to the story about his cousin. He had to expand on the lie with a fabrication about his missing telephone that held all of his phone numbers. He had them all stored by name and had memorized nobody's actual phone number. His cousin was supposed to meet him at the airport, and Salim now had no way to reach him. Neither did Salim know the address. His life was in his phone, he explained. When the phone disappeared, he became disconnected from everyone he knew, and he had no way to get reconnected short of buying another phone and restoring it from the data saved in his computer, which was back in Denver. Salim was pretty proud of the new layer of lies, especially given the circumstances of his current state of health and persistent fever. He wanted to stay in the hospital. The fever had the doctor very concerned. It didn't respond to anything prescribed.

Cynthia Hinojosa had her own thoughts on that subject. She thought Salim was a deadbeat.

So after eleven hours of taking up a bed in the

emergency room, Salim was wheeled out of the hospital and helped into a waiting taxi. One of the nurses made him a reservation at a nearby hotel. From there, Salim could recover for a few days and take the samples of prescription drugs he'd been given. Some time before they ran out, he'd have to walk to the drugstore across the street and get the prescriptions refilled: something for the fever, another for the nausea, the happy little suppositories, and some kind of antiviral medication for the flu. The doctor told him it was no cure, and that viruses generally had to run their course, but the antiviral could help.

It was late in the evening when the taxi driver left Salim standing in front of the hotel, the kind that looked like it might be full of aggressive rodents and hourly renters.

The night air had still not shed the day's heat, and Salim felt sweat run down his face, though he was expending no effort except that of keeping himself upright. He watched the taxi drive away.

A blue and red neon sign flashed "OPEN" at irritating intervals. The asphalt radiated heat up through Salim's tennis shoes. His backpack seemed to have gained weight on its inexplicable journey from the airport, to the hospital, into the taxi, and now back onto his shoulder.

When the taxi's tail lights disappeared into the stream of red pairs of lights flowing down the road, Salim turned toward the hotel lobby's door, but the weight of that backpack pulled him around in a circle that Salim had difficulty stopping. He spun fully around once, almost twice. The dizziness returned. Fuzzy darkness and panic overwhelmed him, and he fell.

Chapter 17

Late in the morning, Austin lay on his back in the remains of Kapchorwa's burned-out hospital, watching some monkeys play on the rafters where the sheet metal had fallen away in the fire. One of the monkeys stopped, rose up on his back legs, and made a show of pissing onto the floor a dozen feet below.

It was when Austin heard the urine splatter on the concrete that he sat up straight, looking around at the charred interior, expecting to be among the hundreds of bodies burned because of Najid's unexpected brutality. The bodies were gone, as was the fire debris. Only the stains on the floor remained.

To Austin's left lay a row—he presumed—of the newly sick. Eleven men in military fatigues, and one mzungu, an older man. Austin had seen enough people sick with Ebola to know that each of them had it.

A noise from the back of the ward announced the entrance of a woman in gloves, goggles, surgical mask, and apron; insufficient protection, as Austin had learned. She spotted him sitting up and hurried over. Swaying in each of her hands were familiar buckets, soiled and splattered; some of the same buckets of waste that Austin had the responsibility for emptying before—

The memories of Kapchorwa's fire and death flashed through his mind, carrying with them a deluge of fierce sorrow and fear, as palpable as they were when the village was burning, and Austin had no strength to run. He gasped and struggled for control of his runaway emotions.

The plastic buckets echoed as the woman set them on the concrete near the other end of the bedridden row. Startled by the sound of the plastic, the monkeys scampered off. The woman said, "You're up."

Austin looked over at her as he drew in a few more deep breaths, and all he saw of her through the plastic she wore were brown eyes and dark hair.

The woman stepped closer. "How are you feeling?"

Austin answered, "Better."

"Better?" She removed an infrared thermometer from a pocket, knelt down beside him, and scanned his forehead.

"Could I have some water, please?" Austin croaked through a dry throat.

He saw a smile in the woman's eyes as she nodded. She jumped to her feet and hurried across the room to where a covered metal bucket sat—a clean bucket. With one of a dozen cups that had been sitting on the floor by the bucket, she came back across the room. She offered it to Austin.

Austin accepted the cup with a nod and started to drink, then gulp.

"Slow down, okay?"

Nodding as he drank, Austin slowed. When he finished, he reached the cup back toward the woman, "May I have another?"

Another smile hidden behind the mask. The woman took the cup and went back to refill it.

When she returned, Austin asked, "How's my temperature?"

"Nearly normal," she said.

He looked down at himself. He flexed his hands. He wiggled his toes and slowly shook his head as he realized what this moment meant. Choking on the words, he asked, "Did I—" But that was all he could get out.

She said, "I think you beat it."

After a moment of looking at the woman's hidden, happy face, he asked, "I'm going to live?"

She nodded.

"Are you a doctor?" Austin asked, looking for a reason to find falsehood in his hope.

"Yes. I'm Kristin Mills."

"Doctor Mills," he said weakly. "I'm Austin Cooper."

Dr. Mills looked around at the charred ward. "I think under the circumstances, Kristin is fine."

"Kristin," he confirmed.

He took another drink of water. "Things have changed a bit."

Kristin nodded. "The soldiers who stayed helped clean up the hospital."

"The ones that stayed?" Austin asked.

"You've missed a lot."

"How long have I been out of it?"

She pointed out through the back of the hospital. "We found you out by the burned bodies four days ago. Do you remember that?"

Austin rubbed a hand over his head, "Barely."

"You told us what happened. At least you tried."

"Tried?" he asked.

"You were mostly delirious, and it was hard to make sense of a lot of what you said, but enough of it came across."

Austin set his cup on the floor and scooted himself back so he could lean against the wall. He looked over at the white guy sleeping on the floor. "There was a man with you."

Kristin looked at the man on the floor. "That's not the

one you talked to."

Austin raised his eyebrows with a question.

"The man who talked to you was Mitch Peterson. He works for the embassy in Kampala."

"So the government knows?"

"He and his men—" Kristin seemed oddly stuck looking for the right words. "They rushed back to Kampala as soon as I was able to collect some samples for him. I haven't seen nor heard from him since."

"And the guy over there?" Austin pointed at the white man on the floor.

"He's Dr. Simmons. He came with me." Kristin sat down on the floor in front of Austin, crossed her legs, and told the story of what had happened while Austin was unconscious.

Once word got around among the soldiers that the burned bodies were infected with Ebola, it didn't take more than a few hours for all the officers and most of the men to mount up in their vehicles and leave. Kristin hadn't been given a chance to protest. She'd been counting bodies and collecting samples when she heard the trucks driving away.

The fleeing soldiers had left one sergeant and nearly twenty conscripts behind. That night, most of Kristin's supplies and equipment disappeared along with the last vehicle and half the conscripts. She was stranded. With the help of the remaining soldiers, she started putting the hospital into a usable state. Some of the soldiers had set out to walk to nearby villages to find transportation or some form of communication. All of those who'd returned came back neither with a vehicle nor word from anywhere further than they could walk. The one thing they did return with was news that the Ebola virus was blazing its way across the countryside, from hamlet to hamlet, village to village. Kristin's fear was for the cities. She made guesses about Mbale and Kampala, but hoped the government roadblocks had contained it.

In a surprise that left Austin's mouth hanging open, Dr. Littlefield walked in through the hospital's open front door followed by a haggard soldier. Austin said, "Dr. Littlefield, you're alive."

Chapter 18

On the day Austin thought of as his first full day back in the world of the living, he didn't have much energy. He was able to get off his bed and use the outhouse. He fetched his own water and sat up with Dr. Littlefield and Kristin when they ate. It was at their noontime meal when Austin asked Dr. Littlefield how he'd escaped Najid's homicidal wrath.

Dr. Littlefield told Austin he'd been taken out behind the hospital by one of Najid's men. This was shortly after he'd heard the gunshots from down the road west of town. Dr. Littlefield had been made to kneel in front of the waste pit and felt the barrel of a gun pressed to the back of his head. He prayed, knowing that he was in the last moments of his life.

At some point though, the gun barrel abruptly went away. Dr. Littlefield didn't take that to mean anything at that moment. He continued to kneel, looking into the pit of human waste, hoping only that he'd die instantly when the bullet entered his brain. The idea of drowning in the waste was horrid enough to make him shudder as he told it.

Seconds passed, then minutes. Nothing happened. Dr. Littlefield didn't know how long he'd stayed there on his knees. When curiosity got the best of him, he looked over his shoulder. The man who'd taken him out for execution was gone. Dr. Littlefield stood up and looked around. He was alone. He wondered if Najid's man didn't have it in him to execute a kneeling victim. Dr. Littlefield took the opportunity and ran into the forest.

He worked his way up Mt. Elgon's slopes and didn't look back until a red glow illuminated the night. From a place maybe a thousand feet up, he helplessly watched the village burn. He was too far away to hear anything but the faintest of screams from those unlucky enough to be alive when their houses were burned. Those indistinct cries and guilt for his impotence haunted his nightmares.

Chapter 19

Najid Almasi sat in what was his father's office. With his father and younger brother gone, everything now belonged to him. The room was expansive—the size of an average house in many Western countries. The desk was cut from a primordial layer of sedimentary stone that encased the fossil of some aquatic dinosaur and spanned nearly twenty feet long. The floor was layered in a rare Brazilian hardwood, illegal to export. The shelves on the walls displayed glittery items, each of sufficient value to make nearly any of the world's dirty grovelers feel rich, even the American ones.

None of it impressed Najid.

He looked out his window at an acre of glare off the ripples in the swimming pool's blue water and thought about all he'd done. He'd told himself as he progressed in his endeavor to bring down the West that he was being decisive, bold. He, Najid Almasi, was walking the path of Salahuddin Ayyubi; *Saladin* to the Western crusaders he drove from Arab lands, in the time when unwashed Christians stank more than the horses they rode, and wore thick metal plate and maille to protect their delicate white skin from Arab blades.

Now, Najid wondered if his ambition had blinded him to the rashness of his choices.

He'd gambled his financial future.

He'd gambled with his own brother's life.

Najid couldn't help but wonder what would have happened if, instead of plotting to spread Ebola to the West, he had spirited Rashid out of Kapchorwa and gotten for him the best medical care available. Would Rashid be alive today? Did Najid sacrifice his own brother on the altar of his ambition?

He'd lost contact with all of those zealous young men he'd co-opted from Firas Hakimi's organization. Najid didn't know what that meant, but it left him with an unease that grew day after silent day. It was the source of his foul mood, a mood that was fertilized by the near absence of new Ebola cases being reported around the world. He hoped for, and desperately depended on, so many more.

Najid's few contacts in Western law enforcement agencies told him eighteen of his unwitting martyrs had been apprehended. How that happened, Najid guessed, was that the young men must have been under the scrutiny of some Western intelligence agency before they'd come into his possession. His mistake was that of trusting Hakimi to do the work of securing his own organization.

Hadi, Najid's computer man and cousin, had been keeping Najid apprised on the progress of his remaining men with a meeting each morning and another in the afternoon. At each meeting, Hadi had reported that fewer and fewer of the jihadists had shown up on flights for which their tickets had already been purchased. Only eleven of the one hundred and eight made it to the end. The last of the tickets had been used the day before by an Indonesian boy who was currently at the Auckland airport in New Zealand. He was the only one responding to messages and awaiting further instructions.

Najid laughed bitterly. Auckland — the hundredth busiest airport in the world. That wasn't the kind of information Najid would ever have been aware of had it not been for Hadi. Hadi had made the ticket purchases, chosen the routes, and optimized the layovers.

Optimize the layovers? Najid didn't follow Hadi's logic

on it. Hadi had first taken a list of the hundred busiest airports—from Atlanta, Georgia, which processed on average over ten thousand travelers an hour, down to Auckland, which processed maybe a sixth of that number at fourteen million a year. Not knowing which of the jihadists would turn symptomatic and when made for a statistical game. Hadi had to schedule infected men to fly through the busiest airports spread across the globe's different regions on laughably circuitous routes.

In Europe, they cycled through Frankfurt and London. In the Far East, they visited Tokyo, Beijing, and Hong Kong. In America, Hadi had seven of the top twenty busiest airports in the world to choose from, not to mention all the others that filled out the top one hundred. For geography's sake, Mexico City, Rio de Janeiro, Moscow, and Mumbai each received extra visits.

He divided individual trips up between coach and business class. In coach, passengers who sat near contagious jihadists were most likely people going to or from an annual vacation; people who could carry the disease on to infect their friends and family where they lived. Those in business class were most likely to fly with great regularity, picking up the virus and perpetuating it through their fellow business travelers even after all of the jihadists had become too ill to continue.

Through careful planning, Hadi had been able to provide Najid with an estimate on the number of people exposed to his infected men through close contact at an airport or on an airplane. Each day Hadi provided a low and a high estimate, all graphed on a pretty curve with a second line for the growth of indirect infections. Unfortunately, the range of uncertainty between the low and high estimate of the number of infected after eight weeks — the range of time over which Hadi projected into the future — wasn't any better than Najid's pure guesswork, somewhere between a few thousand and a few billion.

Najid left the disposition of the remaining jihadist in Auckland to Hadi. Najid suspected that if the man wasn't showing symptoms already, he was probably in the clear.

For Najid, the question of what to do about Firas Hakimi was a more pressing problem. Hakimi had made no attempt to contact him despite the ignorant English boy, Jalal, whom Najid had sent his way.

Had that plan failed?

Had that plan failed, as well?

Najid stared at the water in the pool a little longer and decided he wasn't going to be victimized by his mood. He chose to move forward pragmatically and accept the pain of his mistakes. He picked up one of his telephones and dialed.

When the ringing stopped, Najid heard faint breathing on the other end. "You have not met my emissary," he said.

Firas Hakimi spat, "You know not what I have or have not done."

"My friend —"

"Be careful with your pleasantries, Almasi. They are less true than you know."

"My friend," Najid persisted, "if you had spoken with my emissary, we would now be talking face to face, and you would understand and approve my course of action."

"Do not presume —"

"No," Najid told Hakimi harshly. "Stop with this pettiness. You have sycophants to grovel at your feet. Do not demand such behavior from me. I'm no pet goat of yours. My father has died. His fortune has passed to me. I will use it to pursue our common goals. Will you meet with me to discuss this as men?"

Hakimi's flaring temper was obvious through his sharp breaths. That was good. Hakimi needed to be goaded into action, and Najid needed Hakimi's temper for leverage.

"Search for your emissary's name this afternoon on the Internet." Hakimi paused dramatically. "You will find something of interest."

The line went dead.

Chapter 20

Paul's phone rang. He saw Olivia's name on the screen and looked at the other four people seated around the conference room table. He told them, "I've got to get this." He rolled his chair away from the table and stood up. "Just go on without me. I've got everything I need." Paul left the conference room and closed the door behind him, glad to be out of another pointless meeting. He answered the phone, "Olivia?"

"Hey, Dad. Am I interrupting anything?"

"Just a meeting. Nothing important." Paul looked at his watch. It was nine-thirty a.m. where Paul was, so it was eleven-thirty in Atlanta. "Are you on your lunch break?"

"Yeah."

"You sound worried."

Olivia said, "I've barely said anything."

"I've been your dad for a while now, and I pay attention. What's up? Did you find something out about Austin?"

"No, nothing, but I'm working on it."

"How does it feel to be back in the office?"

"Better than not, but I'm kind of in limbo. My project was taken over by—" Olivia, of course, couldn't say by whom, but she knew her father would guess. He knew what she did and for whom she worked. "Well, I'm between projects at the moment."

"Hmm."

"Did you see the news this morning?"

Paul replied, "I've been in back-to-back meetings since seven. Give me the summary."

"A guy collapsed at the airport in Dallas yesterday. He

was taken to the hospital. They're testing for Ebola."

"I know Heidi probably called you and told you not to talk to me about Ebola stuff anymore, right?"

"Of course she did," answered Olivia.

"Yet here we are." Paul hadn't heard about the case in Dallas, and he was curious why his daughter would call about a single case he was sure to see on the news later in the day. "What's different about this guy?"

"Maybe nothing. I haven't found anything specifically on him yet, but—" Olivia took a long slow breath as she decided whether or not to take the final step in an action that could get her fired and might piss off Heidi. She wasn't sure which was worse.

"If you can't say," said Paul, "then don't."

"I spoke with Mathew Wheeler yesterday morning."

"Mathew Wheeler?"

"Dr. Wheeler," Olivia explained.

"Oh, the CDC doctor you met."

"Yes." Olivia gulped down the last of her reservations. "Yesterday when I talked to him, the CDC was waiting on some Ebola samples out of Uganda. They arrived, and the CDC worked on them all night. Dr. Wheeler just called me with the results."

"And?" Paul asked, into Olivia's pause.

"It's a new strain."

"What does that mean in practical terms?"

"I don't know anything for sure," said Olivia. "I've been reading everything I can find coming out of Uganda and Kenya, for obvious reasons. It might be that the new strain is more contagious than previous strains."

"I've been following the stories and looking at what data

I can find," said Paul, feeling frightened at a confirmation of his belief. "I suspected much the same thing."

"There's more."

"More?" Paul asked.

"The new strain may already be mobile."

"Mobile?" Paul asked, not sure exactly what she meant.

"A German lab matched cases in Frankfurt with the new strain."

"In Frankfurt?" he asked. "I haven't heard anything about those on the news. Well, one or two maybe."

"Dr. Wheeler is getting his information through the medical community, and it looks to me like the government has been keeping a tight lid on Ebola information. They've got more cases than have been reported in the news."

"I've seen news of cases popping up here and there in lots of major cities," he replied.

"Yeah," Olivia agreed. "They may all be the new strain."

Paul didn't follow up with questions about how she jumped to that last conclusion. He knew his daughter well enough to be sure that if she had taken the risk to make him aware, she was certain the information she was sharing was true.

"Dad, I know you can work from home. Can Heidi?"

"Yes."

"Indefinitely?"

"Yes."

"Then I think you should. Hunker down at home, and avoid contact with people. Start today."

Chapter 21

The German Chancellor, in a surprise news conference called to address an Ebola outbreak in Frankfurt, announced that every one of the thirty-eight confirmed cases had been traced back to the airport there. She further announced that the government was considering the drastic decision of shutting down all air traffic in and out of the country.

Lufthansa's stock price in after-hours trading on European markets plummeted by nearly twenty percent. US airline stocks, still trading in New York and Chicago, took a beating. The Dow Jones Industrial Average, the number most laymen thought reflected the pulse of the US economy, didn't contain any airline stocks. One of its components was Boeing, which everybody knew manufactured airliners. General Electric was another component, and in its vast catalogue of manufactured goods were jet engines. Both companies plummeted with the airlines, dragging down the Dow. That spooked an already jittery market, and as the market neared the closing bell, it had shed nearly six percent on the heaviest volume day ever.

The Bear was on the trading floor and investors were stampeding for the exits.

Gold prices were on the rise. Oil prices were on the way down because everyone foresaw an Ebola-related economic slowdown. It was disaster for all the people Najid knew in the oil business. For Najid, it was a good day. The markets had finally turned in the direction he'd engineered. His massive bet—while far from profitable—was losing him less money.

He was in a better mood when an email came from

Hadi. Najid opened the email and clicked the link. In a trite scene soon to turn graphically brutal, Jalal, the English boy, knelt in the sand, nothing but desert behind him and clear blue sky above. Jalal's eyes were red-rimmed from crying. A piece of cloth was pulled tightly between his teeth, presumably tied behind his head. His hands were bound.

Jalal's face was bruised and his clothes were spattered with blood, presumably his. Where other viewers saw needless brutality, Najid saw more chances for Jalal to transmit his gift to Hakimi or someone in his inner circle. Najid didn't harbor any illusions that Jalal had kept anything secret. Najid felt certain Jalal had told Hakimi every single thing he could remember about his time in Kapchorwa, his time in Pakistan, and even how many times he'd had inappropriate thoughts about the young girls in his high school. To Najid, Jalal didn't appear to be strong, and that was the primary reason he'd been selected. Najid was sure that Hakimi's anger would drive him to torture any emissary sent. Jalal, being weak, would make no effort to hide anything, and so would suffer less in being convinced. It was a kind of humanity that made sense in Najid's mind.

A man clad in black, exposing only his eyes, stood beside Jalal, holding a knife in a fierce grip as though he expected any moment to be attacked by a lion. Everybody in the world had seen videos just like it before. There was no lion to come, only poor kneeling Jalal and a loquacious, ranting man, showing his anger through the way he held his knife.

Najid watched with the sound turned down, not interested in the embarrassing ramblings that only served to make the black-clad brute appear mentally unstable. The babbling finally reached its end. The man in black positioned himself behind a struggling Jalal, and then went to work sawing through Jalal's throat until his head came off. Blood was everywhere. The brute didn't know it, but in killing Jalal, he'd infected himself with the Ebola virus and was going to die an even more brutal death. That made Najid smile.

The video didn't end. In an unexpected surprise, Firas Hakimi himself walked into the camera frame with no mask, as bold as a peacock. He picked up Jalal's head by the hair, raised it in front of the camera, and went on a rant of his own.

Najid paused the video a few minutes into the tirade. He took a screen capture of the image and pasted it into a graphic program, not sure he was seeing what he thought he was seeing. Once in the graphic program, he zoomed in on Hakimi's face, angry mouth open in mid sentence. Najid looked closely and nodded as he felt at least one of his troubles start to melt away. Spatters of Jalal's blood were on Hakimi's cheek. Any doubt that Hakimi would also be infected with Ebola disappeared.

Chapter 22

Austin Cooper stood in the center of a red dirt intersection, looking east and waiting for the sun to rise. After a night of fitful sleep, spending a good deal of it watching the moon and stars through the holes in the roof, he'd finally gotten out of bed and decided to walk out to Kapchorwa's main intersection. One of the monkeys who'd taken over the hospital's roof and exposed beams as their new playground squatted at the peak of the roof, as motionless as a furry gargoyle, watching Austin watch the sky.

From inside the hospital, he heard Kristin cough. She'd come down with the fever the day before. Sadly, as Austin's strength grew, hers faded. Now she was on a mat, lying on the floor among the remaining soldiers. One of them had already died.

When someone brushed past a fragment of burned door still attached to a creaky hinge, Austin looked over at the hospital. Dr. Littlefield came out. Austin turned back to watch the sky.

"Waiting for the sun?" the doctor asked, as he walked up.

Austin nodded. "I never appreciated the beauty of the dawn before. I was always rushing off to school or trying to get to Starbucks while the line was still short."

Dr. Littlefield took up a spot beside Austin and turned to watch the dawn come. "Too many neon distractions back in the States."

Austin chuckled. "That sounds like a line from one of those eighties hair band songs."

Dr. Littlefield smiled. "My roots coming out."

Austin drew a big breath of the morning air. "Now that Kristin is down, do you worry?"

"About?"

Austin looked at the doctor. "You've been exposed longer than any of us."

"I was at first." Dr. Littlefield didn't turn away from the sky. "I wonder now if I'm a miracle of immunity."

Austin didn't know what to say in response.

"I was in Gulu in 2000."

"That doesn't mean anything to me." Austin forced a smile. "I've never heard of Gulu."

Dr. Littlefield pointed northwest. "It's a town a couple of hundred miles that way. A little bigger than Mbale. There was an Ebola outbreak there in 2000. It was my first year in Uganda." His face darkened. "I contracted Ebola."

Austin was speechless.

"Obviously, I survived." Dr. Littlefield put a hand on Austin's shoulder. "All this changes you, but you know that, don't you?"

Austin felt the truth of those changes, but was at a loss for putting into words what the differences were.

"After I got better, I wasn't in any hurry to go back to the States. I just stayed on in Africa."

With a question on his face, Austin looked at the doctor.

Dr. Littlefield shrugged. "The money wasn't an issue for me." He looked back at the sky. "Now, when I go back to the States, I feel like I don't belong. Returning to Africa feels like coming home."

Austin changed the subject. "You'll be immune from Ebola forever?"

"No," Dr. Littlefield answered. "Ebola isn't like the

measles or polio. Immunity from a previous infection hasn't been shown to last any more than ten years. With different strains—and the Kapchorwa strain is obviously a new Ebola strain—antigens shift and immunity disappears."

"So you could get it?" Austin asked.

"I honestly don't know."

"Is it safe to assume I won't get it again?"

Dr. Littlefield nodded.

"Am I still contagious?"

"You were only contagious while you were symptomatic. However, that could have changed with this new strain. You're probably not a danger to public safety. Except—"

"Except for what?" Austin asked.

"Studies have shown live virions in the semen of Ebola survivors last for as long as three months after recovery."

"I need to avoid sex?" Austin grinned. "Somehow I think that'll be easy. Not that I want to, but you know...lack of opportunity."

Austin set about rooting through the remains of Kapchorwa, looking for anything that might be of use on a hike to Mbale. With all the road signs listed in kilometers, and kilometers holding no intuitive meaning for him, Austin did the conversion in his head. Sixty kilometers converted to something like forty miles. If Austin was healthy, he figured it was a two-day hike. In his weakened state, just a few days resurrected from his deathbed, he thought it might take four.

It would have been nice to wait another week before heading out, but he didn't have the luxury. He needed to get into contact with his parents. He needed to get help for the few sick still in Kapchorwa. Despite the wispy memory of Mitch Peterson and what Kristin said he'd done, Austin felt a duty to make sure the world knew about Najid Almasi.

Early in his search, he found some empty plastic bottles lying in the grass beside what was left of a house. Those, he recycled into canteens. He found a canvas bag, singed but usable. It wouldn't be as comfortable as his lost backpack, but in it he could carry water, food, a blanket, and a sleeping mat, assuming he could find any of that to take along.

Searching through the remains of another house, he was using a thick stick to push ashen debris away from a pile against the backside wall, hoping to find an unburned, useful *something* underneath. What he found instead when he shoved over a wide piece of tin was the charred body of a parent, clutching a small child with blackened nubs where its arms should have been, a pained scream crisped permanently into what remained of its face. Austin's hate for Najid Almasi flamed hot. He hoped that Najid's stupid plastic suit had failed and that Najid was, even at this moment, lying somewhere in a pool of his own bloody feces, feeling his organs dissolve in his belly. Austin hoped Najid's suffering would last a long, long time while he slipped slowly into death.

Chapter 24

The time Austin spent rummaging through the ruins of Kapchorwa took much more of his strength than he'd imagined. By early afternoon, he'd exhausted himself and spent most of the rest of the day in the hospital being of little help, mostly watching Dr. Mills and the soldiers struggle through an all-too-familiar set of worsening symptoms.

When dawn broke the next day, Austin was up again, standing on the hospital porch waiting for the light in the sky to become bright enough that he'd be comfortable walking up the dirt road toward Mbale. With little surprise, Dr. Littlefield woke early and joined him. Austin said, "You need to sleep more. You'll make yourself sick if you don't."

"You don't need to leave yet."

"I need to get help for you guys." Austin looked back through the hospital door. "I need to find a phone that works and call my dad. At some point—soon, I hope—I need to go back to Denver. That's my home."

"Do you have what you need?"

Austin patted a hand on his bag. He had half a dozen plastic bottles of well water, enough fruit to get him through a couple of meals, and most of a blanket with burned edges. "If I make it to Chebonet today, I'll feel good."

Dr. Littlefield sat down on the porch near Austin and leaned against the wall, his favorite spot. "I think that's good. Chebonet is only seven or eight miles. It doesn't sound like much but—"

Nothing more needed to be said. Two days prior, Austin had come to coherence, surprised to be alive, surprised to be feeling better—not good, but better. His fever was gone. Through some fortunate combination of antibodies and a robust immune system, he'd survived Ebola. Its viciousness took a toll that would require some recovery time.

"Try to walk in the morning or the late afternoon," said Dr. Littlefield. "Rest through midday in the shade. Drink lots of water."

"I crashed pretty hard yesterday," said Austin. "I know I'm weak." Austin pointed at a half-burned cinderblock building out past the northeastern edge of town. "There might be a couple hundred pineapples still in there, plenty of bananas, and some other stuff. I found them when I was searching yesterday."

"Thanks." Dr. Littlefield tilted his head at the ward behind them. "They aren't eating much. Mostly they need water. And who knows, some help might come."

"With any luck, I can find somebody in Chebonet to give me a ride back to Mbale, and I'll be back here tomorrow night."

Dr. Littlefield laughed out loud for a good long time and finished with an apology.

"What?" Austin asked.

"Rural Africa is half of the dichotomy of Africa."

Austin frowned out of the frustration of not knowing what Dr. Littlefield was talking about.

"Some of Africa is modern," said Dr. Littlefield. "Much of rural Africa isn't much different than it was a hundred years ago, and some of it no different than it was a thousand years ago."

"With a lot in between," Austin added, still having no idea what Dr. Littlefield had found amusing.

"It's hard coming here from America," said the doctor,

"and shedding the preconceptions developed in a modern country, that there'll always be something to drink, something to eat, even getting someone to give you a ride—when you really need it—will take little more effort than walking to the nearest house or small town."

Austin frowned again.

Dr. Littlefield smiled widely. "I'm not making fun of you, Austin." Dr. Littlefield lazily waved a hand at a few of the burned houses down the road. "I'm happy that even after all this, your optimism isn't dead. You think— beyond any evidence and almost beyond hope—that you might be able to get a ride from someone in Chebonet."

Sheepishly, Austin said, "There's a chance."

"Going back for a moment to what made me laugh, it's that I've never seen a running car or truck or anything in Chebonet. I don't think anyone there has the money to buy one. That's the funny thing. Back in the States, everybody has a car. Here it's an exception. More so in the rural parts of the country than the cities."

Austin nodded. That was true. "But still—"

"It's a tiny little huddle of twenty or thirty houses."

Austin nodded.

"I applaud your optimism. Be careful when you get there. People will be frightened. Rumors of Ebola and what happened here are halfway to Kampala by now. You'll be walking into that. People won't open their doors for you. You'll be shunned at the least, maybe worse."

"I understand." Austin looked up the road. The morning light was bright enough. He stood up and stretched his muscles, still sore from yesterday's short walk through town. "I'll be back. Probably not tomorrow, but in a few days."

The doctor stood up and patted Austin on the back. "I know you will. And thank you for doing it."

Chapter 25

Olivia was frustrated. She was on her fourth day in bureaucratic limbo. She still had not been added to the team assigned to track down the jihadists out of Pakistan, and still did not have full access to data she'd had before her absence. Eric had explained to her at least once a day that it was the CIA's call to make, and the odd coincidence of her brother in Kapchorwa in the company of terrorists was causing them to balk. It seemed that it was only through Eric's tenacious loyalty to her that she was still being allowed into the building.

She'd spoken with Mathew Wheeler earlier that morning. Countless monkeys were being infected around the world with the new Ebola strain. All of the reported cases in Western countries were being confirmed to match the new strain. The world needed to gain an understanding of Ebola K in a hurry.

More telling than what Mathew actually said was his mood. His humor seemed all but absent, and that had Olivia worried over how dangerous this new strain of Ebola might be.

She was staring at her monitor absently, thinking about everything that was going on, deciding what else to look at before lunch, leaning toward leaving the office early and maybe going for a run. Who would miss her if she did?

Two metallic taps behind her startled Olivia out of her thoughts. She turned to see Barry standing in her cubicle doorway, looking anxious. She pointed to the extra chair in her workspace and in a hushed voice asked, "What?"

Barry stepped over beside her, reached down by her keyboard, and pressed a yellow post-it note onto her desk. As he silently moved away and sat himself in the extra chair, Olivia looked at the note. On it was written a phone number and nothing else.

She turned to Barry and asked, "Is this...?"

He gave her the slightest of nods.

She mouthed a silent "Thank you."

In a normal voice, Barry asked, "Any word from Eric yet on putting you on the team?"

Olivia shook her head. "I'm reading about this scary crap every day, and I feel helpless. Please tell me you guys are making progress, at least."

Barry nodded, but seemed disheartened at the same time. He leaned out into the cubicle aisle, looked up and down the row, and then pulled himself back into the safety of Olivia's cube.

"What?" she whispered.

He scooted forward in the chair and leaned close to Olivia so that he could talk quietly. "You've seen the news."

"Of course," Olivia shot a frustrated look at her computer monitor. She'd been doing little else.

"You know the cities with reported cases of Ebola, right?" Barry rubbed his hands over his face. He looked very tired.

"How many hours have you been working lately?" she asked.

"It doesn't matter," he replied. He spent a moment thinking about what he was going to say next. "You know, we tracked all those guys from Pakistan, then to Dubai, and on to Nairobi."

Olivia nodded.

"You don't have access to the data now to track those guys anymore, do you?"

"Barry, you know I don't." Olivia let her frustration into her tone.

"You don't need it."

A little bit excited, she asked, "Why?"

"I'm not gonna say what you might or might not learn from looking at it, but if you were to look at a map of the world, and then create a time series showing the location of new Ebola cases reported—"

Olivia interrupted, "That might take me the rest of the day to put together."

Nodding, Barry continued, "If you had knowledge of major air hubs, you'd make the interesting connection between the hubs and what might appear to be a spider web of Ebola cases growing outward. First, you might see our old friend, Nairobi."

"Nairobi is going to be in trouble," Olivia confirmed. One news story claimed tens of thousands of cases in Nairobi alone.

Nodding again. "And that surprised no one, really. After all, it *is* in Africa. In the context of what we know already, our Pakistani friends all visited Nairobi."

Olivia gulped.

"Going back to the map we're discussing, you might see something growing out of Frankfurt—"

"A major European hub," Olivia said, mostly to herself.

"Dubai, Mumbai, Singapore, London." Barry shrugged. "You see where I'm going with this?"

"I know you're not telling me this, exactly," she replied. "If I were to map the Ebola cases, would I find that the major airports are the local epicenters, and might I deduce that our Pakistani friends flew through each of those airports prior to the outbreaks?"

Barry nodded. "If you weren't already under a black cloud because of your brother, this morning might be a great time to go short on Airline stocks."

"Germany closed their airports last night," said Olivia. "Is something else going to happen?"

Looking back over his shoulder again. "Just something that should have happened already."

"We're closing down our airports?" Olivia asked.

Barry's face remained blank for a moment before he asked, "Have you talked to your friend at the CDC?"

"Dr. Wheeler?"

He nodded. "Then you're probably hearing the same thing Congress is hearing. People are afraid and rightfully so."

"Oh, my God. The markets are going to crash." Shaking her head as the weight of the human and economic toll became clearer in her mind, her tone turned caustic. "We had these guys. We had all of them on a list. What went wrong?"

Barry sat back in his chair and rubbed his face again, then shook his head. He looked like a beaten man. "Did I ever tell you about a friend of mine name Marco Vasquez?"

Confused about the change in direction, Olivia shook her head.

"My friend Marco was in sales for this computer company, B2B type stuff."

"Business to business?" Olivia asked.

"Yeah," Barry confirmed. "He had to travel to Europe to see his customers, maybe once or twice a month. About half the time when he traveled, he'd get pulled out of line and hassled by customs, coming and going, here and in Europe."

"Why?"

"That's what he asked," said Barry. "After missing some flights and dealing with a ton of frustration, it turned out that he had the same name as some fugitive from a Mexican drug cartel."

"What?"

Nodding, Barry said, "Marco jumped through all kinds of hoops to prove he wasn't this other guy, but the hassling never stopped. Eventually, he had to move his family to Europe to be close to his customers. He was missing too many flights and too many meetings."

"Are our systems really that bad?" Olivia asked. "Surely Marco Vasquez had other identifying data—social security number or its Mexican equivalent, passport number, things like that."

Barry nodded. "Yes, yes, and yes."

She shook her head in disbelief.

"Do you remember our friend Salim Pitafi, one of the original members of our list?"

Olivia nodded.

Barry leaned in close again and in a hushed voice said, "Three Salim Pitafis have been detained, two here in the US."

"But we had more than just his name," she replied. "We have *all* of his identifying information."

He shrugged. "We've got three, and none of them are the one we're looking for."

"You've got to be kidding me."

He shook his head.

"Please tell me he's the exception."

Barry looked at Olivia with a blank face.

Chapter 26

Tiny even when compared to Kapchorwa, Chebonet was the first hamlet on the road to Mbale. Having taken longer and longer rest breaks throughout the morning, Austin walked the dirt road into Chebonet in the early afternoon. A familiar smell fouled the wind. Faint cries carried out of the houses. No people were on the road, on their porches, not working in nearby fields. Chebonet felt like Kapchorwa on the evening when he and Rashid had returned from Mbale to find Ebola marauding through the population.

On advice from Dr. Littlefield, Austin didn't approach any house in Chebonet, though he examined the darkness he saw through open doors and windows. The shadows revealed nothing but an occasional pair of eyes peeking back. At what might have been the halfway point of the village, two teens came out of a ramshackle storehouse and followed Austin, keeping their distance. When Austin stopped and looked back, he saw that each held stones in their hands. Austin waved and said hello, hoping to assuage their fear of him with a smile and friendly words. One of the boys yelled something angry in the local language and hurled a stone. Austin sidestepped the rock, only to see another one hurtling toward him.

Austin lost his smile as he backed away, quickening his steps.

The boys started picking up stones, throwing each as soon as the stones were in their hands.

Austin ran.

The boys chased.

Before Austin's weakened muscles gave out, the boys stopped and went back to standing in the middle of the road, casting themselves in threatening poses and shouting curses. Austin put some distance between him and the boys, but reached a point where he could run no more. He stumbled as he slowed, barely managing to keep his fatigued feet under him. He tried a fast walking pace and found he couldn't even manage that. As he passed the last of Chebonet's houses, he looked over his shoulder.

The boys weren't coming.

Thank God.

Austin passed around a bend in the road. On the edge of a field, he spotted dark shade under squat trees. He left the road and walked far enough into the trees so that he couldn't be seen. He dropped down by a tree trunk and caught his breath, then removed one of the water bottles from his bag and drank it down. His arms felt heavy, and his fingers tingled as he flexed his hands. He felt like he'd just run a fast mile, though he knew he hadn't run more than a few hundred yards.

He felt like he was being lazy, but he couldn't deny the fatigue he was feeling. He had to rest, again. He removed a banana from his bag, peeled it, and ate it. With a few hours of daylight left, he then closed his eyes, waited for his breathing to slow, and passed out from exhaustion.

Chapter 27

Austin woke to the sensation of a large bug crawling on his face. He shot upright, slapping at the bug and shivering at the sensation. He ran his hands over his arms and then rubbed them over his body, checking for anything, bug or reptile, that might have found him to be a comfortable sleeping bag. Thankfully, there were none. He looked around and realized it was morning. He'd slept through the night in the stand of trees by the road.

His muscles ached, reminding him to be careful. Trying to push himself at a pre-Ebola pace was a mistake. He needed to stop thinking in terms of miles. He needed to pay attention to how he was feeling. He needed to rest more frequently and for longer periods.

Austin took his time eating the last of his food: two mangos — one not quite ripe — and he drank the last of his water.

His number one priority for the day's walking would be to keep an eye out for a well. The second priority would be to find some fruit trees growing close enough to the road so that he could harvest — steal — something. Better, he hoped to reach a village where the infection hadn't already arrived. All of Austin's belongings had been burned in the Kapchorwa fires, but he had money given to him by Dr. Littlefield and Kristin Mills. With that he could buy food, water, and more.

Chapter 28

Eric's door was closed. Through the glass wall of his office Olivia saw him sitting at his desk, staring blankly at a computer monitor, doing nothing with idle hands. His shoulders were slack. He looked defeated. Olivia shoved the door open hard enough that it hit the doorstop with a startling bang.

Eric jerked out of his daze.

She stomped in, making little effort to hide her anger.

Eric sighed and motioned toward a chair. He rubbed his palms into his eyes as though his fatigue might be erased through the effort. It wasn't. His eyes were redder than before.

Olivia planted herself between the chair and the desk, pursing her lips and glaring at Eric.

He sighed again. "Please sit."

She stood her ground for a moment longer and then dropped into the chair.

"It's clear you're pissed about something, but I'm not in the mood to be yelled at by anybody." Eric looked absently back at his computer monitor. "You're not the only one with problems, you know."

Olivia huffed once more to clarify the enormity of her effort to restrain her anger. "I read through your email and the attachments."

Eric looked at his watch. "I sent that out like, six hours ago."

"I was busy with something this morning and I didn't read it until I got back from lunch."

"Well you should have read it this morning." Eric waved a hand across the expanse of his office. "You could have come in here and protested with the rest of them."

Olivia's tone softened. Half her anger was over the fact that she thought she was still being singled out. "I know this didn't come from you—"

"I don't make policy," said Eric. "But just to be clear. I'm your boss. You're my subordinate. I sent the email because you're being directed to perform the specific duties listed. I've been directed to ensure that you do."

She huffed again. "You *know* what we do here, right?"

Eric shook his head and rubbed his eyes again. "I told you, I'm not in the mood, Olivia. If you need to go out and run off your anger with another three or four miles, go do that. Get a shower, and then come back up. We can talk about all of this like rational adults. Hell, maybe you can skip the run and find some magical way to calm yourself down." He drilled a pair of hard eyes at Olivia. "Or, and I say this as a friend, you can get the fuck out of my office, and come back another time."

Olivia held Eric's gaze for a moment, then looked out through a window and chewed the inside of her cheek while she thought. Without any sincerity of tone to back it up, she said, "I'm sorry. I *am* angry. I *know* this isn't your doing. I just—" Olivia ran out of words as her anger boiled back up.

Eric leaned forward on his desk, and his face softened. "Olivia, do you know what the average absentee rate across US businesses is?"

"No," she replied.

"Nine percent," Eric told her. "Do you know what it is this week? Nationally?"

"No."

"Just over thirteen percent. What that means is fifty

percent more people than usual decided to skip work last week. You know why?"

"Don't talk to me like I'm stupid, Eric."

"Because they keep reading about Ebola in the news, on Twitter, on Facebook. They hear it on the radio. and everything they hear is exaggerated to scare the shit out of 'em so they'll come back and read or watch or listen some more."

"And?"

Eric continued, "You understand, or should I say that a bright young lady such as yourself—someone who's good with data, good with numbers—should be able to deduce that our economy is going to take a hit. Not to mention what's happening because of the airlines."

Olivia nodded.

"If it all continues, then next week absenteeism will hit fifteen percent, then twenty, then who knows." Eric snorted. "There's no reason for it other than people being scared when they don't need to be." Eric paused and looked her up and down.

Olivia said nothing.

"The directive I emailed this morning—" Eric asked, "what do you think it tells you to do?"

"There's some kind of work queue set up—"

Eric interrupted, "And you have access to the queue. Did you check that your permissions allowed you in?"

"I can access the queue from my computer," Olivia confirmed.

"Good."

She continued, "I read the examples in the directive. I read through some of the cases in the queue."

"And?" Eric asked.

"Some other group, maybe some group at the NSA, is actively censoring the Internet. Anything negative about the pandemic—"

Eric held up a hand to stop her. "Don't use that word."

Olivia huffed.

"You read the directive."

"Dammit, Eric." She pounded a fist on his desk.

"I know you're frustrated."

"Frustrated?" Olivia yelled. "It's not just that I can't use the word *pandemic* even though you and I—and everybody on the planet—can see that's what's going to happen."

"No, I can't," said Eric. "That's part of the problem. Smart people like you believe things are worse than they are. People are sick, lots of them, mostly in Africa. Elsewhere, we've got a few hundred cases getting hyped all to hell."

She ignored Eric and proceeded. "I have to work through a queue of censored web pages, figure out who posted them, and pass those names back through the application to who knows what group. Eric, it frightens me that this application even exists. When the hell did it get written?"

Eric leaned back and looked up at the ceiling. When he looked back down at Olivia, he'd passed his point of frustration and was now angry. "Don't be stupid. Again, I say that as your friend. Don't act like every movie you ever saw about big government conspiracies is true. You get paid to look at data and draw conclusions, and from those conclusions, the government takes action. Well guess what? I know you won't believe it, but there are people in the government's employ who are smarter than you, have more experience than you, have more access to classified material than you—"

"Everybody right now," Olivia sniped.

Eric ignored the dig. "These people think of things that might happen, and then more people just like them decide what contingency plans can be made, and then even smarter people decide which of those contingency plans should be executed. These people are tasked with protecting Americans from tomorrow's threats. You understand?"

Olivia understood, but didn't grace Eric with a response.

"Whether you agree or not, America *is* under attack. You *think* it's from terrorists with Ebola, and I agree that you're right. Those shit stains are screwing the whole world, but it's not as bad as you make it seem. It's not as bad as *anybody* makes it seem. The real problem, and the reason they call these fuckers terrorists, is because right now America is under attack by fear."

Olivia replied with a sneered, "Yes, FDR."

He shook his head at that remark. "It doesn't matter whether that fear is something planned by the jihadists, whether it's a part of some bigger plot to destabilize Western economies, or whether it's just the natural fear people feel over what looks like a disease crisis in the making. All of it has the same effect. People don't come to work. Commerce grinds to a halt. A recession turns into a depression, and who can guess whether America or any Western country survives?"

Eric took a deep, calming breath, his anger having run its course. "The application was written to combat this kind of problem. The news channels, newspapers, websites, blogs, Facebook posts, and tweets are all feeding and amplifying the fear in a self-perpetuating feedback loop. If we can't interdict this flow of information, the very real effects of what at some point will be pure, frenzied fantasy will destroy our economy and our country."

"There are groups out there right now in the government," Olivia asked, "searching through all these media sources and censoring them?"

Eric nodded.

"Then they add them to the queue I need to look at?" Olivia asked. "The people I need to identify and locate?"

He nodded again.

"Censorship alone isn't enough?" she asked.

Eric shook his head.

"What's going to happen to the people I find? Are they going to be warned, arrested—" Olivia gulped before she continued with her accusing question, "or killed by the CIA?"

He said nothing as Olivia waited for an answer.

She said, "Those weren't rhetorical questions."

Eric still said nothing.

"They're going to be killed?" Olivia asked. "We're talking about *American citizens*."

"Olivia, I'm not saying that's going to happen." Eric looked down at his hands on the desk, and seemed to take an intense interest in their inactivity.

Olivia took the opportunity to let her anger run again. "This is censorship in the worst way. We're taking away information the people might need in order to protect themselves. And I doubt—no—I truly hope that the government isn't going to harm the people we've been directed to find. Either way, this whole thing stinks of the rankest form of censorship. This isn't who we are. This isn't the America I grew up in."

Eric laughed bitterly.

"What?" Olivia was self-conscious. "What?"

"This is *exactly* the country you grew up in."

Derisively shaking her head, she replied, "I never took you for part of the tinfoil hat crowd, Eric."

Shaking his head, Eric responded. "You think all that white-cowboy-hat-wearing-good-guy bullshit you learned about in American History in the third grade is true? Is that why you came to work here, Olivia, because you're a true patriot?"

"I can love my country without having to suffer your condescension, Eric."

"Sorry." He settled back in his chair. "That wasn't called for."

"I'm quite aware that America is not perfect. No country is. I do believe we're closer to perfection than the majority of other countries, though."

"I don't disagree with that, Olivia. All I'm saying is censorship has been rampant in this country for a long time. Hell, if you go back and read your history, you'll know that the Espionage Act passed in World War I damn near took away anyone's right to say anything remotely derogatory about the government or its policies."

"I don't understand exactly what we're protecting here," said Olivia, running out of steam.

Eric rubbed his eyes until he renewed the redness. "I'm tired of beating this argument to death." He rolled his head around to stretch his neck muscles, and then looked at his computer monitor as though something there might be urgent enough to cause him to chase Olivia out of his office. "I don't know how much of what I've heard about Ebola is real or bullshit. I do know things will get worse before they get better. I don't know if chasing down the people who are spreading these stories is right or wrong. I'm just as pro free speech as anybody, but principles are easy to hold when you're arguing for them in a college dorm while mommy and daddy pay your tuition. I don't know what will happen to the people whose names we enter into the system. I'd like to believe they'll get a stern talking to, and they'll go back to posting porn pics, selfies, memes, and fart jokes. I have to accept that the ones who persist submit themselves to iteratively more severe punitive remedies."

Olivia scoffed, "Punitive remedies?"

"I don't know where this Ebola thing goes. I know what's happening in Africa better than most. I have two children I've always told myself I'd do *anything* to protect." Eric leaned forward, having finally found his strength. "Well, *anything* is here, and I'll do what I need to do if I believe it helps keep my kids safe."

"This doesn't help your family," Olivia weakly argued.

"You're smart, young, and pretty. You won't have a problem finding a new job if that's what you want. This is what reality looks like now, Miss Idealism. Get on board with it, or pack your shit and go home."

Chapter 29

From the middle of the road where he walked, cautiously keeping his distance from houses, cars, and the few people he saw, Austin suspected Ebola had beaten him to Sironko. He hadn't yet seen a body lying with open eyes staring at an unforgiving sky. He hadn't seen any people with bleeding ears or noses. However, the air did carry the putrid smell of bloody diarrhea. The mournful keen of dying children reached out from dark windows. The feeling of a town full of vibrant people withering into ghosts was unmistakable.

Like it had been in Chebonet two days prior, and like it had been in every hamlet and cluster of houses along the road, people who should have been at work, weren't. Nobody was walking to the market, gossiping on a porch, or working in the fields. They were huddled in their homes, hiding from microbial monsters that stalked their streets. Anyone not afraid of catching Ebola was already sick or dead.

Sironko was a town on the plain in the western shadow of Mt. Elgon, four or five times larger than Kapchorwa. A month prior, the road Austin walked through Sironko would have been abuzz with cars heading north and south, with trucks hauling farm goods to market in Mbale or Kampala.

Now, the traffic was gone.

As the sight of another dying town dragged on Austin's mood, he stopped walking and looked around. He was near the center of Sironko, in front of a closed grocery, just down the street from a modern gas station with brightly colored awnings. A man a few blocks down bounded over a wide puddle of stagnant brown water that had collected along the curb. He hefted a half-full bag of something, glanced suspiciously at Austin, and disappeared down a narrow alley.

Somewhere, a block or two distant, an unseen woman shouted angrily, and another woman argued back. A rickety generator chugged through a holed muffler. Several goats walked out of a side street and started lapping at the water by the curb.

Austin looked back up the road from whence he'd come, wondering for the hundredth time if he'd made a mistake in leaving Kapchorwa. He wondered how Dr. Littlefield was getting along. He wondered if Dr. Mills—Kristin—with her happy brown eyes, was going to die. He felt guilty for not making better time on his trek. Kristin had done her part, and was probably the reason he was alive. All he had to do was walk to Mbale to get her help and he was failing at that.

Austin breathed deeply as he looked up the road, coughed roughly several times before losing his balance and falling to his knees in the road. He realized—or more accurately, he accepted—what he'd suspected since he'd awoken that morning.

He was sick again.

His back ached. His throat was raw and painful when he swallowed. His nose was starting to run with mucus that grew thicker and more greenly opaque with each gob he snot-rocketed out. Some other tropical disease was making a cozy new home in his cells.

Austin laughed ironically as he looked at the dirty road between his hands. He laughed and watched his mucus darken the dust. It never even occurred to him back when he was in Denver that a fever and a sore throat could develop into something that could kill. Now he knew better. He also knew he couldn't spend another night sleeping under the stars. He needed food. He needed to rest. He needed to get himself healthy before pushing on to Mbale.

Standing up and looking around again, Austin saw a woman in the shadows under an awning over the sidewalk. He waved a hand and said, "Hey."

The wide, white eyes flashed fear, and the head slipped back inside a doorway.

Turning around to get his bearings, Austin recalled that an upscale hotel — upscale by African standards — was nearby. On one of his many trips between Mbale and Kapchorwa, he'd been riding in a bus that stopped at that gas station just up the road, the one with the colorful awning. Around the corner and several blocks down stood the hotel. He'd met some Canadian college students on the bus who were staying there, and they had nothing but good things to say about the place.

A good place.

Austin half smiled at the irony of it.

He didn't care if the hotel had a one- or a five-star rating. If someone inside would take his money, he'd be glad to have a bed and a roof. If the hotel had a working phone, then he'd thank his lucky stars. A phone could solve so many problems. He dug around in his pocket and pulled out his wad of cash. It needed to be enough.

Austin removed one of his water bottles from the canvas bag, drank most of it down, and shuffled slowly down the street, keeping an eye out from side to side as he did. Ahead of him, doors were closed. Curtains were drawn shut.

He made a right turn at the closed gas station and saw

his goal. Walking became a little easier.

At the hotel, he crossed a dirt parking lot containing a van and two cars. He felt a pang of hope. A well-maintained sign mounted over the door on the front of the building displayed the hotel name. A smaller sign with red letters hung above a glass door. It said, "Lobby."

Rest was just a few steps away.

After crossing the porch, Austin grabbed the handle on the front door, and yanked. The door rattled against its lock.

"No."

He pulled on the door again. It didn't budge.

That's okay, he told himself. *Of course* it would be locked, given what was going on. Austin knocked and pressed his face to the glass to see inside. Nothing but a small, dim lobby, and a front desk with no one behind it.

He knocked again and waited a patient moment. Someone *had* to be inside.

He waited.

Nothing.

He knocked again and was rewarded.

From a doorway behind the hotel desk, a man peeked around a corner. "Go away. We're closed."

"No," Austin protested. "I have money. I can pay." He grabbed for his wad of cash. He called, "Just one sec."

The man stepped out of the doorway. "You are American?"

"Yes, yes," Austin confirmed, while he pulled out his cash and pushed it against the glass for the man to see.

The man stepped closer and craned his neck to see out into the parking lot. "Do you have a car?"

"No," Austin replied, looking out at the parking lot. "I walked."

"From where?"

Does it matter? It was a stupid thought. Of course it did. He chose to lie. "I've been up in the mountains camping for a few weeks."

"By yourself?" the clerk asked suspiciously.

"My guide dropped me off."

"You said you walked."

Austin huffed, "Yeah, he dropped me off at the gas station," pointing at the bright awnings down the street. "He needed gas."

"They are closed," said the clerk.

"He didn't know—" Austin's temper flared. "Look, you see I have money. Just give me a room for the night, please. I'll be gone tomorrow." Austin needed more than one night with a bed, but he figured he could negotiate a second night later.

The clerk had crossed the small lobby by then and was standing just a few paces behind the glass.

"Please," Austin waved the cash. "I'll pay twice the rate. I need a place to stay tonight."

The clerk stepped close to the door and reached out as if to unlock it. Then he froze, his eyes on Austin's face. The clerk raised a hand and brushed a finger under his nose. "You're sick."

Austin shook his head as he reached up to his own nose. Crap. It was running again. "No, not sick. Just allergies."

"Sick." The clerk stepped back, shaking his head. "Go away. No disease here. Go away."

"I'm not sick," Austin pleaded as he wiped his nose. "I'm not sick."

The clerk hurried around his counter, disappeared through the doorway from which he'd emerged, and slammed the inner door shut behind him.

Austin hung his head, leaned on the glass, and groaned. "Damn."

He turned around and sank down to the ground. Feeling despair, he put his head in his hands. He was sick. He was hungry. Anything that didn't ache from the growing fever in his blood ached from pushing his weak body too many miles. And just on the other side of the glass was access to a bed, a shower, food, and a phone.

He thought about breaking the glass and punching the cowardly clerk.

Where would that lead? No place good. Not in a country full of fear. If he was lucky enough not be shot for breaking in, the police would surely come, and how would he explain himself then?

So Austin sat and looked at the empty street as he rested in the shade of the porch, thinking instead about what to do next. Mbale was still a dozen miles south along the highway. Surely someone there would help him. Somebody had to have a working phone.

"Go away," the clerk called from inside.

Austin held up a middle finger to the glass and yelled, "Fuck you, little man!"

Chapter 30

Sironko, like Kapchorwa, was an agricultural town made up of farmers and merchants, but mostly farmers. Late summer crops were being harvested before Ebola came to town. Just like in Kapchorwa, agricultural warehouses—some small, some large—were scattered up and down the streets and out on the edge of town. As Austin sat in front of the hotel, he gave some serious thought to breaking into one of those storehouses. Such a place would be safe and out of the elements. It might even be free of bugs and vermin—the farmers had to have a way of controlling those. With any luck, he might find something edible in its raw state. A parade of juicy, ripe fruits passed through his imagination, and his stomach rumbled in response.

While his stomach was convincing him to go ahead with the plan, he spent a moment thinking about what the farmers might do when they discovered him in their warehouse, eating their produce. He'd be in the same trouble he'd have been in for breaking into the hotel.

Desperation—and that's what Austin was feeling at the moment, desperation—was driving him to seriously consider bad choices.

"Think, Austin, think," he told himself out loud. And why not? Nobody was around to hear.

Austin thought about Kapchorwa and how the virus had spread so quickly through the village. He thought about all those people in the hospital, those who were dead in their homes, and realized that Sironko was in much the same state Kapchorwa had been. He realized that there might be houses, a lot of them, with no living occupants. Either the residents had gone off to the local hospital, fled from town, or they were dead inside. Any one of those houses might have everything Austin needed for a few days of recovery.

It felt wrong just to consider it, but he knew what he needed to do. He stood up, turned back to the glass door, and pressed his face against it. The clerk was nowhere to be seen. Austin kicked the door as hard as he dared and yelled a curse at the glass. With the dissatisfaction of no response at all, he turned away, crossed the dusty parking lot, and continued up the road.

The afternoon shadows were starting to grow long. Down the dirt road, houses stood on both sides, packed closely together on small lots. The further he walked from the center of town, the further the houses were spaced apart and set further back from the road, hidden among the trees and generally more primitive. Those were the houses Austin was going to visit.

Feeling fatigue start to weigh heavy on his bones, he reached his first candidate. He stood at the ill-defined property boundary, that part of the ground where the grasses had been trampled into red dirt, maybe fifteen feet or so from an entrance protected only by a curtain.

"Hello," Austin called.

He heard some sounds from inside. A metal container hit the ground. A figured appeared in the shadows. The figure said something Austin didn't understand, but the words were accompanied by a gesture one might make when waving away a fly.

Austin understood.

He looked around. Up through the trees on the same side of the road, houses of cinderblock with tin roofs were scattered among round thatched rondavels, traditional buildings for much of central Africa. Austin walked along a path that led to the nearest dwelling. It was one of the round huts.

Before Austin even came to a stop, a thin and angry man stepped out. He scowled at Austin with arms crossed, almost daring Austin to come closer. One glance at the man's boney, balled fists was all the urging Austin needed to hurry by. A second glance at the blood-red color that had replaced the whites of the man's eyes confirmed beyond a doubt that the virus was in this part of town.

Austin told himself he need only persist. Persistence would yield a result. He headed toward a yellowish-orange house that the dirt seemed to be trying to pull back down into its bosom. It reeked of death. Looking back over his shoulder as he neared, the scowling man still watched him, though from a less-threatening posture. He was leaning with his forearm against the wall of his hut, looking like he might retch at any moment.

Austin passed on by the stinking yellowish house.

When he reached the next house, the trees and bushes obscured his view of the scowling man. Nobody was in sight. Austin approached to within a dozen feet of an open doorway, making his way to the squarish little cinderblock house under a rusty roof.

"Hello?" Austin called.

He waited. He smelled the air. He looked around.

"Hello?"

With no response, Austin ventured up to the doorway until he was close enough to rap on the open door. He did so, to no effect. Again, he asked, "Hello?" He listened.

Nothing at all. No verbal response, no sound of movement from within.

Austin gathered up his courage, took a step and a half forward, and peeked inside.

It took a moment for his eyes to adjust to the darkness.

He saw the corpses of a woman and three children under a buzzing fog of flies.

In a basket on the back wall, he saw fruit. In another, he saw yams. Austin looked again at the bodies as he leaned in the doorway. He thought about his aches, and his fever. There was plenty of room on the floor to lie down. He despised the thought of lying down near the dead family, but he didn't have the strength to move the bodies, not even the bodies of the children.

Feeling like a ghoul, Austin stumbled over the dirt floor as he let himself inside. He fell to his hands and knees and decided to lie down in the cool dirt for a moment before he'd trouble himself to peel a mango for a meal. He fell asleep.

Chapter 31

He'd gotten on the road later than he'd hoped. Some mornings, when the weight of his sadness was on him, it was hard to get out of bed. How does a man deal with the loss of a son? The world had turned into a flavorless, bleak place, where music no longer made him reminisce about the good old days, and even the foods at his favorite restaurants lost their spice.

Paul knew he was numb, not dealing with Austin's death in a healthy way. As if there was a healthy way to mourn a child. He also knew the melancholy mood would eventually break, and he would smile again. One day. Until then, he could only go through the motions of living, making the best choices he could along the way.

He'd been on the road for an hour, rolling down Interstate 25, coming into Colorado Springs from the north, seeing Pike's Peak, standing above the Front Range at fourteen thousand feet, its early snows painted pink by the rising sun. Rush hour traffic in The Springs, as the locals called the town, was just starting to pick up. Paul looked at his watch. He was still too early for the stop-and-go worst of it. He'd be out of the other side of town in ten minutes.

On radio's AM dial, where it seemed the earliest news was always breaking, two men were talking about Ebola cases in Beijing and Mumbai. They didn't have numbers, but implied that counts would dwarf anything seen so far in the West. Paul always took AM news with a grain of salt, but lately, the rumors so often passed for fact in that medium, were getting picked up and confirmed by the mainstream media.

He thought about Ebola for the millionth time: the few hundred cases in Western cities, the quarantine in Uganda, the scary news out of Nairobi, and Olivia's warning to start working from home based on the discovery of a new, more virulent strain. Then there was the outbreak in Dallas—the reason for Paul's trip. It wasn't an outbreak, not yet, not really. A half-dozen cases so far, all tied through direct contact to that nameless guy who collapsed in the airport.

Paul passed out of the south side of Colorado Springs, thinking about Heidi. When he'd told her he'd made up his mind on what he had to do, she stopped talking to him. That had been days ago. She told him he was emotional, depressed, and that he needed to go see a doctor. When she was really riled she told him he was irrational, crazy. Paul was tired of hearing it. He argued that his choice was based on data and reasoned conclusions, and that she was the one being irrational. She couldn't accept that an unstoppable Ebola epidemic was coming.

Heidi clung to a baseless hope that a last minute vaccine or serum would arrive to save everyone. She couldn't accept the very real possibility of death. Dying only happened to other people—poor people in faraway lands, people without modern medical care.

But Austin was dead. He was one of those people.

Rumors were all over the Internet about the mutated Ebola strain being airborne. No government agency or reputable medical organization would confirm those rumors. Still, the officials' non-denial denials—as Paul had heard them described in a movie he'd seen a long time ago —came so frequently that Paul took them as affirmations.

Heidi said airborne Ebola was a suspicion he'd had all along, and that he was seeing the evidence through the filter of his fears. That had sparked a fight, one of many. The more they argued, the more they each dug in their heels. They each took every bit of news as proof they were right, even when it was exactly the same news.

How the hell does that even happen?

They were two intelligent, rational adults. They saw the same news on the television. They shared articles and videos they found on the Internet, usually with the statement, "See, I told you so." Nothing was ever proof enough.

Now the discussion was over. Paul was on his way to Dallas to infect himself before the epidemic got out of hand. It was the only sure way to get medical help while it was still available. Afterwards, he'd drive back from Dallas, careful to protect himself and not infect others. That was the reason he had eight full five-gallon gas cans in the back of his truck. He'd need those for the trip. His plan was to stop his truck on remote sections of the road, refill his gas tank, and drive on. He had no intention of making contact with any person on the way back. He didn't want to be the source of an outbreak in Amarillo, Raton, or some such place.

When he arrived back in Denver, he'd hole up in the house until he turned symptomatic. He'd infect Heidi—at least that was Paul's plan—and then he'd call the hospital, concoct some story of how he'd gotten infected, and being the first patient in Denver, he'd get the best treatment they had to offer. Heidi, the second patient in Denver, would get the same. Their chances of surviving were excellent.

Excellent in a relative sense.

Heidi had told Paul the minute he indulged his insanely stupid plan he'd better plan on coming home to an empty house, because she was going to get into her car five minutes later, drive to Denver International Airport, and hop a plane back to San Antonio. She'd rent a car and drive it up to her parents' house in New Braunfels, Texas. That's where she'd wait for Paul's folly to play itself out. She didn't mind adding that she'd take the life insurance when he died and spend it on margaritas and amorous cabana boys in Cozumel.

It didn't matter what she said by then. He was mad, she was mad. Both were past the point where words were anything but painful little hand grenades tossed across the chasm of their disagreement.

A sign displaying the distance to Pueblo stood by the road. Paul passed it and pushed his speed over eighty to flow with the southbound traffic.

Chapter 32

Paul drove through the last of the mountains he'd see on his trip as he left Colorado and entered New Mexico. He turned east at Raton and cut across the northeast corner of the state toward Clayton and Texline, passing little towns along the road that had the look of an apocalypse that left them dead fifty years prior. Whatever reason people had for living, working, and building their little hovel towns so far from any kind of city, the economics of it had stopped making sense a long time ago. Most of the houses, gas stations, motels, and stores were rotting away under sagging roofs. Old cars rusted on flat tires. Trees grew through windows and weeds conquered driveways.

It was a preview of America to come; an America Paul was executing a bold plan to prepare for. Most of it passed, ignored. Paul's plan and his troubles took over his thoughts and left him only enough mental bandwidth to keep his car aimed at the asphalt ahead and his foot on the gas pedal.

He stopped on a stretch of road so deserted he saw volcanic hills pushed up out of the flatness, ten, twenty, maybe thirty miles away. Antelope grazed far out on the horizon-to-horizon carpet of tan grasses. No car was coming or going for miles in either direction. Paul filled his tank from the gasoline cans riding in the bed of the truck and relieved himself without the slightest worry anyone would see.

He crossed the border into Texas and the plain flattened out so much that grain silos ten miles up the highway were visible. To his right and left, irrigated circles of corn a half-mile across bordered the road—dried brown and ready for harvest. Dalhart and Dumas passed his windows. Miles of rolling red dirt hills dotted with smelly oil pumps fell behind.

Oblivious to everything around him and settling into the boredom of the drive, trouble found him.

Paul sat in his pickup, idling on the shoulder. Ahead of him, the hot air shimmered over the blacktop. Behind him, a Texas State Trooper sat in his car, shifting his focus between Paul and the computer that provided him with all the information that he was likely to need about Paul's truck.

"Turn off your vehicle," the officer's voice ordered over his PA.

Paul cut the engine. With the air conditioner off, he rolled his windows down, and hot air blew in. He'd planned to make the entire trip anonymously. If a record of his travel existed, it might turn into a problem later on.

The patrolman walked up to Paul's window, peering into the car through his trite aviator sunglasses. "Driver's license and insurance."

Paul produced the documents with a pleasant smile. "Was I speeding?"

"Do you have any outstanding warrants?" the officer asked. "Anything I need to know about before I run your license?"

"No." Paul was a little offended. Maybe back in his teens and early twenties—his hoodlum years—he'd had a warrant or two.

"Do you have any weapons in the vehicle?"

"No," Paul told him.

"Do you have any drugs?"

Paul looked emphatically around the cab of his truck. "Where would I put them?"

"People find a way to hide them," said the officer,

humorlessly. "Is this your vehicle?"

"Yes."

"Do you live in Colorado?"

Paul wanted to snap back, "I have Colorado plates!" but bit his tongue. "I live in Denver."

"What brings you to Texas?"

Paul's patience was wearing thin, but he didn't want a ticket. He pointed up the road. "I'm just going to visit a friend in Dallas."

The officer nodded and said, "Stay here. I'll be back." He walked back past the bed of Paul's truck, while looking very curiously at the gas cans.

Shit.

Minutes passed. Paul worried. Going back to Denver after all he'd fought through with Heidi would be demoralizing. If he did go back, what then? Paul had no answer. His window of opportunity was narrow.

After a short while, the officer strode back up beside Paul's car, took a long look again at the gas cans, and stopped by the window. "You were going seventy-eight in a seventy." He handed Paul his license and insurance. "I'm not giving you a ticket today. Keep an eye on the speed."

Paul thanked him, smiled, and got back on the road.

Chapter 33

"You were in Kenya, Pakistan, Italy, Germany, England, and here. Which cities specifically?"

Salim looked at the man in the plastic suit standing by his bed, mask over his face, and what looked like ski goggles over his eyes. At the man's side, a silent companion in similar attire scowled. "Frankfurt."

"And?"

Salim closed his eyes as pain throbbed through his head. "Lahore."

"You were in Pakistan for a long time."

"Relatives," Salim said. "Are you a doctor?"

"Why were you in Nairobi?"

Salim didn't need to think about that answer. He'd practiced the lie so many times it almost seemed true to him. "Safari."

"Safari?" The questioner turned to his companion. Doing his best to sound impressed. "Wow. I'm lucky to afford my deer lease. Must be nice."

Salim shook his head and felt gravel roll painfully back and forth inside his skull. "I took pictures. It's not—" He lost his train of thought. "Pictures."

"Is that where you contracted Ebola?" the questioner asked.

"Ebola?" *No.*

"Yes, in Nairobi, did you contract Ebola there?"

"Ebola is in Liberia. I didn't go to Liberia." Salim was confused. He was frightened. Is that what killed everyone in Kapchorwa? "I have Ebola?"

The questions came in a flurry after that, so fast that

Salim didn't answer. Couldn't. He was having trouble just paying attention; what focus he could muster was pinned to thoughts of his death sentence. That's what Ebola was, a painful prelude to inexorable death.

A nurse dressed from head to toe in the standard half-ass space suit, with a big clear plastic shield in front of her face, came into the room. She wore a surgical mask underneath. She did something with a monitor beside Salim's bed and checked the fluid in his IV bag.

"Is my lawyer here?" Salim asked, not sure himself where that question came from.

"You have a lawyer?" The questioner nearly shouted it.

Salim answered, "I don't know."

"Why would you need an attorney?"

"I don't know." Salim asked, "Am I going to die?" Things got fuzzy after that.

Chapter 34

It was one of those bars in the rejuvenated warehouse district—every city had one these days. The building was old and narrow. A hundred years of improvements had been scraped off rough wooden floors and weathered brick walls. Black lacquer tables, gas lamps on the walls, and long shiny bars juxtaposed the new décor with the old, and people piled in after work to drink to the sound of piped-in blues that were played live on the weekends.

Through the light crowd Olivia spotted Mathew Wheeler, already at a table halfway back, by the wall. He stood up in an old-fashioned, gentlemanly way when she arrived. She was a bit impressed. The most she'd gotten in the way of manners from the guys she'd dated through college and since was a "Hey, babe," and a peck on the cheek while leaning over the table.

Wheeler pulled out a chair and said, "You look like hell." He smiled widely.

The nascent bubble of romance burst and Olivia laughed as she collapsed into the chair. "I'm sorry. I'm..."

Wheeler sat and then waved at the waitress. "You need something strong, I think."

Olivia smiled and nodded.

"Work?" Wheeler asked.

She nodded again, adding a shake of her head. "Everything. It's everything, Mathew."

"You okay?"

"Yeah."

Wheeler gave the waitress their order, then turned his attention back to Olivia and looked down at his watch. "Here are the rules. You've got five minutes to vent about whatever you want. I'll listen. I'll nod. I'll say, "Yup." I'll say, "You go, girl." I'll even hug you if you need it. When your time's up, we'll talk about other things. Got it?"

"Why did you get divorced again?" Olivia asked with a wry smile.

Looking down at his watch, Wheeler replied, "You just wasted five seconds. If you want to spend your whole five minutes talking about my troubles...well, that's your prerogative, I guess."

"So, that's how it works?" Olivia asked. "I get five minutes. You get five minutes. And then we talk about the Braves or the Falcons or something?

"Yeah, something like that."

"Fine. My brother is lost in Africa. I called my dad the other day and told him I was worried and he needed to maybe work from home for a while. You know." Olivia looked out through the glass wall at the front of the bar.

"Yeah, I know," said Wheeler. "But that's for my five. Don't steal my material."

Olivia smiled again. "My dad—" she caught herself, not sure what to say, knowing she couldn't tell him all Heidi had said when she called last night, crying. "He's not handling Austin well. I don't know what to do."

"Should you take some time and go home?" Wheeler asked.

"Drive for two days, just to have him insist that everything is fine?"

"Hardheaded?" Wheeler asked.

"You know it."

He looked at her in a way that implied more than he said. "I'm guessing it's a family trait."

"And work." Olivia shook her head. "I can't talk about

work, but it's...it's..."

"Fucked?" Wheeler asked.

Olivia laughed. "Exactly what my dad would say."

Wheeler looked at his watch.

"I don't need my full five minutes. You go ahead." Olivia replied.

Wheeler smiled, but looked serious at the same time. He took his watch off and laid it on the table in front of Olivia. "You're the timer lady. Give me the go."

"Okay." Olivia waited for the second hand to hit the twelve. "Go."

"People are protesting outside the CDC campus every day, and the crowds are growing. This morning somebody threw a rock at my car, and it'll probably cost me two dollars less than my deductible to get the dent fixed. Congressmen are screaming at the director, who screams at my boss, who screams at me—"

"Literally?" Olivia asked.

"Figuratively. Well, not the congressmen part. You know how they are." Wheeler sipped his drink. "We've got eleven labs doing something with the new strain, and that's just here in the States. Everybody in the world is on this one, because it scares the hell out of all of us. We've infected our monkeys, and we're still figuring things out."

"Is it airborne?" Olivia asked.

Wheeler shrugged. "Can't say yet, but one thing we can almost certainly say: the antigens shifted. Any of the experimental treatments for Ebola Zaire..." Wheeler shook his head slowly and looked down at his ice cubes. "They don't seem to have *any* effect at all. We may be starting from scratch on this one."

"That sounds bad."

Wheeler smiled again with the same strangely serious look as before. "Worst-case scenario." He leaned back in his chair and half chuckled. "Back in college we used to dream about finding a new bug. The more dangerous the better. Of course the dream always ended with a miraculous cure, a Nobel Prize, and very few deaths."

"Kind of a cross between '*Luke Skywalker*' and '*Grey's Anatomy*'?" Olivia asked.

"'*Grey's Anatomy*'?" Wheeler grimaced. "Maybe, if you want to put it that way. We don't know what this bug will do. We're still trying to figure out what's happening in Africa. Nobody with the new strain has died yet, but everybody is holding their breath on that one. Maybe it'll turn out to be Ebola Light. People get sick, but very few die." Wheeler shrugged.

"But you don't believe that, do you?"

Wheeler shook his head. "I'm not the believing type. How am I doing on time?"

"I stopped checking."

"You're not very good at this." Wheeler picked up his watch and wrapped it back around his wrist.

"Either the five-minute game doesn't work, or you've still got something else to vent about," she replied.

Wheeler pulled in a deep breath. "Between us?"

Olivia nodded.

"You may already know this..."

Shaking her head, she added, "Long story, but I'm kinda out of the loop on a lot of things right now."

"Do you need another five?"

Olivia shook her head. "What else do you have?"

"Those damned tight-lipped Germans."

"What about them?" Olivia asked.

"How many cases do you know about?"

"The last number I got was thirty-eight," she replied.

Wheeler paused, then said, "The number is higher. A *lot* higher. I talked with a colleague at the European Center for Disease Control and Prevention, and people over there are losing their shit. The Frankfurt number topped three hundred."

Chapter 35

Jimmy Kerr liked to shave his head and wear a goatee to offset his boyish features. He was a big man, standing a good bit taller than average. His big, round belly, wide ass, and meaty shoulders gave him an ominous presence.

Despite the look, Jimmy wasn't the type to intimidate to get his way. He'd never been a violent man. Sure, he had a short temper, but who didn't? He'd been arrested a couple of times on domestic violence charges and didn't mind telling his version of the story: the crazy bitch had been off her meds and had threatened him with a kitchen knife. He'd only punched a few holes in the sheetrock and had never hit her. In a tussle, as Jimmy defended himself, she'd gotten a few bruises that cost Jimmy some time in jail. That was wife number two. The story with number three had different details, but the result was the same.

Wife number four never got a bruise. Jimmy awoke in the darkness after going to bed drunk and angry. Maybe he'd said some things. He couldn't remember. He did remember waking up to the surprise of learning how cold the barrel of the revolver felt pressed against his nuts. More was said. Threats were made. Jimmy left that night with a change of clothes, the cash in his wallet, and his manhood intact.

Crazy bitches!

Jimmy's smile, charisma, and flair for spinning heaping loads of prattle attracted the type. Those same talents came in handy when he mustered recruits for his moneymaking schemes, which were sometimes legal, most often not.

While he was smart enough and inventive enough to come up with ways to steer money into his pockets, he never seemed to have enough of that elusive something to make himself rich. In the early days of high-performance scanners and printers, he'd gone into the business of manufacturing counterfeit money. He saw it as a victimless crime. The trick with printing money back in the eighties — before security strips and watermarks — wasn't getting the accuracy of the print right, it was getting the color and feel of the paper right. It had taken him only a few hours to purchase the scanner and printer, hook them up to a computer, and generate his first counterfeit bill. He'd spent a couple of weeks working out the paper and dye problems. In the end, he was able to produce bills that never raised an eyebrow when passed off to unsuspecting clerks at drive-through windows. The problem with counterfeiting, as he came to learn, was not in producing the bills. It was in passing the twenties off for change, his method of converting fake cash to real cash. By the time he dyed and dried the paper, printed and cut the bills, aged the finished product, and made his way around town passing them off one at a time, he came to realize he wasn't making much more than he would at a legit job.

Fuck that.

Jimmy abandoned the scheme and moved on to Medicare, where he saw himself as something of a pioneer. He'd engineered a process to defraud the government of millions long before anybody knew on what an industrial scale Medicare fraud could exist. Of all the money that flowed through Jimmy's scheme, not nearly enough of it dribbled down to his pockets. He kept himself in late model cars, cigarettes, and beer while managing to pay his child support, but was always living paycheck to paycheck, or however that concept is described in a criminal enterprise.

Identity theft — another product of his criminal aptitude — was a low-risk scheme that generated lots of cash, but it turned out like the counterfeiting scheme: too much legwork to appeal to his lazy nature.

Tax return fraud seemed like pure genius when it came to him one drunk night, while staring at a dollar-desperate stripper with too much cellulite and listening to eighties hair band metal. In that scheme, it had been surprisingly easy to herd several million dollars into accounts he controlled. Getting that money laundered back into his pocket turned out to be too problematic and expensive.

Through all of it, Jimmy had never been caught—well, not for his income-based crimes. He hadn't been so lucky with social malfeasance—domestic disturbances, public intoxication, and the like. Perhaps that was the reason Jimmy always figured his next plot would be the scheme that finally made him rich.

In that vein, he was thinking about scams while sitting in a sports bar with his buddy Larry Dean, watching the San Diego Chargers spank his beloved Denver Broncos. He was two months behind on child support to two mothers and a month behind to the third mother. He couldn't afford his car insurance and was only a week away from a car payment that he didn't have the cash to pay. Things had been lean for most of a year, and the financial pinch was getting real. He was even casting discreet glances at the security cameras mounted on the ceiling around the bar and seriously considering a robbery. How hard could it be? Walk in with a mask and a gun at the end at a busy night, convince the manager to open the safe, and walk out with twenty thousand dollars—or a handful of credit card receipts. Ugh. Nobody used cash anymore.

The Chargers scored. Everybody groaned. The Broncos were down by three touchdowns late in the fourth. Conversation in the bar notched up as people looked to distract themselves. Jimmy sipped at a warming beer and turned away from the painful video feed to watch orange-ish sauce full of cold grease congeal into a waxy coating on the remaining chicken wings. Without taking his eyes off the wings, he said to Larry, "We gotta figure out how to make some money."

Larry said, "I saw this movie the other night about this slave guy."

"The one that got kidnapped and shipped to Louisiana back before the Civil War?" Jimmy asked, wondering why Larry had even watched the movie. It didn't seem the type to appeal to his limited intellect.

Larry said, "Yeah, that's the one."

Guessing that Larry was changing the subject to distract himself from his own financial woes, Jimmy asked, "Did you like it?"

"It was okay."

Jimmy nodded, thinking it was a good movie, though too depressing.

Larry leaned over the table to get close to Jimmy, and said, "I had an idea."

Jimmy put his glass down and started to think of a new way to tell Larry why his idea was terrible. They always were. "Yeah?"

"I was putting it together with something else I saw on TV," said Larry. "These tourists were going to Mexico, getting drunk or something, and waking up with a kidney missing."

And that was the shitty idea. Jimmy bit back his gut reaction but was stuck for some good way to say that selling stolen kidneys was a suck-ass, old idea.

Into the pause, Larry's voice turned animated. "I saw on

the Internet you can get a quarter million for a black market kidney."

"*Two-hundred thousand dollars?*"

Larry grinned and nodded emphatically, oblivious to the mathematical mistake.

Jimmy waited for more on Larry's idea. He looked away from Larry's grin, reached over and poked one of the chicken wings, thought about whether he had any antacids at home to counter the spicy seasonings floating around in his stomach. He decided not to eat any more. "That's interesting. I don't really get how you made the jump from the kidnapped slave to black market kidneys."

"That's the beauty of it, man." Larry scooted his butt anxiously around in his chair as he tried to lean further over the table. "See, there's a bunch of rich people who'll pay a lot of money for a kidney. But waiting for somebody with the right kind of kidney to visit Tijuana takes time. These people don't have a lot of time to wait around, you know what I mean?"

"I guess," Jimmy answered. He didn't know how long someone could live on dialysis while waiting for a kidney.

"What I'm sayin' is, we find their replacement parts around here."

"Here in Denver?" Jimmy asked.

"Denver. Kansas City. Tulsa. It doesn't matter."

"I think there's a bunch of genetic matching or something that goes into that," said Jimmy as he watched Larry's mood start to sink. "Besides, where do you find a surgeon in the States you can bribe to do the work? I think that's the reason they go to Mexico."

Larry slumped into disappointment and muttered. "We'd take the donor to Mexico. Kinda like in the movie."

Jimmy sat up straight and smiled a lie. "I'm not saying it's a bad idea. I'm just saying we need to talk it through, is all."

Larry put on a serious face and said, "You're good with the details. You're smart about this kind of stuff. What do we need to talk through?"

Just humor him.

Jimmy thought about it for a second and said the first thing that came to his mind. "You know, if I was looking for a kidney right now, the first thing I'd be worried about is whether it came from a guy who just died of Ebola. With all that going around right now —"

"Did you see the news about Frankfurt?" Larry's eyes went wide.

Jimmy shook his head.

"They shut down the airport."

"I think they'll shut 'em all down," said Jimmy. "The point I was making is we'd have to find a way to test for Ebola."

"Probably something for it on the Internet, maybe a YouTube video," said Larry.

"Yeah, but..." Jimmy caught himself. Yeah, maybe Larry was right about that. Jimmy hadn't thought about it. Then *real* inspiration hit. "Try this on for size. How about, instead of kidneys, we sell blood?"

Larry made a face. "That's stupid."

Jimmy was unfazed. "I saw this thing on TV about the Ebola epidemic in Africa. They said that taking the blood serum out of somebody who recovered —"

"How's blood serum different from regular blood?" Larry asked.

"Doesn't matter," Jimmy answered. "We can figure it

out. But the point is, if you've got somebody who recovered from Ebola, their blood can be used to cure the next guy. Their blood is like liquid gold to somebody who's sick. They'd pay anything, because if they don't, they'll die. Ebola kills everybody, just about."

"They *would* pay anything," Larry mused.

"Exactly." Jimmy nodded vigorously. "It's easy to get blood out of someone. It's easy to put it back in someone else. I'll bet you could even get those instructions off the Internet, too. Best of all, we might have millions of customers if this Ebola thing keeps going like it is."

"Yeah," Larry nodded, smiling. "Yeah. All we have to do is find the people who've been cured."

"That'll be easy," said Jimmy. "It's a big deal when somebody makes it. It's all over the news when it happens. We just find one at home, pump out his blood, and sell pints of it to as many people as we can."

Shaking his head, Larry said, "Wouldn't we want to keep him alive and maybe harvest a little at a time?"

"Oh, no." Jimmy was emphatic. "That's the beauty of it. We get a few gallons out of the first guy—and hand-deliver that to our customers. A couple of weeks later, we check on our customers to see which ones survived. We pick the easy marks from the survivors, we take 'em out and drain 'em, and sell that blood too. At every cycle, our inventory goes up. The blood from one person treats another twenty or thirty people. From those twenty, we get maybe four hundred doses. From those four hundred...well, you get a bunch."

Larry said, "But...our donors will die."

Jimmy raised his eyebrows and asked, "Will that bother you?"

"Not really. You?"

Jimmy shook his head. "You know me. I don't give a fuck. Tough shit for them."

Chapter 36

Paul was back in his truck, jittery from all the coffee he'd drunk. It was two a.m. He was sitting in the parking lot of a low-rent apartment complex, looking down and across the street at another shabby complex with a few broken down cars in front, dead shrubs, and unkempt trees. Most of the buildings in the complex needed paint, and the grass looked like it hadn't been watered all summer.

A big section of the parking lot in front of one particular building was cordoned off with yellow DO-NOT-CROSS police tape. Two police cars sat on the outside of the barrier parked driver's side-to-driver's side, the cops inside whiling away the dull hours of the night with war stories and talk about their wives.

It had been an easy apartment complex to find, once he recalled the name on the sign he'd seen in a television news story about some cabby in Dallas who'd had the misfortune of picking up the wrong fare. He wasn't the first victim in Dallas, though he was among the first infected. The news liked him because he had a compelling personal story. Now the cabby, the wife, and their infant son were all in the hospital fighting for their lives.

Good luck to him and his kid.

And his wife.

Paul had parked outside a Starbucks, close enough to pick up their Wi-Fi signal. He opened an incognito browsing session on his computer and began searching for the apartment complex by name. Forty-five minutes later, he'd driven by several times and finally parked himself across the street to see what he could see and to make his plan. Or, that's to say, to make his plan B.

He'd started at the hospital, which—if news reports were accurate—housed six Ebola patients. He knew before he'd arrived he wouldn't easily be able to go into a patient's room and get himself infected, but he felt pretty confident about finding a way.

It turned out that more than confidence was required for success.

He'd loitered around the hospital for most of the evening, trying to wheedle and sneak his way into places where he shouldn't have been. He wasn't sure if he'd broken any laws anywhere along the way, but he *was* sure, as he sat in his car looking at the near-vacant apartment complex, that he was about to break at least one law. The cabby's apartment had to be crawling with live Ebola virus, and the only way in was illegal.

Paul thought about his hoodlum days again as he started up his truck and pulled out of his parking space. He drove out onto the street and made an immediate right turn. The primary reason he'd never been arrested back in those days for anything but unpaid speeding tickets was that he was careful and smart. Now he was going to break into an apartment, so he needed to put his truck in a safe place, several blocks away.

After finding what looked like a good spot on a dimly lit street, Paul parked and got out of his truck. He stashed his car keys under the fender, crossed the road, and walked into the darkness of a large, adjacent vacant lot. He checked his pockets to make sure he had all he needed, and none of that which he didn't. He carried no identification. He did carry a flashlight, latex gloves—*no prints, no evidence*—and a screwdriver. All he needed.

Finally getting back to a spot where he could see the apartment complex, Paul watched the two policemen in their cruisers, still talking in the glow of their dashboard lights, taking no interest in anything around them.

The apartment complex backed up to an empty field across from a deserted industrial park made up of tin-walled tumbledown buildings, surrounded by pieces of rusting machinery and stacks of barrels and buckets. A tall chain-link fence topped with three strands of barbed wire surrounded the old lot, and in many places the fence was draped in vines or grown through with bushes—it looked like a good way to sneak behind the apartment complex. There'd be no light to silhouette Paul if either of the policemen happened to be looking between the two-floor apartment buildings.

Paul walked down the block, pushed his hands into his pockets, and crossed the street far from any functioning streetlight. He crossed the field, worked his way around a warehouse, and finally found himself walking along the fence by the industrial park, doing his best to look like just another transient on a casual walk, searching for a dumpster to dive into or a sheltered place to sleep. However, if the police approached him, he'd have to come up with a different story. A missing ID could only get him so far. A trip down to the local drunk tank and a fingerprinting would reveal who he was. How does an upper-middle-class white man who lives and works in Denver explain why he's walking around in the small, dark hours of the morning in the bad part of Dallas?

No explanation came to mind.

All Paul could think to do was simply say nothing beyond identifying himself. As of yet, he'd broken no law—or rather, no law for which he could be detained longer than overnight.

He came to a stop and looked at the backside of one of

the buildings, which was wrapped in a few strands of yellow plastic tape. That appeared to be the extent of the deterrent on this side of the building. Sufficient? Why not? Who, seeing the police tape, would want to cross? Especially given the publicity of the Ebola cases and the high probability of death?

Nobody.

Nobody except for dumbass Paul Cooper.

He pushed that thought aside. He'd been through this a million times—he'd fought with Heidi too many times to back out now.

He glanced to his left, then looked to his right. He listened, but mostly heard traffic noise from the highway on the other side of the industrial park. He inspected the building and figured it held maybe eight apartments: four on each floor, one on each corner with a central stairway. There was a breezeway, open on both sides. The apartment he suspected to be the one the cabby lived in was on the backside, bottom floor, to the right. It was out of direct view of the cops out front. Paul only needed a little luck to get inside. If he was careful, he'd be in and out, and nobody would ever know.

Feeling a strong urge to pee, Paul took a deep breath and ran across a hundred and fifty foot-wide strip of dead grass between the industrial park fence and the apartment complex. He reached the light gray brick wall and stopped. He backed against the wall, looking back and forth and gasping. He squatted down to hide himself in the twiggy skeletons of several dying bushes. Drought had been hard on the shrubs in Dallas.

Paul listened. He looked.

No new noises. No movement.

No time to waste.

Paul removed the heavy flat-tipped screwdriver from his back pocket and pried off a screen, letting it fall to the ground beside him. He cringed at the metallic twang and froze while he looked around. Nothing bad happened because of the sound. He'd gotten away with his first mistake. He jammed the screwdriver beneath the lower edge of the window frame, pried and pushed. Aluminum bent. Metal scraped dully on metal. A windowpane cracked with an audible *plink*, causing Paul to freeze and look around. He held his breath and listened.

He waited.

Still safe.

He breathed again.

He went back to work on the window—more vigorously, less careful about the noise. He was standing out in the open, easily seen by anybody coming around behind the building to investigate unusual noises. He needed to hurry.

With a loud crack, the locking mechanism on the inside of the window popped off the frame. The window slid up with some difficulty on its gritty channels. Paul peeked between the curtains, and seeing no one inside, flung himself through the window. He got back to his knees, grabbed the screen, and pulled it in behind him, closing the window as soon as he leaned the screen against an inside wall.

Breathing rapidly from the adrenaline rush, Paul kept an eye out the window to see if anybody had come around to the backside of the building. He waited for what felt like five or ten minutes, but given the nervous energy and pounding in his heart, it may only have been twenty or thirty seconds.

He pulled the curtains closed and looked around at a messy bedroom that looked pretty much like any bedroom in any apartment. No sign hung on the wall telling him Ebola victims had lived there. He peeked into another bedroom; a queen-sized bed was unmade, clothes strewn on the floor. He checked a hallway bathroom. An air freshener generated an invisible fog of harsh lilac that couldn't quite mask the junior-missed-the-toilet undertones. The rest of the apartment smacked of something musty with an insinuation of rotten.

Note to self: don't open the fridge.

In the kitchen, cockroaches skittered over dishes in the sink and hid under the edges of those cluttered across the countertops. In the living room some kind of disposable apartment carpet had a matted trail of grime fanning out from the front door.

Paul started to fear what he might catch besides Ebola.

Still, there was no sign anywhere that this was the apartment where the Ebola victims had lived. He knew he was in the right building; the yellow tape and the two police cars guaranteed that. He thought how he'd decided to break into this apartment, realizing in his nervous walk along the industrial park fence and his frantic race across the field, he'd only made a guess.

In the dim light coming through the windows, Paul's gaze fell on the front door. He took a few slow breaths and thought. If this *was* the Ebola victim's apartment, outside the front door would be at least a few more strands of police tape and probably other signs to warn people away. He'd have to take a look outside. That was his answer.

He crossed the living room. The door chain hung limply from the doorjamb, unattached. It had to be that way—it could only be attached from the inside. He checked the deadbolt, which thankfully had a little knob lock, rather than a key on the inside as some doors did.

He turned the tiny lock on the doorknob. It clicked open with a muted sound that adrenaline amplified to a firecracker pop in the dark silence of the apartment. Paul grasped the doorknob and turned. The door cracked open and he was happy to see strands of yellow police tape strung tautly across the open doorway. He had the right apartment.

But wait...

What if all the apartments had tape across the doors?

Ugh.

Paul stuck his head out the door to look up the hall. The door just up to the right and across the hall had no tape. Good. He looked left, gasped, and nearly wet himself. There, not a dozen feet away, an officer stood, leaning against the wall, looking out through the breezeway under the stairs, watching the fence that bordered the industrial park.

Holding his breath, frightened out of his mind, Paul pushed the door shut as quickly and quietly as physically possible. He clicked the lock closed and set the deadbolt for good measure. He leaned on the wall and took several long, slow breaths. His heart was beating so hard he felt it pound in his chest. He heard the sound of blood rushing through his ears. He grinned, suddenly giddy, feeling the rush of getting away with something. After so many years of being a good citizen, he forgot how thrilling breaking the law could be. Better yet, he had indisputable confirmation that he was in the right place.

What felt like the best part but probably wasn't, the cop never suspected that Paul was there.

With feet placed softly along the grimy carpet path, Paul walked deeper into the apartment, stopped by the kitchen, and looked over at the cockroaches, which had apparently lost their fear of him and were creeping all over the dishes in the sink, going about their business.

It seemed that everything in the apartment had a layer of dust, smashed with ground-in grime, and was coated in a sticky film of something—and that was as close as Paul could get to a description, of his surroundings. That's the thought that irked Paul the most as he started to think through the unplanned details of what he had come to do.

How does one catch Ebola from an infected someone's personal items? Where might the virus still be alive?

The apartment was uncomfortably warm. Dallas, like most of Texas, spent its summers under a blanket of Gulf humidity that dripped from the nose and put a wet stink in the armpits even at night. Drapes over the windows in the apartment kept most sunlight out—direct sunlight was chock full of UV rays, which could kill a virus—most of the time. If Ebola was going to choose conditions under which it might last the longest outside the body, the apartment was well-suited.

But which surface, tracked over by prickly little cockroach feet through layers of fermenting grime might be best for finding Ebola virions? And how best to get the virus off those surfaces and into his mouth?

Paul shuddered as an idea crossed his mind.

His eyes tracked a skittering roach across the counter, and he shuddered again.

Chapter 37

Paul examined the items he'd gathered from around the house: two toothbrushes and a baby's pacifier taken from the crib in the kid's bedroom; two forks and four spoons, all from the sink of dirty dishes in the kitchen; a bottle of some kind of nasal spray, and a thermometer from the dresser in the kid's bedroom—pretty much anything he found in the apartment that had been in the mouth or nose of one of the victims.

A brave cockroach ran across the counter from the sink and stopped by a tablespoon that still contained small lumps of something no longer identifiable. It waggled its antennae over the spoon, ran over it, stopped on the other side, turned, and prepared to feast.

Paul shooed, but it wouldn't go. He waved his hand closer. Again, it refused to be intimidated. He brushed it with his fingers, but instead of running, it latched on and started prickly climbing over his hand. Paul jumped away from the counter, shaking his hand and brushing frantically, trying to get rid of the bug, shivering at the false sensation of cockroaches all over his skin. In his roach panic, he bumped his back into the refrigerator and sent an empty plastic bowl tumbling. It hit his head before bouncing onto the linoleum floor.

Paul froze for a second and held his breath before dropping to his knees and looking over the kitchen counter toward the apartment's front door. "Shit."

He silently chastised himself. He'd come too far to screw it all up now.

After waiting for what he figured was long enough for something to happen, Paul sucked up his breath, and stood up. He now ignored every inhibition he'd learned since childhood about putting a dirty utensil into his mouth—the worst being the thought of putting another person's toothbrush in his mouth. He tried his best to empty his brain and not to think about what he was there to do, focused only on the fact that he needed to get it done. If a viable Ebola virion was in the apartment, it would most certainly be on the items on the counter in front of him. He needed to hurry, do the deed, and get the hell out of there.

He sucked in another deep breath, picked up the first in the line of items—one of the dirty spoons from the sink—and put it into his mouth. He grimaced but kept his lips wrapped around the handle as he ran his tongue over the stainless steel, soaking it in his own saliva, reconstituting air-dried lasagna crunchies and swallowing down the loosened blobs. After leaving it in his mouth for maybe a minute, he took it out and moved on to the next item.

By the time Paul came to the last of the items, he thought he might puke, but he tried to put the multisensory memories out of his mind. Allowing himself to wretch, allowing his stomach acid to fill his throat and mouth, might kill any virus he'd just harvested.

Fear focused his thoughts externally, taking them off the taste in his mouth. He went back into the kid's bedroom, parted the curtains, and looked outside. It was time to escape. The cop in the breezeway was a worry. Nothing could be done except to mitigate the risk. He'd be silent and keep himself out of any direct view from inside the breezeway. That was all he could do.

Paul slid the window open, stuck his head out, and saw nothing but the wide field and the vine-covered fence on the other side. The distance looked more daunting now that he knew about the cop just around the corner, not thirty feet from where Paul was leaning out the window.

He steeled his nerves and focused.

He pulled his head back in and stuck his leg out onto the ground. Paul was halfway out before he silently thanked the building's architect for designing windows with sills low enough to be stepped over when the window was open. While glancing back and forth, he pulled his torso through and then his other foot. He planted both feet on the ground, pulled the curtains closed, and slowly, so as to minimize the sound, slid the window down. As soon as it closed, he turned and started walking at the angle he'd chosen. The first steps were the hardest to take, knowing that he was at risk of being seen by at least three separate policemen. He knew that once he was far enough away from the building, he'd go back to evasion plan A—keep his mouth shut. If no cop witnessed him leaving the scene, they'd have nothing on him. They couldn't detain him for long on nothing.

But...

And there was a big *but*. If Paul had succeeded in infecting himself, he'd soon become contagious. The last thing he wanted was to be delayed so long that he'd infect someone in a holding cell.

When he was twenty steps from the window, a voice yelled, "Stop! Police!"

Ebola K: Book 2

Paul froze at the sound of the policeman's voice behind him, spent half a second on indecision, and then bolted for the fence.

Please don't shoot.

Options?

Climb the fence? No way. The cop would drag him off and cuff him before he got halfway up. *Unless the cop was fat and slow.* Paul glanced over his shoulder. The cop was lagging, at least twenty yards back, and running awkwardly, losing ground.

Paul sprinted faster. If he could make it to the corner of the property and get out of the cop's sight, perhaps some opportunity to escape might present itself.

As Paul was two-thirds of the way across the field and closing in on the corner of the industrial park, a car engine revved loudly and a police car bounced over a curb. Paul was caught in a pair of bright headlights. The police cruiser accelerated rapidly toward him.

His options were about to disappear. He started to imagine what lies he'd tell. He started to think what Heidi would say. He wondered if his plan to simply keep his mouth shut would work.

He spotted an opening in the chain link fence, cut a hard right, and headed directly for it. He looked back over his shoulder again. The cop on foot who'd wasted his time in calling for backup was way, way behind. The car was bearing down, but wouldn't make it.

Paul hit the gap in the chain link fence. His shirt caught a link and tore—it cut the skin on his arm, but he was through.

Red and blue lights flashed. A siren wailed. Voices shouted.

Paul raced off between two buildings without looking back, moving as fast as he could. He turned a corner and found himself in darkness. That wasn't going to last. Backup was surely on the way. If the cops suspected he'd been in the Ebola apartment, the whole place would be swimming with police before he caught his breath.

But what were his choices now? *Hide? Run?*

Give up? Hell no!

Hiding was futile. At least it always looked that way on the reality cop shows. Hiding perps always got caught.

Paul ran on, hoping another opportunity might present itself.

Throughout the industrial park he passed buildings with sheet metal torn off the sides, leaving plenty of places to sneak inside. An abundance of good spots to hide presented themselves outside among mounds of equipment and rusty machines larger than his truck. Hiding *was* tempting.

Kids and crackheads had likely been using the buildings for secluded underage drinking parties and whatnot. The place was probably crawling with transients. Could Paul find a group of them, and perhaps pass for one?

That might work.

Don't be stupid. Keep running.

Paul slowed his pace and peered into the darkness of one of the buildings. The smell of urine and alcohol served both to confirm his suspicions and to give him pause. What danger might be in there? He reached for the flashlight in his pocket and realized he still had the screwdriver. That had to go. How would he explain that to the police? He pitched it into the darkness inside a building and ran on.

He came to a concrete drainage ditch thirty feet wide and sixty feet long covered over in layers of graffiti and scuffed in arcs like they'd been worn through with skateboard wheels. Down at one end, were four galvanized bars blocking the entrance to a storm drain six feet in diameter. Two bars were pulled away and one was bent out, far enough for Paul to run inside.

He stopped in a shadow. He heard voices shouting from somewhere at the far corner of the industrial park where he'd come in. Blue and red lights bounced off the buildings. Several sirens were inbound and not far away. Paul looked back at the drainage pipe.

Good enough.

He ran down the slope of the ditch, lost his footing and rolled to the bottom, earning more bruises and scrapes along the way. He didn't take time to bemoan his new wounds or catch his breath. If the police caught him, if they decided he'd been in that apartment, that would be the least of his worries. A jail cell might be his home for some time to come.

Paul squeezed past the bent bars and ran into the pipe. Fishing in his back pocket for his flashlight, he stumbled over debris. He put a hand out to use the side of the pipe for a guide. He put the flashlight under his shirt and turned it on, allowing the cloth to damp the light's intensity. He ran as fast as he dared.

It would only be a matter of time before the police, in their search for him, found the culvert, then shined lights down the pipe to see if he was in there. Paul needed to get out the other end or around a corner before that happened.

Chapter 39

A streetlight shining through a storm drain became Paul's beacon for an exit. The cutout in the curb wasn't near wide enough for Paul to squeeze through, but an iron grate that extended the drain out into the street was light enough —Paul only ruptured a single hernia moving the thing out of his way. He struggled through the gap and got himself away from the street as quickly as he could.

He looked around to see if anyone had seen him emerge and happily discovered he was alone. Around him were more apartments with windows closed against the heat and curtains drawn for what privacy could be had in a community of thin-walled apartments stacked one on top of another. After a bit of sneaking around in the shadows, he found himself just a block down from his parked truck.

God must love me.

He probably didn't.

Paul ran around a three-story building as he saw a helicopter arrive above the spot where he figured the industrial park sat, several blocks away. More sirens wailed out of the distance. The helicopter's searchlight pierced the darkness below. Paul reached his truck, got in, and sped away as quickly as he felt safe moving on the deserted city streets.

An hour later, Paul drove through Sherman, Texas on IH-35. Not too long after that, he crossed the Red River and passed into Oklahoma. The trip north through Oklahoma to Kansas, then west to Colorado was the long way home, but it was the quickest path out of Texas, and seemed like the best way to diminish the chance of getting caught. If anyone had spotted a truck with Colorado plates near the scene of the break-in and noticed the truck didn't belong in the area, and if the police canvassed the area and were able to obtain this information, it was best for Paul not to be in the state when that information was disseminated to the highway patrol.

The sun rose as Paul was passing through Oklahoma City. The giddiness of having eluded the police was settling down to general nervousness, aided by enough caffeine pills to make his hands jittery on the wheel and keep him squirming in his seat.

Nine hours later, Paul entered Denver's city limits.

When he got home and pulled into the garage, Heidi's Murano was not parked crookedly inside. She had left, just as she promised she would. Of course, she could have simply been at work, but Paul knew he was lying to himself about that. Heidi was nothing if not stubborn. She said she'd leave if he embarked on his foolish plan. Now he was sitting in his garage with the Ebola virus replicating in his blood, and she was gone.

Paul closed the garage door, then sat in his truck for a long time, coming to grips with the consequences of his choices, mostly feeling alone because of Heidi's absence. He thought about the grimy, roach-infested apartment in Dallas, the police tape, and the quarantine. He thought about his tidy, clean townhouse. If he went inside—hell, if he took one step out of his pickup into his own garage— nobody could come within a hundred yards of the place until after it had been decontaminated. His home, Heidi's home, would be useless.

Heidi needed a place to come back to when her anger finally cooled. Paul needed a place to come back to if he survived—no, *when* he survived.

Paul pushed the button on the garage door remote and the door creaked loudly on poorly lubricated rollers as it rose. Paul started up his engine and pulled out his telephone. He typed out a text message to Heidi—*I know you're mad at me. I'm sorry we argued. We'll talk later. I won't be coming back to the house. I'll find a place to stay. Come home when you're ready. Love you.*

Chapter 40

Austin's fever broke late in the morning after his first night in the hut. It left him feeling weak. The woman and her three dead children had left plenty to keep Austin fed for a week or maybe two, should he decide to stay that long. But that wasn't the plan. He had to get to Mbale. He had to call his dad. He had to do at least that much. His dad was his ticket home.

He also needed to get medical help for Dr. Littlefield back in what remained of Kapchorwa. As Austin looked at the family of corpses, he was disturbed by the fact that he no longer felt anguished by their presence. He realized that help was likely in short supply. Ebola was spreading too fast. Too many mothers, too many children, and too many men were dying.

Thunderstorms dumped heavy rains on Sironko for most of Austin's second day in the hut. To his surprise, the rickety roof had only a few small leaks, one of which dripped onto the face of the younger dead girl. She might have been seven or eight, lying on her back, eyes closed, mouth open, crusted blood under her nose and across her cheek. The drip of water, steady throughout the day, slowly washed the blood away until the girl looked to be sleeping, with her mother's arm draped across her chest.

Austin had many moments on that second day when he thought he had the strength to hike the last twelve miles into Mbale. With strong memories of his second fever reminding him of how fragile he was, and the bodies of the children starting to rot just a few paces across the dirt floor, prudent thought won out. He needed to be careful with his health. He waited out his second day, convalescing in the hut, keeping himself fed and hydrated, swatting at a growing host of insects, and leaning out through the door to breathe air that had no fetid taste.

On the third day, with the morning sun glowing from behind Mt. Elgon, Austin filled his plastic bottles with rainwater and his bag to bulging with fruit and began his hike out of Sironko.

A blanket of gray clouds left over from the storms kept the temperature comfortable. Almost. Austin made good time, walking at a slow pace along the deserted but paved highway. He saw no cars, no buses, no bodas. He saw no bicycles, and no walkers. In the fields he occasionally saw livestock. He heard roosters crow, but saw no farmers. He saw no eyes peeking at him from the darkness inside houses along the road. He saw no doors being shut. No one yelled at him to keep moving, to go away.

Austin felt alone in the world. He'd spent two days sleeping in the company of corpses. The last living person he'd seen was the angry, wiry man glaring at him from the doorway of his hut, and that man had Ebola. He was probably dead.

Austin took a break after walking for a few hours. He sat down under a tree far from the scattered farmhouses. He felt fatigued again. He ate, drank, and watched the wind blow through tree branches across the road. He thought about Dr. Littlefield back in Kapchorwa. He wondered whether Dr. Mills had made it or whether she was still struggling. Probably still struggling with the disease, he decided. He wondered whether the disease had been contained and if he might at some point pass some boundary and walk back into civilization. He wondered about his friend Salim. Had he imagined that encounter back in Kapchorwa? *Probably.* Why would his high school friend Salim show up in Africa? And what about Rashid?

Was he still alive? Najid had brought that doctor for him. It was possible.

The thought of Najid stirred Austin's impotent anger, but he had no desire at the moment to indulge in any Almasi death fantasies.

Finally, boredom set in. Austin figured he was as refreshed as he was likely to get. He stood up, situated his belongings, and started the next leg of his morning hike.

South of Namusi, walking up a long, straight stretch of road, Austin spotted something far ahead that shouldn't have been there, something in the road too distant to make out. Wary about what it might be, Austin walked out of the road's center and to the edge of the asphalt. He'd have walked on the shoulder had it not been muddy from the previous day's rain.

It only took another five or ten minutes of walking for Austin to understand what it was he saw. Parked across the road were two trucks painted military green. A roadblock.

The military must have quarantined the area when word of the Ebola outbreak reached Kampala. Austin walked off the road and leaned against a tree. Initially distressed by the sight of the roadblock, he decided it was a good thing. Containing the Ebola virus in the Kapchorwa and Sironko districts was good, not so much for the people within, but for everyone outside. That also meant that the government and the international community were coming to the aid of these people. With any luck, it also suggested that Najid had been stopped and detained at just such a roadblock.

That left Austin with a dilemma.

If Najid *was* detained, then it might be information Austin could provide that would lead to Najid's punishment for his crimes. Austin would need to make sure that the right people heard what he had to say. The best way to do that would be to talk to the US Embassy in Kampala. The guards at a roadblock in the middle-of-nowhere Uganda would be in no position to have any idea of what Austin was talking about. They would only turn him away.

That left Austin only one choice. He needed to leave the road and start out across the fields. He knew that Mbale was south of him, and with Mt. Elgon as a guiding landmark he knew he could keep himself moving in the right direction.

Austin crossed the shoulder and stepped into a lush field of waist-high tea bushes.

Chapter 41

Early that summer, Paul and Heidi had spent a weekend at a remote cabin up in the mountains near Lake Granby. Paul gave a thought to driving up there. It would get him away from his house and get him pretty far away from other people.

Paul's second thought was that Lake Granby was a few hours up into the mountains. If he fell ill there, what hospital would he end up in? Paul didn't know. What he did know was that he couldn't chance falling ill and waking up in some Podunk hospital with a doctor who earned his degree from a fourth-rate Caribbean island medical school. He had taken an enormous chance by purposefully trying to contract Ebola early. He couldn't afford to negate the advantage of being an early adopter by putting himself under incompetent care.

He needed to stay in Denver.

Inspiration hit.

Paul pulled out of his garage and drove his truck toward Interstate 25.

When he'd first moved to Denver, Paul had been forced to stay in a hotel for two months while he shopped for a house. The hotel he'd stayed in looked nice enough on the outside, and the long-term rates were affordable. The rooms weren't a lot cleaner than the cabby's apartment in Dallas. He'd gotten in the habit of never going barefoot indoors for fear of what he might catch from putting his bare feet on the carpet. He'd have moved out after that first night had he not prepaid for the entire stay. The manager had been a total ass about refunding Paul's money so Paul was stuck for the full two months.

Well, that manager, if he was still there, would earn Paul as a repeat customer, and his putrid little hotel would get itself an industrial-grade decontamination when Paul moved out this time.

Chapter 42

After breakfast on the fourth day of Paul's stay in the petri dish hotel, just as he was starting to worry whether all of his troubles had been for naught, he started to feel feverish. He didn't take any aspirin. He didn't want to mask his coming symptoms. He wanted to be sure he was sick when he made the fateful call.

By lunch, the pain in his head was trying to claw its way through the bone. His muscles knotted themselves into fists of ache, and every organ squirmed through briars and sand. Between trips to the bathroom that were increasing in frequency, he sat on the bed, held his telephone in his unsteady hands, and reviewed his story in his head.

He dialed.

After a single ring, the telephone call connected and the voice said, "9-1-1, what's your emergency?"

Paul quickly provided his name, address, the hotel name, his room number, and then said, "It's possible I have Ebola."

A long pause followed. "Sir, making false statements to the police is a punishable offense in the state of Colorado and is pursued vigorously."

"I understand," said Paul. "Will you please send an ambulance to my location and warn them that I may be infected?"

A sigh and a huff followed from the voice. "Are you able to transport yourself to the hospital?"

"Possibly," said Paul. "I have a fever and the worst headache I've...I feel dizzy when I stand." Paul decided an exaggeration was in order. Well, not much of a stretch. "I don't think I can drive."

"Why do you think you have Ebola?" The operator let her tone convey the accusation in the question. She thought she was being pranked.

"Are you sending an ambulance?" Paul asked.

"Yes, one is on the way."

A new voice—a man—came on the line. "Mr. Cooper, why do you believe you have Ebola?"

Paul said, "I think I've been exposed."

"How so?"

Time for the big lie. Paul replied, "The day after my wife and I had an argument and I left—"

"Is your wife with you now? Is she all right?" the man asked.

"She's fine. I think she flew to her mother's house in Texas after I moved into the hotel."

"But she's in good health?" the man persisted. "Not in any danger?"

"She's fine," Paul told him, thinking that perhaps he was providing too many details. Simple lies are always easier to support.

"Why do think you were exposed?"

"I was driving up Highway 40 toward Granby and I came across a car with a flat tire. The guy didn't look like he knew what he was doing, so I stopped and helped." Paul paused to calm his nervousness.

"And why do you think you have Ebola?"

"Um," Paul said, "He had a Liberian accent."

"And what does a Liberian accent sound like?" the man asked.

"Is the ambulance coming?" Paul demanded. He needed to get better at lying.

Chapter 43

As was her new thrice-daily habit, Olivia dialed the number, and as usual, the CIA operative at the other end did not pick up. She didn't expect him to, but wasn't ready to give up on the endeavor just yet. The phone rang eight times and disconnected. No surprise.

Olivia put the telephone back in its cradle, wondering if she'd have better luck calling from her cell phone, rather than a company line. She looked back at her screen. She'd been working an item from the queue—some person she'd decided to call Blogger X—who had been posting through an anonymous server domiciled in a Norwegian data farm.

Blogger X's posts were written in distinctly American English, with plenty of poor grammar, slang, and R-rated language to prove it. The tone was generally livid with distrust. He believed the government was repressing news about the Ebola outbreak and was trying to drum up public passion to do something—call a congressman, email the White House, *something*.

Unfortunately, as Olivia knew too well, Blogger X was right.

Olivia knew that Blogger X had been shut down twice already. She'd tried to track him down once, as had someone else who worked the queue out of Phoenix. Olivia took a moment to link all three cases together in the application, then called up all the versions of his page cached in the system.

Outside of his seemingly poor mastery of the English language, Blogger X had put together a pleasing color palette, with a nicely limited set of font choices. Graphics on the page were effective, but not obnoxious. She wondered if Blogger X's day job was in graphic design.

That was a clue that might help in tracking him down.

More importantly (for Blogger X, not for Olivia's task), he'd done a fantastic job putting together a time-lapse animation of a global map showing round, red circles over white continents surrounded by teal-colored oceans. A click on the play button started a date counter that coincided with a pinprick of red in Western Africa, the first reported Ebola outbreak.

Visually, it was much more engaging than the version of the same information she'd put together for herself at Barry's behest over a week ago. She watched the video as the pinprick in West Africa grew and multiplied. The size of the spots indicated the number of cases, and she could mouse over any spot to get the date and the count of cases on that date for that spot. A pinprick of red was a single case. A large red spot like the one over Monrovia represented thousands of cases.

Two new enhancements to Blogger X's video had to do with scaling and color. Ebola cases in the new strain were represented by yellow pinpricks and yellow spots. Olivia made a note to look into which information on which strain was public and which was not.

Additionally, at a certain date of the animation, all of the spots shifted to one tenth their previous size to indicate a new scale. A big spot that represented a thousand cases one instant shifted down to the size of a spot that had formerly represented a hundred. It was an unfortunate necessity in order to accommodate the scale of the epidemic, primarily as it was spreading in Nairobi where the case count had just topped forty thousand, though everyone believed the number was higher.

Forty thousand in Nairobi. Olivia took a moment to think about that number and tried to come up with some reason why it shouldn't carry the most ominous ramifications for the rest of mankind.

In the two and a half weeks since Olivia had come back to work, the case count in Nairobi had grown from a few hundred to that staggering forty thousand number. The pictures, videos, and stories coming out of Nairobi were medieval. Bodies were lying in the streets. Hospitals were cesspools where the infected waded in to die. Corpses were stacked in piles of Holocaust proportions. Pyres burned hundreds in squares where markets once thrived. The air was thick with death while armed bandits roamed the streets, victimizing the weak. The police and the army had melted into the chaos.

Olivia wondered if some professor somewhere had put together a measure of social stability for countries around the world, a kind of metric for how resilient a society might be when calamity struck. In other words, what percentage of a city's citizens needed to die in the street before social order broke down?

More to the point, how many *Americans* needed to be dead before Olivia needed to think seriously about barricading herself in her apartment with a gun?

Olivia felt embarrassed for entertaining the thought. Things couldn't get that bad. Not here.

While mainstream American news still reported on the crisis in Africa, the worst of it was repressed. Little mention was made of the distinction between the new strain and the old. Nowhere were deaths counts reported publicly — thanks to Olivia and people like her. That wouldn't last though. They couldn't stifle the information forever.

Already ten thousand had died in Mumbai, and it seemed the first case had just been reported a week prior. Beijing's number carried with it a range of estimates, both on the same scale as Mumbai. Not surprisingly, the Chinese government was doing a better job than the Americans at keeping a lid on the scary numbers. Sometimes censorship had its benefits.

Olivia moved the date slider bar back five days to a time when Frankfurt, the worst-affected Western city, had only — *only* — three hundred cases of the new strain. She let the animation run forward again and watched the few yellow pixels on Frankfurt blossom to a spot that represented over two thousand.

That was what Ebola K looked like in a modern Western city with a proactive government and world-class medical care. Olivia asked herself how long it would be before it looked like Nairobi.

She restarted the animation and watched. The red dots of the first Ebola strain smoldered menacingly but slowly through West Africa. At a point just over two weeks ago, the yellow dots blazed a sudden and spidery path across the globe that made the red dots seem stagnant.

It frightened Olivia as she extrapolated the growth of the yellow in her imagination. It frightened her more because she knew Blogger X's data was accurate.

Chapter 44

To circumvent the roadblock the day before, Austin had exhausted himself trudging through muddy fields that left his shoes caked with wet, red clay that glued his feet to the ground with each step. By noon, he'd found what he could only guess was a barn for some farmer's goats. Its chest-high walls looked like they might collapse in a good wind, and inside, it smelled of manure. It was empty. Austin spent the night.

When he woke in the morning, Austin felt stronger than he had since before Ebola ravaged his body. He fed himself and began early. He crossed a field that was starting to dry out after the rains and came to a road somewhere south of Namusi. The road led southeast, and Austin figured it would either take him into Mbale or to the highway just north of town.

He followed.

Along the way, his spirits lifted. He saw his first sign of normal life—a farmer toiling in his field. Further along, he saw other people both in their fields and working near their homes. He saw a boy herding his family's goats. A car full of people sped by—the roof stacked high with all manner of goods. Later, two more vehicles drove cautiously by on their way out of Mbale.

By noon Austin was nearing the outskirts of Mbale and watching a wide column of tan and gray smoke grow into a crawling stain through the cerulean sky.

Across several fields he saw the Mbale road. At the point where it reached the edge of town, he saw the source of the fire, the Islamic University. At least two of its academic buildings were aflame as were several of the hostels south of campus. People milled about. He heard faint, angry shouts.

Best to steer clear of that area.

Austin left the road and took off across another field toward some neighborhoods on the northeast edge of Mbale. He came to a narrow dirt road and started toward town until he noticed that the road was blocked with debris just where it passed between the first two houses in the neighborhood. He saw the heads of several people behind the barricade. More than one shook a stick at him.

He cut across another field, hoping that whatever unrest was troubling Mbale, it was limited to the northern parts of town. When he saw more pillars of smoke rising from a spot a mile or two to the southeast, he started to doubt that hope.

Staying in the fields, he skirted the barricaded neighborhood and headed south. That's when he saw the source of the second column of smoke, the Catholic University.

Religious unrest?

Austin stopped in the field and watched the smoke rise as he thought again about his options. None of them were particularly rosy. He was just a mzungu in the middle of Africa, and the closest thing to civilization he'd seen all week appeared to be tearing itself to pieces.

Austin looked in the direction of the center of town. Through a haze of smoke from the large fires at the universities, he couldn't tell if anything was burning over there. He listened for the sound of gunfire, more than half expecting to hear it. There was none. He had no doubt the fires at both the Islamic University and the Catholic University were related. One was probably revenge for the other. It was more than possible that the first fire was an accident. Fear, already heightened by the Ebola epidemic in the countryside and the sight of soldiers setting up roadblocks, had turned a previously stable situation volatile.

Austin gave a thought to avoiding Mbale and going—

Going where?

Austin really had almost no other choice. Mbale was the only sizable town within a hundred miles. It represented his only real chance to get in contact with the rest of the world. It represented his only chance of getting help for the survivors in Kapchorwa. He had hoped Mbale would be his first step in getting back home.

No choice but to proceed.

Austin gave the burning Catholic University a wide berth and cut across another field. Near the houses bordering the field he saw more signs of life. Some people were outside their houses watching the fires. Some watched from windows and doors. He started to see people walking on the streets, some in groups, talking, looking almost normal, others carrying goods. He saw a few riding bikes. He even caught sight of a boda.

If he could hire a boda his troubles would be in the past. On the back of one of those motorcycles he could get as far as Kampala and to the American embassy if he had to.

At the southern edge of the field, Austin passed into a densely forested park and felt safe amongst the trees. His worries about Mbale started to recede. When he was deep enough into the park, he took a break to drink some water, eat a snack, and rest. To his surprise, he recovered quickly from the morning's walk. It made him hopeful. His health was moving in the direction of normal.

At the park's southern boundary, he crossed a road and continued south, staying close to a tall hedge of native shrubs along one side of the road. The people he saw were nervous but not threatening.

Though the thought stayed in his mind, he saw no reason to turn around and leave Mbale by the way he'd entered.

While crossing an intersection of two dirt roads, Austin looked to his right and was pleasantly surprised. People were in the street and on the sidewalks in front of the businesses. Several blocks down, the clock tower stood in a roundabout near the middle of town. Oddly, a large bonfire burned on the south side of the tower. From that landmark, Austin would be able to find his way to the parts of Mbale he was familiar with. Better yet, boda drivers liked to park their motorbikes along the outer rim of the roundabout, where they'd wait for fares.

With any luck, at least one would be waiting there today.

Looking down the road toward the clock tower, and seeing the people again, Austin realized he'd misunderstood what he first saw. It was as if the good people of Mbale had disappeared and in their stead, rowdy mobs were on the street looting. A gang of five boys was another half-block down atop a very used cream-colored Mercedes, jumping up and down and pounding its windows and fenders with sticks. Two older men stood to the side, cursing the boys to no effect.

When Austin and Rashid had taken their first trip to Mbale a few months earlier, they'd witnessed a man being beaten severely by dozens of people while two policemen passively watched. Misguided outrage had prompted Austin to confront the police. Laughing at Austin's ignorance, they explained that the man being beaten was caught stealing by a shopkeeper. The people of Uganda didn't tolerate thievery the way Americans did, or so the policeman explained. What Austin was seeing was more than common behavior. It was the rule.

When the crowd had finished their work, the police picked up the bloodied criminal and hauled him to his next step in Uganda's justice system. Austin didn't know whether to feel disgusted by the barbarity or to applaud it. The people had a high moral standard and were compelled to uphold it.

Something very basic had changed in Ugandan society. Was the fear of Ebola so strong it could change so much behavior so quickly?

That worried Austin.

Chapter 45

Still standing in the center of the intersection, Austin was in the midst of deciding whether to leave Mbale. Should he take the long hike back to Kapchorwa, or sneak around town and see if he could find a phone, a hotel, a boda, something? He looked in the direction of the park. He gulped. A gang of armed, angry-faced men wearing shabby military garb was coming up the road—whether toward him, or just coming in his direction, he wasn't sure. Healthy fear told him not to wait to find out.

Austin looked around for a good place to run. He saw two olive drab military trucks drive onto the roundabout by the clock tower and stop. *The army.* They looked to be his safest option. Austin picked up his pace and headed in that direction.

Where the boys were still beating the Mercedes, Austin kept to the far side of the street. They didn't notice him. He looked behind him and saw two of the paramilitary gang stopped in the intersection where he'd been standing just moments before. They were looking around, pointing and talking. Whatever their deal was, it had nothing to do with him. He hurried past another block and then crossed the street to get to the opposite side from the looters.

The last two short blocks were relatively clear of people. He jogged for a bit and then slowed to walking, not because he felt safe, but because he simply couldn't jog anymore. His body hadn't the stamina for that level of exertion yet.

At a cross street he looked right and saw two men— ordinary looking men—using sticks to beat another man. He saw more people far down the road, all carrying pots, bags, and baskets, running as if their burdens were stolen.

Austin stepped over a long, rounded curb at a corner,

the top edge lined with dozens of pairs of shoes—black and brown leather, used but shined, elegant as though purchased from a Wall Street lawyer's estate auction, all ready for sale, with toes hanging out over the gutter. No merchant was in sight.

He hurried on.

Austin made his way down the length of the last block, dragging his feet, each breath burning his lungs. The wind made a slow shift in direction, and the black smoke from the bonfire poured between the two big army trucks and floated over Austin. It reeked with a rotten, bitter taste, and Austin almost gagged. He put a hand over his mouth, squinted to keep the soot out of his eyes, and pressed through.

Finally stepping off the curb that circled the roundabout's perimeter, Austin walked around the front of the first army truck and stopped, horrified. The bonfire was built of corpses with blackened limbs that reached out as though trying to escape.

The soldiers, eight or nine of them, wore green rubber gloves up to the elbows of their yellow Tyvek suits which were spotted with strips of tape to cover holes. Most wore olive-colored gas masks. A few wore filthy, damp cloths the color of dirt wrapped around their faces. All were taking bodies off the backs of the trucks—some in bags, some not—and heaving them onto the pyre.

Austin fell to his knees and threw up. He caught his breath and spit the acrid flavor out of his mouth. Suddenly, feet were on the ground in front of him. He looked up.

One of the soldiers glared down. Silently, he pointed up the road.

Austin looked to see what the soldier was pointing at. It could have been anything, hooligans, looters, an abandoned car. Or he could have been pointing at nothing. Austin looked back up at the soldier, and asked, "What?"

"Go," he said, shaking his head. "Go."

"Where?" Austin pleaded.

"Go."

Austin looked past the pointing soldier to find an officer or sergeant—anyone who might be more helpful.

The soldier took a half step forward, and raised his arm, still pointing. "Go. Now."

Austin nodded, accepting the imperative, but having no idea where to go. He started walking away, slowly and tentatively. He thought of the little restaurant where he stopped in for a plate of ugali nearly every day when he was in Mbale. It was just a few blocks to the east. Surely the owner would remember him and might even have a phone Austin could use. Hell, even a friendly face and a moment of respite would do.

Despite the taste of burned bodies in his mouth, hope renewed Austin's energy, and he headed north on the highway through the center of town, away from the clock tower. He passed the body of a teenage boy lying in a gutter. A woman was sitting on a curb beside it, weeping into her hands. Two men were squaring off to fight as one kept attempting to grab a sackcloth bag away from the other. Three men chased another across the street and disappeared into an alley. A wood-frame building several blocks down had just started to burn. Somewhere, a group of men was chanting some kind of tribal war cry. And every so often, a car screeched out of a side street, slalomed past the road debris, and sped away. North or south, it probably didn't matter.

He turned left off of the Mbale highway, arriving at the

street where the little restaurant was located, and kept to one side of the road. He heard a woman loudly wailing as he passed an open window. He hurried.

Gunshots.

Austin froze and then fell to his knees. More shots echoed through the streets as he looked around for the source. He didn't see any rifles, but he now knew it had been a mistake to come into Mbale.

He slinked around the corner of a building and dropped down behind a decrepit tin fence to collect his thoughts. The gunshots had rattled him. Well, that and everything else he'd seen since foolishly coming into the city.

The restaurant was just another block down and across the street from a bright yellow two-story building.

Would the owner let him in when Austin knocked? Would he even open the door? Or would he pretend not to be home? His wife and kids were probably in the house behind the shop. Austin had to ask himself, would he let a stranger inside under the circumstances? No. That was the simple answer. Austin wondered if he had enough cash to bribe the restaurant owner. No.

Austin realized that going to the shop would be a waste of time and could expose him to more risk.

Other options?

He knew that a river wound its way through the city from northwest to southeast. He wasn't sure where it ran through this part of town, but he was guessing it couldn't be more than three or four blocks north. If he could get to the river, he could easily make his way down along the bank and escape the city in the cover of the trees and thick underbrush. No one would see him. If no one saw him, no one would decide that he was a threat and come after him.

And that was Austin's biggest fear at the moment. He wore a solitary white face in a city full of very frightened, dark-skinned people.

If anyone of them imagined — for whatever reason — that Austin had carried Ebola into Mbale, he wouldn't get out of the city alive.

Unfortunately, no alternative plan for meeting any of his goals presented itself. He could wander around eastern Uganda looking for a phone until he stumbled into enough bad situations that he wound up dead, or he could go back to Kapchorwa.

Eventually, Ebola would run its course, fear would subside, danger would abate, and some kind of new normal would reorder Ugandan society. Austin might have to wait until then before leaving Kapchorwa again.

Coming out from behind the tin fence where he'd been hiding, Austin cast a final glance at the bright yellow building, shaking his head as he did. *Get out of town*, he said to himself.

He crossed the street and looked back toward the center of town.

Oh, no.

Several men in fatigues — some of the same he'd seen coming out of the park on the other side of town — were standing in the road looking at him. The one with a pistol reached up, pointed a finger, and shouted. The ragged young men with him were already racing in his direction.

Austin instincts took over. He ran.

Ebola K: Book 2

Chapter 46

"You're lucky."

Salim looked at a familiar, plastic-draped nurse with the name *Alison* written with a marker on her suit where a breast pocket might have been on a shirt. He tried to reason out why he was the lucky one. He couldn't.

Alison said, "You're AB negative."

"I don't understand."

"Your blood type," she said. "It's the least common blood type."

Salim looked at her blankly.

"This was all explained to you."

Salim shrugged. It did have a familiar ring.

Alison looked over her shoulder as though someone else might have snuck into the room. No one had. She said, "I told them you didn't understand most of what he was telling you."

"The doctor?" Salim asked.

"Doctor Huntley," she said. "He's in charge of your care."

Salim nodded as that name clicked into a slot in his memory. Of course it was Dr. Huntley. He wouldn't have been able to provide the name if asked—still, he knew it was correct. Dr. Huntley, a cold, tactless man had been coming in to see him regularly. "What did he tell me?" Salim asked.

"The only American survivor so far is a doctor who'd been in Liberia."

Salim waited for more.

"His blood type is the same as yours, AB negative. Only

about one in two hundred have that blood type. Dr. Huntley used his blood serum to...to give your immune system a boost."

Salim lifted his head from the pillow and looked down the length of his body. He felt better than he had in days. "I guess it worked."

"His blood serum already had the antibodies to defeat the virus, so it gave your immune system the help it needed until it could manufacture enough to defend itself."

"I'm going to make it, then?" Salim asked, surprised and starting to feel the gravity of the moment. He didn't feel like he was dying. He reached up and touched his ears, his nose, and pulled his hand away to look for the blood. His fingers were clean. He wasn't wasting away like those villagers in Kapchorwa.

Alison looked over her shoulder again. "It seems so. You're doing better. Your body is responding and—"

Alison's sudden stop raised Salim's concerns. "What aren't you telling me?"

Alison stepped closer. "I'm not a doctor so you should take my opinion with a grain of salt."

"Okay," Salim agreed.

"They sent your blood samples off to the CDC. They ran tests. You and the doctor who recovered in Atlanta don't have the same strain of Ebola."

"The surviving doctor from Liberia?"

Alison nodded. "Some of the doctors are saying you survived *despite* the serum, not because of it."

"If I'm surviving, it doesn't matter to me." Salim half smiled.

"That's why they keep coming and asking you so many questions. They're trying to figure out where you contracted the strain you have."

Salim knew the answer. Kapchorwa.

"Other patients are coming in now."

"Others?" Salim asked.

"A lot."

Salim frowned.

"If more than one strain of Ebola is out there, it'll make fighting this more difficult."

Salim's frown stayed on his face. Something didn't seem right about this conversation, but he couldn't put into words what it was.

"What?" Alison asked.

"Why does it matter where I contracted Ebola?" Salim asked.

Alison stepped back from his bed and put her hand on her hip, making a show of thinking about the question and being a little put off that he'd asked it. "I'm just a nurse. I don't know that."

Emboldened and thinking clearly for the first time in days, Salim asked, "If the doctors at the CDC have to test me for my strain of Ebola, won't they have to test everyone?" Salim wanted to pat himself on the back. It sounded like the kind of question one of his smart friends from high school would have asked. "I don't understand why the origin of my infection is necessary."

With her tone shifting from friendly and conspiratorial to authoritative, Alison said, "Tracing the disease back to where you got it, and where that person got it, and where that person got it, is how we get control of Ebola. For all we know, the person who you contracted it from is still out there, giving it to others."

If she wasn't lying about that, then Salim's knowledge of

Kapchorwa had value, maybe even enough value to be bargained for amnesty. On the other hand, if Nurse Alison was sincere, would withholding the information be the cause of more death?

Salim looked Alison up and down. He looked at her mask, her eyes, her empty hands. It occurred to him that she never seemed to be doing anything with those empty hands. She'd been in his room dozens of times, always talking, always asking questions. Sure, she fluffed his pillow and straightened his sheets, but she never injected anything into his IV. She never gave him any pills. She never emptied his bedpan. She never helped him to that weird little chemical toilet in his room now that he was able to get out of bed.

The other two nurses did those things.

Salim suddenly came up with the suspicion that Alison wasn't a nurse at all but an interrogator in disguise.

"What?" she asked, almost angry.

Salim was more certain than ever that he needed an attorney.

Chapter 47

Looking left and right for a place to hide, Austin knew he couldn't stay on the street. He knew the men coming after him had seen the narrow road he'd run down, and they'd be rounding the corner behind him at any moment. He ran past a well-maintained house and saw a row of trees and bushes separating that house from a collection of shanties.

Good enough.

He cut a hard turn and ran into the bushes, bending over at the waist to keep his head down and out of sight. He inched forward at the corner of one of the corrugated-metal shanties. He dropped behind a wall of rotting wood and turned to watch the road.

From inside the shanty he heard the labored breathing of a man with liquid in his lungs. The man's chest rattled through a series of weak coughs. Austin knew the sound. He'd heard it from so many of the dying in Kapchorwa. Ebola would take that man's life within a day.

Austin put the dying man out of his thoughts. He looked between the bushes. He watched the road, seeing nothing, hoping he'd misinterpreted what he saw in the street, that they weren't following him.

Hoping.

It was not to be. A group of men ran by, shouting with frustration and pointing.

They were the same men he'd seen around the corner, the same bunch he'd seen near the park. All doubt was gone. *They were after him.*

Austin crouched and held his breath, afraid his loud breathing would give him away.

Could he hide-and-seek his way to the river? Could he evade them? How many were they, altogether? A dozen? Maybe twenty?

Animal viciousness—angry white eyes and big white teeth—beasts.

Austin was panicking. He was prey.

Why were they chasing him?

I didn't do anything, Austin pleaded silently to himself.

When the shouts and the thump of feet trampling the dirt road faded into the clamor of a city falling apart, Austin straightened back up. He crept along a row of shrubs, going away from the road.

Austin came upon two expansive, rust-colored brick buildings. Each had rows of small, long windows just under the eaves, too high to see either in or out. An alley ran up between them. Austin figured to cut up the alley and start toward the river again. Keeping a cautious eye over his shoulder as he rounded the corner of the first building, Austin wasn't watching where he stepped. His foot slipped and he fell. Involuntarily reaching a hand out to catch himself, his hand hit something slick and went out from under him. Knobby knees and elbows bruised him when he hit.

Urged by dread, he scrambled quickly to get his hands and knees under him as he rolled over. Something was very wrong. He wasn't on dirt. He was slipping on plastic, slick with beads of moisture.

He caught his breath and stopped moving for a moment. No knees were kicking him. No fists were punching him. No red dirt was beneath him.

Austin looked up the alley, and it took a moment for him to understand what he was kneeling on—what was lined up solid along the walls of both buildings—leaving only a narrow, muddy path in between.

Body bags.

Thick, white, plastic body bags, each with the vague form of a human inside, some wet with bleach solution puddled in the folds. There had to be a hundred. Down at the end of the alley, four men in yellow suits entered and tiredly dropped another body at the end of a row. A fifth man with what looked like a pesticide sprayer sprinkled the body bag in bleach solution.

Austin realized that his left hand was pressing down on a face through the plastic beneath him and his right hand on a torso. He jumped off, landing on the muddy trail between the feet of the corpses. His feet slipped out from under him again and he went down in the mud.

I should have stayed in Kapchorwa.

Austin was in real danger. His pursuers could be anywhere. Everywhere.

Inspiration sparked, morbid and disgusting.

He looked up the alley, saw no one, got back to his feet and jogged about half way up the length of the alley, spotted a gap between two of the tightly packed bodies, and dove between them.

The body bags were rectangular in design, much wider than necessary to hold the thin bodies within, leaving large flaps of excess plastic running the length on either side of the corpse. Austin snuggled up to the body on his right until he was partially concealed under the bag's excess plastic. He reached out and pulled on the body bag to his left until the plastic overlapped above, leaving him fully covered, arches to ears. No one looking down the alley would see him. Any armed hoodlum dedicated enough to walk the muddy path between the corpses in search of him wouldn't find him. Only his own movement and breathing could give him away.

Time to think through the next steps.

It was just past midday. Darkness wouldn't fall over Mbale for another six or seven hours. When night came, Austin knew he could make his way out of the city unseen. He resolved to lie between the corpses until the sun went down.

Chapter 48

Twenty minutes passed, maybe a little more, maybe a little less. What at first felt like his skin crawling in tiny tickles turned suddenly into painful pricks of flame, everywhere across his body.

Ants!

Austin jumped to his feet brushing and swatting at his clothes and exposed skin. The ants were all over him. The biting worsened. Ants brushed from his clothes clung to his hands and dug their mandibles into his skin. Cursing and looking for a way to get them off, Austin dropped down on the muddy path between the body bags and rolled. He mashed his hands into the mud to cake them solid. He used the mud as a shield for his hands and as glue to capture the ants still alive and attacking.

He mashed ants against his legs and under his jeans, on his neck, and in his hair. His skin was on fire. He needed to get to the river. That was his only hope of getting rid of them.

Austin ran up the alley, looking left as he passed into the street, then right—a street crossing habit learned in childhood. What he saw when he looked right wasn't an oncoming car. It was two of the men in military fatigues looking up from their conversation with one of the body-carrying men in yellow Tyvek. They were as surprised to see Austin as he was to see them. They recovered quickly from their astonishment and began shouting. Austin was already halfway across the street.

Austin mustered all the speed in his muscles and ran, not looking back. He didn't dare. He heard them coming. He crossed into another alley, his legs getting wobblier with each step. His lungs burned. Desperation pushed him through his body's pleas to stop.

Unfortunately, the mind can only push the body so far.

Austin collapsed and rolled into the rough, musty dirt. He gasped for air and tried to get his feet back under him, but he was pushed roughly back to the ground. One of the paramilitary men pressed a large-barreled pistol against his head and said, "You're mine now, mzungu boy."

Chapter 49

With hands bound behind his back, Austin sat in the center back seat of a ratty, white Toyota compact. A semi-camouflaged thug pressed in on each side. The man with the pistol — the guy apparently in charge — sat in front. A kid who looked too young for a license, drove. They followed behind two other cars, both packed with men and headed east across town.

They crossed the Mbale-Soroti Road, with the Islamic University still burning a mile to the north, and the flaming pyre of bodies at the base of the clock tower to the south. The convoy stopped and a boda driver puttered past with a woman, two children, and their baggage all balanced on top. They passed a barricaded neighborhood and a mango farm bordered on two sides by rows of shanties.

The man in the front seat rifled through Austin's bag, passing his last pieces of mango to the men in the back. He found the stash of cash and pushed it into his pocket, then held up a credit card and examined it. It was one of Dr. Littlefield's cards. "Dwayne R. Littlefield. That is you?"

Austin didn't answer, choosing instead to glare at the man in the front seat.

"You are a fierce boy," the man said with a mocking grin. "What is your pin number?"

Austin ignored the question. "What's going on here? Why have you taken me?"

"You know why." The man laughed. "Your people call it kidnapping."

Austin asked, "Why are you kidnapping *me*?"

"Money." The man laughed, and so did everyone else in the car.

"I don't have any money," said Austin. "My father is not wealthy."

The man flashed the credit card and showed it to Austin. "You are rich."

"Everybody has credit cards. That doesn't make me rich."

"Nobody in Mbale has one." The man smiled. "But now I have one." He put the credit card in his shirt pocket. "Tell me, Dwayne, are you a student, an evangelist, a lost American trying to find himself?" He laughed as though that was the funniest thing he'd said all day and then dug around in the bag looking for more.

"I'm a teacher," Austin answered.

"A teacher?" The man was impressed or at least pretended to be. "At the Catholic University?"

"No. In Kapchorwa."

"Dwayne Littlefield, the teacher from Kapchorwa."

"My name's not Dwayne."

"No?"

"It's Austin."

"Austin?"

"Austin Cooper."

The man in the front seat fished out the credit card. "What of this, then?"

"My things were burned in a fire." Austin paused as he thought about what to say next. "I found the credit card and the money on the body of a dead doctor."

The man scrutinized Austin for a moment and then said, "I do not believe you. I shall call you 'Ransom.'"

The men on each side of Austin laughed.

The man in the front seat put the card back into his

pocket. "You will call me 'General.'"

Austin said nothing.

"You will call me General," the man repeated as his smile seeped away.

The man to Austin's left punched him in the arm and nodded at The General.

Austin understood. "Yes, General."

The General's grin returned. "You understand, Ransom, that I have taken you in order to make some of your father's American dollars into my American dollars. We are at war, and we need money to fight."

Shaking his head, Austin said, "You want money for terrorism."

The General's smile instantly disappeared. He said something, and the driver hit the brakes. Tires skidded on the dirt road. The General nodded at the men in the backseat, and they wasted not a second in opening a door and roughly shoving Austin out onto the gravelly dirt.

The other two cars came to a stop. Men got out, some looking at The General, some looking up the road, back down the road, or out across the open fields. The General pointed at the burning Catholic University. "You see that, Ransom?"

Austin looked at the burning buildings, looking for something distinct in the smoke, flame, and brick. He shook his head.

"You see that building there? The long one, with the terracotta roof?"

Austin nodded.

"Terracotta," The General grinned. "Big word for a black man, don't you think?" He pointed. "I lived in that dormitory when I went to university here."

Austin was surprised.

"You see, Ransom. Americans aren't the only educated people." The General shook his finger at the burning building. "Do you know what happened here?"

Austin shrugged. He could guess.

"Your enemies burned it. America's enemies."

Shaking his head, Austin said, "I don't have any enemies. Except maybe for you."

"You and I have the same enemies," said The General. "The Muslims burned this school."

"The Muslims?"

The General pointed at the smoke rising from the fires to the north. "A band of students from the Islamic University came here and did this. You see, they hate us as much as they hate you Americans."

"Muslims don't hate Americans," Austin muttered. "Not all of them."

The General laughed. "You are naïve, Ransom. That is no matter. Your father's money will help us do what must be done." He looked at his men and nodded at the cars. They pushed Austin roughly into the backseat. Once everyone was loaded, they headed back down the road out of town.

With the smoke from the Catholic University receding behind, Austin asked, "If they burned the Catholic University, who burned their school?"

"There is only one God, and he doesn't love them." The General burst out laughing. The other men in the car chuckled.

The car drove out of town. They came to a stop a quarter mile down the road from an army roadblock. One of the men got out and walked toward it, no rifle in hand. After a brief conversation, the vehicles were waved forward. The convoy of three cars picked up their man as they passed and proceeded through.

Once past, Austin asked The General, "Did you bribe them to let us pass?"

"No, Ransom, some of our soldiers wear a government uniform. Some of my people are government functionaries. Some even run the towns. The shirt they wear at their job is not important. We all work together to do God's work."

Chapter 50

Frustrated and looking at rows of brake lights down the hill in front of her and up the next, Olivia wanted to curse. The one tiny, positive thing she'd hoped would come out of Eric's absenteeism speech ten days ago was lighter rush hour traffic. With so many people skipping work, what the hell were they all doing out here making the drive time worse? She just wanted to get home after another frustrating day, and wondered for the hundredth time why she lived so far from her office.

Her cell phone rang.

She answered without looking to see who was calling. "Hello?"

"Hello."

"Mathew?"

"Yes," he said. "Can you talk?"

"I'm stuck in traffic, but I can talk. I'm mostly parked, waiting my turn to creep forward."

"I'm going to tell you something that needs to stay between us."

"Straight to the ominous stuff." Olivia laughed. "Remember, this is a cellphone we're talking on."

"I don't imagine the news will stay under wraps for long, but—"

"But?" Olivia asked.

Wheeler sighed. "The new strain of Ebola is airborne."

Olivia gasped weakly. Every surprise was bad these days. She was numb.

Wheeler waited a moment for a reply before he said. "I assume you understand what I just said."

"Yes. I—" Olivia pulled over onto the shoulder and put the car in park. "I'm hoping this is one of your jokes."

"Three labs got the same result."

Olivia took a deep breath. "Okay, this isn't the end of the world, but—"

"I'm not sure that's a joking phrase anymore."

"Don't say things like that, Mathew." Olivia collected her thoughts, saw a gap in the traffic, and pulled back out. "If I drive down to Atlanta tonight, how much can you show me?"

"You don't have to come all the way down to Atlanta. I can email you. Still—"

"Honestly, I don't want to go home. I could use some company, and with you, at least I can learn something and maybe even laugh a little. It'll be late when I get there. Can I sleep on your couch? Do you mind?"

"I'd love to have you. There is a better place to sleep than the couch."

"Really?" Olivia said, a little more harshly than she wanted to. "Ebola is airborne, and oh-by-the-way do you want to sleep with me? That's the new pickup line?"

"When you put it that way, it loses its romance." Wheeler laughed. "I was actually offering up the guest room."

"I'll bet you were."

Wheeler admitted, "I left the invitation purposefully vague."

"Back to this airborne thing," said Olivia, thinking about everything flowing through the censorship queue she was working. Emails were in there too. "It'll be better that you don't email me."

"Why?"

"More chance it'll get leaked. I'm getting a little bit paranoid, maybe. So three labs have confirmed that the new strain is airborne."

"Yes, two in Europe and one here."

"No doubt, then?" Olivia asked.

"I'd be surprised if different results came back from further testing."

"Excuse me if I sound stupid now. This is your field. I see data on this outbreak every day." Olivia didn't say that her primary sources lately were leaked data reported on the Internet by people whose governments didn't want them to have it. "Would I be wrong to guess that this strain has a high r nought value?"

"That doesn't sound stupid at all. r nought is the average number of secondary cases that can be expected to result from one infection, though there's a lot of discussion about the effective r nought for any given outbreak."

To make sure she understood, she said, "In other words, how many people will catch Ebola from someone who's already got it."

"Exactly. They calculate it based on transmissibility, the length of time an individual is contagious, and how much time that person might be in contact with others while infectious."

"Sounds vague," Olivia observed.

"Yes, it can be. Lots of factors not related to the infectious agent can affect the result. Only the amount of time a person is contagious is specific to the virus."

"I can see where contact time might change with culture," said Olivia. "I'd imagine New Yorkers who are always bumping into one another on the subway might spend more time in contact than some ranchers in Montana who only see each other at the weekly hoedown."

Wheeler laughed out loud. "The weekly hoedown?"

"Don't pick on me. I don't know why I chose that as an example."

"I haven't heard that word in a long time, that's all," said Wheeler. "Your example puts a simple face on that part of the equation, but it's exactly right. I'm sure you understand the range of complexity involved."

"I don't know, but I can guess," said Olivia. "The part I don't understand is why transmissibility would vary."

"That has to do with the immunity of the population and some other factors," said Wheeler. "If you have a population that's already been exposed or vaccinated, a portion of the individuals will have immunity, so the disease can't be transmitted to them, and the r nought is lower."

"And lower is better, right?"

"Better for us, for sure," Wheeler chuckled.

"Okay." Olivia tried to recall the list of r nought numbers she'd seen. "Ebola has a low r nought, doesn't it?"

"It comes in around two," said Wheeler, "depending on the specific outbreak. These things are often estimated up front but calculated from epidemiological data after the fact."

"Do you have numbers on West Africa yet?"

"One point five to two point five or so. For comparison, influenza comes in between two and three."

"And SARS?" Olivia asked. "The medical community was in an uproar about that a few years back. Where is that one?"

"Rightly so," said Wheeler. "It can be as high as five and very deadly."

"If I remember correctly —" Olivia said.

"You probably do," said Wheeler.

"If I remember correctly, measles topped the list I saw with an r nought between twelve and eighteen."

"It's the kind of number that makes me question the thinking of anti-vaxxers."

"And where does the new strain of Ebola land on the list?" asked Olivia.

"We don't know."

"That's bullshit, Mathew."

Wheeler sighed.

"Don't get all chivalrous now. Keeping me in the dark isn't going to protect me from anything. Tell me what you know."

"Oh, why am I so attracted to strong-willed, young women?" Wheeler mused.

"I'm not going to say what I think you are attracted to, and a strong will has nothing to do with it. Stop avoiding the question, and answer me."

Wheeler surrendered. "One estimate came in at six."

"And?"

"One came in at sixteen. The consensus seems to be that it'll be around eight, give or take."

"Six to sixteen?"

"Yes."

"I'll need to look at this with a spreadsheet, but if each person infects eight more, and —" Olivia tried to do some quick math in her head. "How long after infection does someone turn contagious with the new strain?"

"As early as forty-eight hours. We had one result in twenty-four, but no one has duplicated that result yet. Then maybe as long as three weeks. That's a guess so far based on the strain of Ebola in West Africa."

"The median?" Olivia asked.

"Let's say five days." Wheeler went on to ask, "What math are you doing in your head while you're stuck in traffic?"

After a pause to finish her mental estimate, Olivia said, "It seems to me, the whole world's population could get infected with this new strain in somewhere between four weeks and four months."

"I'll dig up a paper on that subject that you'll enjoy. Very mathematical. It's right up your alley."

"Okay," said Olivia.

"The problem gets complicated. Your assumption by doing your mental simulation based only on r nought is interesting but incorrect. It doesn't take into account heterogeneous and geographically isolated populations."

"Like people in Hawaii, perhaps."

"To oversimplify, yes," said Wheeler. "The upshot of the paper is that it's nearly impossible to infect everybody."

"Even if they're not immune or vaccinated?" Olivia asked.

"Even if the whole population is susceptible."

"So the good news is at least everybody won't die?" Olivia laughed at the gallows humor.

"Yeah," Wheeler joined in. "At least *everybody* won't die."

The joke about dying made her think about her dad and that turned into an emotion that she'd been trying to hide from all day. A sniffle that held back a tear escaped.

"What was that?" Wheeler asked. "Are you okay?"

Olivia didn't want to say anything but with weighty topics on the table, what did one infected parent matter? "My dad caught it."

"Ebola?" Wheeler was taken aback. "Your dad caught Ebola? How?"

"I don't know. My stepmom called. They took him to the hospital. The test came back positive today."

"Where?"

"Denver."

"Your dad is the case in Denver?" Wheeler tried to hide his surprise. "I'm so sorry."

"There's more. I might as well tell you everything."

"Okay."

"I can't tell you how I know this, but Austin—"

"Oh, no."

"I don't even know how to say it." Olivia sighed in a way that sounded a lot like one of Wheeler's dramatic sighs. "He caught it too."

"My God," he said. "How is he?"

"I don't know. I said I couldn't tell you details. I can say the only detail I got was that he had it and he wasn't doing well. That news is nearly three weeks old. And that's all I have."

"I'm so, so sorry."

"I feel like I've been hit by a truck."

"You hide it well," said Wheeler. "Listen. Get down here. I've got wine. I've got a guest room. I may try to get you a little drunk. You sound like you could use some inebriation. And I promise. I'll be a gentleman. No worries there. Okay?"

"I'm on my way if I can ever get through this traffic."

Chapter 51

Paul lay in his multi-adjustable hospital bed blankly staring at a television hanging from the ceiling across the room. He was confused and trying to put the pieces together. Everything seemed jumbled, like broken snippets of video, spliced together and running through his memory —incomplete, out of order.

You might be confused.

That phrase, in a doctor's authoritative voice, repeated itself. Sometimes Ebola affects the brain.

You might be confused.

Paul wondered if he'd suffered brain damage. He wondered if he was going to die.

Wait, he'd been given some drug but couldn't remember which one. He felt better. He was watching TV.

You might be confused.

The news was on the television. It was a story about him, Paul Cooper, complete with an image taken from his Facebook page. The video showed someone on a wheeled stretcher, covered in a thick pup tent of clear plastic, surrounded by faceless people in protective suits, pushing the gurney along.

Paul went to sleep.

Chapter 52

Austin sat alone in a weathered grass hut, looking through the open door, seeing rebels pass in the clearing outside, and hearing the voices of those rising to start their day. Smoke from the morning cook fire wafted in and aroused Austin's hunger for a meager breakfast that would come later.

It was his third day in The General's camp on the southern slope of Mt. Elgon. The routine was the same each day. Austin sat in the hut. Once in the morning, they brought him something to eat. In the late afternoon or early evening, he'd eat again, never anything like a full meal. He was given water when he asked for it, and a few times a day walked out into the woods to the camp latrine. They'd take him more frequently if he begged enough and the guard on duty wasn't feeling lazy.

The sound of two people speaking just outside piqued Austin's interest. A moment later, The General entered the hut. He smiled and said, "Good Morning, Ransom."

Austin said, "Have you contacted my family yet?"

The General waved Austin toward the door. "Get up. I have something to show you."

Wary, Austin pushed himself to his feet.

The General turned and exited the hut. "Hurry."

Austin did as told. Once through the door, four guards in their late teens or early twenties fell in around them. Each of the guards carried an assault rifle, distinct from the others. Two of them wore ugly green and black camouflage military pants. One wore a grease-stained, olive-colored t-shirt with the sleeves cut off. The others wore clothing that could have been worn by a bunch of high school kids—a t-shirt with a football team logo, a red and blue soft drink t-shirt, beige cargo shorts, and silky athletic shorts. Except, all of their clothing was filthy and stained in reddish dirt and green forest hues. Natural camouflage.

Glancing back, The General said, "You are my new houseboy, Ransom."

"What?" Austin asked, understanding the words, just not the meaning.

Ahead, three painfully thin, bruised men—two Asians, and one Westerner—were being herded out of another hut as The General's entourage neared. One of the Asians tripped over his feet and was summarily yanked back up. The General gestured at them. "From now on, you will sleep with them in that hut. You come to me at sunrise. When I dismiss you at night, you go back there and you sleep."

The malnourished prisoners fell in behind The General's entourage. Each of the prisoners had a length of frayed rope tied between ankles crusted with oozing scabs and buzzing with small, iridescent flies.

The General said, "Their names are Ransom too." He loved his jokes.

"How long have they been here?" Austin asked.

The General replied, "I know what you are thinking right now."

Austin, assuming The General was going to say more, waited. Instead, he stopped, and the whole entourage stopped with him. He looked at Austin, his face suddenly harsh. "Ask me."

"Ask you?" Austin queried.

The General nodded slowly. "Yes, ask me to tell you what you're thinking."

Expecting some kind of punch or kick, and wondering a thousand things at once, Austin asked, "What am I thinking?"

The General pointed at the abused foreigners. "You want to know why those men stay when they only have a rope around their feet. They could untie the rope and run. They have no guard, though that may change."

Austin didn't know the other hostages had no guard, but he decided it was best not to point that out.

"They can go anywhere in the camp." The General gestured grandiosely at the muddy ground, the trash, the huts—*his kingdom.* "They serve. They fetch water. They feed us. They do the women's work. They are not watched. Yet, they do not run. They wait patiently for their ransoms to be paid, so they can go home."

Austin looked around the dirty camp. Men were congregating lazily around a central clearing. The jungle rose up on all sides—thick, and full of places to hide. Austin figured he was about to be shackled with a piece of flimsy rope and told like a dog to stay. Well, bad news for The General. Austin knew he didn't have the strength to escape into the jungle that night, not even the next day. Three or four days from now—maybe a week—as soon as his captors got used to the idea that Austin wasn't going to run, as soon as he had a little more of his strength back, he'd melt into the jungle, and run he would. And they'd never find him. Of that, Austin was sure.

The men who'd been gathering into a mob around the center of the camp parted to let The General through. Austin, the guards, and the other hostages followed along. Thirty or forty of The General's fighters started chanting and dancing, with weapons raised in the air.

At the center of the circle, beside a dying cook fire, an

emaciated Asian lay in the mud. Two rebels stood on his hands, pinning them in the sludge. One soldier sat on the Asian's right leg. The Asian's left leg was held with the foot lying on a thick log. The prisoner was crying and pleading in Japanese, or Chinese, or something.

Around the ankle being held down on the log, Austin saw a ring of worn skin and pus-leaking sores. The ankle matched the look of the other prisoners' ankles, only the crying man had no rope.

Growing nervous, Austin looked around for clues as to what might happen next. No one was talking in a language he could understand. The chanting was riding up a crescendo.

A soldier with a worn piece of stained roped walked up to the crying Asian, knelt and pushed it roughly across his face. The soldier cursed and spat. He held the rope up and showed it to The General.

The General nodded in Austin's direction.

The soldier came over, knelt in front of Austin, and tied the rope around each of Austin's ankles. When he was finished, he stood up, drawing a machete out of a frayed canvas scabbard and presenting it to The General. Without any hesitation, without any thought, without any emotion, with all the ceremony of signing a check or entering a pin number while buying gasoline, The General hacked down at the foot lying across the log.

Blood sprayed. The prisoner screamed. Half a foot rolled off the log into the mud.

The General handed the bloody machete back to his soldier and looked at Austin. He pointed to a hut, different from the others, except that its metal roof appeared to have little rust. "Houseboy, be there when the sun rises. Sleep with your fellows at night. Stay until your ransom arrives."

He glanced down at the screaming, bleeding man who'd just lost half his foot. "Or run."

Chapter 53

Olivia had just finished her lunchtime run—four miles at an easy pace. She walked along the edge of a green field bordered by thick trees. The office building, one she'd initially liked, she had come to despise. She turned away from it and looked at the trees. She wasn't happy with the trees, either. Even though it was late September, the trees, for the most part, still held their green leaves. She wanted autumn color.

She took her phone out of her pocket and dialed Mathew Wheeler, hoping to catch him at lunch or between meetings.

"Hello?" he answered almost immediately.

"Hey," she said.

"Hey, yourself. What's up?"

"Have you got time to talk?" she asked.

"Sure."

Olivia hadn't thought that far into it. She'd had the urge to call and talk. That was it. But she wasn't ready to admit that, so she went with the first thing that came to mind, a ridiculous thing that had come up in the queue. Laughing a little, she said, "I came across a story this morning that I started to research. It's probably a waste of time."

"A medical story?" Wheeler asked.

"Yes."

"I've got a few minutes. Maybe I can help."

Laughing again, Olivia said, "The story was pretty much a list of accusations by a guy who's supposedly a doctor. It dealt with misleading work being done by the CDC and the European Center for Disease Prevention and Control."

"What kind of misleading work?" Wheeler asked, concerned.

"I'd say the core of it is that nobody actually isolated the new strain of the virus, and that all of the testing done on the monkeys to show it was airborne—and any work you're doing now on a vaccine—is spurious. Yes, *spurious* is the word he used. He said because you hadn't isolated the virus, you couldn't possibly know if anything you were doing or any conclusions you were drawing were accurate. I laughed, because I knew that you guys had done that first. You guys did identify the new strain. You told me that, right?"

Wheeler paused for a long time.

Olivia stopped walking. "What?"

Wheeler heaved one of his tortured sighs. "The article has *some* truth to it, but at the same time, it's not true."

"That sounds like the kind of thing people tell you when they're thinking up a good lie."

"Don't—" Wheeler stopped himself and said, "If you've got a minute, I'll explain. You're bright. You'll understand."

"Okay." Olivia was starting to feel pretty sure she wouldn't.

"For starters, we ran the new strain of Ebola through our electron microscope. We've tested it nine ways to Sunday. It's unique. Definitely a new strain. That's identification."

"So far. It sounds like there's no problem at all."

"Identifying the new bug doesn't mean all that you think it does. Identification and isolation aren't the same thing. In order for us to be certain that symptoms we're seeing in people and in the monkeys we tested are from the new strain, we would have to find a way to isolate and grow the new strain in some medium. You follow me so far?"

"Yes."

"That's a time-consuming process, sometimes *very* time consuming. If we're lucky, it could take weeks. If not, it could take months, maybe longer."

"Oh, crap."

"Exactly," confirmed Wheeler. "You ran your spreadsheet simulations after I gave you the r nought data. You know each day costs lives, and with every day that passes, the cost goes up. We don't have months to spend on being absolutely certain we have the right bug."

"You're guessing? Are you telling me it could something other than the new strain of Ebola that's making everybody sick, and that the existence of the new strain of Ebola in the samples is a coincidence?"

"That's it exactly," said Wheeler. "I have to tell you, and you'll know it's true when I say it, that all the evidence points to Ebola K being the culprit. Nearly every researcher looking into this—hundreds, maybe thousands—believes it is. A handful don't. Even their concerns aren't so much that we're wrong, as that we're skipping a step in a well-defined, scientific process. We're not doing science now, Olivia. We're just trying to cobble something together to save lives."

"What if you're wrong?"

"Wrong?" Wheeler asked. "It won't matter."

"Why not?"

"Think about it, Olivia. If we spend three months delaying a therapy, delaying a potential vaccine, how many billions, and I did say *billions*, might die?"

Olivia didn't answer. She knew the number was more than one billion and less than seven.

"If we proceed and get it wrong, how many billions will die?"

"The answer doesn't change much," she admitted.

"That's why, in this case, being wrong doesn't matter. We're rolling the dice and hoping for a seven."

Olivia started to say something.

"Let me change that. We're rolling the dice and hoping for anything but snake eyes."

Chapter 54

"The confusion passes," said Dr. Bowman.

"The last few days are a blur."

"The good news is you're responding spectacularly. How do you feel this morning?"

"Better," Paul answered. Throughout the past several days, everything had hurt, he hadn't been able to hold a complete thought in his mind, and then there was extreme gastrointestinal distress. Paul asked, "Did I have Ebola?"

Dr. Bowman's hooded head bobbed up and down. "You were lucky."

"I'm going to make it?" Paul asked.

Nodding again, Dr. Bowman said, "Your viral load has plunged dramatically. You seem to be on your way toward recovery, but don't get too optimistic. We need to be cautious. You've been given an experimental drug."

Shaking his head, Paul said, "I don't remember that."

In a surprisingly defensive tone, Dr. Bowman said, "Your wife approved —"

Shaking his head emphatically, Paul said, "Oh no. I wasn't making an accusation. I just —" He put a hand to his head. "Everything seems jumbled up."

Back in a normal tone of voice Dr. Bowman said, "That's not unusual. Blood clots in the brain. We don't have much information on the long term effects of an Ebola infection, but what we do know indicates that people recover fully."

Paul nodded and asked, "Is Heidi here?"

"Of course."

"Can I see her?"

Dr. Bowman shook his head. "She can't come into the

quarantine room. You understand."

No. He didn't understand. If the doctor could wear a plastic tent, why not Heidi? Paul nodded anyway.

Dr. Bowman pointed at a telephone handset on a nightstand beside the bed. He then pointed over to a smallish window with a metal mesh in the glass, built through an interior wall. Heidi stood on the other side of the window with a handset pressed up to her ear. "You can talk to her through the intercom."

Seeing Heidi's pained smile and tearful eyes, Paul grabbed for the phone. "Heidi."

"Paul," she said as she shook her head and started to sob.

Paul looked over at the doctor then back at Heidi. "Dr. Bowman says I'm going to be fine."

"You're a liar, Paul Cooper."

Paul looked back at the doctor for confirmation. "He said I'm responding well."

"I know more about how you're doing than you do," she told him.

"So you know I'm going to make it, then."

"You're probably going to make it," Heidi agreed.

"Only happy thoughts," Paul told her.

Dr. Bowman excused himself and left the room, presumably into a decontamination area.

Heidi, finding a stable place in her emotional moment, said, "If you ever do anything like this again—"

Paul shook his head then caught himself before he answered, knowing he could never talk about the truth anywhere but in the most private circumstances. "I can only think I caught it from the guy I helped with his tire when I was driving up to Lake Granby."

Heidi paused before she said, "Everybody's looking for him. People on the news are saying he might be the cause of all the cases in Denver."

"What?" Paul hadn't wanted that, and had taken precautions to avoid an outbreak. He was coherent enough to know that his Liberian tire changer was a phantom, and yet was humane enough to feel guilt over the possibility that the outbreak in Denver was his own fault.

"Other news channels say the cases are tied to an airline passenger."

"How many cases?" Paul asked.

"Twelve so far, I think," answered Heidi. "Most of them are at this hospital. Dr. Bowman has been researching an Ebola drug at CU. You were lucky to get it."

"At CU?" Paul asked. "Colorado University? I'm in Denver?"

"Of course. What's wrong?"

"I—" Paul started. "I thought they'd move me to Omaha. They can handle Ebola better there."

Shaking her head, Heidi said, "No, they were overwhelmed with patients from the Dallas outbreak."

"How many?" Paul asked.

"I don't know how many went to Omaha, but Dallas has a whole hospital dedicated to Ebola now. More than a hundred patients, I think. The news has been pretty sketchy on the details lately, and half of what you try to find on the Internet turns into a 404 error."

A lot had happened since Paul went down with Ebola. He asked, "Are the other patients getting the new drug, too?"

"I don't know."

Paul and Heidi looked at one another through the glass

in a silence that was comfortable only because they felt so comfortable together. Heidi finally said, "I'm sorry we fought. If I'd have known this would happen—"

"You'd have upped the life insurance first." Paul grinned.

Heidi rolled her eyes again. "Wow, you're getting back to normal." Dryly, she added, "I'm thrilled." Changing the subject, Heidi said, "They expect—or maybe I should say, they hope—that you'll be virus-free in a couple of days."

"No shit?"

Heidi nodded. "You got lucky."

No, Paul didn't agree, but nodded anyway. What Heidi called luck, Paul called careful planning and execution.

Now, he just needed to protect her. He'd had plenty of time to think during his stay at the petri dish hotel. Heidi would need to stay in solitary confinement in their house. Then Paul simply had to keep the house secure and make sure that he sufficiently decontaminated himself when he came and went. He already had all the food or any other supplies they'd need to survive until vaccines were available.

Now he just needed to convince Olivia to return from Georgia before it was too late. She could stay sequestered with Heidi. Paul had already lost a son. He could bear to lose no more of his family.

Heidi said, "They're planning to move you out of this room and into isolation for twenty-one days—"

"Twenty-one days?" Paul asked, a little angry, even as he was accepting it. He hadn't expected isolation to last that long.

"It's a precaution." Heidi's tone was firm. "They need to make sure you're not going to infect anyone else. It won't be as bad as this. They set up a rec room. You'll be able to walk around, watch TV, read a book."

Nodding, Paul said, "Will I be able to use a real phone. I'd like to call Olivia."

"Don't worry about her, okay? She and I have been talking every day. She's fine. You scared her to death, Paul. You should know that."

Paul understood exactly what she meant. His stupid, selfish choices had effects on other people. "Yes, dear."

"Have you seen the news?"

Paul shrugged, without thinking that the gesture was nearly lost since he was lying on his back in a bed.

"You're something of a celebrity."

"What?"

"For stopping to help the Liberian man," said Heidi. "You did a good deed, and now you're fighting for your life because of it." Heidi dramatically rolled her eyes. "With all the bad news, I think the local stations are infatuated with your story because it's uplifting."

"I'd rather they left me out of it."

"Reporters want to interview you," said Heidi, "I've been putting them off. With you being in the hospital, it's easy so far."

Paul shook his head. He hadn't planned for the possibility of media interest.

"There's something else."

"Yes?" Paul asked.

"The police are probably going to come and talk to you today."

That made Paul nervous. He'd done plenty of things that they might want to talk to him about. "Why?"

Nodding slowly to emphasize her point, she said, "They want to ask you about the Liberian man, I think."

Chapter 55

Crumbled plastic wrappers, dirty sheets, and other clutter gathered on the hall floor, kicked to the sides by the feet of the busy. The trash bins in Salim's room went un-emptied. His isolation room had no running water, so no proper bathroom facilities, just some kind of chemical toilet that was in danger of overflowing. It hadn't been emptied in a week. Nurses came by to check on him with decreasing regularity. In the halls, people passed by his window but they were either draped in protective garb, or were patients being wheeled toward a room. Too frequently, they wheeled other patients away, clearly dead.

From his window on the fifth floor, Salim saw the police cordon all around the property. Police in riot gear walked the perimeter or faced off against mobs of protestors that grew in number and grew in their anger each day. At first, the picketers appeared to be hospital workers, and their signs spoke of unsafe working conditions. The protest changed as locals joined in. They didn't want the infected in the hospital to be there at all.

At first Salim thought the crowd was protesting his presence. As the hospital filled with a sporadic but growing stream of new patients, Salim worried he was witnessing Kapchorwa all over again—only on a grand, modern scale. The protestors outside were shouting their messages but the only thing that really mattered was the emotion that drove them—fear. Fear that Ebola had come to decimate their city.

Salim felt sad for them. They should have worried about annihilation.

Two days before, Salim had taken the chance to leave his room, just to see what would happen. At first, nothing did.

He made his way through an anteroom and into the hallway without anyone taking notice. It wasn't until he neared a centrally located nurse's station that one of his nurses in head-to-toe protective gear told him in harsh tones to get back to his room. She then went back to whatever she was doing behind her desk. Salim accepted his scolding and complied. On the way, he passed an open hamper marked with a biohazard symbol overflowing with sheets, gloves, goggles, and bloody gobs of things that in a previous life Salim wouldn't have touched on a dare.

The situation was different now.

Salim rifled through the bin and gathered up all the pieces he needed to construct his own biohazard suit. Back in his room, he stuffed the suit into a plastic trash bag and stowed it in a cabinet that seemed to have no purpose. That next night, after his nurse's evening rounds, he removed his biohazard gear from the cabinet and went to work cleaning it with alcohol wipes.

The biohazard suit turned out to be his ticket to freedom, at least within the hospital. He donned the gear, wrote the name Dr. Jalal across the forehead of his suit with a discarded permanent marker he'd found, and walked through the hospital unquestioned. He was a doctor, the top of the hospital's social hierarchy.

What Salim found in the hospital was troublesome. He covered three of the hospital's eight floors, and every one of them was the same as his. The only people moving about wore full biohazard gear. He peeked into a dozen rooms, even speaking to a few of the patients to ask how they were doing. His pretense grew easier with each visit. He wasn't qualified to diagnose any of the sick, but he'd seen enough of the dying in Kapchorwa—with their bruises, bloody eyes, bleeding noses, and empty, hopeless stares—to know that all these people had the same disease.

Before going back up to his room, Salim walked into a lounge a few floors down from his own. He found an arrangement of worn couches and stained chairs. The vending machines were a disappointment, with dispensing rows cluttered with those off-brand potato chips that are always stale because nobody buys them, and chocolate bars with unusual names that are so old they're covered in that powdery crust of brown dust.

Just as well, he had no coins to spend. He had no money at all, nothing but his off-blue gown and his newly acquired spacesuit. He leaned against a wall and looked out a window that faced the backside of the hospital. He saw dumpsters and big yellow arrows painted on the concrete to direct trucks into the loading dock. He saw refrigerated delivery trucks—six of them—of the kind they parked behind restaurants for dropping off frozen fish or hamburger patties. Salim felt their idling diesel engines vibrate through the glass.

A handful of people in biohazard suits milled around behind them, seeming to have no purpose other than to look bored. The group perked up and came together. A gurney rolled out from the hospital loading docks, followed soon by a second, each pushed by a pair of plastic-clad people who were obviously tired. On each gurney lay a body bag with what could only be a human corpse.

One of the people who'd been lingering pulled a ramp out from under the back of a truck, walked up, and rolled the door open. Body bags were stacked inside from the floor up to the height of a man. The bodies on the gurneys were hauled up the ramp and added to the piles inside. The rolling door was closed. The gurneys returned to the loading dock.

As he stood there, staring at the truck, watching the men go back to loitering and waiting for the next gurneys, Salim realized the trucks might all be stacked full. How could a modern country develop a problem with corpse disposal so quickly? It shook Salim's sense of security.

Chapter 56

Austin spent most of his first day as The General's houseboy, thinking. In reality, there wasn't much for him to do. The General had a chamber pot—a rectangular plastic pail with the remnants of a mayonnaise label peeling off the side. The General expected Austin to empty the bucket every time he pissed or defecated.

The only significant thing Austin did was to construct a broom from materials he found in the forest close to The General's hut. With that broom, fashioned from a long stick and some leafy tropical plants bound to the end, Austin swept The General's dirt floor. It was an activity meant to demean rather than to clean. At least, that was Austin's guess.

The General dismissed him late in the evening. Austin walked across the dark camp, seeing only a few shadows of rebels; some squatting in the darkness by their huts, some smoking and walking the perimeter. Austin thought for the hundredth time that day of quietly running into the trees and losing himself in the night. Each time he entertained the fantasy of escape, he also thought about the hostage who'd lost half his foot that morning. That bleeding stump of a foot was a powerful deterrent. That and the periodic, mournful moaning of the mutilated man who shared the hostage hut—with the others.

As Austin approached his new home, he noticed two guards sitting with their backs to a tree a short distance across the clearing. No one could enter or leave the hut without being seen. The guards' interest seemed focused on their conversation and some trinket they were showing one another. Neither did or said anything to indicate that they noticed Austin entering the hut.

Inside, a kerosene lamp hung from the ceiling, casting a dim light and dancing shadows across the faces of the hostages. A Chinese man sat on one side of the hut, his butt on his bedding, eyeing Austin suspiciously. The man who'd had his foot hacked lay on his own bedding mat, with bloody, crusty bandages wrapped over his stumped foot. A frail Chinese man was soothing and trying his best to care for the wounded man. The white man—the last of them—sat across the hut from the glaring Chinese man.

Austin looked around. There appeared to be enough mats only for the men already there. All were occupied with the exception of an empty one beside the angry-looking Chinese man's mat. From the way the man glanced at the mat and then glared back up, Austin understood the mat was taken.

Austin looked at the white man and asked, "Where do I get a mat to sleep on?"

The white man pointed to the man with a stump for a foot.

Austin looked at the crippled man, then back at the guy who'd pointed. "What?"

In accented English, he said, "Take his, or wait until he dies, then take it. You decide."

"Take it?" Austin shook his head and glared at each of the sitting hostages before turning around and going back out through the door. Immediately upon stepping outside, the two guards showered him with angry words. Austin stopped. He tried to speak, but both guards jumped to their feet and their words grew angrier as they advanced.

"I need a mat," Austin said, pointing back inside the hut, "a sleeping mat."

When he looked back up, one of the guards punched

him in the face. The other punched him in the stomach. Austin fell to his knees. A boot kicked but glanced off the side of his face and hit his shoulder, knocking him back into the hut. One of the guards leaned in, shouted something Austin didn't understand until it was punctuated with "Stay."

The guards went to their place by the tree. Austin touched a hand to a bruise swelling on the side of his face. He pulled his hand back but saw no blood. He rolled over onto his knees. Outside, the voices of the two guards returned to the low tones of private discussion that they'd been using before coming over to give Austin a lesson in the rules.

He wondered how many rules he'd have to learn.

The guy with the cut foot cried out in a particularly pained series of moans, then hushed.

The white man in the hut said, "We've only got four mats. That's it, no matter how many of us are in here."

"Four," Austin nodded. "And don't go outside at night. I guess that's a rule, right?"

The white man nodded.

Austin crawled over to an empty spot along the wall of the hut near the other white man. "If I sleep here, will they beat me? Is there a rule about where I sleep?"

The man smiled and almost laughed. "They don't care what we do in here as long as we don't go outside until morning."

"Got it," said Austin.

The man pointed at the crippled man. "You should take his mat. He won't live."

The man soothing the invalid turned and gave Austin a look that dared him to try and take the mat.

Austin replied, "I'll sleep in the dirt."

The white man shrugged.

Austin reached out a hand to shake. "I'm Austin Cooper."

The man looked at the hand as though going through some lengthy evaluation on whether to commit to the handshake. In the end, he did. "Sander Desmet."

"Desmet?" Austin asked. "Where are you from?"

"Belgium."

"I'm from America."

"I know."

"From my accent?" Austin asked.

Sander didn't answer. He looked over at the Chinese and back at the dying man. "You should take his mat. His effeminate friend won't do anything."

"I won't," Austin reiterated. "How long have you been a hostage? What's the deal here?"

In a tone just above a whisper, Sander said, "When I said the guards don't care what happens in here, I should have added they sometimes get perturbed if they hear loud talking. Best not to agitate them, yeah?"

Austin nodded.

"The General treats it like a business."

"The kidnapping?"

Sander nodded. "If he gets his money, he sends you home."

"How long does it take?"

"A month or two, sometimes three."

"Did he tell you that?" Austin asked. "How long have you been here?"

"Eight months."

Austin slumped along with his hopes.

Sander pointed at the wounded man, "That's Tian. His boyfriend there is Min."

Min looked over his shoulder and nodded at Austin. Austin smiled in return.

"The silent one over there is Wei. He's always pissed, so he won't say much. They arrived together about a month ago. They work for a mining outfit across the Kenyan border. Too many Chinese are crawling all over Africa right now, trying to schmooze the governments and lock up natural resources. Their companies pay the ransom and they're usually gone inside of a month or two. The General knows that, so he likes to grab the Chinese as much as he can. It's easy money for him."

Austin didn't care about any of that. "If Tian's ransom was going to get paid, why'd he try to run? That is why The General chopped his foot off, right?"

Sander nodded. "He should have stayed but the guards beat him a bit. Maybe a lot."

"Why him?"

"Watch them two," Sander nodded at Min and Tian. "You'll figure it out."

Austin asked, "Why have you been here for eight months?"

"The General likes to grab whites, too. He thinks we've all got rich families."

"We don't," argued Austin.

"You don't feel rich, but to them, you are," said Sander.

"Is yours not rich enough?" asked Austin.

"My mother's got no money. My dad passed away a long time ago. The General asked for something like a million in US dollars to give me back. He likes to start high.

Now he's down to ten thousand. If he can come down to a thousand, like I keep telling him, my mother can pay it. Until then, I'm stuck here."

"How does he contact the families?" Austin asked.

"The General sends one of his men to Kampala. In a couple of days, the man comes back and tells The General what he knows. Nothing ever happens quickly. The General wants to feel out your family to see how much he can get. He stalls. He dickers. In the end, they pay. He sends you on your way."

Austin pointed at the groaning man. "What about that? Is that normal?"

"No," Sander shook his head. "We get beaten. We get fed shit and not enough of it. Sometimes The General cuts off finger or ear to mail to your family. Mostly, fellows leave with all their parts."

Chapter 57

The hospital had converted six rooms at the end of the hall on the fourth floor into an isolated recovery ward for Ebola patients. The stairwell door had been welded shut, most certainly a fire code violation. Extraordinary exceptions were being made for Ebola quarantine. Sheets of plastic were taped in layers inside the door. Paul assumed the other side of the door was similarly shielded.

In the hall itself, an elaborate anteroom had been constructed of thick sheets of plastic, which provided the doctors and nurses a means of entry and egress, and a safe area to don or shed their protective gear. If Paul had taken any live virus into the isolation recovery area, they planned for it to stay there.

Paul was the only current resident, though the nurses promised him company soon.

Every day, somebody came to interview Paul. First it was a detective Curtis, along with a contact tracer from the CDC. Then it was a pair from the FBI. The Colorado State Police stopped by. Each day he sat in a chair on one side of a double plastic wall and talked to officials who sat on the other side. He'd answer the same questions over and over and over again. At first, Paul was sympathetic. The police, the FBI, the CDC, were dredging his memory for any clue that might help them find Colorado's patient zero.

As days passed, activity in the quarantine rooms up the hall grew frenzied with the influx of patients from around Denver. Soon their questioning took on the tone of an interrogation. The investigators reviewed Paul's story for the tiniest inconsistencies, making Paul nervous. He masked it with anger that he finally vented on Detective Curtis. Not quite yelling, but far from civil, Paul asked, "Do

I need a lawyer, here?"

"I don't know," Detective Curtis answered. "Do you?"

The interview ended shortly thereafter. Paul went to his room, sat in the chair by the window, and tried to recall any mistakes he might have made in the telling and retelling of his lies.

By then, the news channels had ridden his Good Samaritan story for all the mileage they could get out of it. He was out of mortal danger now so the story had lost its appeal. More interesting was the projection released by the CDC that Dallas would top a thousand Ebola cases by the end of the week. Two hundred were already dead. The hospital dedicated to Ebola looked like it was under siege. It was protected by uniformed men, all wearing some level of protection—either a surgical mask and gloves, or gas masks and chemical warfare gear. Protestors camped outside wanted the patients moved far from the city. They didn't seem to realize that the hospital was not the source of the Dallas epidemic. Ebola was already on their streets and in their houses. The hospital was simply where the sick went to die.

Atlanta was becoming a big story on the Ebola front as well, and that worried Paul. Olivia lived near Fort Gordon, a few hours east. One of the news channels was projecting that Atlanta would soon overtake Dallas as the most infected city in the country. At least a few dozen other cities had outbreaks in the range of twenty to a hundred cases. Denver was up to forty-three, including Paul. Every time one of the channels discussed Ebola numbers, it was always followed with assurances that government agencies—both locally and nationally—were doing all that could be done, and that the public should take precautions listed on the channel's website, but shouldn't panic. "Go to work. Go to school. Avoid physical contact. Don't let the terrorists win."

Terrorists? Paul wondered. That was a new addition to the news blurbs. He wondered if he'd missed something while he was out of it. He needed a computer and an Internet connection, neither of which were available to him.

A rustling of plastic sheeting from out in the hall alerted Paul that someone was coming through the makeshift anteroom. Paul looked toward the door and waited. Any distraction was welcome.

A few moments later, Nancy, his day shift nurse came in, wearing her protective gear, carrying no syringe, no medication, and no tablet for notes.

"Hello, Nancy," said Paul, curiously.

"Paul." Nancy smiled behind her mask. "How are you feeling?"

"Okay. I don't think I could run a mile, but I could walk it." Paul grinned. "I'm assuming I'm still Ebola-free?"

"Yesterday's test came back negative."

Paul exaggerated a look at Nancy's empty hands. "No blood test today?"

Nancy's expression changed to seriousness. "Have you seen the news today?"

"I'm tired of watching TV." Paul glanced back out the window at the rain falling from the gray sky. "I've been reading a book that Katrina, the night nurse, recommended. It's—"

Nancy was ignoring Paul and fumbling with the television's remote control, but getting no result. She stopped and looked at him. "They're saying things that you should be aware of."

"Saying things?" Paul asked, worried. "What are you talking about?"

Nancy shook her head, and looked at Paul with eyes that he couldn't read. She handed him the remote. "I know you're tired of the news. *We all are.* You should watch."

Paul accepted the device and laid it in his lap.

Nancy turned and walked to the door, where she paused and looked back. "I'll be in to check on you later."

Paul nodded. He looked down at the remote. He looked up at the television with uneasiness. Could it be something about Heidi? Austin? No, surely if something had happened to either of them, the police would come and tell him in person. He turned up the volume.

Chapter 58

It was Maggie's face Paul saw when the television screen flickered to life. The neighbor Maggie, whom Heidi had told about Paul's prepper stash that day after his first trip to Costco all those weeks ago. It was Maggie who Paul was worried would tell everyone in the neighborhood about his fifty-pound bags of rice and other goodies.

Paul got a sinking feeling as though the world had slipped into slow motion, and he watched Maggie's face. She'd been listening to a question from the reporter and in response, her bushy eyebrows wriggled into a pained plea for validation as the rest of her face tried hard to hide the orgasmic joy she felt by tattling on the neighbors.

On the television screen, Paul saw the headline in white text, outlined in yellow on a stylish background of cobalt blue with black pinstripes. Quotes surrounded the words, "Paul Cooper lied."

The guilty weight of all of Paul's choices crashed down on him. Embarrassed pain ripped away the curtain of his self-esteem and sucked the breath out of his chest.

"She likes to talk," Maggie said in answer to the question asked before Paul's television came to life.

The screen split in two with Maggie's face in a window on one side and the anchor's face on the other. The anchor asked, "She likes to talk? She just came out and told you that Paul Cooper was going to infect himself with Ebola on purpose?"

There it was, the paralyzing truth.

"That's right," Maggie nodded. "I usually keep to myself, but Heidi can't. She's always talking to everyone in the neighborhood, just telling them any old thing."

"And what did you do when she told you this?" The anchor asked.

Maggie was put off by the implication that perhaps she should have done something when she'd heard the news. "I didn't think anything of it. His son just died, you know."

"What happened to his son?" the anchor asked, with the appropriate sympathy in her tone.

"He died of Ebola in Africa," answered Maggie. "He was one of those kids wasting their parents' money trying to find himself by vacationing around the world. You know the type.

"Fuck you!" Paul screamed.

Getting the interview back to the pertinent points, the anchor asked, "Did you have any idea that Paul Cooper would carry through with a plan to infect himself?"

"No," Maggie put on a sad face. "He lost his son. He was depressed, I imagine. People don't think straight when they lose a loved one, especially a child."

The television screen dropped the image of Maggie and filled with the news anchor's sad, but pretty, plasticine face. "Loss of a loved one is indeed difficult." Her face changed back to mannequin neutrality, with the hint of a smile. "After the break, we've got a video from the dashcam of a Texas Highway Patrol car that allegedly shows Paul Cooper on a routine traffic stop, at a time when he claimed to be on that much talked-about trip to Lake Granby, where he met the infected Liberian man."

Paul turned off the television and turned his chair around so that he could look out the window again at the rain and the gray clouds. He was screwed.

Chapter 59

"All I'm saying, butt-wipe, is I got things to do today. I don't know why we're driving all the way to this part of town just so you can show me some surprise."

Jimmy made a left turn off the highway exit ramp and then looked over at Larry, asking himself for the thousandth time why he didn't find a new partner. The answer was always the same. Well, the answer *became* the same through the years, after Jimmy developed the capacity to be honest with himself on the subject. Jimmy was too lazy to find somebody else. Larry was loyal enough, productive enough, predictable, and easily manipulated. "It'll be just a few more minutes."

Larry huffed and looked out the window. "All these people down here got their big-ass cracker box houses. Bunch of soccer-mom stickers on the windows of their SUVs. They make me sick."

"Uh-huh," Jimmy agreed, though he didn't care.

"Look around man," Larry pointed down a side street. "Every lawn is mowed and the bushes are all trimmed. You don't see no brown grass. Nobody's got a car up on blocks anywhere. Rich fucks. Dentists and lawyers, all of 'em, I'll bet."

"Probably." Jimmy stopped at a red light.

"No potholes," Larry groused. "That's why we got potholes in our streets. All the tax money goes here to make sure their streets are perfect." Larry pointed at the road ahead of the truck as his anger grew. "Look, man, you see?"

Jimmy nodded as they passed the second road repair crew in just as many blocks.

"Perfectly smooth roads. This place makes me sick."

"Then you'll be happy in a minute," Jimmy told Larry when the light changed.

Larry looked out his side window and said nothing. Jimmy, happy for a respite from the complaining, said nothing more as he drove the truck through two more stoplights. The wide street climbed a hill, and just past the crest, Jimmy took a left turn into a complex of expensive-looking townhouses with perfectly manicured landscaping.

"What's this?" Larry asked as they drove onto a street between rows of new-looking townhouses sided in old-looking bricks.

Jimmy looked at the map on his phone and slowed the truck as he did so. He looked up at a street sign, then back down at his phone.

Larry asked, "What road you lookin' for?"

"This is it." Jimmy took a left turn. A block down, Jimmy made another left turn and slowed to look at the numbers on the sides of the buildings.

"Whose house we lookin' for?" Larry asked.

At a curve in the road, Jimmy pulled over and parked, but left the engine running. Jimmy looked at the buildings again and pointed to a townhouse on the end of a building. "Paul Cooper."

Larry looked at Jimmy while he tried to make the mental connection. His face turned to anger, but he said nothing.

"The guy in the news," Jimmy hinted.

Larry looked back at the building. "The guy in—the guy who infected himself with Ebola?"

"That guy," Jimmy confirmed.

"He's in there?" Larry asked.

Jimmy shrugged. "I doubt it. Last I saw on TV, he was still in the hospital. If the police don't toss him in jail when he gets out of the hospital, he'll be back here soon enough."

"You think—" Larry paused as he put his thoughts together, "since he got better, he's the guy we can get our first batch of blood from."

Jimmy smiled, but it looked more like a snarl. *"He's the guy."*

Larry rubbed the whiskers on his chin. "I know you've been thinking about this, but I've got questions."

"Okay."

"I never paid much attention in school." Larry put his fingers to his lips as if smoking an invisible joint. "Too much of that. Know what I mean?"

Jimmy laughed and nodded. "Yeah."

"But I know if we take the blood out, it'll con—, congranu—"

"It'll coagulate," said Jimmy, knowing Larry would never come up with the word.

"Right," said Larry. "What do we do about that?"

"I got a buddy who works as a plasmapheresis tech down at the donation center."

Larry was confused.

"Where you donate your plasma when you can't make rent. They give you thirty bucks and some cookies."

Larry thumped two fingers on the crook of his elbow. "Been there."

Jimmy reached into his pocket and took out a vial of clear liquid. "I got a whole box of this shit from my buddy." Jimmy handed the small bottle to Larry.

Larry took the bottle and held it up to read the label. "Heparin?"

"And Coumadin," said Jimmy, nodding. "It keeps the

blood from clotting, so you can run it through the machine."

Larry rubbed his whiskers again and said, "Those machines are big and heavy." He pointed at Paul Cooper's townhouse. "Where do we get one, and how do we get it in there?"

"We don't," said Jimmy, shaking his head. "Like you said, they're big and heavy. We don't know how to work it. If we went that route, we'd have to get my buddy, the plasmapheresis guy, in on the deal for a share. I don't know if he'd be down for this kind of work. He doesn't mind stealing a box of Heparin to make a few bucks, but I don't think he'd approve of what we're gonna be doing with it."

Larry put on a confident face as he agreed with Jimmy's conclusion.

"Most people are too afraid of the law to break it by much." Jimmy laughed.

Larry laughed. "That's the truth."

"That's why we just take the blood." Jimmy reached over and took the vial of Heparin back from Larry. "We use this to keep the blood from clotting. I got bags and needles and stuff. My buddy got us everything we need. By the way, that stuff wasn't cheap. I covered the cost, but I'm repaying myself before we divvy up the profits."

"Yeah, man," Larry nodded. "Of course."

"Oh." Jimmy laughed again. "I almost forgot about the best part."

"What's that?"

"Nobody's gonna give a shit."

"How's that?" Larry asked.

"You've seen the news, man," said Jimmy. "Everybody hates Paul Cooper."

"Yeah?"

"Man, you don't play the sympathy thing all over TV, and then have it come out that you lied about everything. People hate that shit. Especially with Ebola in Denver now."

"Over a hundred," Larry cut in. "Maybe two hundred. I heard it on the radio this morning."

"All potential customers." Jimmy laughed. "And they all blame Paul Cooper. If he turns up dead, everybody in Denver will be a suspect. It's the perfect crime. When it comes out in the news that somebody stole all of Paul's blood, it'll make it easier for us to sell our stock. It'll be like the news channels will do our advertising. People will believe we have what we say we have, and they'll pay us top dollar for it."

Chapter 60

Firas Hakimi was dead. That was the news Hadi had just passed along to Najid as he walked in the shade of the date trees just inside the northern wall. After imparting the news, Najid instructed Hadi to find out who Hakimi's successor would be. With every member of Hakimi's inner circle either dead or sick, Najid would be surprised if Hadi came back with any name at all. Hakimi's organization would likely fall apart. If any of his low-level zealots survived the epidemic in Syria, Najid decided he might try to recruit them at a future date. He'd put Hadi on collecting a list, if he could.

But those thoughts were for another day.

This day was for joy.

Najid Almasi, recent heir to the Almasi fortune, had already tripled his wealth. He laughed out loud into the solitude of the grove. The servants knew he liked to walk in the date grove to find his peace, find time to think. They left him alone, except when urgency demanded otherwise.

The wealth was mostly paper wealth. That, and the skyrocketing value of the gold and silver stored in the bunkers beneath the compound. When the international monetary system collapsed, as it surely appeared to be on its way to doing, all of that paper would be worthless. Until then, Najid Almasi—rich already—was in the upper echelons of the list of wealthiest men in the world.

Short-lived though it would be, it felt good.

The morning's best news was that of the Ebola counts. Hadi no longer presented graphs of infection projections. He presented numbers of reported cases. The most infected city in the world was Nairobi, an unfortunate result of its containing an international airport relatively close to Kapchorwa. All of Najid's jihadists had passed through Nairobi.

No new numbers were coming out, however. After Nairobi passed the hundred thousand case mark, the city sank into a chaotic state. The government stopped communicating with the outside world. Everyone speculated that the city's government and the Kenyan government simply didn't exist anymore.

Frankfurt, the most diseased city in the West, reached thirty-six thousand cases, with more reported each day. It seemed to be following Nairobi's path into oblivion. Of the American cities, Dallas was suffering most. Its case count had passed the thousand mark and —

A blaze of brilliant light flashed from out on the water, past the end of the pier.

Najid's skin felt suddenly sunburned.

His beautiful white yacht ruptured in exploding flames.

A second flash. More fire.

The sound of the first explosion shook Najid. The tanker ruptured into flames. Explosions burst everywhere. Najid dove for the ground.

Chapter 61

Giggling, Barry said "See, see."

Olivia did. First the three ships anchored offshore were hammered with a series of missiles that engulfed them in flames and sent one almost immediately under the waves. Najid Almasi's compound lit up next, with explosions ripping through every major structure on the property.

"When is this?" Olivia asked.

"The feed came in last night," answered Barry. "This might be twelve hours old."

The video showing the carnage did so in pixelated black and white imagery. It was nevertheless satisfying to see all those bodies that just moments before had been little black ants moving about—unsuspecting of what was coming, much like the world had been unsuspecting when Najid Almasi launched his attack. After the explosions flashed away, none of the bodies moved. Only the flames and the smoke were alive.

"Remember," said Barry, "You never saw this."

"Gotcha." Olivia couldn't take her eyes off the screen. "I wish—"

"I know," said Barry. "That we'd gotten to him sooner."

"Yeah." Olivia watched the black figures. Still, none of them moved. "Do you think we got him? Almasi himself?"

"Intelligence said he was there."

"Human intelligence?" Olivia asked.

Barry tapped the screen. "We've got him on video in the compound. He didn't leave before the attack. Nobody did, unless they burrowed through the sand."

Olivia nodded. If only they'd gotten to him much, much sooner.

Barry said, "I thought with your brother and all, you'd appreciate seeing it."

"Thanks," Olivia said, putting a hand on Barry's shoulder. "I do appreciate it."

Barry turned off the video. "Did you hear about Eric?"

"No."

"He took a leave of absence."

"I just saw him yesterday," said Olivia.

"It was his last day for a while."

"For how long?" Olivia knew the answer, and she knew the reason. It felt right to ask anyway.

"Don't know," said Barry. "His wife got it."

"Ebola?"

Barry nodded in confirmation.

"The kids?" she asked, hoping they were safe. In truth, if Eric's wife had it, her children would soon follow. That seemed to be Ebola's M.O., to seed one member of the family and then massacre the rest.

Barry shrugged.

Olivia muttered, "It's everywhere."

Barry nodded emphatically at that. "At least Almasi got his."

"At least that." Olivia sat herself on Barry's L-shaped desk, well away from his computer, and leaned against the cubicle wall.

Barry spun lazily around in his chair to face her.

"Who takes Eric's place while he's out?" she asked.

"I don't know," said Barry. "Eric's boss is in the hospital, too."

Before she could ask, Barry nodded.

"Nobody tells me anything since my clearance got

suspended."

Barry looked suddenly very thoughtful.

"What's that?" Olivia asked.

"What's what?"

"That face you just made when I mentioned my clearances. Do you know something you're not telling me?"

Barry pursed his lips and glanced back at his computer monitor. "Your clearances weren't revoked. You know Eric disabled your clearances in the system when the CIA made a fuss, right?"

Olivia shrugged. She didn't have any insight into how the administrative parts of Eric's job worked. "Are you telling me he could have re-enabled it whenever he wanted?"

"Technically, yes," said Barry. "He had the ability to re-enable whenever he saw fit."

"Bastard."

"Don't get offended. It's more complicated than just Eric."

"Now that he's out, are you telling me I'll never get it back?"

"No," said Barry. "I'm not saying that, at all. With Eric out, approval requests automatically go to his boss. With his boss out, they go to his backup approver."

"Wait, you're losing me. Approval requests?"

"If you went into the permissions admin web tool on the intranet, and submitted a clearance request to Eric, the approval would come to me."

"You're kidding me."

Barry shook his head.

"You could take the suspension off my clearances?"

"As long as Eric's out. What he does when he comes back is his business."

Olivia smiled. "Will you come by my desk and walk me through it? That app is too counterintuitive for me. I want to make sure I fill out the forms correctly."

"I'll come by after lunch."

Chapter 62

Where Salim's clothing had gone, he could only guess, and his guess was an incinerator. He assumed his passport was in the hands of his interrogators, along with his billfold and the last of his cash. While not imprisoned formally, he was in effect, trapped in the hospital, completely dependent on the staff to feed him, even to carry out his waste.

Salim appreciated what the hospital staff had done for him. He had his health back. But he had no plans to remain in a hospital-shaped prison.

On his last full night in the hospital, he went through the corridors doing his best to look like a janitor, though most everyone looked alike in head-to-toe plastic. Salim pushed a hamper through the halls, collecting soiled garments from rooms, going through pockets when no one was around.

When he'd found a set of clothes that looked like it would fit, along with enough loose cash to sustain him for a while, he took what he had to a restroom and rinsed the clothes in a sink, cleaning them as best he could. After they were close enough to dry, he put his items in a small, blue, slightly worn duffel bag he'd come across, donned his off-blue scrubs—his doctor disguise—and suited up in his hazmat suit. Salim headed down to the first floor to make his exit through the decontamination tent erected at the hospital's front entrance, hoping he wouldn't be scrutinized too closely. After all he'd been through he hoped luck was still on his side.

Chapter 63

"Who is this?"

Olivia couldn't believe it. She'd dialed the number for the CIA satellite telephone as part of her daily routine, not expecting anyone to answer. "Um, I don't know if I should say, exactly."

"Then we have nothing to talk about. Don't call again."

"Wait. Wait," said Olivia, weighing her options. Could she get in worse trouble by identifying herself? Maybe? With everything else going on in the world, would anybody care? "I'm Olivia Cooper. I'm a data analyst for the Department of Homeland Security." The phone didn't disconnect. She took a little bit of a gamble on the next part. "I found the information about the jihadists with Western passports that was likely the impetus for your trip to Kapchorwa."

Only the hint of breathing on the other end of the phone gave Olivia hope.

Mitch finally said, "I've dealt with a lot of Coopers lately."

Olivia was barely able to contain her excitement when she blurted out, "Austin Cooper?"

Cautiously, Mitch said. "I take it this is not a coincidence. Your real name isn't Heidi, is it?"

"No," Olivia said, "that's my stepmother's name!"

"Good. Because if you'd said yes, I would have hung up. She's the most relentless woman I've ever spoken to."

"You spoke with my stepmother?" Olivia smiled. She *was* relentless.

"It seems. I'll be crystal clear on this point. If you give this phone number to Heidi Cooper and she calls me, I'll destroy this telephone."

"You know about Austin, then."

"She made me aware."

Olivia asked, "Did you find him in Kapchorwa?"

"I'm not allowed—" Mitch paused. "I'll tell you what I can." He let out an exasperated sigh. "Oh, why not? You're the first American I've talked to in two weeks. Yes, I saw Austin Cooper in Kapchorwa, but that was a month ago, and he was in sad shape. I apologize for my tactlessness, but if somebody told me he died five minutes after I left, I wouldn't be surprised."

"But he was alive? When you saw him, right?" Olivia went on to drill Mitch for everything he could disclose about his encounter with her brother. Through it, they developed a rapport. "You said you hadn't talked to anyone in the States in two weeks. I don't have any doubts that you—" Olivia paused as she thought of the best way to say what she wanted to say. "I'm convinced you are the person I had hoped to contact when I dialed your number. I'm also going to make the educated guess that your security clearance is higher than mine. Do you have any questions for me?"

"I can't tell you where I am, but—"

"I should tell you," said Olivia, "I found your number through searching for satellite calls coming from Africa that coincided with some information on record in a report. "I could find out where you're calling from now, but if you ask me not to, I won't."

"What the hell," said Mitch. "I'm in Nairobi."

"Are things there as bad as they say?" Olivia asked.

"However bad they say, it's much worse," said Mitch.

"Honestly, there's nothing coming out of Nairobi

anymore. The reports and pictures I've seen are out of date but they paint a bleak picture."

"It's bad. It seems like everybody's got Ebola here."

Olivia asked, "How are you keeping yourself safe?"

"Lucky so far, I guess. Now I'm holed up in a third-floor apartment. I've got food and water enough to last another week. I don't have to go out and expose myself. When the stuff runs out, who knows?"

"The last number I heard out of Nairobi was a hundred thousand cases."

Mitch laughed. "Do you know what the population of Nairobi is?"

"Three million?" It wasn't a guess. Olivia had seen the number in a report a week or so earlier.

"Yeah," Mitch agreed. "I can look out my window right now and see at least a hundred dead on the sidewalks or in the street. That doesn't count the number they've burned. There's a pyre at the intersection down below me. The fire has been burning nonstop for a week."

"For a week?" Olivia asked, not wanting to believe her projections were true.

"The locals add the bodies of the dead. Every day. Every night. It doesn't stop. Fires are burning all over the city. The smoke hangs in the air all the time. The place reeks. If somebody told me right now that half the population had Ebola, or had died from it already, I wouldn't doubt it."

"My God." She wondered how much of Mitch's assessment was involuntarily exaggerated by a visceral reaction to being immersed in it. Still, the last official number of a hundred thousand had to be low, if Mitch's account was even remotely correct. An irony occurred to Olivia—at the moment, she was a cog in a government machine tasked with repressing the bad news. Were other nations keeping their dirty laundry hidden from the global community? Probably.

Nairobi might have over a million cases.

"I need you to tell me something now," said Mitch.

"Anything," Olivia told him.

"Please tell me we stopped Almasi in time. Please tell me what I'm seeing is just happening in Africa."

"I don't have the full picture," Olivia said. "My clearance was suspended after my brother turned up in Kapchorwa with Najid Almasi."

"They thought he was involved?" Mitch asked, laughing derisively as he did.

"In a nutshell."

"I can tell you one thing for sure," said Mitch. "He wasn't."

"I know," said Olivia. "The good news is, the Navy took out Almasi."

"Fantastic."

"But it happened yesterday."

"Shit," Mitch sounded suddenly despondent. "And his little messenger boys?"

"I don't think they've apprehended all of them yet."

It was Mitch's turn to be shocked. "My God. How bad is it?"

"I think most of the terrorists flew from Nairobi to Frankfurt for connecting flights. Frankfurt topped forty-thousand cases this morning, though they aren't reporting nearly that many. I can't think of a major European or Asian city that isn't dealing with outbreaks of several hundred. In lots of cities the total is measured in thousands."

"How are we doing?"

Olivia knew he meant the United States. "The numbers will seem better, but I believe our numbers are smaller because the terrorists arrived here later, so our outbreak was delayed. Dallas rocketed up from a thousand cases five days ago to over eight thousand this morning. Atlanta is in the same boat. It's everywhere here. Washington seems to be swimming in it, but it's hard to get numbers, even for anybody in this department. We've been actively censoring stories about Congress. Somehow, they got a jump on the population, statistically speaking. The whisper number is sixty-three senators and three hundred and thirty-six representatives ill or dead."

"Well that's a silver lining."

"Yeah." Olivia said flatly. "The serious rumor mill says Congress pulled some strings to get hold of an untested vaccine that backfired—"

Mitch guffawed. "You've got to be kidding me."

"It could be speculation. The second most popular rumor is that a bunch of them were on a fact-finding mission in Kenya—translate that as 'safari'—on some pharma company's dime, about the same time Almasi's boys were flying out of Nairobi. One thing leads to another."

Mitch said, "That sounds plausible."

"The president has been put someplace secure," said Olivia. "The cabinet—or what's left of it—is with him. At least that's the guess."

"I guess that explains why nobody back at the office has time to call me anymore."

"I hate to guess that they're probably dead, but..."

"You know," Mitch paused. "I don't suppose it makes

any difference anymore—my name is Mitch, Mitch Peterson. You may as well know who you're talking to, since you may be the last person I ever talk to. In English, anyway."

"What do you think you'll do, Mitch?"

"I don't know." He sighed. "Staying here is a losing proposition."

"The airlines shut down weeks ago. Most commerce across borders has stopped. I'd be surprised if any ships outside of the Navy are still at sea. Or maybe they all are. You know, people looking to escape the epidemic."

"Yeah."

"Do you have a way to keep your phone charged?" Olivia asked.

"Yes."

"I owe you a favor. Why don't I do some research on my end and see if I can find a way to get you home?"

"Probably won't be much better there than here by the time I get home, but—"

"What?"

"Just thinking."

"About?"

"I'll tell you what, you do your research. You keep in touch. I'll find a vehicle and work my way back to Kapchorwa. If your brother is still there, I'll find him for you."

Chapter 64

Austin stood against the wall, feeling the dirty stiffness of muddy, blood-encrusted clothes. He wondered if he was getting used to his own stink, or if the smell was diminishing on its own. He squirmed at the chafing under his arms and where his pants—getting baggier by the day—rubbed his legs when he walked. He didn't want to think about the rash on his lower legs.

The General looked up from where he sat in his chair next to his window. He put a big piece of dripping meat in his mouth and chewed.

Austin didn't look away. Some days his hate overpowered his subservient sense of self-preservation.

Through his chewing, The General said, "Don't glare at me while I eat."

Austin looked for a moment longer, nodded, and looked toward the open door instead.

"I like defiance," said The General. "I don't like petulance."

Austin nodded.

The General grinned and said, "You didn't think I knew that word, I'll bet."

No, Austin didn't, but he kept that to himself.

The General waved Austin over. "Stand against that wall in front of me. I don't like turning my head to look at you while I'm eating."

Austin did as instructed.

"You're educated, no?"

"I'm a college student," Austin answered.

"In what year?"

"Fourth."

The General sat back in his wooden chair. He looked out his window at the camp and pointed. "Most of them are bushmen. Most have no education. With them, I can speak of devotion and God. We talk of military matters. We talk of hunting in the forest. We talk of our common experiences. As a boy, I was not unlike most of them, but my parents were able to pay for school. I finished at the Catholic University. Most of them farmed or hunted."

Because The General paused, Austin nodded. Acknowledgement of the conversation's ebbs and flows seemed like the polite, safe thing to do.

"Let's be pragmatic, you and I," The General said.

"How so?" Austin asked.

"You know this word, pragmatic?"

"Of course," Austin answered.

The General nodded. He pointed at the chair opposite his. "Sit."

Austin did.

"I can't understand the Chinese accent." The General took another greasy bite of meat. "Sander is a simple man with simple thoughts, not much better than my soldiers. He's been in Africa too long, chasing monkeys to sell to your pharmaceutical companies."

Austin nodded agreement because it seemed like the correct response.

"Sander has no education, no interests beyond finding the company of a woman."

Austin nodded.

"You speak American English. The accent is easy for me to bear." The General sat up and leaned over the table. "But you have an American attitude."

Immediately on the defensive, Austin shook his head. "I...I don't know what you mean."

The General grinned. "Like the English. You think anyone with an accent other than yours is stupid."

"No," Austin shook his head, trying to sell the lie. "I don't."

"You are here because I will make money on you when I sell you back to your rich parents."

"I don't have rich parents," Austin protested.

The General held up a hand to silence him. "You have value to me. I don't hate you. I don't look down on you. I require that you do things while you are in my custody, as a way to maximize your value to me. Do you understand?"

"Sure," Austin replied.

"Hate me if you will," said The General. "Or see the situation as pragmatically as I, and talk to me like one educated man to another."

Austin didn't know what to say.

"I enjoy intelligent conversation," said The General. "I don't get that here."

Austin thought for a moment. "And if you don't like what I say? Then what?"

The General laughed. "I don't need a pretense to beat you, or maim you, or kill you. I do what I want here, Ransom. You choose. Be an adult. Talk if you can accept your situation for what it is, a business transaction—unfortunate for you, fortunate for me. You will be gone in a month or two. If your family cooperates, you will leave with all of your body parts and I will have my money." The General smiled and shrugged. "If you cannot be a man about it, then go back to your wall and glare at me in quiet petulance. You choose. Do it soon." The General looked down at his plate. "I am nearly finished."

Austin looked at the plate, looked back up at The General, and decided, *why not?* "Why don't you feed your hostages more?"

The General laughed. "I had hoped for a better subject for our first conversation." He laid his hands on the table and scrutinized Austin. "Westerners eat too much already. You won't starve on what I give you."

Austin started to argue but stopped himself. He was hungry. He felt like he was starving.

"Think of it this way," said The General. "In this camp, I am the Westerner. You and the other ransoms are the rest of the world. I eat all I want." He patted his belly. "I may even fatten myself needlessly. You?" The General laughed. "You get the scraps from my table. Now you complain, as does the rest of the world. The analogy is perfect, don't you think?"

Austin, without an argument he could put together said, "That's not true."

"I've angered you into sullenness already," The General observed. "I will leave it up to you, Ransom. I will give you a plate as full as mine if you wish. You may eat what I eat."

Austin eyed The General cautiously. "I only require that you eat it in front of your fellow hostages. Their rations will remain the same. Perhaps then, you will understand my point."

Austin looked at the remains of The General's meal.

"You're hungry, right? You want more food, don't you?"

Austin nodded.

"What will you do, then?"

Reluctantly, Austin said, "I'll eat what the others eat."

The General laughed again.

Chapter 65

The General and a dozen of his men lay in ambush across a shrub-covered crest of muddy rock that stretched outward from the base of a cliff rising steeply to their left. Behind them and well down the slope, Austin, Sander, and Wei squatted among the giant tree trunks and underbrush, waiting, silent. In front of The General and his men a path wound along the base of the cliffs on this side of Mt. Elgon. The path took a tight turn around a small pond before starting a series of zigzags down the mountain.

Austin stared into the branches of the trees a hundred feet overhead, seeing sky and mountain beyond. He listened to the howls of distant monkeys and heard the squawk of tropical birds. He wondered what unfortunates would be coming down the trail. Would they be government soldiers on patrol, or farmers hauling their coffee to market?

Either way, slaughter lay in their future.

Austin thought about what he could do to stop the killing before it started and save the unsuspecting victims, warning them away. His only weapon was his voice. A shout would get him a beating, of that he was certain. What he didn't know was how irrationally The General would behave under the influence of his inflamed temper. The General had hacked off part of Tian's foot, and Tian was one of his hostage investments. Now Tian was so sick with infection that his life was in danger. Would an angry General kill?

Probably.

Austin looked up the steep slope at the feet and butts of The General's men arrayed in the shrubs. If Austin yelled —assuming he could somehow select the right time for it—

would anyone on the other side of the rise hear or understand him? If they did, would they even heed his warning?

Instead, Austin went back to wondering why he had been dragged along on a two-day hike across the side of the mountain. Was he to be a stretcher-bearer for the wounded? The thought of schlepping half the weight of a wounded rebel all the way back to camp did not appeal to him one bit. He hoped that any of the uneducated rebels who met the business end of a bullet would at least have the courtesy to die.

Austin leaned close to Sander and whispered, "Where are the stretchers?"

Sander looked back at him, a lack of comprehension clear on his face.

Austin felt a rough nudge at the back of his neck. He looked up at the guard behind him who was prodding with the barrel of his rifle. Austin got the message. Be quiet.

A few small rocks tumbled down the slope and Austin looked up. Feet sticking out of the bushes up there were starting to shuffle with nervousness. At least the end of the ordeal was coming.

Noise, strange and indistinct, bounced around on the tree trunks. It sounded like animals, perhaps oxen pulling carts. Austin guessed coffee farmers hauling a year's worth of their labor down the mountain to sell at a market in Kenya. Austin decided The General wasn't a patriot. He was just a bandit twisting religion around his charisma to keep his impressionable young men subservient.

The animals grew louder and closer. They snorted and stomped. Tree branches snapped. The beasts sounded enormous.

One of the AK-47s fired.

Someone shouted.

An elephant trumpeted.

Two more rounds popped off.

More shouting, and all of the rifles erupted. Elephants grunted and cried out in shrill panic. The ground shook and trees quaked with the impact of the giants turning and bumping.

As suddenly as it started, the shooting stopped. The men atop the hill shouted excitedly as they got up and started forward. From the other side of the mound, the sound of wet wheezing through blood-filled trunks mixed with deep, guttural groans.

"Up, up," the guard told the prisoners. "Go. Go."

Austin, Sander, and Wei shuffled up the hill, feet still shackled with their ropes.

The men on the other side of the hill were joyous.

The General, ebullient, and suddenly unable to keep quiet, came back to the top edge of the ridge saying, "A great day. A great day. A quarter million US, at least. Maybe twice that much. Maybe not. But a quarter, at least. Hurry! Hurry!"

"Go!" The guard urged.

"Two bulls," The General continued. "Maybe a third somewhere up the trail. A great day."

Three more gunshots popped.

After climbing the slope, Austin and his fellow hostages pushed their way through the bushes at the crest and looked down the slope toward the game trail. At the edge of the pool inside the curve lay two huge elephants. One with enormous tusks struggled futilely to right itself, while the other with much shorter tusks, breathed shallowly and bled from a few dozen wounds.

One of the soldiers walked up to the struggling bull, aimed his rifle at the top of the elephant's skull, ripped through six rounds, paused, and fired again. The elephant's massive body settled to the ground, and its last breath flowed out of its lungs in a great groan.

Austin stopped, stunned. A hand pushed him from behind. The death of the great elephant was, in its way, as troubling to him as the death of some of the people he'd seen. It didn't make sense, but there it was, a stark, rasping, and cruel, death, singular but on an enormous scale.

Two of The General's men stepped up to the elephant's carcass and started hacking at its face with machetes.

Sander whispered, "You and I will be carrying those tusks back to camp."

Austin felt ill.

The other elephant, still breathing, with a trunk moving in a drunken snake dance made no move to react when two more men stepped up on each side of its enormous head.

"It's not dead," Austin hollered.

The two men with machetes poised to cut at the dying elephant's face froze. The General started to laugh. He pointed at Austin and said, "Ransom, come down here."

Sander said, "You should have stayed quiet."

Austin started down the embankment, slipped and skidded part way on his back then got his footing and continued. At the bottom he skirted the pool of water and walked over to where The General had positioned himself near the top of the bleeding elephant's head.

"You want to do the humane thing, no?"

Austin nodded, knowing The General was asking him to finish the suffering animal, but at the same time, wanting no part in the slaughter.

The General laughed, and so did the two men with machetes. The General held his AK-47 out to Austin.

Austin looked at it.

"Take it," The General said.

Austin didn't.

"Take it," The General ordered, harshly. "I think you're afraid to kill the elephant yourself."

Austin reached up and laid his hands on the weapon. The General let go as he said, "Careful."

In front of him and off to the sides, several men raised their rifles and aimed them at Austin. His throat went dry. He looked around at the men. And very slowly, very deliberately, he brought the rifle's barrel to bear on the top of the elephant's skull. The elephant's groaning and bloody wheezing didn't change. Its big golden-brown eye looked at Austin, as though to tell of its suffering.

The General leaned close, and in a confidential tone said, "If you're quick about it, you could kill me, you know."

Austin cut his eyes at The General.

The General leaned back and nodded. "If you're quick."

The thought hadn't occurred to Austin, he'd been focused on the dying elephant. The General was right. Austin could swing the barrel around and shoot until the magazine emptied. He'd never shot such a weapon before, but felt positive that enough of the bullets would rip through the evil thug's chest that he would die. Out here in the middle of the jungle, without the slightest hope of getting to a hospital in time, of course The General would die. It would be a trade, Austin's life for a thug's.

Was it worth it?

Austin glanced around at the hard faces of the men with

weapons trained on him, and decided he would not make the trade.

It wasn't fear that stopped him. It was the look on the faces of those rebels. A few bullets in The General's heart would change nothing. While The General was still bleeding, still trying to bite a mouthful of his own last breath, one of those hard men would step in to fill his spot —the new head thug, leading the other thugs on to brutalize good people in the towns and villages below the mountain.

Austin wasn't going to waste his life on futility.

But a time would come, he promised himself that.

Austin snugged the butt of the rifle up against his shoulder, sighted the gun, aimed it at the center of the elephant's head and pulled the trigger.

Nothing happened.

The General burst into a laugh. All of his men laughed along with him.

Austin looked down at the rifle with no idea what he'd done wrong.

"The safety," The General said, reaching over to reposition a large lever just above the trigger. Then he grabbed the top of the rifle and said, "Bullets cost money. Would you like to buy one?"

"You've stolen my money," Austin said, coating his words with vitriol.

"Then you must trade for a bullet, if you want one."

"I have nothing to trade."

"You do," countered The General.

"What?" Austin asked.

The General reached into his pocket and pulled out the credit card Dr. Littlefield had given him. "The PIN number on this credit card."

"For a bullet," Austin confirmed.

"The PIN for a bullet. Yes."

Shaking his head as he thought about what The General might do, what he might buy that could be used to hurt someone else, Austin realized he couldn't know and he didn't care. He cared about the elephant. "I'll give you the PIN."

The General smiled and said, "But if your PIN does not work, if you lie to me, you'll still pay for the bullet."

"Will you beat me?" Austin asked. "Starve me?"

"No," The General said. "The bullet will cost you a finger."

The General reached over and put the tip of his finger on Austin's index finger, still wrapped around the AK-47's trigger. "That one."

"I'll give you the right PIN." Austin looked back down the rifle sight, took a deep breath and squeezed. The gun kicked. Red exploded from a spot on the elephant's head. The elephant's body jerked and the two men with machetes jumped back a step. Still conscious of the rifles pointed at him, Austin slowly lowered his weapon and he waited for the elephant to stop breathing.

It didn't.

He'd only succeeded in making one more bleeding wound.

The General reached over and took hold of the rifle. He asked, "Would you like to trade for another bullet?"

Austin didn't respond. Why wouldn't the elephant just die?

"For a finger," The General said, "You may shoot it again. I'll even let you select the finger."

"Die," Austin said to the elephant. "Die."

"A bullet?" The General asked again.

Austin was very suddenly being forced to put a tangible and high price on a principle he hadn't even known he had. Something about that elephant seemed more sentient than beast, more human than The General. He said, "No."

Very amused by the game, The General laughed.

Austin handed the rifle back, and without consciously choosing to do so, he balled his precious fingers into his palms and pushed his hands into his pockets.

The two men with the machetes stepped up beside the elephant's head and started hacking. The elephant screeched and sprayed blood as the blades slashed into its face.

Chapter 66

The order in the world's endless scatter of arbitrary people, places, and businesses was impossible to discern without the aid of a cell phone. Salim had grown up in the cell phone generation. Any question he had could be answered with a query to the device. It was the conduit through which the world's complexity unfolded in near instant response to his wishes. Without it, tasks once trivial became difficult.

Finding an attorney was among the first of his problems.

Having taken fingertip access to information for granted all his life, it never occurred to Salim to plan the next step during his single-minded effort to get himself out of the hospital. Unfortunately, as he walked hurriedly down the street that night, away from the hospital and the volatile mob surrounding it, he realized he had no place to sleep. He didn't know where the nearest hotel was. He didn't know how much of his meager cash he'd be required to pay for a room.

Worse still, he was clueless on how to find an attorney with the experience and desire to take his case. Indeed, aside from walking down randomly selected streets and reading signs, he had no idea where he was going.

All access he had to telephones and computers—though he had no official access to those—lay in the hospital. Getting out was one thing. Getting back in, even if he became desperate enough to try, would likely be impossible. Doctors, nurses, and the dying were allowed entry, no others.

With no other options, Salim spent the remainder of the night walking down major thoroughfares, reading signs. Another drawback of having no cell phone was that Salim had no place to type in a note to remind him of the locations of the offices he did come across. He had no paper or pencil. After all, who thinks to carry such things these days? All he had was his memory.

After spending the balance of the night searching for lawyers' offices, and then spending the morning and the early part of the afternoon hiking from one office to another, suffering one dismissive rejection by one receptionist after another, Salim finally found himself sitting in an office half-filled with overflowing file folders reeking of old cigar smoke.

Bill Buchanan looked at Salim with two emotionless blue fish eyes, set in a deflated basketball of a head. His mouth smiled in a lie so brazen it dared to be called out. Salim chose not to. He was happy to be talking to anyone with a lawyer shingle hanging on the door.

"So, this nurse, Alison no-last-name, who you think works for the police," Buchanan made a vague waving motion into the air, "or maybe the FBI, told you that information about the source of the virus would help them find a cure."

"Yes," Salim nodded quickly. "Yes, that's exactly right."

Buchanan rolled back in his leather chair. Its oaken frame creaked so painfully under Buchanan's weight, Salim thought it might collapse. Buchanan reached into a desk drawer and took out a disturbingly phallic cigar. He snipped the tip off the cigar with a brutal little flair. Grasping a decorative, metallic brick of a lighter from his desk, Buchanan leaned back in his squealing chair and torched the big cigar. His fish eyes twinkled through a fat puff of smoke as it rose toward the stained ceiling.

Through the pointless cigar show, Salim silently kept his patience.

Buchanan said, "You didn't tell the police anything about where you were, because you were in a camp in Pakistan." Buchanan looked down at Salim. "Pakistan, right?"

"Yes."

"Some short Napoleonic terrorist man took you to a village in Africa, in some town called Kapchorwa, and infected you with Ebola. He then put you on a plane and bounced you around a dozen airports before you got sick in Dallas and wound up in the hospital—a hospital that has everybody in Dallas scared shitless, because people go in there to die." Buchanan put a ridiculous emphasis on the word *die*, so much emphasis that it made Salim feel guilty for not having lost his life there.

"You don't want to get arrested for terrorism. And, I might add, if the people of Dallas thought you brought Ebola here, they might take you out and hang you." Buchanan grinned at that. "Because you don't want to get arrested, you keep mum about the whole trip overseas, even though the police and the FBI have your passport and have seen you've been to Pakistan and Nairobi, and wherever else you claim to have been."

Buchanan puffed an obnoxious cloud of smoke, somewhat at the ceiling, but mostly at Salim. "You think if you tell them anything—the police I mean—they'll haul you off to Guantanamo, and you'll never be heard from again. You think if you get a lawyer first, a lawyer like me, then you'll be able to parlay your knowledge into a deal to get you amnesty. What's more, you want me to take on a job that will likely consume all of my waking hours for the next two years, assuming you're telling the truth. You don't have one shred of identification to prove who you are. I haven't seen one single story in the news to corroborate that you are the guy who passed out at the Dallas airport. It could have been anybody, based on what was reported. Oh, and the best part: you don't have one red cent to pay me for my trouble. Is that about right?"

"Yes," Salim answered. "I mean, no. I mean, not now. I don't have any money." Salim saw that he was losing Buchanan, and given his luck at even finding someone who would take the time to listen, he figured he'd better play all his cards. "I don't know how any of this stuff works, but I may be able to sell my story to Hollywood if you can keep me out of jail—kind of an insider's view of the world of terrorism. I think it has potential. If we can make that happen—"

"We?" Buchanan asked.

"Yes." Salim nodded vigorously, thinking he was somehow agreeing to a partnership. "Yes, if we can make that happen, the fees you earn from—I don't know—being my lawyer through all of that will be significant. That can pay for the services of defending me." There it was. Salim had told Buchanan everything. He slumped back in his chair and waited, while Buchanan filled more of the air around him with pungent smoke.

"Here's what I don't understand, Salim." Buchanan leaned forward and his rolls flowed over his side of the desk, the chair cried out under the shift. "I don't understand why you're not in Guantanamo already." Buchanan drilled Salim with his stare.

"I...I...don't know."

"Because if you came into this country infected with Ebola, and had a Pakistani stamp on your passport with no credible story about where you've been for the last several months, I think the CIA would have your ass slung up in a dog collar somewhere, while some big fellows beat the truth out of you. That's what I think."

Salim shook his head as he looked for a rebuttal.

"I think you're lying to me. I think you're some Mexican kid—"

"Mexican?" Salim couldn't believe it.

Buchanan bellowed right over Salim. "—probably a gang banger who sees this tragedy on the news, and thinks he can capitalize on the suffering with some kind of Hollywood movie deal, and all you need to do is stick to a story. You just need to be a good liar. That's what I think. So why don't you get the hell out of my office, before I come around this desk and kick your skinny little ass out myself?"

Salim was reeling. He thought Buchanan was going to help him. "But—"

"Go!" Buchanan shouted. "Git!"

Chapter 67

Olivia looked through the series of photos taken by the drone for the Battle Damage Assessment. The buildings were crumbled and blackened. Bodies were still strewn. The compound was remote, so it was not surprising that no one had come to investigate or bury the dead. Of course, with Ebola everywhere, who would?

The three ships that had been anchored just offshore were out of commission. One had sunk, and Olivia saw the outline of its broken form beneath the clear water. One, she guessed, was beneath a cloud of oil that flowed down current. The beautiful white yacht had run aground next to the pier, and was listing far to starboard. Its superstructure was burned to the metal framework, and it looked like a hull full of twisted, black, modern sculptures.

Her cell phone buzzed, as she glanced at it sitting next to her mouse pad. Bringing personal cell phones into the building was explicitly forbidden, but with Eric out, the building staff thinning by the day, and every other thing going on in the world, Olivia had a bad case of I-don't-give-a-shit where that rule was concerned.

She picked up the phone. "Social or business?"

"What's the difference?" Mathew laughed. "Seems like all we ever talk about is Ebola."

Olivia chuckled. "Sorry about that."

"How's your dad doing?"

"He'll live."

"Did he really infect himself?" Wheeler asked. "I'm not judging. From a purely statistical perspective, it's not a bad idea."

"I honestly don't even know if its true," she said. "You

know how the media is. But he won't talk to me about it so I can't ask."

"Olivia, don't worry about any of that. Just be thankful knowing that he's got his antibodies now. He won't get sick again. As bad as the rest is, that's an enviable silver lining."

"Can we talk about something else?"

"The NFL cancelled the season, so we can't talk about football."

Shocked, Olivia said, "I didn't hear about that."

"It had to be done. The commissioner just announced it. There's talk of a national ban on assembly but people are in an uproar over that. They may have to word the ban differently, or just be more specific, like closing theaters and malls, shutting down the bus lines and passenger trains, that sort of thing. Otherwise, it's an attack on our constitutional rights. Anyway, I got your message and just now had time to call back."

Olivia told Wheeler about her conversation with Mitch.

"I didn't suspect it was that bad in Nairobi," said Wheeler.

"If you graph out the daily case counts in Dallas," said Olivia, "the graph goes parabolic, and it's headed in the direction of Nairobi."

"I can believe it," said Wheeler. "Dallas announced ten thousand cases yesterday, and this morning they're already over twelve. At least things in Atlanta seemed to have slowed a bit."

"Still under ten?" Olivia asked.

"Yes, but the number of dead is—" Wheeler couldn't find the right words for a moment. "We've got twenty-one hundred dead in Atlanta so far. Those are appalling numbers, but every day, when the mayor announces the numbers, he announces the total case count as well as the number of dead. Two thousand deaths over a little less than ten thousand cases seems to imply a mortality rate of twenty or twenty-five percent."

"But that's not right," Olivia observed.

"Exactly. Eighty-four percent of our cases in Atlanta were reported in the past seven days."

"Parabolic," Olivia confirmed.

"If you look at the mortality rate of cases over seven days old, it's nearly ninety percent."

"Nine out of ten are dying?"

"So far," Wheeler confirmed. "That's with the best medical care we have to offer. It will get worse. We have people who reported over seven days ago and are still sick. I honestly don't know where the mortality rate will peak."

"And when we run out of drugs to treat the symptoms?" Olivia asked.

"It'll get worse."

"Is there anything that can be done?"

"Prevention," said Wheeler. "The President is going to give a speech tonight and go through a series of recommendations. Everybody in the country needs to protect themselves. They need to avoid physical contact. They need to keep their distance. They need to wear masks and gloves."

"Do you think it will help?"

"Yes," said Wheeler. "I just hope we're not too late."

"What about treatments?" Olivia asked. "Any headway there?"

"We're testing treatments with the blood serum of survivors, transfusing it into the newly infected. Preliminary results look promising."

"At least that's something."

"It's full of risk, but if it saves lives—" Mathew sighed. "Hey, I've got to go. A ton of stuff going on over here today. Thanks for the Nairobi info. Can I talk to your contact there?"

"I need to get back with you on that one, okay?"

"Okay. Gotta go."

"Okay. Bye."

Going back to the Battle Damage Assessment, Olivia came across a casualty page with a number of definite casualties, and a number of probable casualties based on estimates of occupants in the buildings and inside the ships. The number that got her attention though was the number known to have survived, thirteen. One of the photos taken just after the explosions showed thirteen of the black bodies outlined on the ground, each with an orange circle. In a photo taken the next day, those orange circles remained but the bodies were missing. All of the other bodies were unmoved.

Chapter 68

Salim looked at the route information on the laminated card attached to the post that held the roof over the bus stop bench. The bus was supposed to run every thirteen minutes, or so the sign said. Salim had no watch, and of course, no cell phone, so no way to know how much time had passed. It seemed like an hour. He looked up and down the street for the tenth time. No bus was coming. It didn't matter. He had no idea where he was going, but he had plenty of time to get there.

He dropped back down on the bench. He thought about the hospital. He wished he'd been bolder as he'd rummaged through the discarded clothes, wished he'd taken a few credit cards, or a cell phone. He looked both ways down the street again. He wished he'd taken a watch. All he had was the cash he'd found—stolen—and the ill-fitting clothes. He wanted to get a hotel room, get into a bed, draw the blankets up over his head, and hide from his problems. His limited pocket of cash wouldn't last long when paying hotel rent. He was smart enough to know that.

Having mined his imagination for all the options he could conceive, having come to the end of his hope, he surrendered the last of his pride. He needed to call his father, admit his mistakes, and ask forgiveness. He tried to resurrect an old habit with a reach into a pocket for a cell phone that wasn't there. He cursed. He stomped away from the bus stop, looking for a pay phone. He saw none. Had modern technology stolen all of those too?

Salim walked down another street and passed business after business, looking for a pay phone that just wasn't there. He got desperate, walked into a convenience store and asked to borrow the telephone, but was told to go away. He went into a dry cleaner and begged, even showing them his money, but was shooed away by two Asian women with distrustful eyes.

He just needed to call his dad. Why couldn't these people be a little more compassionate?

Chapter 69

Olivia answered her phone when she saw who was calling. "Hello?"

"Olivia?" Mitch responded.

"Yes."

"I'm in Kapchorwa, and there's nobody here."

Olivia feared the possibility, but had held onto hope for better news. "What about Austin?"

"I can't say," said Mitch. "We originally found him out behind the hospital, near a pile of burned corpses. He's not there now, but I wouldn't have expected him to be. A couple of doctors were with him when I left and a company of Ugandan soldiers was in town. The hospital looks like it's been cleaned out."

"So there's nobody? Nobody around to tell you what happened?" Olivia asked.

"I've searched the town, I went to some of the nearby farms. I haven't seen a soul."

Olivia sighed as she tried to think of a next step.

"I'm sorry," said Mitch. "I was hoping we'd find him here."

"That's okay. We don't know he's dead. I can still have hope. What happens now?"

"I haven't planned past Kapchorwa," said Mitch. "Besides, it's dark here. I'll spend the night in the hospital, if the monkeys will leave me alone. Any luck yet on finding a way for me to get home? Not that I'm pressuring you."

"Nothing yet. It's more difficult than I thought. I didn't expect to find much in the way of planes or ships, but it seems nothing at all is moving. How did you get across the border into Uganda?"

"I drove. Nobody was watching the crossing. The soldiers on both sides either went home—or hell, maybe they died. Things are bad here."

"How are you keeping your phone charged?"

"That's classified."

"Oh, sorry."

Mitch added playfully to break the tension. "Just kidding. Solar charger."

Olivia actually laughed. "Thanks for that. It seems like I never even smile anymore."

"You know, if you can't find me a way home, I may stay here until everything blows over. You wouldn't believe how beautiful it is here."

"Austin sent me pictures. I'd love to visit one day."

"You can crash at my place. I've got a whole town to myself, you know."

Olivia laughed again. "I need to ask you another favor."

"Another favor? Didn't I just drive to another country for you?" Mitch chuckled to let her know he was still kidding. "Sure."

"I have a friend at the CDC, Dr. Mathew Wheeler. I told him about your observations in Nairobi. I think it would be helpful if you could talk to him directly. As bad as things are, nobody over here seems to have any idea where this is going."

"I don't want to have to sell some doctor on—"

"No," Olivia interrupted, "it's not like that. He's open-minded and smart. We're not getting any information out of East Africa now, and I think if he could pass along what you have to say, maybe we can take some preventive measures over here that will help. Everybody over here is scared, but based on what you told me, I'm think maybe we're not scared enough."

"Sure. Just give him my number.

"There's one other thing I need to tell you."

"What's that?"

"I told you Najid Almasi's compound got bombed, and that he was probably dead."

"Yeah?"

"He might still be alive."

Chapter 70

The morning sweltered in humidity. It was the third day after the elephant slaughter. Storms thundered over the mountain and down the western slope of Mt. Elgon. The rain didn't come to cool the southern slope. The weather brought only sticky air, biting flies, and the stink of overflowing sewer pits behind the hostage hut.

Most of the rebels left the camp early and headed down the mountain. With a quiet camp, Austin sat against the outside wall of the hut, waiting to be told what to do. Through the boredom of doing nothing, the sound of a truck in need of a muffler rumbled out of nothingness and slowly grew louder over the span of an hour or so. It seemed to be coming up the side of the mountain on rugged switchbacks, until unexpectedly, the noise of the engine stopped and brought an end to the most interesting thing to happen since they returned from the elephant hunt.

Sander and Wei were in the main pavilion preparing a midday meal. Usually, it was Min and Wei who prepared the meals, but with everyone out of camp, Min had successfully lobbied a guard to allow him to stay on nurse duty. He knelt inside the hut, holding Tian's hand and dabbing his skin with a wet cloth, trying to control a fever that wouldn't abate. Ominously, Tian had found silence, and no longer interrupted anyone's sleep with his pained sobs. His eyes hadn't opened in days. Nobody said it aloud, but the looks on the other hostages' faces told Austin that they all expected him to die.

Austin wondered if that was to be his fate, as well.

The man The General had sent to Kampala the day after Austin had been kidnapped never returned. Others sent since were likewise not heard from again. The General was worried and the worry carried down in the form of tense nerves to every rebel in the camp.

Austin wondered if it was time to take his chances and escape into the forest. He'd been in the camp for maybe a month. He was wiry, and without any body fat to slow him down. He felt strong, but knew his strength wouldn't last. There had to be a time, a specific day, when his recovery from Ebola and the loss of his body fat would leave him in the best physical condition he could achieve, before the debilitating effects of the starvation diet hit. A window of opportunity would open during which he could run and have a hope of escaping. Once it closed, he'd be at The General's mercy.

Austin put those thoughts aside when The General and two score of his men emerged from the forest on the other side of the camp, hurrying and smiling. Something good had happened.

"Ransom," The General called, pointing at Austin.

Austin jumped to his feet. He'd learned that immediate obedience was the least painful of choices he could make.

The General pointed over at the pavilion and said, "Fetch those two and come."

Austin jogged across the compound, looking back over his shoulder. The General and his men angled off toward another hut—the only other one in camp that was continually guarded. On the day they arrived back in camp after the elephant slaughter, the tusks had been stored in that hut, but had been put inside by the rebels themselves, leaving Austin curious as to what other valuables might be stored there.

As Austin neared the pavilion, he said, "Hey Sander, The General wants us."

"You and me?" Sander asked.

Austin pointed at Wei. "Him, too."

Sander said something. Wei muttered a few angry syllables, threw his utensils on the table, and stomped out from under the pavilion. Austin waved for them to follow, and jogged back across the camp to where The General was standing at the door of the hut that held his hoard of valuables.

As they neared, rebels started coming out of the hut, each with an elephant tusk over his shoulder.

The General said, "Inside, get a tusk and follow."

Austin was the first one in and stopped, appalled, as he counted. Twenty-two elephants had been slaughtered to support The General's cause. Worse still was that most of the tusks were small, hardly tall enough to reach from the ground up to Austin's knee. Austin picked up a pair of the smaller ones and stepped out of the hut, resisting the urge to club The General to death with his prize.

The General, near giddy as he saw his ivory booty hauled out into the sun, didn't see the hate in Austin's eyes as he joined the line of men heading down the mountain.

Chapter 71

They had carried the ivory for a mile when they came out of the forest onto a trail wide enough for a vehicle to pass. Up the road, under the eyes of eight of The General's rebels, a mud-caked white truck sat. Five African men stood behind the empty bed of the truck—three of them armed— their rifles pointed at the dirt. The other two men each wore pistols in holsters, but didn't have the look of fighters. They were both thick around the middle, with soft faces, and eyes that didn't linger for more than a moment.

One of the soft-faced men called a greeting and both of them smiled. Their gunmen wore expressionless faces and cautiously watched The General's men, as if they might be a threat.

The General said something in Swahili, the lingua franca of East Africa. Austin knew it by its sound, but understood only a few words.

Botu, The General's second in command ordered that the tusks be piled in the bed of the truck. Austin followed the line and stacked his tusks among the others. Not knowing what to do next, he meandered a short distance back down the road and stopped beside Sander and Wei. In a low voice, Austin asked, "What's going on?"

Shaking his head, Sander said, "I don't understand all of it. They're switching between Swahili and Bantu."

Wei harrumphed, turned, and walked into the woods, headed back to camp.

Sander said, "That's The General's man from Burundi. He has word on Tian."

At last, a ransom was going to be paid. Austin felt a tinge of hope for his own situation. "Aren't the three

Chinese together?"

"Yes, but Tian is more important than the other two. Min and Wei are just grunts, as far as I know. Maybe the company won't pay for them."

The man from Burundi passed a pouch to The General.

"What's that?" Austin asked.

"Payment," answered Sander. "Looks like Tian is leaving. Just in time for him, I'd say."

More talk followed. The General and his man from Nairobi started to raise their voices. They gestured.

Austin needed no interpretation. "What are they pissed about?"

Shaking his head, Sander said, "Not sure. I think it's about the price on the ivory. It's not what they agreed."

Austin shrank a few steps back toward the trees. Sander did the same. Neither wanted to be too far from cover if tempers led to bullets.

"Something about Ebola," said Sander. "The market for ivory is drying up."

"A lot, I guess," Austin observed. "The General looks really pissed."

More yelling followed. Then came a sudden stop. All of the gunmen were tense. The General turned to his men and yelled an order. His soldiers immediately started unloading the truck. The merchant protested weakly. The General dismissed him.

Sander said, "This is us." He got into the line forming up at the back of the truck. Austin followed.

When Sander and Austin passed by The General, he shouted, "Where is the China man?"

Sander pointed back up the mountain.

The General cursed and jammed a finger into Sander's chest. "You and Ransom will carry his tusks back to the camp."

Sander nodded.

Austin nodded, wondering how he was going to manage two small tusks and more. But that only lasted a moment.

Botu pushed Sander and Austin to the front of the line and said something to the man in the back of the truck passing out the tusks. The man laughed, found one of the largest tusks in the pile and handed it to Austin. Austin took the tusk and laid its curved hundred pounds over his shoulder. He looked at the trees and the slope. It would be a long hike with the burden.

Botu shouted an order and roughly turned Austin so that his empty shoulder was facing the truck. The man in the truck bed laid another tusk of a similar size across Austin's shoulder and Austin swayed.

"Go," Botu ordered.

Chapter 72

With two guards on their heels, Austin and Sander bore their burdens up the mountain with the greatest of effort, stopping every fifty feet or so to lean against a tree and catch their breath. Laying the tusks down for a rest wasn't an option they were afforded.

When they finally entered the camp, it was immediately obvious that tempers were escalating. The General was yelling. Botu was cursing. The men were huddling around the camp's center, near the log where Tian's foot had been hacked off.

The guards urged Austin and Sander over to the hut that contained The General's collection of tusks. As they passed the hostage hut, Austin saw Wei squatting by the entrance, his hand pressed to a wound on his head. He had new bruises on his face and blood dripped from his mouth. Tian was dead. His body had been dragged out of the hut and was laying face down in the dirt

Austin whispered, "What happened?"

The guard behind shoved. "Move."

Covered in sweat, trying to breathe enough air to continue, Austin hurried toward the hoard hut and nearly fell through the door. He crashed into the pile of tusks and let his heavy pair fall from his shoulders. The guard behind him shouted something angry, picking up on the mood in the camp. He hit Austin twice in the back with the butt of the AK-47, and bent over to inspect the tusks that Austin dropped.

"They're fine," said Austin, pointing at the tusks, hoping he would see no chips, no cracks.

The guard glared at him.

Eyes down, Austin retreated from the hut and let Sander drop his load.

A guard pointed at the hostage hut and said, "Go."

Austin needed no further encouragement. Worn out from the hike up the mountain, but light on his feet without his burden, he hurried over to the hut, stepped over Tian, and sat down beside Wei.

A moment later, Sander squatted down beside Austin.

"What's happening?" Austin asked.

Sander spoke to Wei in Swahili. Wei, in an unusual gush of words, pointed at the mass of rebels gathering at the center of camp. He came to a sudden stop and put his head back in his hands.

"What?" Austin asked.

Sander's face grew long with worry. "When The General came up to fetch Tian, he walked into the hut and saw Min kissing him."

Through his surprise, all Austin could say was, "What?"

Nodding, Sander said, "On the lips."

"Tian died while we were on our errand. Min was saying his goodbyes."

Austin pointed at the rebel mob responding to The General's exhortations with raucous howls and jeers. "What's this, then?"

"The General hates homosexuals."

Sander and Austin stopped talking and watched.

A moment later, The General burst out of the mob, his men flowing behind him. In one hand, he held a bloody machete. In the other, he held Min's head, still running blood from the severed neck.

Austin flinched back when The General ran up in front

of him and the other two hostages. He pushed Min's face up against Austin's face, dripping blood down on Austin's clothes. He mashed Min's face into Sanders' face and did the same to Wei. When he'd made that point, he stood tall and yelled, "If you weak women want to lie with a man, then you will lie with Min!" He dropped the head in the mud in front of Austin and turned away.

Chapter 73

Hadi knelt beside Najid's bed. "Every day you get worse."

Najid knew Hadi was right. He didn't want to accept it, because he had no plan to handle it. Dr. Kassis was killed when the Americans bombed the compound. The two doctors he'd hired as assistants to Dr. Kassis, though Najid thought of them as backup number one and backup two, were both on the yacht when it got hit. They were dead. Now Najid had no doctors.

"I have contacted my wife's cousin in Dubai. His compound is as much a fortress as this place, but America will not bomb Dubai, especially since they believe you are dead."

"Are you certain of that?" Najid asked.

"On both counts," Hadi nodded.

"This cousin has a doctor?"

"More than that," Hadi said, "a few doctors and enough equipment for a small hospital. There is nothing you need that can't be done there."

"Surgery on my leg?"

"Without a doubt."

"What does this cousin want?" asked Najid.

"You and I may go. No one else."

Najid didn't like that option, but he accepted with a nod.

"We must both be tested prior to entering the compound."

"For Ebola?" Najid asked.

"Yes."

Najid nodded again. "What else?"

"Ten kilograms."

"Of gold?"

"Yes."

"How will we get to Dubai?"

"It may cost us a few more kilos, but I believe I can arrange it."

Najid thought about the injuries to his leg, felt the pain of the infection, and the fever that had followed. If he didn't get medical help, he would die and the pile of gold in his bunker and in the hold of the burned out yacht would be of no use to him. "Promise what you must. Make this happen."

Chapter 74

Salim woke to the rhythmic thump of cars crossing the expansion joints of the four-lane highway overpass. He'd fallen asleep the night before on a concrete embankment beneath the bridge, near some other people doing the same.

He sat up feeling alone, feeling abandoned in a country he'd chosen to turn his back on, a country that didn't seem to give a care about anything he'd done or who he was. The country had bigger problems than irrelevant Salim Pitafi.

His stomach growled and he reached into his pocket to pull out his cash and coins. He laid the coins carefully on the sloping concrete lest they roll away — he almost laughed at the irony of it. He had a jar on his dresser at home where he dumped coins from his pocket so he wouldn't be burdened with the inconvenience of their jingle in his pocket, not to mention the potential of their little milled edges scratching his cell phone. That beloved piece of technology had been the hub of his high school social life, and in the years since, the hub of everything.

Salim gulped back a piteous sob and resolved not to lose his composure, or lose himself in nostalgia less than three months old. He'd put himself in this predicament. He was taking hard steps to resolve it.

Two dollars and thirty-seven cents in coins. Now the formerly disposable annoyances would pay for a microwavable burrito, or a couple of donuts at the truck stop that sat on a corner adjacent to the overpass.

He counted through his bills. One hundred and eleven dollars. He guessed he could eat on maybe ten dollars a day, less if he were careful. McDonald's had a dollar menu. One double cheeseburger and a refillable dollar soda would be an easy path to stuffing himself for two bucks. Two such meals a day might be enough to keep him going. Hell, if he drank enough soda he might put on weight for four dollars a day.

As dire as his meager bankroll seemed, and as poor as his sleeping accommodations felt, at least starvation wasn't yet an issue. His immediate problems were transportation and communication.

Salim looked at the truck stop again as his stomach growled. The truck stop might have showers for the truckers. Salim looked down at his clothes and sniffed himself to determine whether he stank.

"You don't smell any worse than the rest of us."

Salim turned toward the voice.

A boy sat up next to a sleeping girl, both about his age. Both had backpacks. They didn't look homeless, more like hikers who'd wandered out of the forest. Salim smiled. "I was thinking about getting a shower."

"They charge five dollars for a shower and they only give you ten minutes of water."

"Five dollars for ten minutes?" It was a lot of money to pay, given the state of his assets.

"Yup." The guy crab-crawled across the sloping concrete between them and extended a hand to shake. "I'm Victor."

Salim took Victor's hand and shook it. "Salim Pitafi."

"You on the road?" Victor asked.

Salim shrugged. "I'm not sure what you mean."

"Traveling somewhere?" He looked at the heavy concrete bridge beams overhead. "Nowhere to sleep?"

"Yeah, I guess," Salim said. "I want to get home to Denver."

Victor gestured at Salim's blue duffle bag. Not the kind someone would normally use for travel. It seemed better suited for hauling sweaty shorts to and from the gym. "You don't look like you planned to get there on foot."

"No," Salim said, wondering how much to say. "I flew in before the airports closed down."

"The bus lines shut down, too," said Victor.

"Ugh," said Salim. He hadn't even thought to take a bus to Denver. Now it didn't matter. "When?" he asked.

"A few days ago."

"What about Amtrak?" Salim asked. "Did they shut down the trains, too?"

Victor nodded and pointed at the dozens of people under the bridge.

Salim looked around. Most of them weren't there when he fell asleep.

"Lots of us got stranded."

Laughing, because it seemed better than letting any other emotion win out, Salim said, "So, what are people doing? Living under bridges? Walking home?"

"Yeah, kind of," said Victor. "But there's another way."

"What's that?"

"The truckers."

"What do you mean?"

"Some of them will let you ride in their trailers when they're empty."

Salim perked up and looked at the truck stop, surveying the dozens of tractor-trailers parked behind it. "No kidding?"

"That's why most of us are here," said Victor. "Me and Janet rolled in last night. We're on our way from Montgomery to Phoenix. The guy who dropped us here is heading north to Oklahoma City. We're going to see if we can get a ride west."

"What?" Salim asked. "You just go hang around the truck stop and ask truckers for a ride?"

Victor laughed. "Yeah, pretty much. Turns out most of them are pretty good folks. When the airports and bus lines shut down, I guess some of them decided to step up and help folks out. Lots of them do it now."

Feeling hopeful, Salim looked back at the truck stop. "Thank you, Victor. Thank you very much."

Chapter 75

It was the third time they'd driven by the house that day, and Larry's impatience was coming to the surface. "They're still out there."

"It's okay," Jimmy told him as he drove the pickup past the last news van still parked on the street. "I bet it'll be gone soon."

Fuming, Larry said, "I bet Paul Cooper's not even in there. Nobody's seen him for a week."

Jimmy laughed. "Of course he's in there. People have been out here since he came home. On Channel Seven, they have a Paul Cooper update on the ten o'clock news every night. It's like our own stakeout service. Everybody's wondering when he's gonna come out. People are placing bets on it."

"I can't wait forever on this deal," said Larry. "We've been talking about this for weeks."

"And working," said Jimmy. "The profitable jobs take time. You know that."

"I suppose."

Jimmy reached over and patted Larry on the shoulder. "We're almost there."

Larry pursed his lips, and said, "I got rent dude. The landlord is being a dick."

"Nothing new," said Jimmy. "Just tell him to wait another week or so."

"And if we don't have the money?"

"We will."

"How do you know?"

Jimmy pulled the truck to the curb and put it in park.

"While you've been sitting in your apartment, getting drunk and watching TV every day, I've been busy."

"On what?" Larry asked.

"I contacted some of the people who got family members that tested positive for Ebola."

"And?" Larry asked.

"Not everybody's getting treated, not now, too many people are sick." Jimmy enjoyed a smug moment. He'd called it just right. "There's a drug shortage, just like I said there'd be. People are desperate, and they're willing to pay. I told 'em that I was an Ebola survivor and I'd sell them a pint of my blood."

"What'd they say?"

"They asked questions about blood type, and stuff like that," said Jimmy. "They wanted to know how I could guarantee the Ebola antibodies were in the blood. Right off, they didn't believe it was my blood. They knew they were dealing in black market blood."

Larry nodded. "Nobody's honest anymore."

"That's the way the world works," said Jimmy. "I just told 'em, 'buy it or don't.' It doesn't matter to me. I got plenty of people that will, if they don't. One guy said he knew of a way to do a test, and suggested that if I could test the blood and prove it's safe, I could get a lot more money for it."

"Why'd he tell you that?" Larry asked. "Did he want to pay more for the blood?"

"No," answered Jimmy. "He said I should give him a free pint for the idea."

"Fuck him," said Larry.

Jimmy shrugged. "We'll think about it."

Larry looked back down the street at the group in front

of Paul Cooper's townhouse. "If you've got customers already lined up, we need to get some product to sell them. Your customers won't be waiting around too long, if you know what I mean."

Jimmy turned around in his seat. "As soon as that last news van leaves, I've got a way to get us into the house. I just don't want to go up to the door if somebody is videoing us."

"Go up to the front door?" Larry asked, shaking his head at the obvious stupidity of the idea. "Why would we do that?"

Jimmy leaned into the pickup's backseat, grabbed a paper grocery bag, and set it in Larry's lap.

Larry opened the bag and looked inside. "What the—" He grinned. "I know what you're thinking. This will work."

Chapter 76

The blinds on all the windows were closed, even those upstairs. Due to the neighborhood's hilly terrain, every window in the townhouse was viewable from somewhere. Worse yet, what seemed like a good idea at purchase time, getting a townhouse at the end of the building at the edge of the complex, with more exterior windows and even views across a four-lane road to see the mountains, turned out to be a bad idea. Any car driving on the road passed — it turned out — within easy rock-throwing distance of Paul's house. Most of the rocks hit the branches of the spruce trees or were deflected by the bushes. Many hit the brick wall with a thud inside that made Heidi jump. Enough found their mark that three of the eight windows that faced the road were cracked, and another was shattered, now boarded over from the inside. Paul didn't dare go outside and climb a ladder on that side of the house.

Heidi complained that the place now felt like a cave. Paul felt guilt over it but couldn't argue.

Neither he nor Heidi had been outside since his early ejection from the hospital's isolation ward a week earlier — the hospital needed the space for the tsunami of new Ebola patients. Under a cloud of implicit threats from the Dallas police, the Douglas County Sheriff, the Colorado State Patrol, the FBI, the Texas Department of Public Safety, and other government officials (Paul couldn't remember them all), he'd returned home through a gauntlet of media types lingering on the sidewalk in front of his townhouse and hiding in the bushes at the end of the alley beside his garage. One had even snuck inside while the garage door was coming down, and was incensed that Paul wouldn't grant him an interview right then and there. Paul had agreed, with a few nods and grunts. The gestures were a feint to buy time to get out of the car and get his hands on a heavy-bladed snow shovel. The interview ended when the reporter dodged Paul's swing and ran out of the garage.

A week into his homebound exile, the photo of Paul's angry face and the swinging snow shovel was on television again. The off-camera reporter was talking about Denver hitting a milestone of twelve thousand cases. The news never distinguished between confirmed and suspected cases anymore. Everybody who seemed like they might have it did. The reporter went on to talk about the three weeks since Paul Cooper called 9-1-1 to become the first case in a previously Ebola-free Denver, the implication being that Paul Cooper was the Typhoid Mary seed that grew into Denver's epidemic.

"No! No, I'm not!" Paul yelled at the television. "It's everywhere, dammit!"

Heidi came from the kitchen with two bowls of rice mixed with stir-fry vegetables and chicken. She handed a bowl to Paul and said, "You shouldn't watch that."

"This isn't my fault," Paul answered, as he grimaced at his bowl.

"You bought the rice," Heidi told him.

Paul looked up from the bowl and saw Heidi trying to smile. He said, "I was talking about Ebola."

"I know," she said, smiling again. "But you *did* buy the rice."

"I hate it already," said Paul.

"Not as much as you're going to," said Heidi. "That's the last of the chicken, and we don't have any more fresh vegetables."

Paul looked down at his bowl. He had no appetite.

"One of us should go to the store soon and get something else while there's still something to get." Heidi looked at the television. "I know I haven't said this yet, but it looks like maybe you were right about all of this from the start. I'm sorry for not believing."

Shaking his head, Paul said, "You don't think this is all my fault, do you?"

"Of course not. You know it isn't. You're still wallowing, and you shouldn't be. I know you accepted that Austin was dead, but with what Olivia told us, he might not be."

Paul tried to smile.

"How many cities are reporting outbreaks?" Heidi asked.

"Just in the US?" Paul asked.

Heidi nodded.

"I don't know. It's literally in every major city. It's in Fort Collins, Boulder, Colorado Springs. It's up in Cheyenne and out in Steamboat Springs. It's everywhere."

"Exactly," said Heidi.

Paul nodded.

Heidi pointed at the TV. "They're blaming you to put a face on their audience's fear. Because they think they can get better ratings out of it."

"Everybody hates me, Heidi."

Heidi failed at a smile. "It'll pass. I got over it." Then she did smile. She sat down and put her bowl on the coffee table. "If you keep being right about the epidemic, all of them will be dead soon, so who cares what they think?"

Paul laughed as he shook his head. "That's *so wrong*."

"I know," Heidi agreed, as she laughed too, embarrassed that she'd made such a crass joke.

Paul took a few bites of his rice, sat his bowl on the coffee table, and rubbed his hands over his face. He felt the bristle of a beard coming in, just a week old.

"I could go to the store today," said Heidi. "Stock up on whatever we can get."

Paul shook his head emphatically.

Heidi nodded toward the TV. "When I was upstairs, there was a story about people panic-buying at the grocery stores."

Paul absently said, "You can't go."

"One of us has to, Paul. And you can't."

"I have to." Paul turned toward Heidi, certain and firm. "We've been through too much to get here." He pointed at one of the shaded windows. "The thing out there we have to fear most is Ebola. Sending you out into that kind of risk isn't something we can do. I'll go. I have to go. As much as it's going to suck, until this thing blows over, you're going to be stuck here. I—" Paul smiled again, but it was just a mask for feelings of loss. He couldn't buy into the hope that Austin was alive, just to reset the grieving process. "I can't lose you, too."

Heidi got up off the couch and came over to sit on the coffee table near Paul. She took his hand in hers and leaned over to kiss him. "There are too many of them out there."

"Not that many, now," Paul said. "I think maybe only three or four reporters out front, and—you know, some protestors."

"Protestors?" Heidi laughed.

Paul laughed, too. "Yeah, I know. Protestors? I guess I've made it to the big time now."

They both laughed some more.

When they got past the humor of the situation, Paul

said, "I've got a plan to get myself out undetected."

"Is that why you're growing the beard? Why don't you just wear a disposable facemask like everybody else? You have a case of them in the basement."

"You'll need those more than me." Paul walked over to look at himself in the mirror above the fireplace. His hair was longish, thick, and brown with a bit of gray. He wore it the same way he'd worn it since forever ago. "If I use that beard trimmer under the bathroom sink—"

"If it even works anymore," Heidi cut in.

"—to cut my hair off and put on some sunglasses, I don't think I'll be recognizable."

.

Chapter 77

With a stubble of hair on his head and a goatee changing the look of his face, Paul quietly dismantled the shelves on the wall of the garage. On the other side of the shared wall lay his neighbor's garage. Inside was a Toyota Camry in that weird metallic beige—so unnatural, but at the same time effective for suburban camouflage. Barb and Bill, their retired neighbors, lived only part-time in their primary residence. They spent several months of the year traveling in their RV. While they were gone, Barb left her house keys with Heidi, so that Heidi could keep an eye on the place. It was a matter of luck that Barb's key ring also had a key to her car.

That one fact made Paul's plan palatable to Heidi. As Paul explained, since Barb had placed the key to her car in Heidi's hand, using Barb's car wasn't theft. Legally, Paul was in the clear. The same extended to the house. The only legally fuzzy part of Paul's plan was the part about how he let himself into Barb and Bill's garage.

Paul couldn't leave through his front door and go into his neighbors' adjoining townhouse. Any stragglers out front would see. The back way into both townhouses was through the garages. Paul couldn't be seen leaving his own garage, either. That left Paul one choice.

With a utility knife in hand, Paul found a sheetrock seam which had to run over a stud. About one inch to the right of the seam, Paul cut a long vertical groove. Three more cuts created a rectangle, which Paul punched a few times, knocking a five-foot tall, thirteen-inch wide section of wall out. Paul saw no insulation in the adjoining wall, just the backside of the sheetrock nailed to Barb and Bob's garage wall.   A few minutes later, Paul passed through his new makeshift doorway and slid a key into the door of Barb's Camry.

Chapter 78

Because of the layout of the buildings and the limited space along the curbs for legal parking in the Coopers' townhouse complex, nobody standing in Paul Cooper's front doorway, or looking out one of the front windows, could see a car parked in the street. Not from the first floor, anyway. That was a bit of luck that Jimmy hadn't thought about as he climbed the stairs from the sidewalk up to the front porch.

Jimmy stretched his neck and jiggled at the knot of the uncomfortable tie that felt like it was choking him; it wasn't. It was the shirt that was too tight. He checked the mask over his mouth and nose. Like everyone else, everywhere, he'd become so habituated to wearing his mask that he sometimes didn't notice it on his face, and had to check to be sure it was still there.

Larry followed Jimmy up the stairs. When they got to the door, Jimmy needed to do the talking and Larry simply needed to wear the police costume, keep a serious face, and a silent mouth. That's why Jimmy wore the suit. He needed to appear naturally in charge.

Jimmy rang the bell and stepped back so that he and Larry could stand shoulder to shoulder in clear view. If they looked like cops, no one would request their identification, let alone scrutinize them when showed. The only real concern was the cooler in Larry's hand — not large, big enough for three or four six packs and some ice, but large enough to contain their supplies. Most importantly, it was big enough to contain what they hoped to leave with: all of Paul Cooper's liquid gold blood.

Jimmy heard a sound inside the house and rang the doorbell again. A moment later, the door unlocked and opened a crack. Jimmy said, "Mrs. Cooper, I'm Detective Smith and this—" Jimmy panicked. He hadn't planned an alias for Larry. Crap. Think. "—is Officer Friday."

Heidi said nothing, but her face told Jimmy she was suspicious.

Jimmy smiled warmly, not thinking about the mask over his mouth and nose. "Sorry to bother you." He reached into his jacket and pulled out a sheath of papers he'd printed up the night before. "Is your husband, Paul Cooper, home?" Heidi's eyes followed the papers in Jimmy's hand. She looked a little bit frightened of them. That was good, exactly what Jimmy had hoped for.

Heidi said, "Paul went to the store."

"The store?" Larry asked in a tone that advertised his disbelief.

"Yes," Heidi said, offended. "He left just a little while ago."

Jimmy looked over at Larry, who was looking back at him with a question on his face. Jimmy didn't believe her, either. "How long ago?"

Tentatively, Heidi answered, "Um, maybe...? I'm not sure. A little bit. Can you come back?"

Jimmy didn't want to have to come back. In fact, if Heidi was alone, things would go much better. He and Larry could grab her, tie her up—or whatever—and ambush Paul once he returned. Divide and conquer. Oh, yeah. Jimmy congratulated himself on that phrase. He'd picked it up one night watching the History Channel when his premium channels had been disconnected.

Jimmy tried his best to sound charming, non-threatening. "Mrs. Cooper, I know this is hard. It's hard for everyone, you know. I'd rather be home right now with my wife and kids. You'd rather not have us here on the porch. We're just doing our job."

The charm seemed to be working. Heidi's attitude softened a bit. "What exactly do you need?" Heidi looked down at the papers again, then suspiciously eyed the cooler.

Jimmy lifted the papers to emphasize their authority. "It's a court order to draw a sample of Paul's blood." Jimmy pointed at the cooler. "It was the smallest one we had. For the sample, you know."

Heidi looked at the cooler still. "It looks like you bought it at Walmart. Don't they have a special cooler for that sort of thing?"

"Well, yes. No," Jimmy corrected himself. "This is unusual for us."

"And why send the police?" Heidi asked, her suspicion growing. "Why not send a medical...I don't know, a nurse or something?"

Jimmy smiled again. "The nurses are all busy with, you know...at the hospitals. They sent me because I used to be an EMT before I became a cop." That lie seemed to have worked, and Jimmy congratulated himself for it.

"May I see those papers?" Heidi asked, reaching out from behind the door.

Jimmy lowered the folded pages out of her reach. "These are for Paul Cooper, ma'am."

Heidi left her hand extended. "I'm his wife."

"Ma'am," Jimmy started.

"Then you'll have to come back next week. Paul had to travel to the hospital in Omaha. He won't be back until Thursday."

Larry's temper flared. "Ma'am. You said he went to the

grocery store."

Heidi glared at Larry defiantly. "It's not uncommon for women to lie to strangers about whether their husbands will be returning soon."

Jimmy smiled and nodded, doing his best to look defeated. He handed the papers to Heidi. Heidi accepted them without a word and immediately unfolded them and started to read. Jimmy yawned, pretending boredom and looked around for any neighbors in the streets — none — any open windows, any open blinds, any peeping neighbor eyes. None, none, none.

He gave Larry a nearly imperceptible nod and Larry understood.

Heidi flipped to the second page of the document, giving it her full attention. She said, "I don't under—"

Jimmy rushed at the door with his shoulder, flinging it open and knocking Heidi back on the floor. Larry charged in behind and jumped on top of Heidi, who struggled and screamed. Jimmy quickly pushed the door shut.

Chapter 79

The Safeway by the house was closed. It had a sign on the door promising to reopen in a few days. The Sharpie scrawl on a pink neon-colored poster board taped inside the glass went on to explain the store's woes over frightened employees after one got sick. Their stock of grocery items was low because delivery drivers were refusing to come to the store.

Paul peeked in through the windows. Shelves were mostly empty. Items were scattered. A few dented cans, mashed boxes, and torn packages lay on the floor.

He left and drove down the road to the King Sooper, where the story was much different. Paul had to wait in a line of cars on the street for a half hour before getting into the parking lot, all the while muttering to himself about the pussies at Safeway who were afraid to open their doors. At least the King Sooper managers had the good sense to keep the doors open and price gouge—he was just guessing on that point not having seen the prices yet.

Once parked, he waited in a line of widely spaced people, all suspicious, most with some kind of facial mask. All wore gloves: some latex, some rubber house cleaning gloves, some wore ski gloves—better than nothing. Not being concerned about Ebola, Paul hadn't thought to wear gloves of his own. Now he realized that was a mistake. It made him stand out, made him look like a careless danger.

Few people conversed. The grocery store itself was admitting no customers. They had a system. Armed security guards—eight or nine—patrolled around the store entrance, keeping the crowd in order, enforcing the rules. At one door, customers lined up to use unwrapped crayons to write their orders on laminated sheets of white notebook paper. At the head of the line, they dropped their crayons and the plastic-coated paper into a tub of bleach water. Store workers wearing the requisite protective gear used tongs to take sanitized order sheets out of the tub, one worker and one sheet at a time. The worker would take a basket into the store and collect the items, while the customer went to the other entrance, paying upon delivery of the order. All transactions required a credit or debit card —enter your PIN on the keypad at your own risk. A box of bleach-wipes sat beside each keypad for customers to use in sterilizing the pad prior to touching. Cash wasn't being accepted. Anybody with half a wit was afraid to touch a porous paper bill, home to who-knew-how-many viruses, collected from any number of grubby hands.

Paul stood in that line for over an hour, working his way toward the front, only to be disappointed when it was his turn.

"Write your items on the list, prioritized by which you want first," the woman draped in plastic said from her station on the other side of the bleach bath. "We pick them from the shelves in the order on the list. If we don't have something you've selected—and we're out of a lot—we'll skip to the next item. You can buy a maximum of twenty-five items or spend a maximum of fifty dollars, whichever you reach first."

Paul, his patience worn to nearly nothing by that time, swore at the woman and told her just how stupid he thought the whole system was. He started to expound. Two guards with guns drawn ejected him from the line.

Paul protested further, telling them that he had every right to stay and shop for his bullshit allotment of fifty dollars' worth of groceries and if they didn't like it, he'd just call the police. Through the harsh laughter, one of the guards told him they *were* the police, and that he should get the fuck off the property.

Chapter 80

Larry came back in from the garage, muttering and cursing. Jimmy was sitting in a dining room chair in front of Heidi, who was fuming, but unable to do anything with her anger. They'd stuffed her mouth with a mildewed dishrag from the kitchen sink, and they unwound nearly a full roll of duct tape in attaching her to another of the dining room chairs.

Jimmy called across the living room, "What's wrong?"

Larry pointed back toward the garage. "He cut a hole in the sheetrock and stole his neighbor's car."

Jimmy laughed. "You gotta give him credit for that."

"No, I don't," Larry grumbled. "We need to get this done and get out of here."

"We can be patient," Jimmy told him.

"If one of the neighbors saw what we did when we came in, the police could be on their way."

Heidi nodded emphatically.

Jimmy said, "If the police were coming, they'd be here by now."

"No, no," Larry protested. "They're shorthanded, like everybody else. Nobody wants to come to work, with the virus everywhere."

Jimmy sighed and looked at Heidi. As much as he wanted to dissuade Larry, he knew Larry could be right. "What do you suggest then? That we just leave?"

Larry was in the dining room by then, glaring down at Heidi, looking at her breasts, and at the constraints keeping her legs and arms from kicking or punching. Larry reached out and put a hand on one of Heidi's breasts. "Nice."

"Be careful," said Jimmy. "If you give yourself a hard-on

and decide to rape her, you might catch it."

Larry dropped a hand and huffed.

Jimmy laughed.

Larry grimaced, he raised a fist to punch Heidi but he hesitated, simmering while he thought about whether to proceed.

"Stop," Jimmy told him. "There's no point in that."

Larry dropped his fist to his side and started to pace. "I don't want to wait around. I'm getting a bad feeling."

"We wait, or we go," said Jimmy. "If we go, we've got to start over somewhere else, and we have to do something with her."

Heidi protested again, as much as she could, through the dishrag in her mouth.

Larry glared at Heidi.

Heidi glared back, daring him with hate in her eyes.

"She's a feisty one," said Jimmy.

"You know what I think?" Larry asked.

"Yes," answered Jimmy, hoping Larry wouldn't go on to tell him anyway.

Larry shook his head and took his eyes off of Heidi's breasts. "I think we don't need to wait for Paul Cooper. Hell, she might be telling the truth. He might not be back until next week, like she said."

"I don't know what he'd be doing in Omaha, or how he'd even get a travel pass to cross the state border, but you never know."

"I think if he came home, he gave her Ebola and she survived, because Paul gave her some of his blood."

Jimmy looked at Larry and shook his head at the stupidity of what he'd just said.

"No, I'm serious," said Larry. "Think about it. He was with her, fuckin' her and stuff, before he went to the hospital. She had to catch all of his germs. I guarantee you he did her when he got home. After being locked up in a hospital isolation room, where you don't even have the privacy to spank it, you know what he did when he got home, first thing." Larry nodded at Heidi. "She had to have caught it. And this Paul guy, he's too smart to take her to the hospital. Hell, he can't. He knows everybody hates him. I'll bet he had the same plan we did. If he was smart enough to get himself infected early, so he'd get the good drugs while they were still available, then he was smart enough to make her immune, too." Larry took a deep breath. He was finished with his theory.

Jimmy looked at Heidi, who was as flabbergasted as he felt, though for different reasons. In all the years Jimmy had known Larry, he'd never once come up with such a complex explanation. As much as Jimmy wanted to discount it out of hand, simply because Larry had spoken it, he couldn't. The more he thought about it, the more it made sense. This Paul Cooper guy was smart. They'd said so on TV. He did infect himself on purpose. Everybody knew that. He was devious, in his own way, as devious as Jimmy and Larry. Jimmy believed Larry's theory about Heidi. Why would Paul go through all the trouble to infect himself early, unless he had a plan for Heidi too?

Heidi had to be immune.

Ebola K: Book 2

Angry and empty handed, Paul exited the highway. The only good thing about his day had been the light traffic. People were skipping work. Many were hunkering down at home, praying Ebola would pass them by.

Costco was the last store Paul had the patience to shop. Their employees were decked out in whatever they thought would pass for protection. Some wore military-style gas masks, some wore surgical masks, and more than a few wore something that looked like what the paint and body guy might wear when he was spraying on a coat of lacquer. All wore gloves—thick, heavy, and designed for use in an industrial chemical plant. They'd probably come off the shelf at ten bucks a dozen.

A quarter million dollars worth of flat-screen televisions previously stacked into a tunnel through which customers entered the store in prior weeks had tumbled down to form an obstacle course. Paul pushed his basket back and forth between the TVs.

Once past the television graveyard, Paul faced the second obstacle between him and the food shelves. A grid of folding tables covered a rectangle the size of a football field in the center of the store. The tables had been stacked high with jeans, sweatshirts, t-shirts, underwear, and the like. All those neatly folded piles of clothing, organized by color, style, and size, now formed a carpet of undulating soft mounds—some waist-high—that could only be crossed on foot.

Orange, painted pallet shelving forty feet tall was visible across the clothing quagmire. Empty wooden and fiberglass pallets sat on the shelves with long sheets of torn shipping plastic draping down. Pallets hung precariously halfway off a shelf, half on. Giant cardboard boxes had been torn open, spilling their economy portion packages, family-sized plastic bins, and one-gallon glass jars. An army of the afraid —seeing starvation in their future for the first time—had attacked the store with oversized baskets and overdrawn debit cards. The store lost the battle. The stock had been massacred.

Paul worked his way to the far side of the store to search the processed, pre-packaged, HFCS-laden, no-salt-added, carrion for edible remains.

The only other customers in the store were scavengers, sorting through the trash on the floor, looking for survivors with inner packages intact, unbroken seals, food that could be purchased, taken home, and added to a hoard like the one in Paul's basement.

Paul found himself staring at a woman picking crushed granola bars out of a pile of smashed boxes, checking each individually wrapped bar and tossing away those that spilled crumbs. Paul wondered how long it would be before the next person came through that aisle and collected even the packages that were open, but still contained something. It wouldn't be today, but he knew the day would come. That would mark the beginning of humanity's most desperate times.

Paul shivered.

After more than an hour of searching, Paul drove out of the parking lot with three bottles of soy sauce, a fat jar of brilliant red maraschino cherries—what the fuck do people use those for—some severely dented cans with missing labels containing mystery vegetables, a torn, half-full bag of dog food he planned to give to one of the neighbors, and a surprise treasure, a bottle of wine.

The sun was down behind the mountains and it was

dark enough for headlights when Paul drove Barb's Camry past his townhouse on the way around to the alley entrance to the garage. He noticed no glow of light seeping past the closed blinds in his townhouse's windows. With all that was going on, it put Paul on edge. The unusual and surprising so often these days were wrappers hiding bad tidings within.

Paul pulled into Barb's garage and used the remote to close the door behind him. He took a moment to get his items transferred from Barb's car in through the hole in the wall to his garage. Once finished, Paul took the bottle of wine in one hand and held it like a club, torn between his probably-pointless fear that something was wrong inside the house, and the possibility of looking like a fool storming into the house brandishing his wine bottle club.

Paul put a hand on the garage door handle, and muttered to himself, "Don't be a fool, Paul." He took a deep breath to calm his nerves and went through. Heidi must have fallen asleep on the couch or foolishly gone stir crazy in the house with no one to talk to. It would be just like her to sneak out and go talk to one of the neighbors when Paul was out.

Paul cautiously turned the knob on the back door and let it swing into the house. He gripped the neck of his wine bottle, listened, and wished he'd brought his new AR-15 shopping with him, wished he was brandishing *that* instead of the stupidly inadequate bottle. The rifle was in the closet upstairs, exactly where it had been since he shot it that one time after purchasing it a month or so back.

Paul called, "Heidi?"

The house was quiet.

He raised his wine bottle high and reached inside the door to flip up a light switch. The porch light illuminated the courtyard and a little of the living room. Everything seemed to be in its place.

Paul entered the house, and crossed into the shadows of the kitchen, where he flipped the first switch for an interior light. All sixteen decorative bulbs in lines across the kitchen ceiling lit up the kitchen and the living room. Paul spotted feet just inside the dining room. His heart skipped. "Heidi?"

He bounded into the dining room, flipping the light switch as he entered.

Heidi was on the floor, blood on her arms and around her neck. Her eyes were wide and staring. Her mouth hung open. Her skin was hoary pale.

Paul dropped to her side, howling out. He put his fingers on her cool neck to check for a pulse he already knew wasn't there.

Chapter 82

Paul woke up on the floor of the dining room. He'd been sitting on the floor since finding her, leaning against a credenza, waiting on police who never came.

On his eleventh attempt at calling 9-1-1 the night before, he'd gotten through and had told the operator to send an ambulance, even though in the next breath, he told her his wife was dead. She'd asked a meager few questions. The words *blood* and *dead* were sufficient cause for her to tell him to go to a web address for instructions on handling the body. *Click.*

Paul was enraged, and dialed back more than a dozen times to get back through. He asked for the police to come because his wife had been murdered. *Dead?* Yes. *Blood?* Yes. Website address. *Click.*

He'd persisted into the evening, finally convincing one of the operators—a middle-aged woman with a bureaucratic, nasally voice—to lie to him about sending the police to investigate the obvious murder of his wife.

The police never came. Nobody did.

Seeing Heidi's body under the blanket he'd covered it with, Paul restarted his dialing campaign. Though he tried through the morning, he only got through to an operator twice, each time with the same result as he'd gotten the night before: the web address, a token "Sorry for your loss," *click.*

Nobody in all of Denver—not the police, not the sheriff's department, and not the highway patrol—gave a shit that Heidi had been murdered in her dining room. He'd pleaded with one operator, telling her that the government shouldn't target him just because of what he'd done. She responded by asking who he was. He told her, Paul Cooper. She asked, "*Who?*"

That's when Paul gave up and cried. The cultural infrastructure was buckling and society's veil of sanity was slipping away, exposing its uncharitable Id.

Chapter 83

They'd been following a troop of black-furred monkeys for nearly an hour, never seeing more than a few at a time. The monkeys moved through the tree branches high overhead, far enough away that neither The General, nor the three men with him, dared a shot. To shoot and miss would be to frighten the troop away. His men, with their old, worn, inaccurate AK-47s needed to be pretty close to hit a small monkey up in the trees.

Unfortunately for the monkeys, their troop had made enough chatter that it was easily heard in the camp earlier that afternoon. The General had decided on a specific craving for dinner: monkey meat.

The General and the other hunters stalked through the trees, talking in whispers and spreading out. Austin stayed near The General. It was his place, as The General's houseboy.

"Monkeys are like men," said The General in a soft voice.

Used to the conversations now, Austin asked, "How's that?"

"Monkeys fear us."

"You have guns," said Austin.

"Yes, but you oversimplify," said The General.

"How so?"

"Monkeys did not always fear men. Not the way they do now. Men would hunt in the forest and the monkeys would not flee. They might sit safe in their trees. The belligerent males might throw shit or sticks. They'd try to drive men from their territory."

"And the men shot them," Austin concluded. "Now the

smart ones run away."

"That is one way to look at it," said The General.

"What's the other way?"

"More and more men came into the forest, with better and better weapons, and killed what you would call all of the dumb monkeys. I would say they killed all the brave monkeys, all the defiant monkeys, all the strong monkeys. Now, most of the monkeys are gone, and only the weak, fearful ones remain."

Austin looked up for the flashes of shaggy white fringe on the black monkeys up ahead. He heard them. He just didn't see any, and hoped it would stay that way until it got dark or The General got bored.

The General stopped and turned to face Austin. Clearly, he had an important point to make. "That is why monkeys and men are the same."

Without looking away from the treetops, Austin said, "I'm still not seeing your point."

"Genocide," said The General.

Austin walked past The General, trying to keep roughly abreast of the hunters a dozen paces to the left and right. Wherever The General's crazy bullshit was going, Austin wasn't in the mood to hear it. "I think we're losing the monkeys."

"All the monkeys that carry the valor gene are dead," said The General. "That is genocide."

"I'm not sure that's right, but I don't know the exact definition of genocide," said Austin.

The General moved ahead of Austin again. "Man has won the war with the monkey."

Austin didn't say that he didn't agree with the concept of war with the monkeys, either.

"War with men is the same. It never ends until you kill all of your brave enemies, leaving only the weak and fearful. War cannot be won without genocide."

Austin followed in the wake of The General's dramatic silence. Long silences often followed when The General said something he thought was profound. This particular thought sounded like total craziness, so Austin figured he'd let it slide without comment.

The General wanted to discuss it further. "Tell me what you think."

Crap. Austin thought through something tactful. "What about...what about...?"

"What about Hitler?" The General interrupted. "That's what you're going to ask, isn't it? American's favorite metaphor for anything they don't like, especially given the topic of genocide."

"I was going to say, peace," said Austin. "The two sides negotiate a peace and the war ends."

"Wars are only postponed by negotiated peace."

Shaking his head, Austin said. "I don't agree."

"You don't have to." The General smiled back over his shoulder. "The facts exist, whether you agree or not."

When The General looked forward again, Austin rolled his eyes.

"History is full of examples of slaughter and victory. Did you know that King David slaughtered every person in Jericho when he took the city?"

"No." Austin didn't remember much from his Sunday school classes.

"It's true. Caesar did it to the Germanic tribes. Europeans did it to the Indians—smallpox helped a lot. Stalin did it to everybody who disagreed with him and a lot more. It is the only way to win."

Austin shrugged. He really didn't care. "Okay."

"It is why your America will lose its war with Islam. America is too weak to do that which is necessary."

"Kill all the Muslims?" Austin asked trying to keep the scorn out of his voice.

"Yes," said The General. "The Muslims want to kill Christians."

"Just the extremists," Austin argued, as he recalled his experience in Kapchorwa, trying to figure out how he'd been backed into a conversation in which he was defending Muslims. He reminded himself that the men in Kapchorwa — the men he was truly angry with — were terrorists who just happened to be Muslims.

"That's why God put me here," said The General. "I understand what must be done." The General pounded his chest with one fist. "I am strong enough to do it."

One of the other hunters signaled and pointed. Half a dozen of the Colobus monkeys were up ahead, sitting on the branches of a tree without enough leaves to conceal them. The hunters raised the AK-47s. One shot; more followed in rapid succession. Monkeys tumbled through the branches.

The General turned back to Austin. "Fetch."

Chapter 84

Sander and Austin were the only two hostages left. Two of the Chinese were dead. The third, Wei, was sent as a consolation to the company that paid the ransom for Tian. That put Austin on double duty for cooking and cleanup, as well as being The General's houseboy. Austin didn't mind. Being The General's houseboy was mostly a boring job of doing nothing. Cooking for the rebels and cleaning up after them was tiring work, but it kept him busy. It also held a secret benefit that Sander shared as the reason he'd stayed healthy during his eight-month internment. Cooking gave him the opportunity to pilfer extra food. Austin followed Sanders' example, grabbing nibbles when there were no watchful eyes around.

With the increased rations, Austin's health fully returned, and his spirit grew strong. He spent a good deal of time thinking about his ransom. No word had ever come back from Kampala. Austin worried what would happen when The General concluded that kidnapping Austin had been a waste of time, because Austin had no monetary value. Despite Sander's insistence that The General was a businessman, it didn't bother The General to beat his hostages, and he appeared to suffer no qualms about killing them.

Escape was at the center of Austin's thoughts as he watched six monkey carcasses lying across a grate of rusty metal, with the cooking fire's coals beneath. His job was to turn the monkey carcasses from time to time and to keep the fire hot enough to cook.

The process disgusted Austin, not for the fact that he was cooking skinned monkeys to be dined on by rebels; Austin had seen too much brutality for much to affect him anymore. It was when the monkey carcasses lay on the fire too long on one side, the flesh blackened on the edges and produced a pungent smell that reminded him of Kapchorwa with all of its burned human bodies. It made him nauseous.

"How are those monkeys coming?" Sander asked from under the pavilion, where he was preparing yams.

"About done," Austin answered standing from his perch on the same log where Min had lost his head and Tian his foot. With a sharp stick, he poked the wiry flesh on one of the monkey's arms and peered inside. The meat was ready. Austin lifted it off the grill with a stick and leaned the roasted carcass against the log he'd been sitting on. He checked another monkey. Its meat was still bloody and red. None of the other four monkeys was finished cooking. Austin turned the monkeys over and sat down on the log beside the one that was cooling off.

He thought about his dilemma, the beatings to come, and the brutality of The General and his men. Austin couldn't help but think he was a depreciating asset. He started to believe he was going to die and never see anything but jungle and unwashed men for the rest of his life. He grated at his captivity. His mouth sometimes said things that his brain wished it hadn't. He was sure a day would come when The General would put an end to it.

Austin stared at the fire and tried to come up with a solution that didn't involve his running through the forest, without a direction or a plan, in hopes of escaping sixty men with rifles, all of whom knew the trails and hiding places on this side of the mountain better than he ever would. They were all in fine, lean shape, looking like marathon runners with weapons. Austin had no idea how long he could elude them in the forest. It was an uncertainty that kept Austin from trying.

On the far side of the camp, two rebels came running out of the forest, yelling, alarmed, and a little frightened. Suddenly, the whole camp was scampering, weapons in hand. The General strode through the chaos. All of the rebels formed in a huddle around the two who'd just come into camp.

Austin was on his feet, looking at the huddle, and glancing back toward Sander, who'd also stopped working to watch. "What's going on?"

"Not sure."

Austin was hoping a regiment of government troops was on its way to save him, although he had no realistic expectation that it would happen.

The rebels hushed. The General spoke. Then, as suddenly as they'd all gathered, they burst into a run, disappearing into the forest. Only three rebels remained, disappointment clear in the way they frowned and sulked. Two of them started talking. The third crossed the camp toward Sander and Austin.

"Did you understand anything that was said?" Austin asked.

"I think they spotted somebody." Sander replied. "Maybe a rival faction? The army? I don't know."

"They're going out to fight them?" Austin smiled. A firefight should kill some of the rebels. It might wipe them all out. Not likely, but possible.

That *was* something to hope for.

The two guards on the far side of the camp seemed content to stay where they were. The guard who'd come toward Austin walked up to the fire and looked at the monkeys. He spotted the one leaning on the log and tore a piece of meat away. He turned and headed off to make himself comfortable at the base of a tree a short distance away. He absently watched Sander and Austin as he gnawed on his piece of monkey thigh.

Austin checked his remaining monkeys. They were ready. He removed them from the grill one at a time, and leaned each against the log, he remembered something Dr. Littlefield had said to him before he left Kapchorwa. He smiled as an evil and disgusting—but workable—inspiration came to him.

Austin was as alone as he'd been since arriving in the rebel camp. If he was going to do anything, ever, then now was his chance.

Austin glanced at the guard who was bored and staring. He looked at Sander who'd gone back to his work. He started walking toward the latrine pit that lay in the trees a short distance behind the hostage hut.

When Austin had walked just a few paces, the guard said some words that Austin didn't know but he understood. He stopped, turned to the guard, put on a pained face and put a hand to his belly. He groaned to sell the act.

The guard said a few harsh, undecipherable sentences and then laughed.

Austin looked to Sander for an interpretation.

Sander said, "Don't run away. It's too obvious if you go now. He's expecting it. Indeed, he says he hopes you run. He says you're the ugliest mzungu he's ever seen and he'd like to take a machete to you before The General returns."

Austin looked at the guard, repeated the act and said, "Thanks." To Sander, he called, "I'm not going to run." He headed for the latrine.

Once there, Austin dropped his pants and leaned on a tree. The smell was a problem but he did his best to ignore it. He looked over his shoulder. The guard hadn't followed him. The last thing he thought before he went to work conjuring up a pornographic fantasy was what Dr. Littlefield had told him about how contagious he was after he'd recovered from his fight with Ebola. The bottom line was that Austin wasn't contagious, except for one possibility: the Ebola virus might live in his semen for another few months.

Austin had a secret weapon.

Chapter 85

Getting his zipper up and his belt tightened with one hand presented a problem that Austin hadn't anticipated. At the moment, Austin only had one hand available for doing things. In his other he held a gift for The General. After some struggling with the zipper to get it partially up, he cinched his belt snug and tucked the end back inside his pants to hold it secure enough so that he could return to the kitchen pavilion.

Surprised that he'd even managed to get a result, given the conditions, Austin walked back through the trees and came out by the hostage hut. In the clearing, the guard was no longer eating. He was no longer sitting. He was staring angrily. Austin smiled, covered his loaded hand with his empty one, and pushed them against his belly. "I'm okay now. I'm okay. No problems."

Austin looked away from the guard and headed toward his monkeys, still by the cook fire. The Guard didn't follow, but he didn't sit either.

"Are you okay?" Sander asked.

"Yes," Austin answered.

Sander cocked his head and furrowed his brow.

"Something in the water, I think." Austin stepped over the log on which his cooked monkeys were leaning. He glanced up at the guard who had just sat back down, going back to whatever thoughts kept him occupied when he was guarding the mzungu hostages.

Austin heard the sounds of men moving through the forest on the other side of the camp. The two guards over there half-raised their weapons and watched the trees. The guard who'd been keeping an eye on Austin stood back up.

They were concerned, but not alarmed. No guns had been fired. The General was probably returning.

Austin took the opportunity to kneel down by the monkeys. He laid a hand on a plump one, still warm from the fire and moist with its own cooked fats. He rubbed his hands together then rubbed them up and down on the warm monkey's legs, arms, and torso. He moved to the next monkey, not sure if the slippery mess on his hands was monkey fat or not. He rubbed the second monkey.

"You."

Austin nearly fell over as he jerked around to look at the source of the voice. The guard was standing over him, irritated again. He spat a string of syllables.

Austin looked to Sander. "What'd he say?"

Sander said, "He wants to know what you're doing."

Austin looked at the monkeys. He looked at the guard. He looked back at the monkeys and rubbed a hand across a third monkey's back. "Tell him I'm brushing off the burned pieces so the monkeys will taste better." Austin yanked a small flake of burned crust, grimaced at it, and threw it on the ground.

Sander said something to the guard.

The guard pointed at Austin and said something back.

Sander said, "Stop."

Austin took his hands away from the monkey. Was he busted?

Sander said, "He says he likes the burnt bits. Leave them."

Austin looked up at the guard, smiled widely, and said, "Okay. Okay." He picked up the two monkeys he hoped he'd infected and carried them to the pavilion. The guard went back to stand by his tree.

When Austin stepped up into the pavilion, Sander pointed at a table. "Lay them there."

Austin nodded toward the noise coming from the far side of the camp. "I guess everything is cool."

Nodding, and pointing at the forest behind them, Sander said, "If it wasn't, these guys would already be running into the woods that way."

Austin took two more trips down to the fire to bring the remaining monkeys under the pavilion.

"Help me with these yams," Sander said.

Austin looked over at the guard to make sure that his attention lay in the other direction. Austin whispered, "Don't eat the monkey tonight."

"What?" Sander asked.

Austin caught Sander with a serious look. "Don't eat the monkey. Not a bit. Okay?"

With a look of confusion, Sander nodded, and said, "Okay. No monkey. Help me with these yams."

Chapter 86

When all the rebels were back in camp, Austin had trouble hiding his giddiness. He didn't know if his plan was going to work. He only knew that he felt a sense of power at attempting to retake control of his life. The monkey meat had a thin layer of Ebola virus. If enough of those virions were viable, then one of the rebels might get infected. Austin only needed one. One victim would spread it to the others. It would be Kapchorwa all over again only with sick people who deserved their fate. Austin might be walking out of the rebel camp by the end of the week, maybe next week, free.

Austin prepared a plate for The General. That part of his houseboy duties didn't disappear after The General killed Min and ransomed Wei. Austin tore pieces of meat off the first monkey he'd infected, spooned some yams onto the plate, and carried it out of the pavilion.

The General sat on his execution log, watching the fire, laughing with those who sat beside him or stood around nearby. No one had yet eaten. The General always ate first. That was the rule.

Austin stopped in front of The General and presented the plate.

The General looked it over, smelled it, smiled, and accepted. He then looked over Austin's shoulder with a question on his face.

Austin looked back to his left. Inexplicably, Sander stood there, not back in the pavilion with the food where he should have been, but right behind Austin with a pained expression on his face.

What the hell?

Panic rose in Austin's blood. He smiled at The General and stepped away as though to go back to the pavilion, as he always did after serving The General.

Sander looked at Austin one more time and said, "In light of my ransom problems, General, I must beg you to hear an alternative deal."

The General laughed. "I am intrigued." He reached onto his plate and picked up a piece of meat.

Sander nearly jumped forward with an open palm.

That shot the tension right through the roof, and several of the rebels were immediately on their feet. Everybody froze.

"Please," Sander begged, "don't eat yet. Hear my proposal first."

Austin couldn't believe what he was hearing, what he was seeing. He inched toward the pavilion, hoping to sneak out of sight. He eyed the woods. How close would he have to be to the tree line before he made his sprint?

The General's smile was gone. He was suspicious. "Why not eat?"

"Allow me, please," Sander said. "I have information that I want to trade for my freedom."

Austin took two more quick steps. He stopped when a hand grasped his shoulder. It was the guard, who'd been watching him and Sander cook. No surprise, he wasn't happy.

"What information?" The General asked.

"I will trade it for my freedom," said Sander.

"I will judge whether your freedom is worth this information," said The General.

Sander looked around while he considered his position. He licked his lips. He wrung his hands. He delayed.

The General's face showed his impatience, and just as he started to speak, Sander interrupted him, quickly blurting, "I trust The General's judgment and fairness." He gulped a big breath. "Don't eat the meat. It's been poisoned." Sander slumped and took a half step back.

Shit.

The General jumped to his feet, his face twisted with rage but he said nothing. He poked Sander in the chest with his finger. He poked him a second time, but with his fist, knocking him back a step. He punched him hard in the chest again, knocking Sander back to the edge of the fire. In a venomous voice, The General said, "Tell me everything."

In a flurry of frightened words, Sander pointed at Austin and told The General exactly what Austin had told him, and what he'd seen Austin doing, when he was for some odd reason running his hands over the cooked monkey carcasses. The guard, who'd seen Austin do it, confirmed.

The unhappy rebel dragged Austin over and pushed him down to his knees between The General and the fire pit.

Sander started to say something else, but a raised hand from The General silenced him. The General glared down at Austin and spat the words, "You would kill me after all the kindness I have shown you?"

"No he's—"

The General cut Austin's words short when his boot kicked Austin's stomach. Austin fell and rolled perilously close to the flames. The General kicked him twice more and stomped on his back.

The kicking stopped, when Austin was struggling for breath and racked with pain.

The General knelt down beside Austin and put the barrel

of his pistol to Austin's head. "Tell me the truth and I'll let you die without pain."

Austin struggled for breath and said, "Sander lied."

"Lied?" The General laughed. "Two lying hostages." He jumped to his feet and theatrically asked the audience of his soldiers, "What am I to do?"

None of them responded. Everybody knew the question was rhetorical.

The General knelt down beside Austin again, used the barrel of the pistol to push Austin's head against the ground and said, "Tell me more, Ransom."

Having caught enough of his breath to speak, Austin said, "I lied to Sander. I told him the meat was poisoned so that he wouldn't eat it. So there'd be more for me, after your men ate what they wanted."

The General laughed again, "Is that so? Is that so?" He stood up.

Sander shouted, "He's a liar. He poisoned it. I saw him do it. Don't eat it!"

The General yanked Austin up to a sitting position and smiled wickedly down at him. He pointed to his plate, which lay on the ground nearby. One of his men jumped to retrieve it. He handed it to The General.

With the plate coming his way, Austin guessed The General's intent. It wasn't a Mensa test question. The General was going to make him eat the suspect meat. Any hesitation to do so would earn Austin a bullet in the brain. In that moment, Austin learned just how far he was willing to go to save his life.

The plate passed in front of Austin, and before a single word came out of The General's mouth, Austin grabbed a handful of the monkey meat, stuffed it into his mouth, and started to chew.

The General was stunned, clearly expecting a different outcome.

Austin swallowed his mouthful and greedily took another handful, stuffing it into his mouth and chewing.

Laughing, The General took the butt of his pistol and bashed Sander in the side of the head. "Fool."

Sander crumbled to the ground, covering his wounded skull with one hand, while raising his other to defend against a second blow. No second blow came. The General turned back to his seat, telling Austin, "Finish your plate, then—" he stopped.

He spun back around, looked down at Austin, and said, "Stop eating."

Austin froze.

To Sander, he said, "Eat the rest."

"But," Sander started to say something, then froze his face in fear.

The General leaned over Sander and in an acid voice said, "Eat."

Sander took the plate from Austin and with the greatest reluctance put a small bite of the meat into his mouth.

The General raised his pistol and pummeled Sander again. He fell. The plate spilled. The General looked at Austin. "Get him another plate. A full plate."

Austin hurried back to the pavilion, filled a plate with a big helping of monkey meat, and brought it back out.

"Hand it to him," The General told Austin.

Austin did so.

The General leveled his pistol at Sander. "Eat it all. Quickly."

As Sander ate, the soldiers started to jeer and bet on whether he'd finish. The General simply watched with no expression on his face. Austin watched The General, wondering what was to come next, and wondering if Sander was going to earn more justice than he deserved for his betrayal of Austin's secret.

When Sander finished eating the meat, he laid the plate on the ground and looked at it with a sickly expression.

Don't vomit, Austin silently pleaded. If you vomit, they'll think the meat is poisoned. That would be the death of them both.

"Sit." The General told them. "Both of you."

Sander dropped down. The General silently watched them. Minutes passed. The rebels watched too, at first, looking for whatever The General was looking for. After a few minutes of nothing happening, they got bored and went back to talking amongst themselves.

For what may have been a half hour, The General simply watched Sander and Austin. By that time, the men were starting to grumble. They were hungry and Austin was starting to worry. Though it was Sander who spoke up and took center stage by delaying the meal, any rebel with half his wits about him knew the dinner fiasco was Austin's fault.

Eventually, The General stood back up, walked up in front of Austin and Sander, and said, "You're not going to die, are you?"

Shaking his head, Austin said, "It's not poisoned."

The General turned to a few of his men and said something in Swahili. The men ran up to the pavilion and started putting together a plate for The General. It only took a moment. He motioned more of his men to come. He pointed at Sander and Austin and said, "I don't like to wait for my meals. Teach them a lesson. Put them in their hut when you are done."

The first blow on the side of his head was the only one that Austin felt.

Chapter 87

Six days in Amarillo, Texas. It had been six days, and Salim's money was bleeding away.

That first ride was easy. He'd walked over to the truck stop with Victor and his girlfriend—Salim forgot her name—Victor did the talking, and arranged a ride for Salim in the back of an empty cattle truck. The floor wasn't *covered* in manure, but there was plenty of it. Still, Salim found himself a relatively clean spot for the six-hour drive to Amarillo. From there, the driver was headed south to Lubbock, and left Salim at a truck stop on Interstate 40.

Salim thanked the driver, went inside, bought himself a microwave burrito for a dollar ninety-nine and a fifty-two ounce soda for eighty-nine cents. He ate alone on an orange bench at a sunshine-yellow Formica table, one of a couple dozen in a dirty lounge that reeked of cigarette smoke. The other customers, two of them, kept their distance from Salim and each other.

He felt good, and seriously thought he'd get a ride in the empty trailer of another truck and be in Denver by midnight.

That didn't happen.

Each day, as he sat there in the shade of the twenty-five foot high awnings, asking the favor of truckers, none of them admitted to heading north or west. Maybe their first impression of Salim rubbed them the wrong way. Maybe he was too young. Maybe too dirty. Maybe too brown. Maybe they were all liars.

Each day, the traffic out on the highway thinned a little more and Salim wondered if a day would arrive when no cars, no trucks rolled. What would he do then?

In his boredom, he became preoccupied with The Big Texan Steak Ranch, a quarter-mile up the highway from the truck stop. With signs so large and gaudy they might be visible all the way back down the highway to Oklahoma City, Salim couldn't help but spend too many thoughts on the promise of a free seventy-two ounce steak, under the condition that he eat the entire thing, and the sides, in less than an hour.

Salim, as hungry as he was, convinced himself he could beat that game. He skipped his breakfast, not an uncommon occurrence anyway, waited until lunchtime, left the truck stop, and walked down to the Big Texan Steak Ranch. The parking lot was near empty, but that wasn't a surprise, given the light traffic and everyone's fears about going out in public.

He crossed the parking lot and noticed a sign taped to the front door. By order of the governor, along with several lines of legal jibber jabber, the restaurant, like all other restaurants in Texas, was closed until further notice.

Chapter 88

Most of the rebels were gone when Austin found the energy to crawl out of the hut around noon. His eyes were swollen and painful, his nose full of crusty blood, his lips split. It hurt to move. He had bruises all over.

Using the hut's doorframe, he dragged himself upright and looked around the camp. A couple of guards sat in the shade of a tree, one napping, the other staring into the jungle. Their lackadaisical attention shamed Austin. The rebels had beaten him so badly the night before that he couldn't have run away if he'd wanted to.

He hobbled out into the woods behind the hostage hut and found the latrines. As he relieved himself, he smiled up at the sky and laughed—not too loudly. Given what little power he had to do something to save himself, he'd done it. He paid a price, an affordable price. His bruises would heal. His scars would fade. All he had to do was grovel and smile falsely at his captors for a few more weeks.

That was the hope.

When Austin got back to the hut, he sat down in front where he could feel the sun on his face. Over his shoulder through the hut's doorway, he saw Sander's feet but couldn't see anything above his waist.

"I'm awake," said Sander.

"What the fuck do I care?" Austin snapped, causing his lower lip to start bleeding from beneath a scab.

"Are you all right?" Sander asked.

"I'll live."

For nearly a minute, Sander stayed quiet and Austin wondered if he'd gone back to sleep. "I don't think I will," he said.

"Will what?" Austin asked, though not caring whether he heard the answer.

"Live."

"Just get up," Austin told him. "Move around. You'll be fine in a couple a days."

Sander started to sob. "I hurt."

"Good." Austin gave a thought to stomping into the hut to kick Sander a few times. That was only a fantasy. Sander had paid for his mistake, too, and would likely pay a lot more.

Sander got control of his sobs and asked, "Why?"

"Why, what?"

"Why did you tell me you poisoned the meat?"

"Why did you have to say anything?" Austin asked. "If you'd just stayed quiet, none of this would have happened."

Sander groaned and shuffled on his mat. Austin turned around to see him trying to push himself into a sitting position. Half way up, he clutched at a pain in his belly and fell over with a grunt. The sobs came again. He was in bad shape, much worse than Austin.

Thoughts of empathy and coarse justice flipped through a hundred reversals as Austin listened to Sander's pained breaths.

"You have a hope to get out of here," Sander muttered. "Your ransom will come. For me —"

Austin said nothing.

"I told The General because it was my way out," Sander explained. "He would have let me go."

"And killed *me*." Austin's ambivalence disappeared.

Chapter 89

One hundred and eleven thousand cases of Ebola in Denver. So fast. Holy Christ, it was hard to believe.

Addicted to the repetitive speculations and random nuggets of information, Paul couldn't bring himself to change the channel to anything other than another news station, so he pushed the off button on the remote and watched the TV screen go black. He got up from the couch and paced a path through the first floor, around a dozen circuits, rushing through the dining room each time, not wanting to linger in the space where Heidi had breathed her last. He rounded a quick U-turn in the guest room at the front of the house that faced the patio where Heidi's body still lay, bundled exactly as described by that fucking website. Why the hell wouldn't they come and pick her up?

Oh, right. One hundred and eleven thousand cases.

How many bodies lay bundled up on how many patios? How many more were coming?

The whole God-damned world was going to shit.

Paul pulled his cell phone out of his pocket. Well, not *his* phone. That device was a casualty of his Ebola mitigation plan. He had it when the paramedics put him in the ambulance, and like his tainted clothing, it had been destroyed. Now, he had Heidi's phone. He'd restored it from his computer, so it had all of his application data and contact information, but something was wrong with it. It made barely perceptible chirps when calls came in, and Paul couldn't figure out how to make the contrary thing ring. Looking at the phone, Paul saw that he'd missed another call from Olivia.

"Damn."

He called her back, but got no answer.

He tried a second time, with the same result.

Paul climbed the stairs and wandered through the bedrooms, checking the blinds that—of course—were closed. He hadn't opened them, and no one else lived in the townhouse, not anymore.

He was feeling stir crazy. That, and depressed, the only two things he ever felt anymore. He stared at the ceiling at night until he got tired of the feelings that lurked in the dark corners of his bedroom. He turned on the TV and watched until he passed out. He woke too early every morning, usually before the sun was up. He rolled out of bed and started his day, a repeat of the one before.

He realized he needed to get out of the house. It was that simple.

To leave the house unnecessarily was a violation of one of hundreds of new rules, some contradictory, random, thrown together in a rush by mayors, city councilmen, or state legislators, alarmed and trying to do anything that felt like something. Most of them had ridden a well-financed, mud-slinging campaign into office. They'd spent their time learning how to smear opponents and win elections. Governance? Fuck that! None of them knew how to manage a pandemic. None of them had time to learn.

Paul felt rebellious, the first new *anything* he'd felt in weeks. He went out of the house through the garage. The corpse on the front porch made the front door an undesirable exit path.

Paul crossed over the busy road that ran past his house, the one from which passing assholes threw rocks at his windows, back when enough of them were healthy enough to drive a car. He admitted to himself that was an exaggeration. Still, just a small percentage of citizens had contracted Ebola. All the rest of them were afraid though. That kept most of them in their houses, a great plan until the food ran out. Then what?

God, what a question that was. Paul at least had enough food in the basement.

He stepped onto one of the concrete-paved hike-and-bike trails, one of those he and Heidi had walked on countless evenings, watching the sky turn to hues of orange and red as the sun sank behind the Front Range.

Forty-five minutes passed. The trails were his alone.

Moving his feet along the meandering trail system was doing nothing to quell his dark emotions. He stopped, got his bearings, and found the nearest path back to a road. Cutting back through the residential streets would be the most direct route back home. Once there, he resolved to find an on-demand movie to watch on his giant television —something with no depth and lots of violence—he'd drink a beer, or two, or more, and forget everything, at least for a little while.

As he passed the houses, the parked cars, and the uncollected garbage at the curbs, Paul noticed the homemade flags, strips of black or red cloth, hanging from doors. Red meant sick. Black meant death. As if a body, lying bundled in plastic on the front porch wasn't enough of a warning. Paul, too, had a black T-shirt tied to the railing on his front porch. The mandate declared it to be so, fines and incarceration for violators.

Everything carried a penalty these days.

Even bad choices.

Paul started to count—not flags, but bodies he saw on porches. He'd reached seven when he saw two heavily-taped cardboard boxes, each with its own flag, each labeled according to the law: body inside.

Each box looked new, purchased from a do-it-yourself moving company, and put to use as a makeshift coffin — there were no more real coffins in Denver. Those ran out in the first week. Paul stopped. He stared at the two boxes, not lengthy enough by far to contain a person. Not even long enough for a child. He imagined the tears of the parents in that house as he thought about his own son. He couldn't imagine how much it pained them to fold their two dead children into packing boxes.

Maybe in their minds it was better than wrapping them in garbage bags. Heavy-duty plastic sold out shortly after the coffins went. Now, duct tape was absent and people were using ropes made of torn cloth to wrap and bind.

The law required so much with the limited resources remaining.

Grandparents couldn't grieve. No, the law didn't say that. If any of those two boxed children's grandparents lived out of state, they'd never get a pass to cross state lines. Only smugglers, out-of-state aliens, and truckers carrying the trickle of the nation's commerce were moving between states these days.

Neighbors couldn't help a bereaved parent. They could only send an email or make a phone call. To cross the street and give the neighbor a hug was now illegal. Between the myriad of government agencies, all physical contact between people was banned unless their jobs required it.

Going outside without a mask or gloves now carried a fine and a year in jail.

Spitting on the sidewalk, or anywhere, for that matter — a law from the past that seemed so silly to modern Americans — was illegal again.

Ebola K: Book 2

Paul hung his head and watched his walking feet. He wanted to see no more.

He crossed the wide road that passed beside his townhouse complex. A car drove by, giving him a wide berth. He passed onto a street just a block over from his townhouse. He didn't look at the flags on the doors.

He rounded the last corner and was startled by the yap from a tiny mop dog on a leash. Paul looked up. His tattling neighbor stood a handful of steps in front of him, surgical mask over her face, latex gloves on her hands, goggles covering her wide, frightened eyes.

"You stay away from me, Paul Cooper."

The dog growled. It yapped some more.

Paul pointed up the street and muttered, "I'm going that way." Maggie could cross the street to get out of his way. Paul had no civility left for her, not after what she'd done by spilling all of his and Heidi's secrets on the news. "Get out of my way."

Maggie backed up a step, found her courage and stopped. "No." She pointed across the street. "You go over there."

"Fuck you and your stupid rat!" Paul lunged forward, not to attack her, but to frighten her as he pushed past. Maggie screamed. She bolted to her right, dragging her yappy mop thing by its leash.

"Stay away from me!" she shrieked as she squeezed through a gap between two cars parked at the curb.

Paul caught a glimpse of a blur of blue, and heard the revving whine of a tiny engine, followed by a wet thud.

A Prius took Maggie down as she stepped into the street. The dog yelped and its leash flew into the air.

Tires screeched, but the Prius didn't slow, not at first.

The driver had been speeding.

Paul ran out into the street. The Prius came to a halt half a block up. It sat there idling, sitting at an odd angle. A bloody smear ran out from behind, to the spot where Maggie had been just an eye blink before.

The yappy little mop dog, recovered from the shock of seeing its owner taken by the Prius, returned to frantic barking.

The Prius engine whined again. It lurched.

Paul ran up to the car and saw Maggie mashed between the front bumper and the road. He looked at the driver, mouth agape, still in the front seat, stuck in the shock of what had just happened, perhaps stuck in the limbo of having to choose which law to break: the old requirement to render aid after an accident, or the new one, not to touch a stranger.

It was an easy decision for Paul. He slipped his hands into his pockets and had the very black sense that something right—disproportionate, but *right*—had just transpired. God had a very dark sense of humor.

The driver of the car looked at Paul. Paul shrugged and turned away toward his townhouse. He heard the engine rev again. The car's suspension creaked and it rolled off of Maggie's body. Tires screeched again as it sped off.

Paul didn't look back.

He was walking.

He was thinking.

When would his own disproportionate, deserved justice come?

Chapter 90

The second day after the beating, most of the rebels were still gone. The dozen left in camp, apparently spooked by the poison scare, didn't put Austin to work preparing their meals.

Sander didn't wake up in the morning, which didn't concern Austin. Sander was hurt. He needed the sleep to aid his recovery.

By early afternoon, Austin started to worry and tried to shake Sander awake. It didn't work. Austin told the guards that Sander needed medical attention. Neither guard cared. In fact, they looked at Austin while he spoke, then turned away when he stopped, not even troubling themselves to verbalize their apathy.

Austin took to putting damp compresses on Sander's face. He washed the cuts and rolled Sander onto a clean mat after he'd soiled his.

Three more times before Austin went to bed that night, Sander had accidents. After each, Austin rolled him onto a freshly-cleaned sleeping mat. Through all of it, Sander didn't regain consciousness.

When Austin woke on the morning of the third day, Sander was dead. Austin went out to tell the guards, but had to wait until late in the morning for one to show up. Austin asked, "Is it just you today?"

"Sick," said the guard nodding in the direction of one of the huts.

Biting his lip to repress a smile at news of the guard, Austin said, "Sander died. We need to bury him."

"*You* need to bury him."

Chapter 91

The metal patio chair wasn't cheap, but it wasn't expensive. It was resilient under layers and layers of flaking paint. The townhome's previous owner had abandoned the table and chairs on the front porch, leaving them to be treasured to an equal measure by Paul. The chairs weren't comfortable. The tabletop metal mesh left waffle prints on his elbows when he leaned. It stayed on the porch because it was there, presence being its salient quality.

Heidi's corpse was also present, lying along the side railing, bundled in a sheet and favored down comforter, wrapped in the mandatory layers of plastic and tape. Paul had plenty of tape and plastic in the basement, part of his prepper hoard.

That website, with its pitiless packaging and disposition instructions, assured that the body would be collected in a "safe and respectful" manner and taken to a local interment annex. The bereaved, Paul, would be provided details of the location of the buried loved one after the pickup took place. They'd email him.

Email: subject porch corpse. *Are you fucking kidding me?*

In the event that the transport service became backlogged, the responsibility fell to the closest living relative of the deceased to transport the body in a sanitary fashion to the nearest interment annex. Bodies left out, especially in the suburbs, would attract vermin (rats), scavengers (coyotes), and opportunistic predators (bears).

Much was made on the webpage, of the deadlines and shifting responsibility covering that part of the process. It was ambiguous, at best. The only thing that was certain was when Paul violated the rules surrounding corpse disposition, he was subject to a punishment, including two years in jail and a ten thousand dollar fine.

The government seemed determined to stop the epidemic, even if it had to jail the entire population and ensure that everybody contracted Ebola from one another that way.

"So be it," Paul muttered as he came to a decision. No matter what the government said he couldn't or shouldn't do, his heart couldn't start letting go of Heidi until she was at least off the front porch.

He got out of his ugly metal chair, crossed the porch and knelt in front of Heidi's body. He gently stroked her face through the layers. She was cold. The last several nights, the temperatures had dipped near freezing and the days had been cool. Feeling a shiver down his spine, Paul prepared himself for what he had to do next.

He leaned over and lifted her onto his shoulder. He carried her unnatural, cold body into the house, through the dining room, the kitchen, the TV room, and out the back door. He crossed the small courtyard and went into the garage. He squeezed his way between the two cars, and when he turned to put Heidi in the bed of his truck, he lost his balance. She fell, bouncing against the side of the truck before banging down in the bed.

"Dammit!" Paul yelled out. "Dammit! Dammit! Dammit!"

He pounded the truck's fender with his fists. The tantrum did nothing to ease the pain in his broken heart.

Paul went back into the house, locked the front door, checked all the windows, gathered up his car keys, and stopped. He looked up at the ceiling, knowing that in the room upstairs, in the closet, in the bedroom he used for an office, was the AR-15 he'd purchased in an act that he'd been ashamed of at the time. And though that choice now seemed prescient, it hadn't saved Heidi's life.

Paul went upstairs and found the weapon in the corner of his closet. He didn't yet have a good way to store it, but he decided in that moment that weapon storage was a concept from the past, not for the future. From now on, the rifle would always be with him. Just let those fuckers who killed Heidi come back. Paul yearned for that to happen.

He gathered up a couple of spare magazines and checked that they were full. He ejected and checked the magazine in his rifle. He checked that the safety was set, and headed back downstairs. Once back in his truck, he leaned the rifle against the seat with the barrel pointing at the floor and the handgrip within easy reach, ready for use in the space of a few heartbeats.

Paul was stuck in the black molasses of a foul mood that nothing would wash away. He had lots of bullets, though, and thought that sharing those bullets with just the right kind of people might help free him of his sticky darkness.

Chapter 92

Paul didn't see a single—living—person as he drove through his neighborhood. That wasn't unusual. The townhouse residents seldom ventured out on foot, even when there was no disease. Driving out of the townhouse development and through his generically placid suburb, Paul felt like he was passing through a cemetery of house-sized tombstones, waiting for years of seasonal storms to come and grind them to shards of iridescent glass and crumbles of spotted brick. He didn't see an automobile in motion until he reached the highway.

At the second exit, Paul followed the ramp off the highway and made a left turn at the intersection. Heading north on a road that used to be full of traffic, he saw a few more cars than had been on the freeway. At a red light, two cars lined up behind him, making this the first intersection since leaving home at which he wasn't alone.

In his rearview mirror, he looked suspiciously at the driver behind him. He reached over to touch his rifle, feeling a measure of strength in its solid weight.

The driver leaned her head against her steering wheel and shuddered with silent sobs. Paul put both his hands back on the steering wheel. The woman behind him was probably on her way to the same place as Paul, carrying in her trunk a similar burden.

The light changed to green, and Paul rolled down the street. At Arapahoe Road—it seemed every town in Colorado had at least one street named Arapahoe—Paul turned right and started looking for the repurposed plot of land now named The Denver Southern District Interment Park. The map on the website showed it to be a short distance east of the intersection.

He crested a hill while looking down a side street and a flash of movement burned an image into his mind. Several people were beating something in the street with baseball bats or boards. He glanced at his rifle. He thought about Heidi and mashed the brakes.

Down the hill and halfway up the next, vehicles with red brake lights glowing were stopped in his lane, waiting to make a left turn.

At the head of the line, soldiers in camouflage fatigues, with gas masks over their heads and rifles on slings, directed traffic off the road. Two tan Humvees parked in the lane impressed the weight of their authority on the drivers. One of the soldiers pointed at Paul and was probably cursing him for speeding up to the end of the line like an idiot and almost causing an accident.

Paul settled in to wait.

The line inched forward and Paul eventually came up beside a soldier. He tapped the glass on the passenger side window. Paul rolled it down and the soldier's gas mask-covered head angled a look toward the AR-15 leaning on the seat. The soldier tensed, but looked back up at Paul. It wasn't the first weapon he'd seen. In a voice turned Cylon-mechanical through the filter of the gas mask, the soldier asked, "Interment?"

Paul nodded and made a feeble gesture at the bed of the pickup. "My wife." An ache in his heart ambushed him, and he said no more.

The plastic-headed, glass-eyed, lethal thing nodded gravely. "Stay in the line. When you turn into the park, you'll be told where to go. Do you have your interment sheet?"

"My what?" Paul asked.

"Did you print your interment sheet?"

"I—" Paul wanted to curse. What the hell was he talking about?

"Did you call for pickup?" The soldier nodded at Heidi's body.

Paul wanted to say yes, but when he spoke, the mix of anger and grief threatened to turn into tears. His mouth opened, but nothing came out. He settled for a nod.

"I'm sorry for your loss." The soldier didn't sound like it. He pointed forward. "Just stay in line. There'll be someone ahead to direct you."

Paul nodded and sniffled.

In an effort to convey empathy, the Cylon asked, "Do you have someone at home to talk to?"

Paul shook his head.

"Check the website. They have some virtual support groups. Trust me, I know that sounds like it sucks already, but it helped me." The soldier stood back up, paused, and then leaned back into the window. "Suicide's a thing now. Don't go that way. Try the website."

Paul nodded again. He didn't dare risk a thank you. Tears might have come.

The soldier rapped twice on the hood with his knuckles and stepped away from the truck.

Chapter 93

Paul rolled along on autopilot until he found himself parked among dozens of other cars, next to an expansive field of grass, green and lush from a mild summer. Bordering the park, the tall trees were starting to show their fall colors of brilliant yellow and blazing red against a perfect blue sky. Far past the trees, the mountains touched the heavens, the tallest peaks already dusted in snow.

Paul killed the engine and sat. The parking spaces around him used to fill with cars of parents hurrying their children to soccer games as they promised them an ice cream cone for a victory. Mothers hugged their daughters and assured them that losing a game wasn't the end of the world.

The end of the world.

The end of the world was watching the man in the next car wrestle a small, plastic-wrapped body out of the backseat of a subcompact. The body was wrapped in a too-small baby blanket, decorated with fat, pastel-colored numbers, letters, and cartoon giraffes. Clear plastic and packing tape covered most everything but a child's white-socked foot, dangled limply from an open end.

The man trudged away with the tiny weight of the boney child, and the crippling burden of its death. He crossed the emerald grass on a path worn thin under the traffic of too many feet. He followed it toward a herd of dirty yellow backhoes, snorting plumes of diesel stink while they gouged long pits into the field. The man took up a place at the end of a widely spaced line, holding his burden tenderly in cramping arms. When his time arrived, he dropped his child into the bleak hole and collapsed as though all the life in his soul had just flitted away.

Paul wept.

Chapter 94

With Heidi's body in his arms, Paul crossed a fading chalk line that defined the boundary of a soccer field, walked in front of a goal, and between two long, rectangular mounds of dirt. A dozen other mounds, eight feet wide and forty feet long, formed neat rows across the soccer fields. At the head of each, a stone the size of a coffee table stood, each carved with the names of the people buried under that particular mound.

Following the general path of others carrying bodies, Paul passed between more rows of mass graves, neat and straight. He arrived at a row of open pits. In front of each, a hand-written paper sign on a wooden pole displayed some letters, A-B, C-D, and so forth. C for Cooper. Paul headed for the C-D pit.

Beside each pole, one of the coffee table-sized stones lay. Seated in front of the stone by the C-D pit, a man worked at carving the names of the deceased being dropped in by family members. The carver had an assistant close by, tablet computer held in gloved hands. Soldiers and policemen posted themselves with hands on weapons, keeping things in order, standing in carefully selected spots, out of the flow of foot traffic, away from contact with any human, away from any corpse.

Paul queued up in a line behind three people, one with a baby, one with a child, and one dragging an adult. Each person in line maintained a gap of six feet between the others, the new invisible boundary of personal space, defined and mandated by the city of Denver. The federal requirement was just five.

Paul came to the head of the line and he stared absently at the row of bodies in the pit.

A thoroughly hazmat-protected man with a tablet computer and a barcode scanner in hand, said "Show me your interment ticket."

Paul looked at him blankly, as he thought about what the traffic-directing Cylon had told him.

"Your interment ticket." The scanner man had no patience, and had no qualms about letting Paul know it. Paul looked down at Heidi's body, growing heavy in arms that had gone numb from the load. Did the man not understand why Paul was here?

Slowly and loudly, in a tone meant to tell Paul that he was an idiot, scanner man, said, "Your interment ticket. Did you call in? Did you register online?"

"I—" Paul had called for Heidi's body to be picked up. They'd taken his information. "I called."

"Did you print out your interment ticket?" The scanner man looked emphatically past Paul to remind him that others were in the line, good people who'd followed their instructions. Paul's stupidity was prolonging their grief. "It had the bar code with your—" scanner man waved little circles in the air toward Heidi's body.

"Wife," Paul said.

"Your wife," scanner man confirmed. "I scan the information from the sheet." He pointed to the tablet computer. "The information goes here. We have to keep track of who's de—"

Dead? Of course, that was the coarse word the scanner fuck was going to use. He'd stopped. Maybe he'd already been punched in his tactless goggled face.

A policeman walked over and positioned himself several paces behind scanner man. The six-foot gap was maintained, but he was close enough to let Paul know that scanner man had backup. Paul took the cop's stance as a dare, and in his roiling sorrow and stoked anger, he gave a thought to taking it.

With an air of bureaucratic authority, scanner man said, "We have to keep track of the numbers. We have to have the information to track the disease. We have to know we're beating it. And—" Scanner man let the "and" hang in the air for a moment, emphasizing the importance of what was to come. "Your wife's information goes in here," he tapped the screen of the tablet. He pointed to the stone carver's assistant. "Then your wife's information goes over there, so her name can be added to the stone. You do want to know where your wife is buried don't you?"

"Of course," Paul spat, wanting very much to punch the officious fuck. "Her name is Heidi Cooper. I don't have an interment sheet. I called it in a few days ago."

A soldier, sensing the tension, took up a position to Paul's left.

Scanner man typed on the screen of his tablet and his expressive brows wrinkled in frustration. "There's no record. You'll just have to dump her in the unmarked pit." He pointed to the end hole on the row, where no coffee table-sized stone marker lay, where no stone carver sat, where the handwritten sign on the post said "Anonymous." A line of excruciatingly sad people stood near that hole with the burden of their departed loved ones in their arms.

Shaking his head, Paul said, "You have my wife's name. I called it in."

"No ticket." Scanner man shook his head to punctuate the discussion.

Turning around, Paul called, over his shoulder, "I'll print a ticket and come back."

"No!" A shout from behind him. "Sir!"

"Stop!" another voice ordered.

Paul stopped and turned back toward scanner man. The policeman had stepped forward, his elbow cocked out and his palm on his pistol, ready to draw. The soldier had his rifle halfway up. The policeman said, "Sir, take your loved one to the anonymous line. It is illegal for you to take a body away from the interment site. Do you understand?"

"I don't have a ticket," Paul pleaded. "I don't have a ticket." He felt his anger turning into futile sadness. "I don't have—"

Scanner man had stepped forward again to cement his own authority. He pointed. "The anonymous line."

"I want to be able to come back and visit my wife's grave," Paul begged. "I love her. Can't you just take her name and add it to your list?"

Scanner man pointed again. "You're slowing the line."

Paul shook his head. Everything he felt turned to tears. He started toward the stone carver, "Heidi Cooper. Please add her name. Heidi Cooper."

The stone carver and his tablet computer assistant jumped to their feet and stumbled away, as though Paul might be a fountain of Ebola virus.

People yelled.

Uniformed bodies ran.

The commotion was invisible to Paul. He only wanted one thing in that moment, the tiniest scrap of dignity for the woman he loved, the dead woman he still loved. He needed to have her name carved in the stone. "Please!" he shouted.

Something hit him hard in the back of the head and he fell forward. Heidi's body rolled out through the dirt and grass in front of him. A boot landed on his back.

Scanner man prattled something, ordering and yelling.

Paul no longer cared. He no longer cared about anything. He only wanted to bury his wife. He wanted a place to come and to say his goodbyes for as many days or years as that might take. With a heavy boot on his back and Heidi's plastic-wrapped corpse in the dirt, he tried to sob out his explanation, over and over. If he said it enough times, maybe—just maybe—they'd hear.

A gloved hand touched his shoulder and patted him, and as the boot lifted, he suddenly realized how much he missed the gentle touch of another human being.

"Look, mister," a voice said beside him, "I know this is hard for you. This is hard for all of us."

Paul turned his head to look. A masked and goggled policeman said, "Let me help you get your wife to the anonymous grave, okay? I'll get you the information on the grave number. We'll get her added to the list. There won't be a marker today, but it'll get there. Okay? Maybe in a week or two. It'll be there. I promise."

Paul nodded.

"You gonna be all right?" the policeman asked.

Paul nodded again, though his tears still flowed.

The cop put a hand under Paul's arm and helped him to his feet. Heidi was still on the ground, dirt all over her clean plastic wrap. The cop knelt down to pick up her body.

"You don't have to—" Paul started but the cop already had her in his arms. He turned and Paul put his arms out to take the weight of Heidi's corpse. "Thank you. Thank you."

"C'mon. I'll walk you over."

Chapter 95

Mitch said, "I talk with Mathew almost every day."

"Good," Olivia responded absently.

"He's a good guy. He seems to have a thing for you."

Without the energy to smile, she said. "Yes, he does."

"None of my business, of course."

Olivia laughed, but it was so hollow, it sounded forced, even to her. "It's okay. You and I have probably broken half the secrecy laws on the books. If we can't be confidants, who can be?"

"Then you won't mind my saying so, but you sound off."

"The world," Olivia mused.

"Ebola has been making a mess of things for a while now. If it's because of Austin—"

"No," Olivia told him, "I...it's my dad and stepmom, and —"

Mitch drew an audible breath. "I don't have to tell you this, and I know it's no comfort, but you knew things could get bad. Everybody is catching this thing."

"Everybody but you," said Olivia.

"Lucky, I guess. Tell me about your folks."

"I probably didn't tell you this, but my dad caught Ebola and recovered."

"That's great."

"Yeah," Olivia said, but in a tone that didn't convey any of Mitch's enthusiasm over the point. "My dad called and told me my stepmom, Heidi, was murdered."

"People can be shitty. Really shitty. Were you close with her?"

"Not really, not at first I guess. It took a while but we became friends."

"I only talked to her a couple of times, but she really loved your brother."

"I know."

"Are you dealing with it okay?"

Olivia thought about it for a moment then stopped. That was how she was dealing with it. She was hiding. She was numb. She just had to keep working, keep moving. "My dad's not taking it well. I think he never got past Austin. He never believed that he might still be alive."

"About that," said Mitch.

Olivia gulped. "If you have bad news just tell me."

"No, nothing like that. Before I tell you, though—"

In more of a command than she intended, Olivia said, "Just tell me."

"As much as I wanted to stay in Kapchorwa and ride this thing out, Dr. Wheeler has had me running all over Uganda and Kenya, trying to learn what I can. What else am I gonna do? I think everybody at Langley who knew I existed caught Ebola and died. I just hope payroll doesn't forget who I am." Mitch laughed.

"Are you actually in a good mood?" Olivia asked, "Or are you pretending, just to cheer me up?"

"Good. I got into Mbale today. This thing is bad here, Olivia. Before I got to Mbale, I hadn't seen a single living person in four days."

"I'm missing something," said Olivia.

I'm getting to it," said Mitch. "I was in the hospital, and I ran into a Dr. Kristin Mills."

"Is she cute?"

"As a matter of fact, yes. Two important things came out of that conversation."

"If you don't just tell me—"

"She was one of the doctors I told you about that I left in Kapchorwa."

Olivia stopped breathing.

"She caught Ebola while she was caring for your brother. She said he made it."

Olivia's preferred numbness crumbled and she started to cry. "I swear to God—"

"I'm serious. She said there's another guy, a Dr. Littlefield, who treated her. He was in Kapchorwa all along, through the whole epidemic. He knows Austin. I haven't caught up with Littlefield yet. She said he'll be in the hospital later today. He'll know more, but she said he told her that your brother came to Mbale to get help for them."

"So he's in Mbale?" Olivia asked through her tears.

"Nobody's seen him since Kapchorwa, so don't get your hopes too high yet. All we know is that he survived the virus."

Olivia gathered her composure and said, "Thank you, Mitch. Thank you so much. You don't know how much this means."

Then, she just cried. Too much pent up pain over too many awful things finally found a release.

To his credit, Mitch said nothing until she reached the end of her tears. "You know," he said, "if I run over on my minutes, the phone company charges me extra."

Olivia laughed. "You must be a real catch."

"I guess," Mitch laughed. "Here's the other thing I mentioned."

"Yes?"

"Dr. Mills was with another doctor in Kapchorwa besides Littlefield. She said a dozen or so Ugandan soldiers stayed with them, and every one of them got sick."

"Okay." Olivia wasn't surprised. "Everybody catches this thing. Everybody but you."

"Yeah," Mitch chuckled. "I'm immortal."

"That'll be funny until you get infected. You be careful. Okay?"

"Yes, mom." Mitch got back on track. "This thing is killing over ninety percent, right?"

"Those are the numbers I'm hearing," Olivia agreed.

"Only that other doctor and four of the soldiers died."

"Wait. What?"

"I told Dr. Wheeler about it a couple of hours ago. He said it's statistically possible for a small pool of cases to show a low mortality rate. He also said it was possible the airborne strain mutated again but with an attenuated mortality rate."

"My God. That could be huge."

"Absolutely," said Mitch. "It's all preliminary at the moment, but he said he was going to see what he could do about getting a jet sent this way to collect samples."

"Then you'll have a ride home."

"Or I could stay and look for your brother."

"Don't be stupid," Olivia told him. "Now I've got some news for you. I'll apologize first, because it's not as good as what you told me."

"Shoot."

"I got this from Barry, a coworker of mine. He's in contact with somebody at Langley who's not dead yet. They got information that Najid Almasi is alive and recovering from his wounds in Dubai."

"I—" Mitch choked on something that sounded like anger. "Killing him won't change anything now, but that piece of shit needs to suffer and die."

Olivia said, "I saw an assessment report this morning estimating that twenty-three percent of the global population now has Ebola, or has already died. Half of the infections occurred in the last seven days. You're smart enough to know what that says about where we'll be next week. Africa, the Asian subcontinent, and the Far East are getting hammered the worst. Some of it sounds like your experience in Nairobi. The infection rates in India are shocking. What I'm getting at is yes, I couldn't agree more. Najid Almasi needs to pay for what he's done. I'm only afraid that with the state of things, that might never happen."

"I don't know about that."

Chapter 96

Paul drove the pickup into the garage, squeezing in beside Heidi's crookedly parked SUV. Heidi was a terrible driver. She'd always insisted the opposite, so she and Paul often argued about it. Such is marriage.

Paul turned off his engine and closed the garage door. In the dim light coming in through the closed window blinds, he sat. He wondered what he should do with Heidi's car. He only needed one. He thought about giving it away. He remembered Austin's little pickup, still parked out at the curb, collecting dirt and rusting. It hadn't moved since Austin left for Africa four months ago.

So Paul had three cars: his, his dead wife's, and—

He didn't want to think about it.

He reached into his pocket for his phone. He wanted to call Olivia and tell her he'd buried Heidi, but saw that he'd missed another call from her. He dialed her back, but his signal dropped. He'd have to go upstairs. It was the only place in the house where the cell phone signal didn't get randomly dropped.

Paul stared at the garage wall a little while longer, not feeling enough motivation to do anything, wondering how long he could sit in the dim comfort and pretend life didn't hurt. He wondered how long he could hide from the guilty suspicion that Heidi's death was a result of his choices.

Someone drained her blood when they killed her. Only one reason existed for that behavior and it came back to Ebola immunity. If that was true, then a series of tautological steps traced back squarely on Paul. It was his fault and nothing could be done now to change it. All he could do was pay for his sins with his tears.

It was the missed call from Olivia that finally gave him enough motivation to get out of his truck.

He took his AR-15 out of the cab and carried it with him into his desperately silent house, losing track of what he was thinking about in the garage, forgetting even about the call to Olivia.

He thought about preparing himself something to eat as he stood with rifle still in hand. It was well after noon, and he hadn't eaten anything all day. Feeding himself seemed, at the moment, like an onerous, pointless endeavor. Standing in the kitchen, he was able to see most of the living room and a good part of the dining room. He looked up toward the top of the stairs. So much space, for just him and his ghosts.

He looked across the dining room and thought about his empty front porch, empty of all but that black flag of a T-shirt that he didn't need anymore—refused to have anymore. There was no Ebola in Paul Cooper's house and there were no dead.

Fuck the government. Fuck the neighbors. The T-shirt had flames in its future.

Paul stomped across the dining room, and flung the front door open.

"Freeze!"

Startled, Paul faced policemen on his porch. They were wearing black riot gear, gas masks, and thick gloves, standing in a shoulder-to-shoulder wall behind their rifle barrels and pistols, all pointed at him.

"Drop the gun! Now!"

Paul was confused and didn't move.

"Drop it!"

Paul's attention locked on his AR-15—solid, lethal, a

conduit for all the anger anyone might deserve. And these cops standing on Paul's porch, they wanted a dose. They needed a dose.

He looked back up at the gun barrels pointed at him, and in his mind, he imagined himself dodging those bullets long enough to bring his untested weapon to bear on the offensive pricks. He saw himself shooting them down with bullets wrapped in his hate. He saw them suffering, gasping, and bleeding. And somehow, he imagined that those bullets ripping their flesh would make him feel better.

"Don't do it," a voice behind one of the gas masks ordered. "Drop the weapon."

The rational Paul knew he'd be dead before he fired one bullet. If he tried to raise his AR-15, he'd have so many bullet holes in his chest, neck, and face, that he'd never feel the pain. He'd die before he hit the floor where Heidi had taken her last breath.

Maybe raising the AR-15 was his best option.

Maybe that was the best way to end his deep, empty sorrow.

"Drop the gun, right now."

As he thought about Heidi, he thought about the kind cop at the interment center, who'd helped him there, at the end. He knew that each of those thirty rounds in his magazine was just a new sin, waiting to be added to his debt of tears. His hands relaxed. The AR-15 hit the floor, and just that quickly, Paul was on the floor as well.

Chapter 97

Paul was no longer in control of his body. His hands were cuffed behind him, and he was seated on one of his own dining table chairs. Strong hands held his shoulders still.

The black-clad posse—he wasn't even sure how many there were—fanned out into his house, knocking things over, stomping up the stairs, kicking in doors that could easily have been opened with the turn of an unlocked knob. They yelled a lot at the empty house. All warnings and threats. They hollered at one another, their standard form of communication, macho fucks wagging their Kevlar-protected little dicks.

A guy in a suit—protected with the usual gear, of course—asked, "Are you Paul Cooper?"

Paul said nothing.

"Are you Paul Cooper?"

A hand dug into Paul's pants pocket and produced his billfold. Paul smirked. The billfold was empty of everything except some cash and Heidi's credit cards. All of Paul's stuff had been incinerated with his telephone.

One of the macho cops thundered down the stairs and jogged across the kitchen in boots that must have been weighted. He handed a passport to the suited questioner.

The questioner gave it a look and then held the photo up beside Paul's face. "You've put on weight."

"Your mom always makes me cookies when I come over to fuck her." Junior high snark seemed appropriate.

Unfazed, the guy said, "Me, too. She's nice like that."

Everybody laughed, though it was clear nobody found it funny.

The questioner asked Paul to confirm his social security number and his date of birth. Paul didn't cooperate.

The suited guy said, "You are Paul Cooper. You have contracted and survived Ebola. I am Lieutenant Harper, Douglas County Sheriff's Department. In compliance with the United States Ebola Resources Act, all blood sera previously the personal property of any Ebola survivor has been designated a strategic resource."

"What?" Paul shouted.

"You, being a human," the Lieutenant Harper continued, "and a living person, are not separable from your blood serum, and you continue to produce blood serum. You are hereby notified that you are to report to a strategic resource extraction facility until such time as The United States of America has deemed your blood serum to be of no more strategic importance. Do you understand?"

Shaking his head and weighing the price he'd have to pay in punches for pointlessly spitting onto Lieutenant Harper's gas mask, Paul said, "I do not understand. Why don't you get the fuck out of my house?"

Lieutenant Harper looked down at Paul through his gas mask lenses, and Paul imagined that Harper was glaring, so Paul glared back. When Harper raised a hand, Paul expected he'd get punched, maybe he just hoped for it. Instead, Harper waved a hand to brush away the hands holding Paul's shoulders.

"Don't get up," Harper told Paul. Harper's tone held no threats. He grabbed a chair and scooted it over in front of Paul. He sat down and looked silently at him while men continued ransacking the house.

"What are they looking for?" Paul asked in a civil tone.

The gas mask shook back and forth. "Blood plasma.

People have been selling it online. Can you believe it?"

"No."

"Crazy times bring out the crazy people. If there's any serum here, we'll find it."

Paul thought about Heidi. He looked down at the spot on the floor where he'd found her, bloodless. All resistance in Paul drained away. He didn't care what happened to him.

Harper sighed in what sounded like a long metallic hiss through his gas mask. He grabbed the front of the mask and pushed it up off his face. He looked to be about Paul's age—haggard, and frayed, no longer a robotic government thug, but a tired man, a neighbor even, just doing his job. He said, "I hate this shit. Sorry if they bruised you up a bit."

Paul shook his head feebly. With no energy left to hate, he said, "I'm fine."

"My partner got shot the day before yesterday," said Harper.

Paul looked over at his AR-15, which leaned in a corner. "What happened?"

"Same as you, a survivor." Harper reached up to rub his gloved hand over his sweaty face, froze, looked at the glove as if it were a poisonous snake, and put his hand back down. He attempted a pained smile. "Old habits." He looked at his hand again and shook his head. "We'll probably all kill ourselves before this is over. It was a guy with a hunting rifle who shot Bill when he was getting out of the car. We never even got to the door."

"How's...Bill?"

Shaking his head, Harper said, "Couldn't take him to the hospital. No room there. No doctors available, even if we could. No way he'd live through that, anyway. Too much

Ebola there. The men call it the petri dish, you know." Harper chuckled at the joke, but only in the most perfunctory way. "The petri dish. That's a one-way ticket now. You go there, you bleed out. I guess Bill should have gotten there first, like you did."

Paul didn't respond.

"He died." Harper sucked in a sharp breath. "A few months ago, we'd have called an ambulance. He'd have gone to the hospital, maybe stayed a week or two, and come away with a scar and a commendation." Harper lost his line of thought, staring at the shiny lenses of his gas mask.

Paul said, "You said you went to a survivor's house?"

Harper perked up. "Like you, a guy who contracted the virus, but beat the odds." Harper leaned over to get closer to Paul, "You and this other guy, you've got the golden ticket—you're immune now, full of all the right antigens."

"Antibodies," Paul corrected.

"Whatever," said Harper. "You're gonna get through all this. You'll still be alive. But the rest of us—" Harper shrugged.

Paul looked around the house. "I took my wife—" Paul choked and his eyes watered again. "—to the South Denver Interment...oh, whatever. The mass grave. I put my wife's body in a pit this morning. My son—" Paul looked down at his lap to hide the shame of his tears. "My son is in Africa. I haven't heard from him in over a month. He's probably dead. Not a very golden fucking ticket, is it, Lieutenant Harper?"

Shaking his head, Harper said, "My wife passed last week. Only one kid." Harper looked off into the distance. "She's fine, so far. You've got a daughter, right?"

Nodding, Paul said, "Near Atlanta. Government job."

"She okay?" Harper asked.

Paul nodded.

"That guy with the hunting rifle who shot Bill," Harper said, getting back on topic. "We didn't shoot him. We didn't even hurt him."

"Wait. What?"

"He's got the Ebola...antibodies. His blood is a strategic resource. It's been nationalized. Technically his serum. Specifically, his antibodies. The ones he has now, and all he is going to produce in the future." Harper's face grew deadly serious. "And yours too, Paul."

"Bullshit."

Harper pushed a hand into a pocket on his vest, drew out a sheet of folded paper, showed it to Paul and pushed it into Paul's pocket. "That's yours to keep. That's the court order."

"I'm calling a lawyer." Paul said it because that's what a TV character would say in the same situation. He didn't have the conviction for it, though.

"That's what everybody says."

"This can't be legal," Paul stated but it sounded like a question. "This isn't right."

"Yeah," Harper nodded. "I'm sure you're right. I think this is the most un-American bullshit I've ever heard of, but at the same time, this might be the only way we can save what's left of us."

"What exactly is going to happen to me?"

"You'll be put in a camp out east of town. You'll be taken care of. You'll be protected. Your blood serum will be harvested at least bi-weekly. Every time it's harvested, it'll be used to save lives. You'll be a hero."

"Whether I want to be or not."

"Will you come along?" Harper asked.

"Do I have a choice?" Paul answered.

"No," said Harper. "But it'll be easier for everybody if you just walk out with us."

Paul looked around. "Will you at least lock up the house?"

Chapter 98

Two days after Sander died, Austin heard voices coming from the forest on the south side of camp. The General and his men were returning. By then, three of the soldiers who stayed in camp were sick. Nobody told Austin what their symptoms were, but he had his hopes.

After a few minutes, Austin saw the first men come out of the trees. They carried a stretcher. All four had anguished faces. More men came into camp. The soldiers who'd stayed ran over to the others, talking, pointing, agitated.

Austin stood up for a better view.

Some of the men coming were supported by their comrades. Austin looked for signs of gunshot wounds, but couldn't see any. He walked a few paces forward, wondering who was on the stretcher, telling himself it had to be The General—who else would the rebels carry?

In truth, that was an unfounded guess, built from a handful of capricious hope.

Rebels kept straggling in.

Austin decided it was a good time to be out of sight. Angry rebels liked to kick and beat conveniently proximate hostages and Austin was the only one left. He decided he'd be well-suited to slip into the most shadowy corner of his hut and pretend to be asleep, or better yet, feign illness.

After lying for a while and coming to think he was developing a talent for evasion, Botu stuck his head in the hut and said, "Come with me."

Chapter 99

Austin knelt beside The General's cot and put a hand across his forehead. The General was burning with fever. Austin looked up at Botu, who was standing behind him, keeping a distance, and asked, "What happened to him?"

Waving a hand at the obviousness of it, Botu said, "He's sick."

"With what?" Austin asked, showing enough exasperation to demonstrate his frustration, but not enough to earn him a beating. It was a necessary risk. He didn't want any wandering imagination to connect the accusation of poisoning to The General's current condition.

Botu scowled and headed for the door. He said, "The black shits."

Botu stopped and turned back. "Take care of him. Don't leave this hut. Food and water will be outside the door when you need it." Botu left.

The black shits had to be Ebola.

Austin got to his feet and crossed over to the door to look outside. At least five rebels were staggering toward huts or collapsing in the shade. Austin bet himself they all had Ebola.

Behind him, The General said, "Bring me water, Ransom."

Austin looked around the hut and spotted a pitcher on a shelf with some cups. The pitcher was empty. He said, "We don't have any water. I'll get some." Austin took the pitcher, stepped through the hut's doorway and stopped, recalling Botu's orders.

"Go," The General told him.

Austin took another step outside.

Botu hollered at him from across the compound. He was pissed and marching angrily back.

In his defense, Austin said, "The General is awake. He needs water."

Fuming, Botu said, "Go back inside. Do as I told you."

Austin retreated inside and Botu yelled some orders.

Looking around in the dim light inside the hut, Austin didn't know what else to do except go back to The General's side. "Water is on the way." Putting as much concern into his voice as he could muster, he asked, "What happened?"

The General's smile flashed through his pain. "More hostages. More ransoms."

"You went to get more hostages?" Austin asked.

"I only have two," The General told him. "Hostages are a good business for us."

"Unless you brought some back, you only have one."

The General raised his eyebrows in a silent question.

Austin said, "Sander died."

"How? Did he try to escape?"

Shaking his head, Austin said, "He died from the beating. He never got out of bed. It took a few days."

"Did he suffer?" The General asked, in what seemed like sympathy.

Austin wasn't sure how to answer, but decided that with The General unable to stand, unable to do anything with his anger, it was safe to tell the truth. "He did suffer. A lot."

The General stared at the ceiling for a moment, his face blank. He said, "Good."

Chapter 100

The trucker was kind enough to pull off at the Lone Tree exit long enough to let Salim out of the trailer. The Denver air held a crisp chill, exacerbated by the long bumpy ride up Interstate 25 in the trailer. Salim thanked the driver, who made a point of keeping a wide gap between them. The driver closed up his trailer, got back into his cab, and Salim watched the tractor-trailer roll back onto the northbound highway as the rumble of its engine faded.

Eight miles from home, Salim stood in the middle of the night, back in the mundane familiar where every sign displayed a name he'd read before, in a nauseatingly bland font; where every wide, clean road rolled smoothly past one block just like the last block, all the way to more of the same; where the dry, cool air smelled of nothing in particular, and everybody he'd ever met readily accepted him into their Facebook-sized circle of acquaintances, but few treated him as a friend or equal. He talked like them, dressed like them, liked the same TV shows, lusted after the same silver screen hotties, and daydreamed of the same shiny future. He had that funny name that they Americanized to Sam, and they always, *always* assumed he was just as Sunday-Christian as they were.

Now, none of it mattered. He wasn't yet ready to admit it, even to himself, but he longed for a hug from his mother, a snarky smile from his sister, and a nod from his father. A future in a pastel-ified, earth-tone, three-sides-brick, uni-box, Cal-Style, assembly line neighborhood, with thoroughfares lined in drive-thru franchise grease-kitchen clichés wasn't the deepest pit of hell. It was just life.

Salim walked.

The first mile of Lincoln Avenue going west from the

highway was lined with strip malls and big-box stores, all with strangely empty parking lots. Salim had expected to see at least a few cars, not zero. Traffic on Lincoln Avenue's six lanes had also gone truant.

At the intersections, Salim didn't bother to stop and wait for a favorable signal at the crosswalk. He had no need. He was alone on the street, walking at a brisk pace to keep himself warm.

The longer he walked, the closer he came to home. He eventually passed the store where his mother usually purchased her groceries. He passed a burger joint that he and his high school buddies visited when taking long lunches and skipping fourth period. He walked by a paved trail on which he rode his bicycle to soccer practice.

Finally, he turned off the main road and entered his neighborhood.

Lights gleamed on front porches and windows glowed dimly behind closed curtains. Cars sat in driveways, waiting for owners to wake in the morning. Trashcans sat at curbs in the company of an unusual number of overflow bags. Every house had an excess of garbage. Many had refuse on the porches.

He rounded a long curve and spotted his house on the corner of a cul-de-sac. He saw his father's car in the driveway—his mother always had too many of her excess purchases piled in the garage to put the car there. Salim crossed the street and made the final, anticlimactic step onto his own lawn and breathed relief. Though he'd hoped and endeavored all along the way, he'd never truly expected to see his home again.

He looked up at a second floor window at the corner of the house. That was his room in there—his bed, his computer, his television, his clothes, his box of condoms stashed in a drawer in the desk, of which he'd thrown half away. When his snooping mother found the half-empty box, she would of course tell his father, and his father would look at him from that day forward, always hiding a bit of jealousy. Salim was having sex with American girls — plural — and Salim's dad had only ever bedded his frumpy mother. Ha! Salim had made plenty of mistakes, but at least he had that.

He stepped onto the porch and noticed two bundles wrapped tightly in thick black plastic trash bags, secured in rolls of silvery tape. Salim tripped up the last step and caught himself on a support post as a realization came to him. His eyes had seen more corpses than any boy should ever have to.

Two corpses were on his porch, corpses matching the size and shape of his mother and sister.

Salim gulped and rushed at the door, jiggling the locked knob and ringing the bell. He heard no sound but the bell from inside.

Panicked, Salim ran around to the side of the house, let himself in through the gate and skirted the shrubs to reach the back door, which his parents never locked. He leapt over an herb garden, crossed the porch, and flung the door open.

Kapchorwa smell punched him in the face. He cried his sister's name. He yelled for his mother and his father, but only got a mouthful of humid, stinking rot.

Salim ran up the stairs and checked his sister's empty room. The sheets were gone, but the carpet and the mattress told the story of Ebola. He ran to the other end of the house and into his parents' ridiculously large master bedroom. At the center of the long wall, on a king-size bed constructed of the heaviest looking oak-veneer particle board, lay the body of his father, contorted with pain, frozen by death, in an evaporated pool of all the fluids that ran out as the Ebola virus rotted his body from the inside out.

Salim collapsed onto the stained carpet as the toll of his decisions crushed any desire he had for his heart to pound out one more beat. The only people in the whole world that Salim loved had been killed by the virus that traveled to America in his own blood.

Chapter 101

Two days passed, and Austin didn't see Botu once. At first, food and water arrived as promised, placed outside the door by a rebel who hurried away. Then delivery stopped. For The General, food deliveries didn't matter. He wasn't eating. Austin was, though, and the generous portions helped a great deal with his strength and stamina.

Without Botu around to threaten him, and The General slipping between consciousness and delirium, Austin sat on the ground outside the door and leaned against the wall, breathing the fresh morning air. Around the camp, in the other huts, rebels were dying, and not doing it quietly.

A troop of monkeys was making a racket about something far up the mountainside. A couple of soldiers shuffled through the center of the camp, looking nervously from side to side, carrying their weapons, but carrying other things too: their few belongings, and food, pilfered from the camp stores. Austin looked on without interest. Soldiers had been deserting for days, running away from Ebola, taking a chance on survival.

Inside the hut, The General started to hiccup and woke himself.

For Ebola patients, hiccups were the death knell.

Weird, but what the hell.

Austin had no doubt this moment would arrive. He only wondered how he'd feel when The General finally died. He'd seen rebel bodies being dragged out into the forest for disposal, but all of them seemed oddly anonymous. To him, they were beings of one dimension that ignored or beat him, nothing else. When Ebola took them, the passing left no grief or guilt for Austin to feel.

The General called out and Austin looked into the hut's darkness. He got up and went in to kneel by The General's bedside. "Would you like some water?"

The General shook his head.

He was a charismatic sadist, but he was a helpless victim of Ebola, too. Austin despised, even hated The General, but it didn't trouble him to fill the role of nurse. Austin dipped a cloth into a tub of cool water and laid it on The General's forehead.

"You should run," The General said.

Austin shrugged, impressed that The General was still coherent. "I will."

"When I get better—" The General whispered wetly, as though the effort of those few syllables had taken all the energy he could muster. "When I get better, I'll kill you, if you're still here."

Austin patted The General's shoulder. "You won't get better. You'll be dead by sundown."

The General slowly shook his head. "I'm strong."

"Doesn't matter," said Austin. "All you have left now is prayer."

The General's head lolled to the side and he looked out through the door. "Bring Botu to me."

"He's dead, or gone. I haven't seen him in days."

"Their faith was weak."

"Yeah," Austin agreed.

The General's eyes closed and he seemed to go to sleep.

Austin stayed by his side. For hours, bubbles of blood started to grow out one of The General's nostrils when he exhaled. Each would pop and another would form. Austin dabbed the blood away in an endeavor that grew more futile with each breath.

Night fell, and The General made a liar out of Austin by clinging to life.

"Ransom."

The General's voice startled Austin out of his thoughts. The General's red eyes were open again.

"Yes?"

"After I die, will you take me to Masindi?"

"Masindi?" Austin asked. He'd never heard of the place.

"I was born there. I wish to be buried there."

"I don't know."

The General's hand reached out with surprising quickness, and even more surprising strength. It gripped Austin's wrist. "Promise me, Ransom. Promise me you'll take me back to Masindi."

Lying, Austin said, "I will. Is Masindi in Uganda?"

"Masindi is in Africa." The Generals eyelids fell shut again and his hand fell away from Austin's wrist.

Austin continued to dab at the blood.

The General died.

The next morning, just as the sky was starting to lose its nighttime blackness, Austin disappeared into the jungle.

The End

Book 3 in the Ebola K Trilogy will be out in 2015...when, you ask? We'll let you know as soon as we firm up the date.

We do let readers know through our newsletter, so if you'd like to be notified, we'll send you a message. Just sign up at http://www.bobbyadair.com/subscribe.

Or if you're into Liking, Pinning, or Following, the links to social media sites where you can do that are below. I try to keep everyone up to date with upcoming releases... oh, who am I kidding. Mostly I post random, silly crap that I find interesting or amusing.

My website

http://bobbyadair.com/subscribe/

Facebook

https://www.facebook.com/BobbyAdairAuthor

Pinterest

http://www.pinterest.com/bobbyadairbooks/

Twitter

https://twitter.com/BobbyAdairBooks

Do you have a moment for a review?

To quote Shakespeare...to review, or not to review, that is the question. No, really. They had reviews back then, too. They call them "tomatoes."

Ebola K, Book 2 was an extremely emotional book to write, and an extremely complex project. If you have a moment, I would be forever indebted if you could give any feedback on the site where you purchased the book. As an indie author, the visibility of my books is very much tied to the ratings and reviews, and for that reason we solicit your feedback a little more aggressively than the big box stores and publishers. We also really care about what you have to say, and look to that feedback when thinking about new and exciting things to write for you.

Also, if there's something you find that's a blatant error, I would really appreciate your input in a private message through my website (please don't vent on Amazon if I really screwed up!). I'd appreciate the opportunity to fix it before it goes into a permanent review.

Here's the place to report any typos:
http://www.bobbyadair.com/typos

Oh yeah, I almost forgot. Please leave a review on the website *where you bought the book.* My landlord likes it when I pay my rent on time. Reviews (especially the good ones) help make that happen.

NOTE TO LANDLORD: Seriously, Rusty and Stephanie...I am a writer....no, I know that people say that all the time. :-)

Other Books by Bobby Adair

**Also, check out my audiobooks
on audible.com to "live" the story!**

Thriller, Dystopian, Horror, & Post-Apocalyptic Fiction (okay, Zombies)

Slow Burn: Zero Day, book 1

Slow Burn: Infected, book 2

Slow Burn: Destroyer, book 3

Slow Burn: Dead Fire, book 4

Slow Burn: Torrent, book 5

Slow Burn: Bleed, book 6

Slow Burn Box Set: Destroyer and Dead Fire

The Last Survivors: a joint collaboration with
T.W. Piperbrook

Satire

Flying Soup

Science Fiction

Ace Gonzo (no longer in print, but may be re-released)

Made in the USA
Middletown, DE
29 November 2022

16453842R00245